K'Ehleyr emerged from the mist behind Picard.

"I thought you didn't care about the rebellion. Because it sure sounds like you do."

He looked back at her to find himself the object of three different stares. K'Ehleyr was amused; Barclay looked hopeful; Troi wore a mask of desperation. Picard looked back at Saavik. "I'll ask for the last time: Why am I here?"

Saavik was composed, calm, and dignified. She spoke without emotion or hauteur, but with simple, direct honesty. "We have watched you for a long time, Mister Picard. I believe that because of your history and your inherent good nature, you are the sort of person who can help us reach out to the Terran Rebellion, by carrying our offer of support and leadership to them. We need someone from outside our sheltered society, someone with a reputation beyond reproach who is known to the rebels, to act as our ambassador. I wish you to be that ambassador.

"And you are correct in your assertions about Spock's timetable. His projected timeline of events was off because he did not account for further interference in our affairs by persons from the alternate universe. Thanks to events that have transpired on and around Bajor, the future has taken shape far sooner than Spock expected. Consequently, we—and you—must act now, before this pivotal moment in history slips away from us."

Shocked and intrigued, Picard asked, "What pivotal moment?"

Saavik placed her hand upon Picard's shoulder.

"The one at which a rebellion becomes a revolution."

STAR TREK®
MIRROR UNIVERSE

RISE LIKE LIONS

DAVID MACK

Based upon
Star Trek and
Star Trek: The Next Generation®
created by Gene Roddenberry

Star Trek: Deep Space Nine®
created by Rick Berman & Michael Piller

and *Star Trek: Voyager*®
created by Rick Berman & Michael Piller & Jeri Taylor

POCKET BOOKS

New York   London   Toronto   Sydney   New Delhi   Memory Omega

Pocket Books
A Division of Simon & Schuster, Inc.
1230 Avenue of the Americas
New York, NY 10020

This book is a work of fiction. Names, characters, places, and incidents either are products of the author's imagination or are used fictitiously. Any resemblance to actual events or locales or persons, living or dead, is entirely coincidental.

First Pocket Books paperback edition December 2011

POCKET and colophon are registered trademarks of Simon & Schuster, Inc.

For information about special discounts for bulk purchases, please contact Simon & Schuster Special Sales at 1-866-506-1949 or business@simonandschuster.com.

The Simon & Schuster Speakers Bureau can bring authors to your live event. For more information or to book an event, contact the Simon & Schuster Speakers Bureau at 1-866-248-3049 or visit our website at www.simonspeakers.com.

Cover design by Alan Dingman

Manufactured in the United States of America

10 9 8 7 6 5 4 3 2 1

ISBN 978-1-4516-0719-2
ISBN 978-1-4516-0720-8 (ebook)

For those who continue to fight the good fight

Historian's Note

Rise Like Lions begins in January 2377, immediately following the events of the *Star Trek: Deep Space Nine* novels *Fearful Symmetry* and *The Soul Key,* and concludes in 2381. All events occur in the alternate universe first seen in the *Star Trek* episode "Mirror, Mirror" and revisited in several *Deep Space Nine* episodes, starting with "Crossover."

Freedom suppressed and again regained
bites with keener fangs than freedom
never endangered.

—Cicero

'Rise like Lions after slumber
In unvanquishable number,
Shake your chains to earth like dew
Which in sleep had fallen on you—
Ye are many—they are few.'

—Percy Bysshe Shelley,
The Mask of Anarchy

PART I

Ferro Comitante

2377

1

Keener Fangs

M'k'n'zy of Calhoun knew there were only two ways
this would end: He would win, or he would die.
And Mac didn't plan on dying—not here, not like this.

He barked orders over the thundering explosions
that rocked the *Excalibur*. "Roll to starboard! Keep our
shields toward the surface!" The tactical display next to
his command chair flickered with new data indicating
that defensive systems were activating on the planet's
surface and targeting his ship. "Tactical! Report!"

Soleta—his half-Vulcan, half-Romulan lover and de
facto second-in-command—responded without looking
up from her console. "I see them. Coordinates locked.
Transmitting now."

At the comm station, Robin Lefler shot an anxious
glance at the nerve center's main screen, which showed
a brilliant, crimson barrage streaking up at them from
the planet. "Let's hope the Romulans come through."

Mac scowled. "They'd better."

"They won't let us down," said Edward Jellico, his
clenched jaw betraying his fear even through the camouflage of his meticulously groomed white beard.
"We're the only hope they've got."

Changing course and speed—emergency evasive. The
warning, heard only in the thoughts of Mac and Soleta,

had come from McHenry, an extraordinary human who lived aboard the *Excalibur,* cocooned inside a nigh-invulnerable null sphere from which he provided the ship with its near-limitless energy and borderline pre-scient navigation. *Angling deflectors to shield aft quarter.*

Mac looked at Jellico. "Ed, check our tail!"

Jellico turned and keyed commands into the panel behind him. "Incoming!"

Thumbing open an intraship channel, Mac declared, "Brace for impact!"

Excalibur pitched and yawed, and the command crew in its nerve center clung white-knuckle tight to their sta-tions as the ship's inertial dampers and artificial gravity modules struggled to compensate and then reset them-selves.

Pushing sweaty strands of his long, black hair from his scarred face, Mac slapped the side of his malfunc-tioning tactical display, which stuttered and went dark. "*Grozit!* Soleta! What just hit us?"

"Secondary batteries, on the planet's moon. Updating target profile—"

"Make it quick," Jellico said. "It's locked on and charging up fast!"

Mac sprang from his chair, too keyed up to stay seated. "Hard about! All power to aft shields and for-ward weapons!"

Soleta looked up, her exquisite, angular face a mask of confusion. "What? Mac, what the hell are you—"

"We'll take out the secondary guns. Give Hiren the signal—*now*!" *McHenry, give me everything you've got—we're about to need it.*

McHenry's telepathic voice was calm and certain. *Ready, Captain.*

Excalibur's impulse engines filled the ship with an almost musical droning, the product of a resonant frequency traveling through its spaceframe. Mac relished the steady vibrations traveling up his legs; they made him feel almost like a living part of the ship, and in such brief moments he wondered if he understood even a fraction of what McHenry's union with the Thallonian-built vessel must be like.

Not even close, Captain.

Just fly the ship, McHenry.

An alert shrilled from Jellico's console. He silenced it with the side of his fist. "All enemy guns are set to fire!" Then his eyes widened, and his voice pitched upward. "Romulan ships decloaking, bearing one-three-five mark two! They're firing torpedoes at the artillery bases on the planet."

Mac made a fist and barely suppressed the urge to punch the air. "Fire!"

The *Excalibur*'s forward cannons unleashed a fearsome barrage toward the Klingon border world's solitary moon. Half a second later, a massive detonation flared on its surface. "Direct hit," Soleta said. The firestorm faded from view in a matter of seconds, leaving nothing in its wake but barren wasteland. Looking up from her instruments, Soleta added, "Enemy firebase destroyed."

Jellico cracked a rare smile. "The Romulans did their bit. All gun installations on the surface have been neutralized."

"Good work, everyone. Soleta, arm torpedoes and lock onto our primary target. Robin . . . hail them."

Everyone carried out Mac's orders. Lefler nodded. "I have them."

"On screen." Mac stood as Lefler patched the subspace feed to the nerve center's forward main viewer.

The image of Tranome Sar's cinnamon-hued surface, now scarred by dozens of mushroom clouds climbing into its upper atmosphere, was replaced by a signal from inside the massive anti-deuterium refinery on its surface. A gaunt, weather-beaten old Klingon squinted at Mac, then bared his jagged teeth in a mirthless grin and expressed a contempt beyond measure in a single, rasped word: *"You!"*

"That's right, K'mtok: *me*."

The refinery boss furrowed his thick, ash-colored brow. *"Don't think you can extort us into refueling you or your Romulan lapdogs."*

Try as he might, Mac couldn't purge the mockery from his tone. "We're not here to raid your refinery, K'mtok." He smirked. "We're here to blow it up." A single nod to Soleta, and she began locking the *Excalibur*'s weapons on target. Mac looked back at K'mtok. "I'm giving you and your crew fifteen minutes to evacuate the refinery and leave in that empty freighter parked in low orbit."

K'mtok narrowed his eyes, clearly suspecting treachery. *"That freighter is unarmed. Once aboard, we would be defenseless."*

"You're *already* defenseless. At least on the freighter you'll be mobile and able to swear your revenge. But if it makes you feel better, I swear that the freighter will be given safe passage away from here." He nodded to Jellico. "Start the countdown." Then, to K'mtok, he added, "Fifteen minutes. Anyone still in the refinery after that is going to have a *really* bad day."

"You'll pay for this, you filthy petaQ!"

"So you keep telling me. Fourteen minutes and fifty-three seconds. *Excalibur* out." He nodded at Lefler, who terminated the transmission, then stood and said to Jellico, "Let me know as soon as that freighter breaks orbit. Soleta, if it leaves before time's up, blow the refinery early. Robin, remind our Romulan friends not to fire on that freighter. When I promise safe passage, I mean it."

Minutes and seconds bled away, until, with less than thirty seconds remaining in the countdown, the Klingon freighter broke orbit at full impulse, on a bearing away from the Klingon-Romulan border, back into the heart of Klingon space. Mac watched the ship shrink to a pin-point on the forward viewscreen, and then he looked at Jellico. "Any Klingons still on the surface?"

"Not a one. The refinery's deserted."

"Good. Signal the fleet to cloak and meet us at the rendezvous point."

"Hang on," Lefler said, swiveling her chair away from her post to face Mac and Jellico. "We're not just leaving behind all that fuel, are we? There must be enough down there to power this fleet for the next nine —" A brilliant flash from the main viewscreen forced her to shut her eyes, and she raised her arm to shield her face. After the blinding glare faded, Lefler stared in slack-jawed horror at the screen but said nothing.

Mac didn't need to look back to know what he would find: the refinery vanished and most of Tranome Sar's atmosphere blasted away by a massive antimatter explosion. "The Klingons had no intention of letting us capture that valuable a resource," Mac said to Lefler. "Standard operating procedure in a situation like this is either to defend it to the death or booby-trap it to prevent it from being used by the enemy." He stole a glance at the smoldering devastation on the screen, and he sighed. "At least they saved us a torpedo." He thumbed the switch for the ship's PA long enough to say, "All hands, secure from general quarters," and then he silently attuned his thoughts to address the ship's true master: *Take us out of here, McHenry—maximum warp.*

As you command, Mac.

Six hours later, Mac sat at the head of the table inside the *Excalibur*'s conference room, flanked on his right by Soleta and on his left by Jellico. None of the three stood as the door opened and a line of Romulan starship commanders entered, led by Hiren, their former praetor. Trailing them were a handful of Xenexian captains, whom Mac had promoted whenever he and the Romulans had captured Alliance ships to add to their armada. Hiren claimed the seat next to Soleta's, and the other commanders settled in around the table, on which sat several bowls of fruit.

As the last of the Romulans sat down, Mac leaned forward. "Who can guess why I've asked you all here today?" His rhetorical question was met with blank stares and averted gazes. "Hit-and-run tactics can take us only so far. We need to think bigger if we want to make real progress against the Alliance."

Hiren steepled his fingers on the table in front of him. "I disagree, Captain. The biggest mistake we could make right now would be to overextend ourselves." He looked around the room, directing his next remarks to the other commanders. "With patience, we could expel the Klingons and their Cardassian lackeys from Romulan space in less than a year."

"Don't count on it," Jellico grumbled. He raised his

voice as he continued. "The only reason we've made headway against the Klingons is that most of their forces have been tied up fighting the Talarians."

"Who have inflicted serious losses on the Alliance," Hiren said. He plucked a large, ruby-colored fruit from the bowl nearest him and started peeling away its rind to reveal the glistening pink flesh underneath. "Their divided attention presents us with an opportunity."

Soleta bowed her head slightly. "True. But Edward is correct. When the Klingons once again make their conquest of Romulan space a priority, we will almost certainly see our recent victories reversed. It is only a matter of time."

"By then we will have expanded our recruitment efforts," Hiren said, popping a wedge of peeled fruit into his mouth. Chewing, he added, "We'll be ready to whip those Klingon animals back to their wilderness."

Mac shook his head slowly. "No, you won't. You need to face facts, Hiren. We've commandeered almost every available ship in your former empire, and we've pressed into service every warm body we could find. We're as strong as we're ever going to get—but it won't be enough to stop what's coming. If you're serious about helping me save your people, you need to stop thinking in terms of reclaiming what *was,* and start dealing with your situation as it *is.*"

The mood in the room chilled as the gathered Romulan commanders bristled at Mac's implication. Hiren set down his half-eaten fruit, took a deep breath, and clenched his fists on the tabletop. His voice was quiet and sharp, like an assassin's blade. "We will not abandon what is rightfully ours, Calhoun."

"I'm not saying you should. But if you don't stop

being so provincial about its defense, you *will* lose it, and a lot sooner than you think. The truth is, we're outnumbered. So, unless we make some new allies, and soon, we're screwed."

Temolok, one of the senior warbird commanders, piped up. "And to whom should we turn? Our old foes, the Patriarchy? The First Federation?"

"The Terran Rebellion," Soleta said.

Hiren let slip a derisive snort. "Don't be absurd. The Terrans are as good as dead. Once the Alliance finishes with the Talarians, they'll wipe out what's left of those pathetic rabble-rousers."

Calhoun spoke softly, his focus on Hiren intense. "Not if we join them."

The former praetor of the defunct Romulan Star Empire chortled. It was a grim, world-weary sound. "Are you *mad,* Captain? The Terran Rebellion is over a hundred light-years away, on the far side of Alliance territory."

Jellico interjected, "So what? Your ships have cloaks, and the *Excalibur* is a stealth ship. We can outrun anything the Alliance sends after us."

"My point is not to ask how we would reach them," Hiren replied, with more condescension than he would dare employ when speaking to Mac. "My point is that once we deploy so far from our own space, we will have all but ceded it to the enemy." He glared at Mac. "And *that* is entirely unacceptable."

Mac fought to rein in his temper. Behind his bloodred veil of anger, he heard McHenry's telepathic voice: *I sense that you wish me to arm* Excalibur*'s internal defenses and terminate the Romulan commanders. Shall I commence firing?*

No, McHenry, thank you. He pinched the bridge of his

nose and sighed. *I suspect that would cause far more problems than it would solve*. Placing his palms flat on the table, he said to Hiren, "I've never made any secret of my agenda to join with the Terran Rebellion. And in case you've forgotten, you swore to defer to my judgment on all matters pertaining to this fleet. *My* fleet."

"I said I'd lost the taste for power, and that I was willing to defer to your authority." He looked at the Romulan commanders, several of whom nodded in Hiren's direction. A sly smile tugged at his mouth when he looked back at Mac. "Lost appetites can be regained. Past indulgences can be revoked." His mien darkened, and a note of menace crept into his voice. "Most of your fleet consists of Romulan warships and support vessels, many of them crewed exclusively by my people. While we are, understandably, grateful to you for rescuing as many as you did when the Alliance destroyed Romulus, our gratitude doesn't extend so far as to abandon the remainder of our empire merely on your say-so."

The challenge provoked nothing more from Mac than a slow nod.

McHenry silently alerted Mac, *I have the information you asked me to find*.

Well done. Start using it. Mac reclined his chair, set his hands on the armrests, and looked at Hiren. "Should I interpret your refusal to obey my orders as a 'vote of no confidence'?"

"If you like."

Eyeing the other Romulans in the room, Mac asked, "What about the rest of you? Can I see a show of hands? Who agrees with Hiren?" One by one, every Romulan except Soleta—who, Mac reminded himself, was half Vulcan, and therefore didn't deserve to be lumped in with her countrymen—raised his or her hand. Mac frowned. "All right. I've heard your position. Here's mine." He pushed his chair back from the table and stood. Leaning forward on his knuckles, he fixed Hiren with a baleful stare. "This ship—and, by extension, this fleet—is *not* a democracy. We don't take votes, and I don't give a *targ*'s ass whether we achieve consensus. I give orders, and you follow them. That's how it works. Anyone who doesn't like it is free to leave. But ask yourself this, Hiren: How long will you and your people last without me and mine?"

"Longer than you will without the safe haven of Romulan space." Hiren held up a hand to stifle any replies from Mac or his senior personnel. "Let's not be hasty about this, Calhoun. I still believe our forces are stronger united than separate. Splitting up now doesn't benefit either of us. Let me suggest a compromise."

"No."

Soleta touched Mac's arm. "Maybe we should hear him—"

"No," Mac repeated, with more force. "I'm not making any deals. Hiren, if you want to take your fleet and go home, be my guest. But if you want to stay and be part of *this* fleet, you and your men need to submit to my authority. I won't be threatened, second-guessed, or extorted." He shot a withering glance at the other Romulans. "And just in case any of you are thinking you can pledge your loyalty now and stab me in the back later, you might want to take a moment to check in with your ships." He motioned for them to do so. "Go ahead. I'll wait."

The Romulans traded bemused looks, and then they began muttering into their wrist-mounted communicators. A soft chatter of comm traffic, of harsh whispers and tinny, filtered replies, filled the conference room. Mac waited until all his guests had finished verifying the current status of their respective ships.

"By now, you should all be aware that each of your vessels has targeted one of the others, and that your crews are locked out of all command functions." Mac smiled. "I can just as easily turn your ships' intruder countermeasures against your crews, any time I wish. Remember that the next time you get the urge to mutiny."

Hiren quaked with rage. "What kind of treachery is this?"

"The kind I resort to when I suspect my so-called allies are going to betray me. Now, let's cut to the heart of it. Do you accept my authority or not?"

Seething but visibly diminished, Hiren mumbled, "Yes, Captain."

"Yes, *what?*"

"Yes . . . I accept your absolute authority over this fleet."

"Good. I'm glad we sorted that out."

The ex-praetor forced out bitter words. "May I make a *request,* Captain?"

"You may."

"Before you take the fleet out of Romulan space to join the Terrans, might you consider making one more major tactical strike against the Alliance in the Acamar Sector—to replenish our supplies and provisions and delay the enemy's inevitable counterstrike against the Romulan colonies there?"

Mac gave a half-nod. "I'll take that under advisement."

"Thank you, Captain."

"Dismissed." Mac remained standing as he watched the procession of ship commanders leave the conference room, once again following Hiren. When the door slid closed behind the last of them, Mac dropped heavily back into his chair.

Jellico folded his arms. "That was some stunt you pulled, turning all those ships against each other. Care to tell me how you did it?"

Mac cracked a wan smile. "Maybe some other time, Ed." He caught a sly glance from Soleta, who knew that Mac had enlisted McHenry's help, by having the psionic prodigy lift the various starship captains' command codes from their minds and use them to usurp control of their vessels over a subspace channel.

Soleta cocked one eyebrow in curiosity. "Orders, Captain?"

"Find our next target," Mac said. "Something we can use to hobble the Alliance and keep them busy licking their wounds while we join the rebellion."

2

The Messenger

Miles "Smiley" O'Brien faced his closest adviser and fellow rebellion general, Michael Eddington, across the situation table in Terok Nor's Operations Center. Eddington was the portrait of calm. Tall, thin, and soft-spoken, he was the polar opposite of stout, irascible O'Brien. With a few gingerly taps, O'Brien highlighted part of the station diagram on the tabletop display between them. "The outer sections are vulnerable. Let's move their occupants to the inner edge of the Habitat Ring and gut those areas for parts."

"That causes more problems than it solves." As usual, Eddington pulled no punches. "The Habitat Ring is already too crowded, and we won't get anything useful out of those sections except cables and some plasma relays."

"It's better than nothing," O'Brien snapped. Of all the people who had flocked to the Terran Rebellion over the years, Eddington was the only one O'Brien felt he could really trust to always tell him the unvarnished truth—but that didn't mean O'Brien had to like it. "I don't give a damn how crowded the ring is. There'll be plenty of room after we're gone." Noting that his raised voice had prompted anxious looks from the other senior personnel manning the Operations Center, O'Brien took a deep breath before adding in a more subdued tone, "Repairing the fleet has to be our top priority, Michael."

Eddington took a second to consider his reply. "I agree with you, Miles. But I don't think we should be so quick to write off the station. The move to the wormhole inflicted only minor structural damage, and the deflectors are intact. It's still a highly defensible base of operations."

"No, it's a damned target, the first thing the Alliance will shoot at." O'Brien sighed, his shoulders slumped beneath the weight of years on the losing end of a war. "We're low on torpedoes, half our phaser banks are broken, and we don't have the time or manpower for another raid on the Cardassians' weapons depots. I think our best bet is to redistribute what we have left to the fleet and retreat to the Badlands before the Alliance comes back for a rematch."

"Miles, most of what we can salvage from the station will be useless to the fleet. Half the components are incompatible with anything non-Cardassian, and the rest will take more effort to adapt than they'll be worth. We'd be gutting a valuable resource for no good reason." He called up a new screen of data on the table-top. "Since we can't fix the engines on the *Rescorla,* why not salvage it for parts and use its weapons to repair the station?"

"The *Rescorla*'s parts and munitions are already earmarked for the fleet."

Eddington nodded, not in accord but out of frustration. "All right. If we're committed to abandoning the station, can I make a few recommendations?"

"By all means."

"First, we should move it away from the wormhole."

O'Brien frowned in confusion and felt his forehead crease. "Why?"

"To hide the wormhole from the Alliance. It's a potentially useful tactical asset, not to mention a point of major religious significance to the Bajorans."

O'Brien rolled his eyes. In the weeks since Iliana Ghemor, a Cardassian and former agent of the Obsidian Order, had returned from the wormhole—after being pulled into it beside her counterpart and the Kira Nerys from the alternate universe—the people of Bajor had become engulfed by an intense religious fervor. They had started calling Ghemor "the Emissary of the Prophets." He'd never before heard of these Prophets, but apparently they were the deities of an ancient mythology, and the Bajorans believed they lived inside the wormhole.

"I'll concede the second part," O'Brien said. "What makes you think the wormhole is tactically valuable?"

"As far as we can tell, the Alliance still doesn't know it exists." Eddington called up a star map on the tabletop screen and began drawing tactical diagrams. "If we stage a fleet on the far side, we can fool the Alliance's long-range recon into thinking we're weaker than we really are. Meanwhile, we'll use cloaked subspace radio buoys on either side to maintain communications. They'll size their assault force based on what they think is the minimum necessary to ensure victory. Then we'll lure the Alliance fleet into a battle around the station, and—when they think they have us—we'll call in our reinforcements and blast the Alliance fleet to bits."

Knowing that Eddington was a shrewd tactician, O'Brien took a moment to study the details of his colleague's plan. "It's a good idea. But it has one flaw."

"What's that?"

"You're assuming the Alliance will continue its past tactic of minimum engagement. They've done nothing but escalate this conflict since it started. When they finish their war with the Talarians, they'll come for us—and it *won't* be with the bare minimum. The last time they tried that, the Klingons lost their flagship, the *Negh'Var*. Martok won't tolerate another defeat like that. The next time the Alliance comes here, it'll be to crush us. They'll hit us with everything they can." He tapped the tabletop display and dispelled Eddington's schematics, leaving the screen blank. "By the time that happens, I plan to be long gone."

Eddington seemed to have run out of counterarguments. O'Brien was set to move on to other pressing business when chief of security Luther Sloan joined them. "Excuse me, but there's something you'll want to see." He patched in a feed from the sensor console, and the oval holoframe suspended high overhead flickered to life and showed a small Bajoran spacecraft heading toward Terok Nor. Sloan nodded at it. "We picked it up about ninety seconds ago. Its shields are up, and it's following the stealth trajectory we used to use to visit the planet without being observed by the Alliance. But no flights are scheduled today."

O'Brien and Eddington traded worried glances, and then O'Brien looked over his shoulder toward Ezri Tigan at the tactical station. "Hail them."

The young Trill woman pushed a lock of her wild black hair from her face with one hand while operating her console with the other. "Bajoran vessel, this is Terok Nor. Identify yourself and your passengers." Several seconds passed without a response. Tigan looked at O'Brien for guidance. "Lock phasers?"

Before O'Brien could answer, a female voice crackled over the subspace audio channel. *"Terok Nor, this is the Bajoran transport* Yolja, *requesting permission to dock."*

O'Brien's expression of worry became one of suspicion. "Transport *Yolja*, identify your passengers, or you will be fired upon."

Eddington looked askance at O'Brien and whispered, "That seems extreme."

"That ship could be loaded with explosives, for all we know." Anxious, O'Brien folded his arms. "Ezri, stand by to raise shields."

"Terok Nor, this is transport Yolja. *Can we switch to a secure channel?"*

O'Brien nodded at Tigan, who keyed in the commands. "Encryption's up," O'Brien said. "Go ahead, *Yolja*."

"This is Iliana Ghemor. I've come to talk with O'Brien. It's important."

"First, you'll have to lower your shields," O'Brien said.

Ghemor sounded annoyed. *"Sorry. Force of habit. Shields down."*

Cocking one eyebrow, O'Brien looked at Sloan for confirmation. The lean, fair-haired man checked his console, then nodded at O'Brien. "One life sign, Cardassian female. The ship's clean."

That satisfied O'Brien for the moment. "Transport *Yolja*, dock at airlock three. Terok Nor out." He closed the channel, then snapped orders as he moved toward the lift. "Michael, with me. Luther, clear the corridors near the airlock. Ezri, have Keiko meet our guest and bring her to the wardroom."

Iliana Ghemor had hardly expected a hero's welcome upon her return to Terok Nor, but she certainly hadn't anticipated being treated like a prisoner.

The station's first officer, a slender human woman named Keiko Ishikawa, had met Ghemor at the airlock, backed up by a trio of armed rebels led by the one named Sloan. Ishikawa led her away from the airlock, with Sloan following a few paces behind Ghemor, his blaster drawn and pointed squarely at her back. By the time they arrived at the wardroom, Ghemor didn't know whether she was being marched to a parley or an execution. Though she hadn't wronged the rebellion during her last visit to the station, she knew all too well that people had an unlimited capacity for irrational behavior in times of war.

Despite reports Ghemor had heard of the station being overcrowded, the corridors seemed deserted. Then she noticed fresh boot stains on the deck, bits of trash littering nooks along the passageways, and a faint odor of unwashed bodies, and she deduced that the corridors through which she was being led likely had been packed with people only minutes earlier. A sardonic smile lifted the corner of her mouth. *They must have cleared them just for me. How considerate.*

Ishikawa stopped beside the wardroom door and pressed its visitor signal. "We're here," she said.

O'Brien's voice squawked from the speaker beside the control panel. *"Enter."* The door slid open, and Ishikawa motioned Ghemor inside.

Standing on the far side of the meeting table were O'Brien and Eddington. Ghemor strode in, followed closely by Ishikawa and Sloan, who shut and locked the door. The svelte Cardassian woman stopped directly across from the two rebellion leaders and nodded politely. "General O'Brien. General Eddington. Thank you for seeing me."

"Have a seat," Eddington said, gesturing toward a chair. He and O'Brien settled into their chairs, so Ghemor did likewise.

O'Brien skipped the pleasantries. "What do you want?"

"I came to bring you important news, and to make a request."

Eddington offered her a pained smile. "You'd better start with the news."

"Sixteen hours from now, Bajor will secede from the Alliance and abdicate its role as power broker and mediator between the Cardassian Union and the Klingon Empire." Her pronouncement was met by wide-eyed stares.

Ishikawa looked stunned. "How did this happen so quickly? I thought the Bajoran government was destroyed when the Intendant torpedoed Ashalla."

"Ironically," Ghemor said, "the loss of the civilian government streamlined the political process. Opaka Sulan has been selected as the planet's *kai,* or spiritual leader, and the senior members of her underground religion have come out of hiding to reconstitute the Vedek Assembly for the first time in centuries. In the absence of other leadership, they've become Bajor's de facto government."

Sloan shook his head and wore an incredulous expression. "From tyranny to theocracy. I'm not sure that counts as progress."

Ghemor shot a pointed look at him. "Considering that it's also changed Bajor from your enemy to your ally, I would argue that it does."

"No offense," O'Brien said, "but don't you think it's a bit too soon to call the Bajorans our allies?"

"Not necessarily. That brings us to the second reason for my visit: a request. The government of Bajor wants me to ask you not to abandon Terok Nor."

O'Brien chortled and looked around at his comrades, who seemed uneasy. Grinning at Ghemor, he asked, "Why, pray tell, would the Bajorans want that?"

"Because that's what the Prophets told me to tell them."

Another awkward silence settled over the rebels.

Eddington folded his hands on the tabletop and leaned forward. He looked Ghemor in the eye. His mien was focused but his voice remained calm and quiet. "Could you clarify that, please?"

This was never going to be an easy sell, Ghemor knew. Despite having made personal contact with the Prophets, even she was not entirely certain which of their predictions she believed or which of their adjurations she was willing to heed. She was not one to believe in gods, but even she could not deny what she had witnessed firsthand. She needed to make the humans understand, and her best chance of doing so was to phrase this in a way they might be willing to accept.

"Sentient beings created and live inside the Bajoran wormhole," she said, doing her best to sound clinical and detached. "They exist without physical form and don't perceive time in the same linear way that we do. To them, there's no difference between the past, the present, and the future. They experience it all at once. When they tell us what they see in the future, for them it's reporting—but to us it seems like prophecy. These are the beings the Bajorans call the Prophets." She cast expectant glances at each of the four humans. "With me so far?" They all nodded, so she continued. "After I made contact with them, they started using me as a mouthpiece to give messages to Bajor. One of those messages was about you."

Ishikawa asked, "What was this message, exactly?"

"That Bajor needed to help the rebels, or else its people would die."

Sloan shrugged. "That sounds pretty cut-and-dried."

"Yes," Ghemor said. "Which makes it a very unusual statement for the Prophets, but that's a topic for another time. The bottom line is that Bajor is prepared to help you repair and defend this station."

O'Brien sounded suspicious. "What can they do for us that we can't already do for ourselves?"

"Restock your torpedoes, for one," Ghemor said. "For another, they can fix your broken phaser banks and guide you to orbital coordinates from which their planetary defenses can give you maximum covering fire."

The rebel leader held up his open hand, palm out. "Hang on. Do you mean to tell me Bajor's had spare munitions for the station all this time?"

"Of course they did. The Alliance has maintained a sizable weapons cache on the planet's surface ever since Terok Nor was built."

"Then why the bloody hell are we finding out about it only now?"

"Because when someone puts a gun to your head, you don't offer them free ammunition."

Eddington muttered to O'Brien, "She has a point."

O'Brien grimaced at his friend, then turned his attention back to Ghemor. "So, what does the rebellion have to do to win these favors from Bajor?"

"Move Terok Nor away from the wormhole and back into orbit. Once you're in position, we'll begin shuttling up munitions, provisions, and personnel."

Nodding, O'Brien said, "We'll have to discuss it."

"Talk if you must, but do it quickly," Ghemor said. "The Talarian Republic is about to collapse, probably within a few days. Kai Opaka has already sent out a message offering Talarian refugees safe haven on Bajor. It won't be long before the Alliance retaliates. The sooner Terok Nor is back in orbit, the sooner we can begin making ready for war."

"If we stay here," O'Brien said, "we can't expend all our efforts on defense. Fortifying a home base is all well and good, but the only way we're ever going to win this war is to expand and start playing offense. Will Bajor sign on for that?"

Ghemor nodded. "Yes, it will."

"All right." O'Brien looked around at his comrades. "Show of hands: Who's ready to move the station back to Bajor?" He raised his hand first, and the others did the same almost immediately thereafter. "Motion carried, then. Miss Ghemor, tell Kai Opaka that Terok Nor's coming home." He offered her his open hand, and she reached across the table and clasped it. Shaking her delicate gray hand in his callused fist, he smiled and added, "Welcome to the rebellion."

3

Plans of Attack

Secession?" Supreme Legate Skrain Dukat knew that laughter was a grossly inappropriate response but chuckled despite himself. He smiled at his best friend and chief adviser, Gul Corat Damar. "That's the best news I've had in weeks."

Damar looked perplexed. "By what measure, sir?"

Dukat cleared his throat and shot a glance through narrowed eyes at his old comrade. A by-the-book soldier, Damar had many fine qualities—courage, loyalty, efficiency—but a gift for grand-scale strategic thinking was not among them. "This is a gift, Damar. Bajor just spit in the face of the Alliance—and after all we've done for them! We freed them from the Terrans. Gave them privilege and power. Shared our technology." He leaned forward, his countenance darkening. "And how did they repay us? With *betrayal*."

"Forgive me, but I still fail to see the opportunity in this."

"All crises are opportunities, Damar. The key to leadership is not to waste them." He got up from his desk, walked to a low triangular cabinet tucked into the corner behind him, and opened it, revealing his private stock of rare-vintage *kanar*. He chose a tall bottle that resembled a coiled serpent, then took two squat, cut-crystal tumblers from the upper shelf, set them on top of the cabinet, and closed the doors. "You know better than most how hard I've tried to be a friend to Bajor."

Damar nodded. "Of course."

As he filled the two glasses with the thick, burnt-orange liquor, Dukat reflected bitterly on the wrongs the Bajorans had done him in recent months. He had influenced their Chamber of Ministers to appoint his ruthless mistress Ro Laren as Bajor's Intendant, only to see her convicted soon after on trumped-up charges of treason and handed over to the Klingons. Then the Bajorans had added insult to injury by reappointing Kira Nerys to the office. Now that scheming *pulyot* was dead, a casualty of her own hubris, and that fact was the sole reason Dukat was able to marshal a smile as he handed Damar his drink.

"Ever since this 'Emissary' appeared, Bajor has been caught up in a religious mania run amok. It's clear to me that what the Bajorans need now, more than ever, is someone who can restore order to their society. I am that person."

"On that we agree, old friend." Damar raised his glass to Dukat, and they clinked the tumblers in a toast. "Though I have to say, that sounds more like a chore than a gift."

"You need to see the big picture." Dukat stepped in front of his office's trio of oval windows and admired his sunset view of Cardassia Prime's capital city. "By bringing Bajor to heel without Klingon interference, we'll shame Martok's empire and give the Union back its pride." He sipped his *kanar*. "But to do that, we'll need to move quickly, while the Klingons are still bogged down subduing the Talarians. How soon can you mobilize the Ninth Order?"

"Ten days."

"Too slow. Make it five."

Damar frowned. "With respect, Legate, I don't inflate my estimates, and the timetable is not flexible. The Ninth Order can't deploy until it's refueled and resupplied—and that will take ten days."

Dukat grumbled in frustration. "Very well. I just hope we can secure Bajor before the Klingons regroup."

"May I offer an opinion, sir?"

"By all means."

Setting his untouched beverage on Dukat's desk, Damar said, "We might not want to commit ourselves to the Bajor mission."

The suggestion triggered Dukat's temper. He faced Damar. "Why not?"

"Destroying Bajor would be simple, but subduing it will require a large-scale invasion and occupation. It normally requires years of planning to prepare the battlefield—to stage personnel and supplies and compromise the enemy's infrastructure and institutions. My concern is that our forces will become bogged down without clear objectives, and we'll wind up occupying Bajor for decades."

"You say that like it's a bad thing."

"I say it because it would be a costly thing, sir. It would consume far more of our budget and resources than we can afford, and it would leave us vulnerable on other fronts. And for what? Bajor has surrendered its influence within the Alliance by seceding. What will Cardassia gain by conquering one planet?"

"Revenge!" Dukat hurled his glass at the wall. Crystal shards ricocheted like shrapnel from the impact. Tiny fragments remained stuck inside the syrupy stain that dripped in slow tendrils to the black granite floor. "Don't talk to me of budgets or politics! You and I— we're *soldiers,* Damar! Men of action!"

The door to the antechamber outside Dukat's office opened, and two young Vulcan women entered carrying janitorial implements. They seemed to glide in graceful silence, heads bowed, moving on a direct path toward Dukat's latest mess. With practiced choreography they set to work, cleansing the shards of crystal from the floor and the stain from the wall. Dukat admired their efficiency, obedience, and apparent humility. To his trained eye, their species' reputation as perfect slaves seemed well deserved.

While the women worked, Dukat returned to the bar cabinet and poured himself a new drink. "I want you to take direct responsibility for planning the invasion and occupation," he said. He returned to his desk and sat down.

"If that's your wish, Legate."

"Be merciless. Don't concern yourself with preserving Bajor's value to the Alliance. It's more important that we make an example of them. The greater the collateral damage, the more effective a demonstration this will be. Understood?" Damar nodded once. Dukat grinned. "Splendid. Report back when the invasion plans are ready for my review."

Damar stood. "As you command, sir."

"Dismissed."

Dukat watched Damar turn and leave his office. The two Vulcan servants followed him out, and the door shut after them with a soft hiss. Downing another swig of his *kanar,* Dukat swiveled his chair to gaze once more out his windows at the deepening dusk. Night would soon descend on the Cardassian capital—but it was nothing compared to the darkness Dukat had resolved to unleash on Bajor.

"I'm surrounded by fools!" Regent Martok slammed his fist on the arm of his throne. The smack of flesh against stone reverberated off the walls of the High Council Chamber, which was deserted except for Martok and his chief of staff, General Goluk. The two Klingons regarded each other in the half-light, Martok glaring at Goluk's war-scarred visage. "Kopek and his band of cronies got us into this quagmire with no plan for getting us out! What could they have been thinking, starting a war with the Romulans?"

"No doubt trying to boost their own pathetic credentials," Goluk said. "For what it's worth, My Lord, I've downgraded their security clearances and adjusted their portfolios to cut them off from the High Command."

"It's too late. The damage is done." Martok stood, stepped off his throne's dais, and walked past the grizzled, gray-maned old veteran. He paced atop the imperial emblem that adorned the chamber's floor, and clenched his shaking fists. "We had one hand on the throat of the rebellion and the other on a *d'k tahg* set to stab the Talarians in the heart—but two wars at once wasn't enough for them! They had to lay waste to Romulus and open a *third* front. Make no mistake: I enjoy a good war as much as anyone, but I prefer to wage them on my own terms."

"I think that is precisely *why* Kopek sent Krone and his Cardassian allies to Romulus." Goluk noted Martok's questioning glance. "They may have instigated the conflict with the Romulans, but now that it's engaged, its resolution is your responsibility."

Halting in the middle of the room, Martok considered the implications of that point. "You think they've set me up to fail."

"Yes."

It made sense. The first sign of weakness on Martok's part would be all the justification any of his rivals on the High Council would require to challenge him to ritual single combat for the regency. "I refuse to give them the satisfaction," he rasped. "What will it take to neutralize the Romulan threat?"

Goluk crossed his arms and stroked his bearded chin. "The Romulans are rigidly hierarchical in their thinking and behavior, so the surest way to break their resolve is to strike at their leadership."

"Are you talking about that *toDSaH* Hiren?"

"No, My Lord, the Xenexian, Mac Calhoun. Hiren and the other Romulans have rallied to his banner, and he seems to have been the architect of their recent victories, including the strike on our refinery at Tranome Sar."

Martok returned to the dais and settled onto his throne. Though he had heard Calhoun's name a few times before this, he hadn't realized just how substantial a threat the rebel leader had become. "How strong is Calhoun's fleet?"

"Strong enough to be called an armada. He has hundreds of ships, most of them built and crewed by Romulans, as well as several dozen vessels crewed by Xenexians he liberated from the Danteri."

The regent's thick brows knitted together in fierce concentration. "Not enough to invade our territory, but more than enough to inflict serious damage."

"Exactly. Though I would be more concerned about Calhoun's plan to unite his forces with those of the Terran Rebellion."

The very notion prompted a gruff *harrumph* from Martok. "The Terran Rebellion will be gone long before he reaches them. Dukat will see to that."

The general bristled at the mere utterance of Dukat's name. "Must we let him seize the initiative against the Terrans and Bajorans? If his forces pacify those sectors without us, he'll fill dozens of worlds' governments with his puppets."

"So? It's not as if the Alliance Council wields any real authority. If Dukat wants to waste Cardassian blood and treasure jockeying for control over a bunch of useless *jeghpu'wI*, let him." Martok reached down to a low table beside his throne, picked up a stein half-filled with *warnog,* and guzzled it dry. The last drops of pungent liquor dribbled through his black whiskers until he palmed them away. "Do you trust Klag to finish off the Talarians?"

"Yes, My Lord. He may have only one arm, but he's still a great warrior."

"Good. Then our only concern is Calhoun. Where is he now?"

Goluk took a small device from a pocket inside his cassock and used it to activate a holographic star map that filled the chamber. Manipulating its controls, he enlarged a section of the galaxy along the Klingon-Romulan border. "In the week since the attack on Tranome Sar, we've received reports of intermittent contact with single Romulan ships at numerous points along the border. We presume those ships are performing reconnaissance for Calhoun."

"No doubt. Illuminate all points of contact." A few taps on the control device by Goluk peppered the projection with more than two dozen pulsating red points of light. Martok studied the pattern and cracked a lop-sided grin. "Curious."

"My Lord?"

"Carraya, Lorillia, Celes . . . Those systems lie along an old trade route inside what used to be Terran space. Calhoun's looking for a convoy, something big enough to be worth his while. He probably thinks that if he hits us hard enough, we'll cut our losses—and give him the breathing room he needs to reach Bajor."

"Then he's hunting in the wrong place," Goluk said. "He's light-years from any active trade routes."

"True . . . but he doesn't know that." Martok punched his open palm and smiled at his good fortune. "If it's a convoy he wants, let's give him one. The biggest one he's ever seen. Fuel tankers, heavy freighters, medical frigates, all on a regular schedule between H'Atoria and Celes—a target so tempting Calhoun won't be able to resist going after it, even if he suspects it's a trap. But don't make it look weak—he'll see through such an obvious ploy. Defend it well. And make sure it passes within two light-hours of the Joch'chal Nebula."

Goluk looked at the nebula in the holographic star map and nodded. "You think that's where he'll stage his forces for the ambush."

Martok grinned, a predator preparing to feast. "Of course. Because that's where we're going to stage ours."

4

Death Is a Name for Beauty

S ensation and awareness returned to Saavik in a sudden flood as she emerged from the prismatic fury of the transporter beam. She had materialized on a platform inside the new Memory Omega command headquarters, which lay hidden deep inside an ostensibly unremarkable asteroid orbiting Zeta Serpentis.

A pair of familiar individuals manned the transport console a few meters in front of her: a slender, balding human man with a kind face, and his lanky, supremely self-assured half-human, half-Klingon female comrade-in-arms. The two stepped around the console to greet Saavik as she stepped off the platform.

The woman spoke first. "Welcome back, ma'am. It's good to see you."

"Thank you, K'Ehleyr." She nodded at the man. "Mister Barclay."

He acknowledged her greeting with a shy smile. "Ma'am."

"We are all in your debt," Saavik said to them. "Your actions at Gamma Pavonis prevented what might have been a calamitous reversal. I commend you."

K'Ehleyr bowed her head slightly. "Kind of you to say."

Dark emotions crossed Barclay's face like a shadow.

"We did what we had to, ma'am." He gestured toward the door. "The others are waiting for you."

"Of course," Saavik said, leading them out of the transporter room. It did not surprise her that neither of the two field agents wished to dwell on their most recent assignment; it had been a most unfortunate affair from its inception.

One of the movement's top strategists, General Alynna Nechayev, had absconded with Memory Omega's master quantum transceiver during the emergency evacuation of the Regula base. When her absence had first been noticed, most of her peers assumed she had either become lost or stranded, or had been captured by the Alliance, so Saavik had sent K'Ehleyr and Barclay to rescue Nechayev. Soon afterward, the duo had discovered Nechayev's lost ship in Alliance custody, and they tracked Nechayev to a remote Klingon outpost on Gamma Pavonis III—only to discover that Nechayev was not a prisoner of war but a defector, a traitor to Spock's underground movement. In the end, after recovering the quantum transceiver, Barclay had been forced to kill Nechayev to prevent her from escaping and seeking another opportunity to betray Memory Omega.

Since his return, Barclay had seemed to harbor profound guilt for his slaying of Nechayev. Saavik regretted that the man's conscience had been so cruelly burdened, but it also reassured her. Barclay's remorse was further proof that Spock had been right about the malleability of human nature. If a Terran could exhibit such a noble regard for life and obvious disdain for murder, perhaps Spock's vision of a better future for all sentient beings truly was possible.

The two agents followed Saavik down a broad, drab

gray corridor stacked high on either side with battered old shipping containers. The contrast between the newly manufactured metal flooring and the century-old crates was striking. Saavik saw her reflection underfoot with almost mirrorlike quality, while flanked on either side by a hundred years' worth of scuffs, scratches, dents, and gouges. That was nothing, however, compared to the contrast that awaited her.

As she neared the end of the long passageway, a pair of massive doors joined on a diagonal slid apart, revealing the lush splendor that lay beyond them. Intense artificial sunlight streamed through the portal's widening gap, followed by a flood of warm air heavy with the perfume of flowering plants and ripe fruit. White noise greeted Saavik's sensitive ears, which distinguished the hush of mechanically generated breezes from the susurrus of water crashing down from carefully engineered waterfalls. Her eyes adjusted to the brilliant glare as she passed over the threshold into an Eden born of science: a Genesis cave.

It looked like a paradisiacal jungle valley on any of a number of Class M worlds, with its clear blue sky and misty horizon beyond forested hilltops, but those details, Saavik knew, were only illusions. In reality, the cave, though vast, was entirely self-contained deep inside the asteroid. The sky was generated by a sophisticated holomatrix that provided the cavern's flora—and inhabitants—with necessary cycles of nourishing daylight and restful night. The air and water were filtered regularly by machines buried in the bedrock, and concealed portable fusion generators supplied the base's nearly two hundred occupants with clean energy. Advanced septic systems helped recycle waste into fertilizers and biofuels that were used to perpetuate the secret colony's agricultural resources. Replicators were used sparingly, to fabricate precision parts for scientific research and high-tech repairs, while such essentials as clothing and daily meals were made by hand.

Remarkable as the cave was, it was not at all unique but rather only one of dozens of such redoubts created throughout local space by Memory Omega. Some were optimized for research and others for data archives; many were tasked solely with preparing to secure a future that now seemed to be at hand. This, however, was the command base that coordinated the actions of all the others, and it was the only one that dispatched field agents into the galaxy at large.

Saavik stood atop the broad cliff that overlooked the ersatz valley and basked for a few moments in the tropical microclimate while K'Ehleyr powered up one of several open-topped antigrav hovercraft parked to the right of the entrance.

The tall, athletic half-Klingon nodded to Barclay, who beckoned Saavik into the vehicle. "Ma'am, we're ready to bring you down to the meeting."

Despite being over a century in age, Saavik was still quite fit by the standards of most humanoids, and she moved with alacrity and grace as she boarded the hovercraft. Once she sat down, K'Ehleyr piloted the craft away from the cliff and down into the deep basin. The speed of their descent whipped the women's hair behind them. Raising her voice to be heard above the rush of wind, Saavik asked, "Are we really in need of such haste?"

"Yes, ma'am," K'Ehleyr said, "I believe we are."

Less than a minute after lifting off from the cliff, the hovercraft dropped through a break in the forest canopy and settled gently into a clearing ringed by a tight cluster of prefabricated structures. There were fleeting signs of activity in all of them, but the closest of them, the dining hall, was alive with agitated voices. Saavik stepped out of the vehicle and climbed the steps to join the discussion. Barclay and K'Ehleyr followed close behind her.

Standing off to one side of the spacious hall were two Vulcan undercover operatives, Tuvok and Chu'lak. They were a study in contrast. Tuvok was of average height but quite muscular; he had deep brown skin and wore his hair shorn tightly to his skull. Chu'lak was tall, pale, and gaunt, and his silvery gray hair had grown a bit wild during his years lurking among the cells of the Terran Rebellion. Standing a short distance from them was Tuvok's wife, T'Pel, who was a member of Memory Omega's senior leadership alongside Saavik.

None of the three Vulcans were speaking, and Saavik realized all the shouting she'd heard from outside was coming from just two people in the center of the hall: Martin Madden, a high-strung human man who was part of Memory Omega's operations team, and Curzon Dax, who, in addition to being the galaxy's only remaining Trill joined with a symbiont, was the most ill-tempered and foul-mouthed old man Saavik had ever encountered. Dax's invectives and Madden's protests bled into a wall of impenetrable noise—which crumbled like a sand castle in the tide when K'Ehleyr bellowed, "Both of you, SHUT UP!"

The sudden silence remained tainted by the two men's vitriol. Saavik studied them with her cold gaze. "What are we discussing?"

Madden pointed at Dax. "Don't listen to him! It wasn't my fault!"

Dax snapped, "Of course it's your fault, you *chuQa*! It was *your* job!"

A hint of Saavik's temper, dormant but never extinguished, put an edge in her voice. "A *topic*, gentlemen, *please*."

From the side of the room, Tuvok interjected, "Kes is missing."

K'Ehleyr shot back, "*Missing*, as in, we've *misplaced* her?"

"No," Dax said, "as in, Madden let her escape!"

"It wasn't my fault!" Madden pointed at Tuvok and T'Pel. "They were supposed to be in charge of moving her from the old HQ to this one, not me!"

Tuvok arched one eyebrow in a distinctly accusatory fashion. "There were exigent circumstances, Mister Madden, as you well know. We had no choice but to entrust her safe passage to you."

"She used her powers to scramble my memory. That's not my fault!"

"That's quite enough," Saavik said, in a quiet voice that forced the others to be silent in order to hear her. "Cease your protests, Martin. No one will blame you for Kes's escape. You had been assured"—she aimed a keen stare at Tuvok—"as we all were, that Kes lived among us of her own free will. You couldn't have known she meant to flee during our forced evacuation of Regula." She folded her hands behind her back. "We need her back in our custody before the Alliance finds her. She's dangerously unstable, and will inevitably draw attention. If they learn how to clone her talents as B'Elanna did, all hope for the revolution will be lost."

Barclay and K'Ehleyr exchanged determined looks, and then she said, "We're ready to go find her, ma'am."

Tuvok stepped forward. "With respect, I should be the one to pursue Kes. I was the one who brought her into the movement and vouched for her. That makes her, and the potential threat she represents, my responsibility."

Saavik looked at K'Ehleyr. "Tuvok is correct. He is the

one best qualified to bring Kes back into the fold. More important, I have an urgent assignment for you and Mister Barclay." She faced Tuvok. "Time is against us. Go now."

"Yes, ma'am."

Tuvok walked quickly toward the door but halted when K'Ehleyr caught his arm and asked, "How the hell are you gonna track a superpowered telepath who doesn't want to be found?"

He pulled his arm free of K'Ehleyr's grasp and resumed walking. "By reaching her destination before she does."

Kes drifted like a ghost through the back alleys of Okara, a dilapidated spaceport on the planet Tammeron. The young Ocampa woman traveled alone, a picture of innocence, beauty, and frailty—a magnet for all manner of degenerates and thugs.

They were everywhere, lurking in shadowy doorways below street level, watching her through windows and from rooftops, observing her from vehicles that crossed her path—all of them oblivious of the malevolent energies they projected and the intentions they telegraphed, emanations that only Kes's telepathic skills could detect; unaware that as they watched her, she watched them.

All around her, alien minds blazed in the night, psionic beacons announcing their presence to a deaf world. Daydreams and revenge fantasies mingled with lies still being honed to perfection before being spoken aloud. Emotions of every color bled together into one without a name, and Kes had to concentrate to keep her telepathic barriers raised, to filter out the sheer noise of so many untrained minds trumpeting their desires to the universe at large.

For a moment it was almost enough to make her miss the relative tranquility of the Memory Omega base inside the Regula asteroid. Most of her close company there had been Vulcans, natural telepaths who had developed great discipline to shield their own thoughts and conceal their talents from a galaxy of hostile neighbors. Before Tuvok and his wife, T'Pel, had taken her to live there, Kes had been indiscriminate in the use of her abilities, and until she met Tuvok she had never even considered the need to actively mask her gifts. T'Pel, Saavik, and several other Vulcans had shared a great deal of knowledge with her, and their teachings had helped Kes hone her abilities and magnify them many times over.

But as grateful as she was for their tutelage, she had never stopped thinking about Neelix, the only person in the galaxy who loved Kes for who she was rather than for what she could do, the one who had risked his life to save her when her first steps into misadventure had led twice to her capture—first by the Kazon-Ogla and then by the Alliance. When T'Pel and Tuvok liberated Kes from the clutches of Intendant B'Elanna of Ardana— who had tasked her minions with unlocking the secrets of Kes's abilities so that they could clone them into any- one they wished, starting with B'Elanna herself—the Memory Omega agents had told Neelix some absurd tale about Kes transforming into a being of pure energy, as if such a thing were the least bit believable. From that moment, Kes's and Neelix's lives had been forced onto separate paths. This had been done not only for Neelix's safety, Tuvok had explained, but for the sake of the en- tire Terran Rebellion, whose status within the Alliance would have been elevated from "nuisance" to "primary target" if it was believed to be harboring a telepath of such unrivaled potential as Kes.

She was not unsympathetic to the rebellion's cause, and

she bore more than a small measure of lingering hatred
for the Alliance, but Kes was no longer content to live as
a prisoner for someone else's sake. After aiding a mission
years earlier to capture the psionically enhanced B'Elanna,
Kes had gone so far as to take the precaution of switching
the holocube inside which B'Elanna's consciousness had
been imprisoned, reasoning that she could use it as lever-
age against the Alliance when the time came for her escape
from the rebellion. Unfortunately, the complete lack of
response by the Alliance to B'Elanna's disappearance had
soon made it obvious to Kes that the renegade Intendant
of Ardana was worthless as a hostage, so she had erased
B'Elanna's quantum pattern and discarded the cube. As
best she could tell, no one within Memory Omega had
yet detected her deception, which made it clear how little
value they, too, placed on B'Elanna's life.

No sooner had she made that choice than the Memory Omega leadership had declared that a security breach
required them to evacuate the secret base inside Regula.
During the chaotic exodus to the new safe haven in the
Zeta Serpentis system, senior personnel such as Tuvok
and T'Pel had been consumed with many pressing duties, and it had been a simple matter to persuade them to
let Kes travel with young Mister Madden. An ordinary
human male, Madden had a mind like soft putty, and
Kes molded it to suit her aims. After he had dropped her
off in Okara, he helped her erase his ship's navigational

logs, and then she sent him on his way with a delayed-onset episode of transient global amnesia.

She had spent the days since his departure discreetly acquiring a ship and arranging to have it fueled, provisioned, and armed. Now she was on her way back to her tiny vessel, the *Valaria,* having completed an impromptu visit to the home of the spaceport's Cardassian chief administrator, whom she had compelled to issue immediate departure clearances that would guarantee her safe passage to Bajor.

Turning a corner toward the docking slips, she halted abruptly as three brawny male aliens blocked her path. Warts and freckles covered their hairless heads, which each sported a prominent bony ring stretching around the back of the skull from ear to ear. Attired in dark garb and brandishing blasters, they advanced on Kes. She tried to reach inside their minds to turn them away and make them forget they had seen her, but their minds were utterly unreadable, as if they weren't even there. The leader bared a sharp-toothed grin. "What have we here?"

Rather than retreat, Kes stood her ground. "Move aside and let me pass."

One of the henchmen chuckled and said to the leader, "That didn't sound very friendly, did it, Gorta?"

"No, Paluk, it didn't." He stopped in front of Kes and teased her blond hair with the muzzle of his blaster. "Maybe we need to teach this little *veska* some manners." He traced the line of her jaw with his gun. "What's your name, girl?"

"Holster your weapon and walk away. I won't warn you again."

Gorta swung his arm up and back to pistol-whip her.

Their minds were impervious to telepathy, but Kes

had many other talents, not the least of which was tele-kinesis—which meant their bodies were fair game.

The blaster in Gorta's hand collapsed into its con-stituent parts, which warped and twisted as they fell to the ground. His hand remained trapped high above his head—and then his arm twisted right as his torso was wrenched left. The sickening crack of breaking bones and ripping ligaments was crisply audible in the stillness of the night. As the two henchmen behind him backed away, Gorta met Kes's hard, unblinking glare with a look of terror. Then his rib cage imploded, his femurs snapped like dry twigs, and his head was forced to turn 180 degrees, shattering his cervical vertebrae.

His broken corpse dropped to the pavement with a dull *thwap*.

The two henchmen turned to run. Kes knew they couldn't be allowed to escape. If they ever spoke of what they'd seen, the Alliance would initiate a hunt for her unlike any in its history. For her own sake as well as Neelix's, Gorta's partners in crime had to die, but that didn't mean they had to suffer. She gave them swift deaths—telekinetic stabs through their heads. Blood, bone, and brain matter erupted from the aliens' fore-heads, and they collapsed instantly to the sidewalk.

Kes stepped over Gorta's body and resumed walking. She had waited long enough for her reunion with Nee-lix, and this world had nothing else she needed.

Minutes later she was aboard the *Valaria*, riding a black wind into space and charting a course to the stars. *Be strong, my beloved*, she projected, hoping desperately that Neelix could hear her. *I'm on my way.*

5

The Promise of Shadows

Sweat dripped from Jean-Luc Picard's forehead and soaked his loose-fitting linen shirt. Sand filled his boots and caked his pants, and he was surrounded by mounds of excavated dirt. A sharp scrape echoed inside the cave as his entrenching tool made contact with something metal. He cast the shovel aside, dropped to his knees, and pawed at the rocky sand, clearing it from the container, a cube whose edges each measured fifteen centimeters. *Right where the legend said it would be,* he rejoiced, and a rare, broad grin brightened his usually grim countenance.

He had just begun translating the symbols on the cube's exterior in a bid to open it and retrieve the ancient treasure locked inside when he heard the telltale hum of the Vorgons' transport beam reverberating off the cavern's walls. He glanced up at a high ledge that overlooked the subterranean chamber and was unsurprised to see Ajur and Boratus gazing back at him. Equally expected, the two criminals from the future were brandishing small handheld weapons.

"You've found the Tox Uthat," Boratus said, "just as we predicted."

Picard stood, still holding the box. "Indeed. But you don't think I'll simply hand this over, do you?"

Ajur cocked her head at an odd angle. "Not without persuasion. That is why we have come prepared to use force."

"So have I."

A scathing blue beam shot from a pitch-dark tunnel behind Picard, sliced through the hazy air above his head, and slammed into Ajur's chest. The female Vorgon rebounded off the wall behind her and pitched forward off the ledge. Her unconscious body struck the rocky ground with a heavy crunch and kicked up a choking cloud of dust.

Deanna Troi emerged from the tunnel, garbed in olive khakis, an off-white linen shirt, and well-weathered knee-high boots. She kept her plasma rifle steady and aimed squarely at Boratus. "I think it's time you left."

Boratus seemed to smile, though it was hard for Picard to be sure what emotions might be at play on the Vorgon's hideously ridged face. "An obvious strategy," he said. "One for which precautions have been taken." He raised his voice. "Gul Edoka?" A lanky Cardassian man with a high forehead and heavier-than-usual ocular ridges stepped slowly from the darkness behind Troi. As he raised his weapon, she grudgingly lowered hers.

"Put the box on the ground or she dies," Edoka said.

Picard dropped the box. Boratus said with smug self-satisfaction, "You and your companion will be remanded to the custody of Gul Edoka."

"And in exchange he's letting you take the Tox Uthat?" Picard huffed derisively and shook his head. "He doesn't know what it is, does he?"

"He does not seem to care. Your capture appears to be his sole desire." He looked at Edoka. "You may arrest him now, but please do not harm the artifact."

At first, Edoka didn't move or speak. Then the gul gently lobbed his disruptor away. The weapon clattered across the rocks, stopping at Picard's feet.

Keenly aware that Boratus was still aiming at him, Picard made no attempt to pick up Edoka's discarded weapon.

The Vorgon hollered at Edoka, "What are you doing?"

Troi moved aside as Edoka took another step forward, and it became clear that there was someone behind the Cardassian, prodding him forward at gunpoint. The trailing figure edged into the pale moonlight that illuminated the cavern through a hole in its ceiling. It was a male human, slight of build, with fair but thinning hair. He was clad all in black and wielding a compact hand weapon unlike any Picard had ever seen. He smiled meekly at Boratus. "Pardon the interruption."

Boratus's hand began to tremble. Apparently, Picard surmised, the Vorgon hadn't anticipated this turn of events and was now aware that the odds were turning against him. "Most ingenious, Picard. But do not think this is over. You cannot hide the Tox Uthat from us forever."

As if from thin air, a female voice that Picard didn't recognize said, "He won't have to." Then an angry red streak of energy slashed through the tiny artifact from the future and destroyed it in a brilliant flash. Picard stumbled backward from the miniature conflagration and recovered his bearings in time to see a tall and strikingly attractive woman of partial Klingon ancestry shimmer into view between him and Boratus. She wore the same solid black body suit as the man who had rescued Troi. The half-Klingon woman pointed her peculiar weapon at the Vorgon. "Your little toy is dust. And unless you feel like joining it—"

Boratus pressed a button on his wrist bracer. A red swirl enveloped him and Ajur, and they teleported back to the future from which they'd come.

The man in black gestured with his weapon at Edoka and asked his female compatriot, "What about this one?"

"Heavy stun."

A blue pulse lit the cavern as a screech split the air. Edoka collapsed face-first to the ground, unconscious. The two strangers holstered their weapons, and the woman smiled.

"Jean-Luc Picard, I presume?"

Picard's cool façade gave way to fiery indignation. "Do you have the faintest idea what you've done?"

The woman shrugged. "Saved your life, for starters."

He pointed at the blackened scorch on the floor. "That was a weapon of inestimable power! Its value was beyond measure!"

"Actually," said the man in black, "it was worthless, booby-trapped by its creator. Anyone who tried to use it would've blown themselves to bits."

Picard glanced at Troi. She gave him an almost imperceptible nod that confirmed the strangers were telling the truth. He continued, still upset but less overtly hostile. "Be that as it may, it was a unique artifact, with intrinsic archeological value. Do you have any idea how long we'd spent looking for it?"

The woman cocked one eyebrow. "According to your dossier, five years."

"That's right! Five long, miserable—" He stopped short and considered the first part of the stranger's answer. "Did you say *dossier*?"

She nodded. "I did. We've had a file on you ever since you assassinated Lursa and B'Etor at the Sacred Chalice on Betazed."

"Actually," Troi cut in, "I was the one who shot the Duras sisters."

"We know," said the male stranger. "We have a file on you, too, Miss Troi."

The half-Klingon moved closer to Picard. "You two make quite a pair. Not many people have survived planetside encounters with the Crystalline Entity. And I'd love to know how you talked the Romulans into saving Drema IV."

"It was easy," Picard said, "once they found out the planet was full of dilithium." He still regarded the interlopers with suspicion, but his mounting curiosity came to the fore. "Who are you?"

The woman offered him her hand, and he shook it. She had a powerful grip. "My name is K'Ehleyr, and this is my partner, Reg Barclay."

Picard released her hand. "Charmed. But if you're here to recruit us into the Terran Rebellion, don't bother. We left that behind years ago."

"We're not from the rebellion," K'Ehleyr said, "though I'd be lying if I said we weren't on their side." She loomed over Picard as he squatted and gathered his digging equipment into a canvas roll-up. "We've been directed by our superiors to invite you to a meeting."

He tied the roll shut and looked up at K'Ehleyr and Barclay. "Your *superiors*? Who do you represent?"

Barclay said, "No one you've ever heard of."

"That doesn't answer my question."

K'Ehleyr sounded impatient. "Edoka's men are going

to come looking for him, probably sooner rather than later. We should go."

"No," Picard said. "Not until we get some straight answers."

Barclay and K'Ehleyr looked at Troi, who held up her palms. "Don't look at me. He's in charge."

"Fine," K'Ehleyr said. "We belong to an organization called Memory Omega. It was a secret program initiated nearly a hundred years ago by Emperor Spock, to preserve the knowledge of the Terran Empire after its fall, and to help steer the galaxy toward a new age of freedom."

It was all Picard could do not to laugh. "Preposterous." Then he looked at Troi. Her eyes were wide, her jaw slack. This time there was nothing subtle about her nod of affirmation. Picard was struck by the sensation that he stood on the cusp of a discovery that was as remarkable as it seemed improbable. "You expect me to believe that a century-old resistance cell can stand against the Alliance?"

Barclay stepped forward to reply. "It's not some mere 'resistance cell.' It's a vast network representing the finest scientific minds in the galaxy. We have access to technology more advanced than anything the Alliance has ever seen. And we're gearing up to put the full weight of our support behind the Terran Rebellion."

"I won't deny that your equipment is impressive," Picard said with an envious glance at their stealth suits and sidearms, "but the rebellion is doomed. We've tried to help them, but they're hopelessly disorganized. They have no viable strategy for victory, no consensus, no *unity*. Soon they'll be gone, and once more the law of survival will become every being for itself."

K'Ehleyr fixed Picard with a bold stare. "The rebellion's fortunes are about to change, Jean-Luc."

"Call me Luc. I've only ever let one person address me by my full name, and it was a privilege she had to earn." The memory of Vash's death at the hands of the cybernetic horrors known as the Borg still felt like an open wound to Picard.

"My apologies," K'Ehleyr said. Her contrition caught Picard's attention. It sounded genuine and was, as far as he could recall, the first time any Klingon—or half-Klingon, in this case—had ever apologized to him. "You don't know us, and you have almost no reason to believe us. But we're not asking much, Luc. All we want to do is bring you safely to a meeting so you can hear what our leaders have to say. Then you can decide for yourself what to do, and if you choose to go your own way, no one will stop you. But I promise you—this is an opportunity unlike any you've ever had, or any other you're ever going to have. You need to trust us."

He was torn. As much as he treasured his independence, he knew that alone he and Troi were vulnerable. Sooner or later the Alliance would catch up to them, and then there would be hell to pay. These people seemed competent and earnest, and their comportment suggested that the organization backing them had the kind of discipline and foresight that the rebellion had sorely lacked.

Weighing even more heavily upon his thoughts was his concern for Troi. He had long felt a quasi-paternal obligation to the young half-Betazoid woman, whose mother and sister—and, for that matter, her entire life as she had known it—had been destroyed by a chain of events he had set in motion. It had taken him and

Troi years to heal all the lingering hurts between them, to forge an emotional bond. Now she was woven inextricably into the tapestry of his life, and he loved her like the daughter he'd never had. He couldn't bear the thought of her coming to harm.

Troi looked at him, her eyes shining with the promise of tears, and Picard knew it was because her empathic and telepathic gifts enabled her to perceive his unconditional affection for her. She shot subtle looks at Barclay and K'Ehleyr, and then she nodded to Picard, who took her meaning clearly.

"Trust," he said, choosing his words with care, "is a hard thing to come by." Harsh Cardassian voices echoed from the passages behind him; the enemy was drawing near. It was time to make a decision. He slung his equipment roll over his shoulder, beckoned Troi to his side, and took his transporter-recall controller from his pocket. "Where and when shall we rendezvous?"

K'Ehleyr handed him a data rod. "These coordinates in ten days."

Picard pocketed the data rod. "See you then." Then he triggered the beam-up sequence, and the cave seemed to vanish in a flood of white light as he and Troi returned to their ship with an appointment to keep.

6

Storm Sign

O'Brien joined Eddington at the railing on the upper level of a bar that once had been called Quark's but now was a space with no name. The shelves were bare, its bottles stood empty, and its replicators had been looted. Like most of the former shops along Terok Nor's once-bustling Promenade, the place was just a shell.

The two leading generals of the rebellion looked at a long row of pushed-together tables on the level below. Around them had gathered the senior members of the rebellion—cell leaders and ship commanders, most of them recruited in the last few months. "Here we go again," O'Brien said under his breath.

"Let's hope it goes better than our last war council."

The mere mention of that day drew a grim look from O'Brien. It had been nearly two years since Julian Bashir and his Ferengi cohort Zek had, in this room, usurped control of the Terran Rebellion from O'Brien and Eddington, only to blunder into an ambush that cost the rebellion hundreds of lives, eleven *Defiant*-class ships, and the vital tactical advantage of an untrackable Romulan cloaking device. O'Brien's only bitter solace was the knowledge that both Zek and Bashir had paid for that catastrophe with their lives.

Eddington straightened and clasped O'Brien's shoulder. "Ready?"

"Let's go."

Side by side, they descended the spiral staircase to the lower level. Together, they looked mismatched—O'Brien stocky and heavy-jowled, Eddington tall and square-jawed—except for a passing similarity in their receding hairlines. The hushed babel of overlapping voices dwindled to silence as they approached the head of the table. Standing at the far end were Sloan and Keiko. Gathered on either side were nearly two dozen of the rebellion's most experienced commanders, all looking lean and hungry for action.

Resting his fingertips on the tabletop, O'Brien looked around and met the stares of the men and women gathered there. "Good morning, and thank you all for coming. Some of you took great risks to join us today. For that, we're grateful." He glanced at Eddington, who took the cue to continue where O'Brien had left off.

"We'll cut straight to business. The rebellion is stronger now than it's been in over a year, and we need to change our strategy from defense to offense."

Anxious murmurs rolled through the room. O'Brien raised his voice to stifle any nascent protests. "Now that Bajor is helping us defend this station, our ships are free to take the fight to the enemy—and that's exactly what we're going to do."

"Nothing personal, General," said Steven Wexler, a bearded Terran man whose compact physique had been honed by years of forced hard labor and clandestine martial-arts training, "but this sounds a lot like the hot air General Zek was blowing before he got all those people killed at Empok Nor." The criticism drew fervent nods and mumbles of agreement from around the room.

Another dissenting voice rose from the murmurs. "How can you say this is the time to go on the attack?" The wall of bodies parted, and a striking brunette named Rebecca Sullivan leaned forward to question O'Brien and Eddington. "Any day now the Alliance'll come gunning for us *and* Bajor. No matter how well armed the planet is, it's still a stationary target. Making a stand here is suicide. My entire crew wants to run for cover in the Badlands. And frankly, so do I."

Eddington answered her with his trademark preternatural calm. "Yes, it's true: The Alliance is gearing up for a siege of Bajor and this station. Our long-range recon suggests it will be a unilateral action by the Cardassian Union. If our intel is correct, we have roughly a month before they attack. But if we can hit them first and inflict enough damage, we could throw them off balance and force them to play defense instead of us."

No one said anything, but O'Brien felt the air thicken with doubt. He felt compelled to rail against it. "Don't you see? This is our chance to start fighting the war on our own terms."

"What war?" The question had come from Alan Kistler, an irreverent, cocky young Terran who in recent months had orchestrated dozens of guerrilla attacks on several high-value Alliance targets. "Up till now, all we've been doing is sabotage and terrorism. No offense, but monkey-wrenching and limited collateral damage hardly counts as a 'war,' in my opinion."

"Technically," Eddington replied, "what we've been engaged in might be categorized as a 'low-intensity conflict.' The Alliance refuses to call it a war only because they fear doing so will legitimize us in the eyes of their labor class—and the last thing they want to deal with is an interstellar slave uprising."

L'Sen, a Vulcan woman who had come to the rebellion as a gunrunner and in short order had risen through the ranks to command one of its captured warships, leaned apart from the throng and looked O'Brien in the eye. "General, for the sake of discussion, let us presume that we choose to join you in this preemptive attack upon the Alliance. What would be the intended target?"

O'Brien cleared his throat. "Olmerak Prime." Stunned gasps were followed by whispered variations of *Is he out of his mind?* After giving the room a few seconds to recover its composure, O'Brien continued. "This target is a triple threat, people. It's a major shipyard, the Cardassians' main port of call for this sector, and the Alliance's joint intelligence headquarters. Destroying this will be like cutting off the enemy's right arm in the Alpha Quadrant."

It was Sloan's turn to protest. "Miles, we don't have that kind of firepower. Even if we send every ship we've got, we'd be lucky to get within two light-years of that system. What makes you think this is even remotely possible?"

"I have a plan."

Kistler lifted his hands and raised his voice as he addressed the other commanders. "Did you all hear that? He has a plan! That changes everything!"

L'Sen planted a hand on Kistler's shoulder. With alarmingly little effort, the lithe Vulcan woman forced the husky, black-haired young Terran back into his chair. Her voice was low but rich with menace. "Sit down and be quiet while the general is speaking."

O'Brien ignored the kerfuffle and continued as if it had never happened. "Fifteen days from now, a massive ion storm is going to pass through the Olmerak system. For approximately eleven hours and forty-seven minutes, every sensor, comm system, and defense screen in that system will be inoperable. So, that's when we're going to blast it all to hell. By the time the Cardies find out they've been hit, we'll be long gone."

"Whoa, hold on," Wexler said. "In a storm like that, we'll be just as blind as they are. How can we attack when we can't even navigate to the target?"

"We won't have to," O'Brien said. "By the time that storm hits Olmerak, we'll already be in attack position, under cloak, locked on with visual targeting. The moment the Cardies' sensors go dead, we fire. Game over."

Nodding heads and excited grins.

"We need to move quickly to make this happen," Eddington said. "Any ship that needs parts, personnel, munitions, fuel, or supplies, get your requests in to me by 1300 hours today. Ship commanders, we'll meet back here tonight at 1900 to start hammering out the tactical details. Bring your XOs and tac officers. Any questions?" None came. "Dismissed."

As the commanders filed out of the defunct bar, their collective mood had an electric quality that O'Brien hadn't experienced in a very long time. Belatedly, he realized the feeling he was struggling to name was *hope*.

Eddington gave O'Brien's shoulder a fraternal slap. "Nicely done." Before O'Brien could respond, his fellow general fell in with the departing commanders and rode the tide of bodies out to the Promenade.

His last companion in the bar was Keiko. She looked worried as she kissed his cheek and held his hand. "Congratulations, General—now it's a war."

L'Sen made haste from the war council and returned to her private quarters aboard her ship, a stolen Trill freighter she had renamed the *Free Rein*. Once her door closed and locked, and her anti-surveillance systems were engaged, she prostrated herself on the deck, reached under her bunk, and pried open a panel beneath which she had concealed her Memory Omega–issued quantum transceiver.

She sent a test signal back to her superiors, activated the holographic interface, and awaited a response. Within seconds, a humanoid shape shimmered into the air before her, a ghostly simulacrum of the person at the other end of the untraceable and untappable channel, which was based on the entanglement of subatomic particles inside her portable transceiver with those inside another unit kept secure at the leadership's secret redoubt. Standing before her was the spectre of Saavik, who had only a few decades earlier succeeded T'Prynn as director of Memory Omega. *"You are not due to report for another twelve days, L'Sen."*

"This regards a time-sensitive matter, Director."

Saavik made a nigh-imperceptible nod. *"Continue."*

In as brief a manner as she was able, L'Sen explained the Terran Rebellion's new plan to attack the Alliance shipyards at Olmerak, and the short timetable for the assault. "General O'Brien seems unaware that the Cardassians are mobilizing too quickly for such an operation to succeed, but I cannot warn him or his people without attracting suspicion."

Saavik arched one eyebrow and asked coolly, *"What do you propose?"*

"Can other assets from our organization take covert action to delay the Cardassians' response? Even a few days might buy the rebellion the time it needs."

The request drew a tight grimace of disapproval from Saavik. *"Our people are vulnerable. Such direct interference now could compromise us all."*

It was difficult for L'Sen to strip the urgency from her tone and preserve her detached façade. "With its entire fleet deployed against Olmerak, the Terran Rebellion will be unable to defend Terok Nor when the Cardassians attack. Unless we intervene, the Terran Rebellion will not survive"—she added a note of gravitas to her voice—"and Spock's plan will be put in jeopardy."

The director seemed pensive. L'Sen, not being prone to hyperbole, hoped that she had not overstated the matter by implying its stakes had escalated to the level of the existential, but it had been Saavik herself who had impressed upon Memory Omega's field operatives the vital importance of the Terran Rebellion to Spock's long-term strategy for the quadrant's political realignment.

"It is too soon for us to foment open hostilities between the Klingons and the Cardassians," Saavik said. *"At best, we might instigate diplomatic difficulties, but I cannot guarantee such squabbles will hamper the Cardassians' war effort."*

That was not the answer for which L'Sen had hoped. Her thoughts went to dark places. "If that proves to be the case, can the necessary intelligence be provided to the rebellion without compromising our operational secrecy?"

Saavik folded her hands in front of her. *"Yes, though it will take time to mask its true source and provide Agent Ishikawa with a plausible scenario to explain its acquisition. How long before the Terrans' fleet deploys against the Olmerak shipyards?"*

"To be in position at the day and time specified by General O'Brien, and taking into account the speed of the fleet's slowest ship, they will need to depart no later than seven days from now. Can a warning be ready by then?"

"Perhaps. Do your best to prevent their fleet from departing early."

L'Sen bowed her head. "I will, ma'am."

The elder Vulcan woman raised her right hand, fingers spread in the traditional V-shaped Vulcan salute. *"Live long and prosper, L'Sen."*

"Peace and long life, Saavik."

The connection was terminated at Saavik's end, and her holographic image stuttered, fractured, and faded away. L'Sen returned her transceiver to its hiding place, then unlocked the door of her quarters and exited, in a hurry to rejoin the other rebel commanders on Terok Nor's busy Promenade. A postponement of the Terrans' assault against Olmerak would almost certainly dispirit General O'Brien and his followers, but L'Sen knew that would be a far better outcome than watching them add their fragile army to history's parade of failed revolutions.

7

Whispers in the Wind

After years of service within the Great Hall in the First City on Qo'noS, Taurik still could not decide which olfactory sensation he found more revolting: the stink of the various delicacies he was compelled to serve to the regent, councillors, and their guests—or the Klingons themselves. Portering a platter of *pipius* claws into the imperial dining room, the Vulcan servant-spy mused, *For a species that prides itself on its keen senses, Klingons seem nose-deaf to their own odors*. If it wasn't the musky scent of their perspiration assaulting Taurik's nostrils, it was the sour reek of their halitosis, which they expelled with every throaty exclamation.

He neared the main dining table, upon which he had set a lavish feast of Klingon fare: ornate platinum trays of *bregit* lung arranged artfully around hearts of *targ*; silver bowls teeming with *gagh* or its smaller cousin, *racht*; deep-dish stoneware plates loaded with *rokeg* blood pies; a tureen of *bahgol,* a decadently rich soup; and a steel platter stacked high with *krada* legs. Dotting the table were pitchers of *warnog* and onyx decanters brimming with bloodwine.

Regent Martok sat at the head of the table, half a heart of *targ* clutched in his fist and its other half stuffed into his copious maw. Syrupy blood squirted and oozed from the raw cardiac muscle as Martok masticated it into pulp. Thick, magenta-hued goop dribbled from the corners of his mouth, and chunks of torn meat were snared in the wiry black whiskers of his uneven beard. He made a hacking noise as he swallowed, then snapped up his *warnog* and guzzled a long swig to wash down his overflowing mouthful.

Taurik averted his eyes from Martok and focused on rearranging the dishes on the table to make room for the *pipius* claws. Setting down the tray, he stole a glance at Martok's dining companion and honored guest, Darhe'el, the Cardassian ambassador to Qo'noS. The young Vulcan's face betrayed not one bit of the profound satisfaction he derived from noting Darhe'el's appalled reaction to Martok's barbaric table etiquette. Tellingly, the ambassador had not eaten a single bite of his own meal, apparently finding the cuisine less than palatable.

Martok slammed his empty stein on the table. "More!"

Mindful of his role as a servant, Taurik moved in quick, soundless strides to the head of the table, lifted a pitcher of *warnog,* and refilled Martok's carved-metal mug. Though no Klingon had ever complained about a bit of spillage here or there, Taurik's technique was precise and flawless, wasting not a single drop due to server error. He set down the pitcher and backed away from Martok, taking care not to turn his back on the notoriously irritable Klingon head of state.

The regent unleashed a belch that shook the walls, then asked Darhe'el in his rasping growl of a voice, "So . . . what does Dukat want?"

Darhe'el affected an air of confusion. "I beg your pardon, Regent?"

"Spare me the preamble. You didn't come here for

the *gagh,* and you drink like a *taHqeq.* So what are you doing here?"

The Cardassian picked up his onyx goblet and sipped his bloodwine—no doubt, Taurik surmised, to buy himself time to mentally rehearse his reply. Darhe'el drew out the process of swallowing and setting down his goblet. "The Bajor situation is one that demands urgent attention, My Lord Regent."

"Yes, yes. After we crush the Talarians, we'll deal with the Bajorans."

"With all respect, My Lord Regent, the Cardassian Union is prepared to take immediate action on the Bajor crisis. Supreme Legate Dukat made it a priority."

A fearsome grin possessed Martok's face. "Has he? Good for him." He resumed gorging himself on *krada* legs, cracking open the shells with his back teeth and pulling out the meat with his incisors.

Darhe'el tilted his head back and drained his goblet. Emboldened, he continued. "Supreme Legate Dukat requests that your empire share with our scientists what they've learned from the Romulan cloaking device captured from the rebels by the late Captain Kurn."

Martok peered inside the gutted shell of a *krada* leg and, satisfied it was empty, flung it away. "And what will your scientists do with that knowledge?"

"I presume they would equip our fleet in anticipation of the attack on Bajor." Receiving no response from Martok except a noncommittal grunt, the ambassador pressed onward. "Under the Articles of Alliance, technologies captured by either side from third parties are to be shared without delay or restriction." He pulled a small data device from his coat's deep pockets. "Need I cite chapter and verse?"

A tired growl rolled behind Martok's clenched teeth. Taurik had read the Articles of Alliance and knew that Darhe'el's invocation was entirely within the spirit and letter of the law. The regent's capitulation was a foregone conclusion. All his bluster had been for nothing but show, a bid to save face politically.

Taurik kept his head down and his hands folded at his waist, drawing no attention as he circled behind Martok. Situating himself a few meters directly behind the regent's chair, he knew he would be all but obscured from Darhe'el's field of vision by Martok himself. Like all the best servants, he became invisible.

I must focus my thoughts, was his silent mantra. *See the regent's mind, like an island in a dark ocean. My mind to his mind, a whisper in the wind, felt but not heard.* He reached out with his psionic abilities and made contact with Martok's turbulent subconscious. Having spent years as one of Martok's servants, Taurik had on several occasions, when Martok was submerged in alcoholic stupors, made physical contact and primed the regent's mental pathways for this sort of touch-free invasion. The churning emotions that impelled the Klingon's psyche made it easy for Taurik to push and probe the regent's unconscious thoughts without giving away his own telepathic presence. He began polluting Martok's mind with inflammatory questions. *Who are the Cardassians to demand anything? Why should the Empire aid the weak?* Feeling the regent's ire rising, Taurik stoked it into a bonfire of rage with fleeting images of Cardassian depravities and of Klingons being dominated by Cardassians. A wave of prejudice and resentment surged through Martok's thoughts, and he banged his fist on the table.

"How dare you come into my hall and demand I sur-

render what my soldiers have claimed as spoils of war!"
He pushed away from the table with such fury that his
chair fell over behind him. He stalked beside the table
toward Darhe'el, who froze at the regent's advance. "You
Cardassians are all the same. Sniveling opportunists, always ready to profit from other people's sweat!" Martok
swatted the goblet from Darhe'el's trembling hand.

As the onyx vessel shattered across the floor, Darhe'el
scrambled from his chair. The Cardassian spluttered angrily as he backed toward the door. "This is an outrage,
Martok! The supreme legate will be told every word of
your treachery!"

"Is that supposed to be a threat?" Martok unsheathed
his *d'k tahg* and continued prowling toward the retreat-
ing Darhe'el. "Let me show what a real threat looks like,
you bloated *petaQ!*"

Darhe'el quickened his pace, only to trip over his
own feet. He fell backward and landed roughly on his
copious buttocks.

The ambassador's predicament drew howls of laughter from Martok. As Darhe'el floundered on the floor,
the regent kicked the portly diplomat in his posterior,
and Darhe'el face-planted into the stone floor. Taurik
almost let himself feel pity for the middle-aged Cardassian, who, soft from years of state-sponsored debauch-
ery and gluttony, clearly was no match for the Klingons'
warrior-king.

Visibly disgusted with Darhe'el, Martok sheathed his
dagger and spat on the ambassador. "Go back to your
embassy and cry to Dukat. Tell him the Union can have
the Romulan cloaking device when it's ready to offer
something of equal value to the Empire! Until then"—
he grabbed the edge of the enormous and frightfully

heavy dining table and flipped it on its side, scattering food and drinks across the floor—"don't darken my hall again."

The regent marched out through his private access door at one end of the dining room, and Darhe'el stiffly collected himself from the floor and slipped out the main entrance with his head hung in shame.

Lingering in one shadow-steeped corner, Taurik gloated. *All too easy*. He took stock of his intervention's aftermath. Then, having done his part to nudge the galaxy one step closer to freedom, he went in search of a mop.

"That arrogant animal!" Dukat paced inside the sauna chamber. "Who does Martok think he is, that he can treat our ambassador that way?"

Damar cracked open one eye. "He's the Klingon regent. He can do whatever he wants." His voice was muffled because his face was pressed against the padded headrest of the massage table, luxuriating in the soothing fragrance of mint-scented oils while his Vulcan masseuse, T'Lana, kneaded the muscles beneath his neck ridges with exceptional skill and precision. He didn't care how many times Dukat complained that it was a disgrace to bring a slave inside the executive bath house; the woman had uniquely talented hands, strong and supple, as well as an intuitive knack for releasing the tension from Damar's aching joints and muscles. It also helped that, unlike the Terran and Bolian women who had preceded her in recent years, T'Lana seemed well adapted to the extreme heat and high humidity of a Cardassian sauna. The only way Dukat could ever force Damar to exclude his most-prized servant from the bath house would be to pass a law against it—and risk aggrieving the scores of high-ranking officials from the civilian government, Central Command, and Obsidian Order who had followed Damar's lead and begun bringing their own Vulcan slaves to service them in the sultry twilight.

Dukat ambled back and forth beside Damar's massage table, his bare feet slapping on the tiled floor. "Mark my words, Damar: The Alliance is devolving into a farce. What kind of nation treats its allies the way Martok has abused us?"

"The Tholians, for one. Would you relax? You're making me tense." He glanced back at T'Lana. "A bit more oil, and focus on my lower back."

Ignoring Damar's advice, Dukat continued to tread from his table's foot to its head and back. "I grow weary of Cardassia being treated like a second-rate power. Where would the Klingons be without us? They needed our strength to stop the Terran Empire, to pacify local space, to keep order. We've borne their burdens long enough, Damar. It's time the Klingon Empire gave us our due."

"As I'm sure they will," Damar mumbled, lost in the bliss produced by T'Lana's thumbs exorcising his pains and cares, one circular motion at a time. "But there's nothing to be gained by confronting them now. It will just make the Alliance look weak and divided to its enemies."

"Far from it." Dukat circled around to stand at the head of Damar's table, which he grabbed with both hands as he squatted to talk directly into Damar's face. The Supreme Legate had a crazed look in his eyes. "We'll strike fear into our foes and put the Klingons in their place at the same time when we crush Bajor!"

Damar grunted and glared at Dukat. "Skrain, we've been over this. We don't have enough ships to guarantee a successful assault unless we can cloak them. Since the Klingons won't share the Romulan cloaking device, we need to wait until the Seventh Order can be regrouped and transferred from Arawath, or until the Klingons finish off the Talarians and send us their Sixth Fleet as reinforcements."

"Nonsense. We just need to be decisive."

Laying his head back down, Damar replied, "I *am* being decisive. I've decided to postpone the attack until the odds tilt in our favor."

Dukat walked away, fuming but silent.

T'Lana continued unraveling the coiled spring of tension in Damar's lower back, and as she kneaded the pain from his hip sockets, he considered directing her efforts toward a more intimate form of release.

Tepid water crashed over Damar's head and back, and he leaped to his feet in a rage to find Dukat standing naked in front of him. The leader cast away the sauna's now empty water bucket and regarded his dripping-wet nude subordinate. "If I tell you to attack Bajor with the forces you have, you do not question me, Damar. Your role is to obey and secure a victory for Cardassia."

"Damn you, Dukat! You put me in charge of the assault. How can I command our military if you undercut my authority?"

Dukat stepped forward, invading Damar's personal space. "In public you will have my full support, but remember that I gave you your authority, which means I can take it away. You serve at my pleasure, Damar. Never forget that."

"I assure you, Supreme Legate, I never do."

Dukat's mouth curled into a smile, but there was no mirth in his eyes. "Good." He turned and walked away.

Damar called after him, "I still don't think Bajor is worth the risk."

"I do." Dukat threw open the sauna's glass door, which spidered white as it rebounded off the wall outside. As it drifted shut, Dukat added, "Get it done." The door closed with a soft click, and Damar felt the kiss of cold air on his feet. He stared at the door for several seconds, seething with a resentment he could never voice for fear of summary execution.

His diminutive Vulcan handmaiden sidled cautiously into his field of vision. "Pardon me, master," T'Lana asked in a near whisper. "Do you wish to continue your massage?"

He looked at her, then reached out, lifted her chin, and gingerly traced her lower lip with his thumb. "You know how I like it finished, yes?"

She flashed a lascivious smile, just as he had trained her to do. "Of course, master."

"Very well, then." He reclined on the massage table, made a pillow of his hands behind his head, and surrendered to T'Lana's exquisite ministrations.

Minutes later, as she coaxed the last bit of tension from Damar's body, he caught himself entertaining a deeply seditious notion: *Maybe it's not the Klingons who are the problem, but Dukat himself.* It was a dangerous idea to consider, and its only possible solution was unthinkable—but also, at the same time . . .

Logical.

8

Trinity

Three ships converged in the endless darkness.

Prefect Zogozin stood on the bridge of the Gorn battle cruiser *Shozsta,* waiting for its command crew to confirm that the other two ships at the rendezvous coordinates had transmitted the proper, prearranged recognition codes. Low hisses of muted communication passed between the officers surrounding him, underscored by the feedback tones from the ship's consoles.

On the main viewscreen, a Tholian battleship and a Breen assault vessel held station less than a tenth of a light-second from the *Shozsta,* and at an equal distance from each other. The Breen had come the farthest distance to join this conference, which the Tholians and the Gorn had decided would be held at a point of particular, mutual historic significance. More than a hundred cycles earlier, these coordinates had been occupied by one of the late Terran Empire's most fearsome installations: Starbase 47, or, as it had been more commonly known, Vanguard. Under the command of the ruthless Commodore Diego "Red" Reyes, it had served as the epicenter for a reign of terror that had been excessive even by the cruelly depraved standards of the Terrans.

That starbase was long gone, destroyed by the Tholians. Today, in this place of death and destruction,

Zogozin hoped to inaugurate a new order for the galaxy.

The *Shozsta*'s commanding officer, Rezkik, received a report from one of his officers, then looked at Zogozin. "The codes have been verified, Prefect."

"Excellent. Hail both ships on a shared channel."

Zogozin waited while the bridge crew opened a frequency to the Tholian ship, the *Lanz't Tholis,* and the Breen vessel, the *Artosk*. Seconds later, two faces appeared on the split screen. On the left was Azrene, the appointed delegate of the Tholian Assembly; on the right was a snout-masked visage of a Breen that Zogozin had to accept on faith was that of Thot Gor, the Breen delegate.

"Greetings," Zogozin said. "I come bearing the proxy of the Imperator. The Gorn Hegemony is prepared to act. What news do you bring?"

Azrene's screech of a reply was filtered through the universal translator. *"The Ruling Conclave of the Tholian Assembly has invested me with executive authority in this matter."*

Thot Gor's helmet vocoder spewed mechanical noise that ultimately was translated as *"I speak for the Breen Confederacy."*

The Gorn Prefect walked slowly toward the viewscreen as he addressed his peers. "We face uncertain times. The political dynamics of local space are in flux."

"A poetic way of saying the Alliance is disintegrating," Gor said.

"Quite," Zogozin said. "Each passing moment brings the Cardassians and Klingons closer to the dissolution of their bond. If the Alliance should fall, their absence will leave a profound vacuum on the political stage."

Azrene cut in, *"One we are prepared to fill."*

"Unilaterally? I think not. Even with the Romulan Star Empire beaten and the Alliance on the brink of collapse, Tholia is in no position to exert dominance over local space. None of us is." Zogozin nodded to Rezkik, who took the cue to transmit an annotated map of local space to the other ships. "Separately, each of us is likely to remain contained and marginalized during the coming Klingon-Cardassian conflict. United, however, we would be in a position to dictate terms."

The Tholian delegate uttered a string of clicks and scrapes. *"What of the Terran Rebellion? It appears to be a growing source of chaos and unrest."*

"The Cardassians will put it down. It is of no concern to us. Soon all of explored space will be ripe for new overlords. If we pursue our courses at odds with one another, our most reliable strategic models predict a Klingon resurgence inside of a decade, followed by total Klingon dominion within a century. But if we unite, we can master the Klingons, seize control of known space, and usher in a new age of order." He held his clawed hands apart, palms open and facing up. "What say you? Do we part ways as rivals—or unite as equals?"

A long pause followed Zogozin's ultimatum.

Thot Gor answered first. *"The Confederacy will join this new order."*

Chest puffed with pride, Zogozin asked, "Azrene? What say you?"

The Tholian's countenance coruscated for several seconds, and then she responded, *"The Conclave pledges its fealty and cooperation to you both."*

"History will mark this day as a turning point," Zogozin declared. "It will be remembered as the genesis of the Taurus Pact."

9

On the Hunt

Gamma Pavonis III had been a miserable hunk of worthless rock for eons before Duras had come there, it had continued to be a joyless mud pit every day since his arrival, and he had every reason to believe it would go on serving as the rectum of the galaxy long after he had left it behind.

It had one saving grace: It was a fine place to go *targ* hunting.

Decades earlier, some fool or other had loosed a handful of the coarse-furred, sharp-tusked, barrel-shaped scavengers on the planet's surface and lost track of them. A few years later, the countryside was over-run with *targ*s. The snorting beasts defoliated the forest floors and generally made a mess of things while growing fat on an unlimited diet of protein-rich fungus and insects.

Then the hunters came and thinned the herds, but the animals continued to multiply. Had the planet hosted more than a handful of Klingons at any given time, they might have rid this world of *targ*s decades ago, but with only a few dozen warriors resident, there were more than enough *targ*s to go around.

Thanks to frequent rains in the region around Du-ras's outpost, the ground often was muddy and peppered with *targ* tracks. Whenever he got a hankering for fresh meat, he grabbed a spear and took the day off. Today was a perfect day for the hunt: cool and damp, with little wind. Wet, rotting undergrowth muffled his footfalls as he crept through the brush, tracking a fat male *targ* by scent alone in the gray predawn hours. Then he caught sight of it in the distance, rooting in the mud for rare and fragrant fungal blooms. A deep breath, and Duras's heartbeat slowed, steadying his hands. With slow, fluid grace, he lifted his spear above his shoulder and visualized its trajectory through the trees.

Half a breath later the spear was aloft, sailing true.

It pierced the *targ*'s neck, cutting the major artery and its opposing vein in one strike, and the beast toppled onto its side, felled in a single blow. Duras bounded through the brush, heedless of his clamor now that his prey was immobilized. He dropped to his knees beside the expiring animal, plucked his spear from its neck, and drew his *d'k tahg*. Into the creature's ear he growled, "Noble beast! Tonight I shall eat your heart. Go into the darkness knowing your strength shall become mine, and you shall live on within me." He plunged his blade deep into the *targ*'s chest just below the sternum and twisted. The animal expired with a final rasp and rattle, and then it was still.

All was silence for a moment. Then Duras heard his pulse hammering in his ears. When it faded, all that remained was the soft patter of rain dripping through the boughs of trees and the low breath of the autumn wind.

He looked up at the pearl-gray sky and grinned as cool rain kissed his face. *This is a good day to live.* He trussed the slain *targ,* ran his spear shaft between its bound feet, and hefted it across his shoulders. He would eat heartily tonight.

Marching back to the outpost, he reveled in the nights he spent on the hunt, and in the back of his mind he knew he would miss them when he left this world.

Not that his departure was at all imminent. In fact, he had every reason to believe he would remain in exile on this rock for years to come. His first sin had been an accident of birth; as the eldest son of Ja'rod, scion of the ancient and powerful House of Duras, he had inherited the everlasting enmity of the House of Mogh, one of the key players in the politics of the Empire. After Mogh's elder son, Worf, ascended to the regency, Duras had been forced to call in every political favor owed to his House just to retain command of a starship.

Worf's capture by the Terran Rebellion the previous year had proved briefly fortuitous for Duras. With the House of Mogh temporarily descendant, he had maneuvered his way into command of the *I.K.S. Negh'Var*. As the right hand of Bajor's then-Intendant Ro Laren, Duras had wielded tremendous influence and achieved an unusual degree of notoriety within the Klingon Defense Force, despite being disliked by Regent Martok.

Then it all had come crashing down, thanks to Kira Nerys and Worf's younger brother, Kurn. The pair had formed an alliance, circumnavigated Duras's authority, and scored a major victory for the Empire against the Terran Rebellion. In the process they had exposed Ro as a traitor, Kira regained her title as Bajor's Intendant, and, with Kira's backing, Kurn succeeded Duras as the commanding officer of the *Negh'Var*—with the intended consequence that Duras was relegated to commanding the strategically unimportant outpost on this backwater rock.

As if all that had not been enough to ensure the premature demise of Duras's career prospects, a few months later he had been forced to take the blame for a major blunder. A Terran woman who identified herself as Alynna Nechayev had been captured by one of Duras's patrol ships and brought in for questioning as a possible member of the rebellion. During her interrogation, two other individuals—so far officially unidentified—had infiltrated the base, wreaked havoc, killed multiple Klingon warriors, including Duras's second-in-command, Colonel Gowron, and escaped with the Nechayev woman's personal effects. Nechayev had been found dead in a passageway beneath the shuttle platform, most of her head and face blasted into smoking goop. If not for some artful excuses and a few friends in high places, Duras might have found himself facing execution or, at the very least, incarceration on Rura Penthe. Instead, he had retained this useless command assignment on a world about which no one gave a damn.

And that was exactly as he preferred it to be.

On the *Negh'Var* he had been too visible, a victim of his own success. His every action and communication had been recorded and analyzed as a matter of routine counterintelligence. Under such intimate scrutiny he had been all but unable to carry out his clandestine duties as a secret asset of Memory Omega. Here on Gamma Pavonis III, however, discipline was lax and security was an afterthought. The planet had nothing of value, so Imperial Intelligence paid it no mind. It was just a bare-bones listening station and sensor outpost, a way station for secure information passing between Qo'noS and its fringe territories.

In other words, a perfect place from which to intercept communiqués and track the deployments of Alliance forces.

As he neared the outpost's main gate, he called up to the sentries in the guard tower, "I come bearing today's lunch. Open the gate."

A young guard peered down through the morning fog, squinted until he recognized Duras, then nodded to his comrade, who opened the main gate. Duras marched slowly, bearing his heavy burden into the compound. He dropped the carcass unceremoniously in the dirt at the feet of his new second-in-command, J'mkor. "Have that cleaned and ready for midday," Duras said. "And make sure the chef saves me the heart this time."

"Yes, My Lord." J'mkor handed him a data slate. "The morning reports."

Duras grabbed the data device and perused it as he walked to his office. J'mkor followed him, as if expecting some manner of reward simply for doing his job. Duras ignored his sycophantic executive officer and kept his attention on the morning reports. They seemed to be the customary mix of routine data traffic, ship movements, and security advisories. Then he saw there was nothing typical about them. Just outside his office he stopped, turned, and pointed at the slate as he faced J'mkor. "Is all this confirmed?"

J'mkor stiffened. "Yes, sir. Directly from the High Command."

Duras frowned as he reread the specifics. This was not good. Not at all. "Dismissed," he said, and then he continued into his office and locked the door behind him, stranding the bewildered J'mkor on the other side.

Not being given to sentimentality, Duras kept his office spartan and functional. He had a work station, a chair, a desk, and a window whose smart glass he kept in an opaque "privacy" mode. No personal items adorned his desk, and the walls were as bare as they'd been the day he'd arrived.

He settled into his chair, logged into a secure channel of the base's data network, and proceeded to verify the information brought to him by J'mkor. To his dismay, it all checked out. Massive redeployments of ships and personnel were under way throughout multiple sectors along the Klingon-Romulan border—not that such a territorial distinction meant much in the wake of the Romulan Star Empire's collapse. Enormous convoys were being formed and dispatched at regular intervals on a route that linked H'Atoria and Celes. Though the convoy vessels had no cloaks, they were assigned several defenders that did.

The convoy deployment was unusual but not unheard of; it suggested a major project was under way in the Celes system. The first item that bothered Duras was the slipshod tactics being employed by the convoys' protectors. Instead of deploying from multiple points, cloaking, and joining the convoy at random intervals along the start of its route, all its defenders were deploying and arriving with the convoys themselves, meaning that any reasonably observant enemy could make an accurate estimate of the convoys' strength.

The second item in the morning report that troubled Duras was a set of military redeployments that tasked dozens of Klingon warships from a number of ports to rendezvous under cloak at a precise set of coordinates inside the Joch'chal Nebula. Though these orders were not officially related to the convoys, Duras noticed immediately that the convoys' regular route passed within a hair's breadth of the nebula. It stank of a trap as clearly as his hands still reeked of dried *targ* blood and mud. Clearly, a snare of unprecedented size was being laid, and it seemed apparent to Duras for whom it was intended.

Martok is goading the rebel Calhoun, he concluded. *And if Calhoun and his Romulan allies take the bait, they'll be walking into a slaughter.*

Duras reclined his chair and fought to focus his thoughts. He needed to warn Calhoun and his fleet, but how? He had no direct line of communication to the Xenexian commander or anyone in his armada. His only option, as far as he could tell, was to send the warning to Memory Omega and trust them to relay it in time to Calhoun. Unfortunately, he had no idea how long that might take; despite his many years of covert assistance to Memory Omega, they had never seen fit to grace him with one of their remarkable quantum transceivers. Consequently, he would have to send his encrypted message to an Omega-compromised relay buoy and hope that they received it before Martok's forces sprang their ambush.

Resigned to operating within his limitations, Duras began composing the most dire missive of warning he had ever written, and hoped to *Sto-Vo-Kor* that it would not prove to be in vain.

10

Eve of Destruction

Oh, bloody hell." O'Brien shook his head, dismayed. "Are you sure?"

Eddington enlarged the sector map on the situation table between them. "Positive. The entire Ninth Order is leaving Olmerak right now."

At the narrow end of the vaguely teardrop-shaped table, Sloan betrayed his frustration with a narrow frown. "So much for a sneak attack."

Opposite the security chief, Keiko planted her hands on the table's edge and leaned forward to study the map. "Can we can hit them en route?"

"Not a chance," O'Brien said. Anxiety propelled sour bile up into his throat, and he grimaced as he swallowed it back down. "If they're deployed, it's too late." He thought for a moment and felt every canyonlike wrinkle in his forehead. Then he looked at Keiko. "How reliable is the source of this intel?"

"Very. He's the captain of a Xeppolite freighter that has free passage between the Tzenkethi Coalition and the Cardassian Union."

Suspicion gnawed at O'Brien, an occupational hazard of a life lived entirely in slavery and wartime. "How did a freighter captain come by intel like this?"

"The Cardassians forced a last-second change to his

flight plan," Keiko said. "After he diverted to the new course, he scanned his original path and picked up signs of a major fleet deployment."

O'Brien nodded. "Uh-huh. And why would he risk telling us?"

"Officially, he's neutral. Unofficially, he's rooting for us."

It sounded plausible enough to O'Brien, but it didn't lessen his black mood. "Wonderful," he grouched to Keiko. "Let me know when this freighter captain's ready to pick up a gun and join the fighting." He looked down the table at Sloan. "Have we confirmed the Cardassians' course and speed?"

"Yes, sir. Straight for us, hell-bent for leather."

"Of course they are." He asked Eddington, "Why did the Cardies leave Olmerak in such a hurry?"

Eddington looked perplexed. "Probably to avoid the ion storm."

"Hang on," said Sloan, sounding worried. "Do you think they found out we were planning an attack? Is it possible we have a mole?"

"Stop right there," O'Brien said. "This is no time to start rumors. It's possible the Cardies are getting clear of the storm, but I think we need to assume the worst: They left earlier than expected for one reason—to get here sooner. They're coming for us, which means we need to be ready."

Keiko asked, "Then it's official? We're scrubbing the Olmerak mission?"

"No choice," O'Brien said. "We need everybody here."

Sloan kicked the side of the table. "Dammit! We were so close!"

As usual, Eddington remained the coolest of the four minds in the room. "We should begin evacuating people to the planet's surface."

O'Brien shook his head. "There's no time. We need everybody we've got, working on repairs and offloading munitions."

"Michael's right," Keiko said. "There are hundreds of noncombatants on the station, Miles—some of them kids. Let's move them to Bajor while we still can. Later, if we have time, we'll evac the support personnel."

All three of his subordinates were nodding in agreement, so O'Brien relented. "Fine. Luther, tell Bajor we need extra transports up here on the double. Michael, what's the ETA on the Cardie fleet?"

"Sixty-one hours. I've summoned as many reinforcements as I think can get here before then, but it looks like the Cardassians will have us outnumbered roughly five to one." He frowned, a rare admission of pessimism. "We'll have to hope the station's weapons and the planet's artillery can hold them off."

Steeling his nerve, O'Brien put on a brave face. "If we can get the shields back to full power, we should be able to hold our ground. It won't be pretty, but it'll be possible. Keiko, get anyone who knows how to hold a tool onto a work detail. Fixing the shields is our top priority, even before weapons. Understood?"

"Yes, sir."

"All right," O'Brien said, straightening his back. "Let's get to it." He shot a look at Eddington and tilted his head sideways toward his office. Eddington nodded in reply, and the two men climbed the stairs to the upper level and continued through the parting doors into O'Brien's sanctum. As the portal shut behind Eddington, O'Brien circled behind his desk and slumped into the chair. "Of all the bloody bad luck." He made a fist. His rage made it quake. "We were about to seize the momentum. Now we're back on defense. Again."

"I share your frustration, Miles. And I don't deny this is a disappointing setback. But I believe we can survive this."

The prediction drew a derisive grunt from O'Brien. "Survive it? Sure. But for how long, Michael? We'll take heavy losses this time, no matter how much firepower the Bajorans lend us." Driven by fear and fury, he got out of his chair and turned to stare out the window behind his desk. He spoke to Eddington's reflection in the window. "No one's ever won a war fighting only defense. If we can't shift the momentum, we're finished. So, you tell me"—he turned and looked at Eddington—"are we ever getting off the ropes again? Or are we just biding our time until the Alliance puts us down for good?"

A grim affect descended upon Eddington. "I don't know, Miles. I'm not a fortune-teller. But if this is the end for the rebellion, I plan to face it standing on my feet with a gun in my hand."

O'Brien took two glasses from a drawer on his desk, then filled them from a half-empty bottle of some alien liquor he kept hidden beside them. He handed one to Eddington and raised the other in a toast. "Bloody well right."

A clink of crystal, and they drank to their impending doom.

Surrounded by abandoned furniture inside an evacuated suite in the Habitat Ring, Keiko faced the life-sized holographic projection of Saavik generated by her quantum transceiver. The Vulcan woman stood with her hands folded primly in front of her. *"Did O'Brien and the others heed the warning we sent?"*

"Yes," Keiko said, leaning against the side of an overturned sofa. "O'Brien seemed suspicious of the source, but I persuaded him it was reliable."

Saavik nodded. *"Has the rebellion abandoned its assault on Olmerak?"*

"Reluctantly, but yes. They've turned their efforts to fortifying the station."

That news seemed to disappoint Saavik. *"The Cardassians are sending their entire Ninth Order. The rebellion will not be able to repel that great a force."*

Keiko's temper was stoked by Saavik's matter-of-fact tone. "Be that as it may, they've chosen to stand and fight."

"Have they formulated any contingency plans for tactical withdrawal?"

"We're working on some, yes. But our top priority—"

"You mean their *top priority."*

Feeling her anger rising from a simmer to a boil, Keiko fought to keep a civil tone as she replied, "*Our* top priority is defending Bajor and the station."

"But if necessary, the station will be abandoned, correct?"

"Yes, Director."

The older woman's countenance took on a grave aspect. *"In such an event, the rebellion's casualties are likely to be severe. What preparations have you and the other embedded operatives made for your escape?"*

"None," Keiko said, holding up her chin with prideful defiance. "And I've ordered the other Omega agents in the rebellion not to do so."

Confusion furrowed Saavik's upswept eyebrows. *"This is in contravention of my express orders."*

"I'm aware of that. My order stands. No one leaves."

Her overt challenge seemed to draw out a hint of anger from behind Saavik's cool Vulcan demeanor. *"This is highly illogical and extremely dangerous. We cannot risk any of our agents being captured and interrogated by the Alliance."*

"Oh, please. We have agents all over the Alliance! In the capitals, on the ships, in the hidden bases. My people aren't in any greater danger."

"Quite the contrary." Saavik unclasped her hands. It was a small gesture but enough to tell Keiko that she was eroding her superior's patience. *"Those agents have cover stories prepared decades in advance. Yours are in league with the rebellion, which makes them all potential prisoners of war. They need not do anything more to attract the Alliance's attention than survive. And if even one of them—or yourself—should be subjected to a Klingon mind-sifter, all for which we have struggled and sacrificed will be lost."*

Keiko folded her arms. "Well, then. It sounds to me as if we have a vested interest in not letting the rebellion fail."

"That is a non sequitur. The safeguarding of our operational secrecy does not necessitate our intervention in the affairs of the Terran Rebellion. In fact, just the opposite is called for."

Overcome by rage, Keiko wished Saavik's holographic image were real so that she could throttle the Vulcan. "So we do nothing? We just sit by and watch them get slaughtered? Then what the hell are we even doing here? Why send us to infiltrate the rebellion if we're not going to help them when they need us?"

"Our objective is merely to steer them toward nobler paths, so that when the time comes for their ascendance they will possess the requisite qualities to establish a stable and benevolent society."

"It's awfully hard to be *benevolent* when you're *dead*, Saavik!"

"Restrain your passions, Miss Ishikawa. They cloud your judgment."

Saavik's arch condescension was more than Keiko could take. "Don't tell me to act like a Vulcan! If I'm emotional, it's for a good reason."

"If your fellow embedded agents' reports are correct, your reason seems to be that you have developed an unhealthy emotional attachment to the rebellion's leader, Miles O'Brien."

"It's not an unhealthy attachment. I *love* him. And he loves me."

A subtle sigh of disappointment. *"This was not part of the plan."*

Keiko closed her eyes and pressed her hands to the sides of her head, as if to stop the pressure she felt building inside her skull from splitting it in two. "God help me, I am so sick of hearing about the plan!" She glared at Saavik. "As a set of objectives, it's fine. But why must you be so slavishly devoted to its details?"

"It has carried us through many decades of suffering and deprivation, and its predictions have, for the most part, been accurate."

"All except for when the rebellion would come," Keiko shot back. "Spock didn't see the Alliance falling for another twenty years! I don't know about you, but I'm not prepared to wait that long just because Spock said so, when there's a viable rebellion happening right now."

Arching one eyebrow, Saavik sounded skeptical. *"So, you now consider yourself a strategist on a par with the late Emperor Spock?"*

"Don't twist my words," Keiko said. "And don't

lecture me about my emotional link with O'Brien when your own emotional biases are just as obvious."

Saavik recoiled, offended. *"Who are you to accuse—"*

"I know about your history with Spock. He was your mentor. Hell, from what I've heard, he was like a second father to you. So don't tell me you don't have a personal stake in protecting his legacy, because I know that's a lie."

Her accusations were met with several seconds of bitter silence from Saavik. Then the Vulcan recovered her blank mask of composure and folded her hands at her waist. *"If you wish to defy my orders, so be it. But I will not permit you to condemn our other agents within the rebellion based on your emotional impulses. Henceforth, I will issue my directives to them through L'Sen."*

Keiko seethed. "You're relieving me of command?"

"Correct. For your sake, I hope you can maintain operational security. It would be a pity if an agent of your caliber had to share General Nechayev's fate."

Saavik's threat sent a chill through Keiko. "Secrecy will be maintained."

Lifting her hand in the Vulcan salute, Saavik replied, *"Then live long and prosper, Keiko Ishikawa."*

Suppressing her anger, Keiko reciprocated the gesture. "Peace and long life, Saavik." Upon the last syllable of her valediction, the transmission ended, and the image of Saavik flickered and vanished, leaving Keiko alone in the darkness. She tucked the quantum transceiver back inside her boot and heaved a dejected sigh.

So much for calling in the cavalry.

11

The Path of Most Resistance

Picard didn't like going into any situation blind, but this time he had no choice. Navigating inside the Klach D'Kel Bracht—a dense nebula of supernova remnants that was packed with false vacuum fluctuations, littered with innumerable pockets of metreon gas, and laced with shifting zones of metaphasic radiation—was nothing less than a nightmare. He had been forced to reduce the speed of his Trill-made outrider, which he had named *Calypso,* to less than one-third impulse, to avoid triggering a meltdown in its impulse manifolds.

Troi stood behind his right shoulder, peering with a fearful gaze through the forward canopy at the roiling, bloodred maelstrom that seemed to have swallowed them whole. "Are we sure these are the right coordinates?"

He glanced at the helm controls and verified their position. "We're within two hundred million kilometers. It can't be much farther." He pointed at a display along the starboard side of the cockpit. "Is there anything on sensors?"

She leaned over and poked at the console. "Nothing but static."

"Merde." Swallowing his suspicion that they had been led astray—or, worse, into a trap—Picard focused on steadying their passage through the fiery tempest.

Menacing forks of lightning flashed through distant clusters of churning gas, and thunderstrokes shook Picard's tiny vessel. The erratic energy fields inside the nebula had made it impossible to raise the *Calypso*'s shields, which had only exacerbated Picard's already serious misgivings about coming there.

Then, all at once, the walls of fog and dust parted like a curtain revealing a grand stage, and what Picard saw directly ahead robbed him of his breath. They had penetrated a pocket of near vacuum more than half a billion kilometers in diameter. At its center was a yellow main-sequence star, and orbiting it, squarely inside its habitable zone, was an Earth-like planet with the most eerily beautiful blue rings Picard had ever seen. Barely able to raise his voice above a shocked whisper, he told Troi, "Verify coordinates."

Troi checked the sensors, then looked back in awe at the planet. "Confirmed. That planet's position matches the coordinates Barclay and K'Ehleyr gave us."

"A world like that, hidden in the midst of all this . . ." He couldn't help but smile. "How remarkable." He set an approach course. "Strap in for landing. There's no telling what kind of weather might be waiting for us."

Minutes later, he found that his precautions, though prudent, had been entirely unnecessary. Only minimal cloud cover lingered above their specified landing point, a broad prairie shining with waves of tall grass bowing before a stiff afternoon breeze.

As the *Calypso* neared its precise touchdown location on top of a small knoll, another ship shimmered into view there. It was sleek and feminine in its slopes and curves, pale gray and pristine, beautiful yet imposing. Picard had never seen anything remotely similar to it. He admired it more profoundly the closer he came to it, and it was an effort to tear his eyes from it as he completed his landing procedure. The *Calypso* touched down with barely a tremor of contact, and he gently cycled down the engines and thrusters to standby.

Troi was already lowering the aft hatch and hurrying out to go see the other ship. Picard struggled to unfasten his seat's safety harness as he shouted at her back, "Deanna, wait!" It was no use—the woman was already outside, sprinting through waist-high grass toward the other ship.

He grabbed his blaster on the way out and followed Troi. When he caught up to her, Barclay and K'Ehleyr were walking down their ship's port-side ramp. Noting Troi's excitement as she circled their vessel, Barclay said to her, "She's a beauty, isn't she?"

"It's amazing," gushed the half-Betazoid. She threw a wide-eyed look at Barclay. "What's it called?"

K'Ehleyr answered, "The *Solomon*. It's named for a king of ancient Earth, one known for his wisdom and good judgment." She glanced at Barclay. "How it ended up as the name of *our* ship, I still don't know." She stepped off the ramp and met Picard with a taut wrinkle of a smile. "Thank you for coming."

"The pleasure's mine." He pivoted one way, then the other, and marveled at the lush, untrammeled world that surrounded them. "What is this place?"

"A well-kept secret. People have died to keep it off the Alliance's star maps, so we'd appreciate it if you'd lose these coordinates after you leave here."

Picard nodded. "Of course."

The half-Klingon seemed bemused. "Don't you want to know why?"

He drew a deep breath and savored the perfumes of flowers whose scents he didn't recognize but that reminded him of a dozen others on worlds scattered across the galaxy. He exhaled and asked K'Ehleyr, "Does it matter?"

A stifled chortle and a small shake of her head. "No, I guess not."

"Though I am curious about one thing." Now he had K'Ehleyr's attention. "If you're capable of preventing the Alliance from discovering an entire star system in the middle of their own territory, just how much influence do you have? How far does your organization's reach extend?"

"Even farther than you might imagine."

"That's not an answer, dammit. Be *specific*. Is this Memory Omega really powerful enough to take down the Alliance?"

K'Ehleyr and Barclay exchanged what seemed to Picard like a meaningful glance. Then she said, "Yes . . . with the right allies."

"With the right allies," he parroted. "And you think I fit that bill?"

A noncommittal sideways nod. "Our superiors do."

The cynic in Picard told him to walk away, to trust in himself and no one else, to remember that the cardinal rule of survival is "never get involved." But part of him wanted to believe that he might still make a difference. That his life might amount to more than decades spent digging in the dirt, looking for fragments of other people's great labors. That, just perhaps, he might contribute something of value himself, some work of noble note. And he couldn't deny there was at least a small appetite for revenge demanding to be sated; he had endured a lifetime of injustices and abuse at the hands of the Cardassians and the Klingons. They'd beaten and killed those whom he had dared to take into his heart; they'd robbed him of his freedom and his pride, smashed the last token of his heritage and left its dregs in a stain at his feet. They deserved to pay. To fall. To face justice.

But above all, he had to do what was best for Troi. He watched her smile and laugh as she cavorted around and beneath the *Solomon,* all her attention on young Mister Barclay. In all the years Picard had spent with Troi, he had never seen her react that way to anyone else. She clearly was smitten, and he doubted it was a physical infatuation. Barclay was not an unattractive man, but he was hardly a chiseled Adonis or a fountain of charisma. *Whatever she's reacting to,* Picard speculated, *it's something in the man himself. Something in his nature.*

He couldn't know what was in Barclay's soul or Troi's heart, but he saw an undeniable connection being made between them. Such moments, in his experience, were beyond rare. Most people he had ever known, himself included, had never experienced anything like it. And here, Troi had found it—or it had found her. Either way, it seemed wrong to Picard to take her from it. And if the mere presence of such a man could transform Troi's mood so dramatically, then that alone was a reason to consider taking the path of most resistance.

Picard asked K'Ehleyr in a low voice, "Why me?"

"Because you have a reputation that precedes you," she said. "Because you have intelligence, and education, and experience, and courage. But most of all because the future needs people like you: men of conscience. Natural leaders."

He shook his head. "No. I can't. And besides, the rebellion's finished."

"Not yet. Let us prove it to you. If we can't, you go your way, we'll go ours. But give us a chance to show you what's *possible*."

Wiping a sheen of perspiration from the top of his bald head, Picard sighed. "I've never been what one would call a *joiner,* K'Ehleyr."

"This is worth joining." She stepped in front of him and clasped his shoulders. "Emperor Spock once said that one man can summon the future, if he has the courage to do so. You say you're not a brave man, Luc, but I know you are. For the good of the many, I'm going to beg you: Please be brave now. *Trust me.*"

Picard couldn't remember the last time anyone had said "please" to him, or had begged him to follow the better angels of his nature. He didn't know if it was what she had said or the heartfelt way that she had said it, but it moved him.

"How do we begin?"

"Follow us," K'Ehleyr said, "and we'll show you the future."

12

Invisible Effects

The airlock portal rolled open ahead of Kes, and she stepped over its threshold into a corridor of Terok Nor's huge Docking Ring. Bajor's orbit had been crowded with small ships flocking to the Terran Rebellion or fleeing to the planet's surface, and the station's interior was just as busy. The curved, dark gray corridor teemed with travelers arriving and departing, all of them toting heavy duffels or packs, or towing bags laden with personal effects, a mad frenzy on the cusp of battle.

No one seemed to spare Kes a second glance as she drifted through the raging currents of running people. She had dyed her hair dark brown and styled it to cover her distinctive Ocampa earlobes, and then, with the aid of some simple cosmetics, she had disguised herself as a Trill by stenciling beige spot patterns from her temples to the back of her jaw, and then down the slope of her neck and under her tunic to her shoulders. Her legs were covered by dark tights, so she had seen no reason to extend the ersatz spots beyond her clavicle.

A few meters from the airlock, traffic bottlenecked at a security checkpoint. Four armed Terran men manned the post: One watched the crowd, two directed people through a sensor arch, and one monitored a control panel. Kes was not armed, but she had no intention of being stopped because her internal anatomy didn't match her outward appearance. Cautiously, she extended her psionic awareness beyond her telepathic shield of privacy. The mind of the young Terran watching the sensor display was easy to isolate and easier to deceive. Only the merest tickle of suggestion was needed to draw his eyes to hers, and once he met her gaze, she smiled. He smiled back. One of his older comrades waved Kes through the arch, and as she stepped through, she reached into the younger Terran's thoughts, extracted the image of what he expected to see when a Trill woman passed through the sensor, and then she showed it to him in vivid color.

Moments later she was on the crossover bridge, moving at a quick step toward the station's Habitat Ring. She attuned her thoughts to Neelix and sensed him somewhere nearby. He was in a hurry, making preparations for war, getting ready to leave the station.

Fear flooded Kes's thoughts. *I have to reach him before he goes!* At first she resisted the impulse to run, worried it would draw attention to her, but then she saw that everyone was scrambling toward or away from something. Reaching out with her empathic senses, she nearly drowned in the tidal wave of anxiety flooding through the station. *Something terrible is about to happen,* she realized, and then she was running, too.

So much emotional noise pressed in on Kes that she could barely focus on finding Neelix. She found the terror deafening, smothering, and paralyzing all at once, and it assailed her on more levels than she could filter out without losing her sense of Neelix's mind amid the madness. Other people's emotions bled into hers as she raced past them—a flash to passion, a cold burn of resentment, a sick churn of worry, an empty burst of bravado. The din was painful to bear and impossible to ignore, like a force of nature.

She kept her mind trained on the beacon in the night, the one thing that mattered, as she stumbled through gaggles of rebels and staggered around corners and down passageways that had been gutted to their frames, cannibalized for parts.

Instinct and desperation carried her forward until she reached an unmarked door and slumped against it. The call button was gone, so she thumped the side of her fist against the door, then forced herself to stand straight and take a breath.

The door slid open with a harsh scratch—and then there was Neelix, right in front of her, as dashing and heroic as Kes had remembered, though his face looked leaner and his rust-hued mane now sported a few streaks of gray. Kes had imagined this moment countless times in the five years they had been apart, had rehearsed a seemingly infinite variety of greetings and declarations, but now that she was in the moment, all she could do was smile and try not to cry.

Neelix flinched at the first sight of Kes, and his eyes widened. A wave of fear rolled through his thoughts, and she heard him ask himself whether she was a ghost. Alarm turned to confusion, then to cautious hope. "Kes?"

"Hello, Neelix." She threw her arms around him and held him as tightly as she could. He stood there like a statue, as if he were paralyzed, for several seconds before returning her embrace. Kes opened her mind to drink in Neelix's thoughts and was dismayed to find them awash in fearful doubts. Leaning back to look into his eyes, she saw through his happy charade. "Neelix, what's wrong?"

"Nothing's wrong."

She pressed her palms to his cheeks. "I can feel your emotions, Neelix. You're scared. You don't believe it's me. Why not?"

He reached up and gently guided her hands away from his face. "Well, it's . . . it's not that I'm not happy to see you, I am, I'm thrilled to see you . . . but . . . the Vulcan man, Tuvok, told me you'd transformed into pure energy. That you'd left this plane of existence." He hung his head. "I thought you were gone forever."

"He lied to you, Neelix. They all did. They lied to me, too." She cast nervous looks toward each end of the corridor. "Can I come in, please?"

"Of course." As polite as ever, the Talaxian man stepped back and aside, then ushered Kes into his quarters with a low sweep of one arm. "Come in." She hurried inside and he shut the door behind her. He clasped his hands and rubbed his palms together, a nervous habit. "So, you didn't turn to pure energy?"

An amused smile and a shake of her head. "No."

"Then where have you been?"

"Tuvok's people have a hidden sanctuary. I lived there and learned from Tuvok's wife how to control my powers."

Suspicion tainted Neelix's tone. "That's where you've been for five years?"

"Yes. Why?"

"Well, pardon me if this sounds indelicate, but . . . shouldn't you be . . . ?"

"Old?"

He looked embarrassed. "Yes. You told me your species only lives about nine years, and if memory serves . . . you recently turned eight."

She put on a disarmingly sweet smile and stepped

toward him. His mind radiated alarm, but she projected waves of calm into his psyche, along with her telepathic voice. *Tuvok's people wield amazing technologies, Neelix. Biotemporal accelerators, advanced genetic therapies, nanotech medicines. They changed me, made me young again. I can live as long as I want.* She caressed his neck and pressed her forehead to his. *Even as long as you.*

She heard his unspoken question: *How do I know it's really you?*

She projected into his mind one of her most cherished memories: the first time she met him. Letting it unfold inside the theater of his imagination, she let him experience that event from her point of view.

I was younger, then, not yet three years old. I had found a secret passage out of the underground oasis of the Ocampa, a gap in the protective force field generated by the Caretaker to keep us safe from intruders. But as badly as I had wanted to escape that place, there were others who had wanted just as desperately to find a way in: the Kazon-Ogla.

A band of them had set up camp near the entrance to the caverns, and they had captured me almost as soon as I had set foot upon the surface. They found my pale skin and golden hair repulsive, which was only fair, since I thought they were the ugliest brutes I'd ever seen. They beat me, tortured me. Broke my bones. Fed me slop and made me live amid my own putrid filth, like an animal. They promised me a lifetime of suffering that would end only when I showed them how to enter the Ocampa city, so they could plunder its resources for themselves.

All I knew was agony and loneliness, Neelix. During the day I wilted from the heat. At night, the cold left me shaking until it pierced me to my bones.

First Maje Jabin wanted me only for the knowledge I refused to share. His underling Raltik thought the best way to make me talk was to rape me. But none of them compared with Kabor, my torturer. He showed me what pain is. He taught me to despair. To give up hope. To pray for death.

But then, from the darkness, there was light.

I knew you were different the moment I saw you. When you saw what the Kazon-Ogla had done to me, you were overcome with pity. I felt your heart break, the tears you forced yourself not to shed, the rage you felt at their cruelty.

Your memories came so clearly to me. Your homeworld of Talax scoured of life by the Haakonians' metreon cascade weapon, the loss of your entire family, all your friends, your entire civilization. You were alone, grieving, in the dark.

You were just like me.

I knew your heart in the span of a moment, and I knew that I loved you.

That night you came to me, found me while the Kazon were asleep. You brought me real food and clean water. You did your best to clean my wounds. And you promised that one day you would take me away from there, to someplace where the Kazon could never touch me again.

You kept your word, Neelix. You came back for me. Now I've come back for you, so that we can be together, and no one will ever separate us again.

Tears of joy rolled from Neelix's eyes. "It's you! It's really you!" He hugged her, without a trace of hesitation. "Oh, how I've missed you, my sweet one! Not a day's gone by that I haven't thought of you. I won't lie—I've tried a few times to take comfort in the arms of women I've met here. But none of them ever meant to me what you do. None of them could ever take your place."

She kissed him and ran her fingers through his crest-like mane of hair. "You don't have to explain yourself, Neelix. You thought I was gone. I understand."

"But you're here now!" He bubbled over with excitement. "This is fantastic! With your help, the rebellion can have a real chance!"

Kes recoiled half a step in confusion. "I'm sorry. What?"

"I remember how powerful you are," Neelix said. He grabbed her shoulders. "And if Mister Vulcan's wife taught you how to control your powers, I can only imagine how much stronger you've become. With you on our side, we'll show the Alliance we mean business."

She lifted her hands and aggressively waved off his suggestion. "Neelix, no! That's not why I came back! I'm just here for *you*. I came back to find you so that we can leave together, get away from all these people, and start a new life."

Her declaration left him taken aback. "Kes, I can't leave—not now. We're on the verge of the biggest battle we've ever fought, and I'm a ship captain. These people are counting on me, Kes. They *need* me."

"Not like I need you! You were mine before you were theirs!"

"And I'm still yours, Kes. But I made promises. Pledged oaths. I'm fighting to help billions of people gain their freedom. To help make a better civilization." He offered her his hand. "And I want you to be a part of it. Join us."

She looked at his open palm, extended with virtue and innocence. He was still the same man she had always known: true and brave, faithful and generous. Even half a decade living amid peoples torn by war, corruption, and villainy had been unable to taint him or quell his spirit. Hesitantly, she stepped forward and clasped his hand. He smiled.

She frowned. "I'm sorry, Neelix."

Then she reached into his mind and found its deepest core of consciousness, the kernel of self that all beings try to hide and protect from suggestion, the part that most sentient creatures delude themselves into believing is private and inviolable . . . and with the slightest twist of thought turned it to her will.

"It's time to leave here, Neelix."

His gaze was empty, his voice flat, his smile weak and contrived, and the words that issued from his mouth were the ones that Kes wanted him to say. "Yes, my sweet one. Lead the way."

Taking her misguided but beloved Talaxian in tow, she guided him out the door and down the corridor, committed to rescuing him in spite of himself. He walked beside her as if in a daze, a puppet on invisible strings.

It's for his own good, Kes consoled herself. *He'll thank me when we're safe.*

They walked quickly but did not look out of place amid the frantic knots of people coursing in both directions over the bridge to the Docking Ring. Every few seconds brought another urgent announcement over the station's PA system, but Kes tuned them out, keeping her focus on controlling Neelix and shielding her own mind. *All we need to do is get back to my ship,* she reminded herself. *Once we're away from here, we'll be free. No one will ever find us again.*

She gripped Neelix's elbow and guided him through a right turn into the main passageway of the Docking Ring. Less than fifteen meters ahead stood the same security checkpoint she'd transited earlier, the last hurdle to her escape. *I already have a window into the young Terran's mind. This will be easy.* She led Neelix into the line of people waiting to depart the station.

Pain like a needle of fire shot through Kes's skull, from temple to temple. Her vision turned white and then purple, vertigo swept her legs out from under her, and as she struck the floor she was overcome by the urge to vomit. Sour bile preceded a rush of emesis that left her coughing and gagging. When the vile episode ended, she lay weak and spent—and noticed only then that she had gone telepathically blind. She could no longer sense the minds around hers, which meant she had lost her hold on Neelix. Struggling to focus her eyes, she looked up.

Neelix stood over her, looking down with an expression that was equal parts horror, fury, and pity. The throng gathered at the checkpoint backed away, forming a wide ring around Kes, and armed Terran sentries pushed through the crowd.

Someone else stepped through the wall of onlookers first, from the other direction, and kneeled over Kes with a concerned look on his face and a peculiar small device in his hand. It was Tuvok. "Do not try to move, Kes. The sickness will pass in a moment." As the Terran guards approached, Tuvok said to them, "The situation is under control. Please contact Colonel Ishikawa." The two Terrans nodded. One stepped away to do the Vulcan's bidding, and the other corralled the gawking bystanders back into motion, hurrying them away from Tuvok and Kes.

Fighting not to weep, Kes grabbed Tuvok's shirt. "Why?"

"You put yourself and others at great risk by coming here. For your own safety and the greater good, I had to stop you from abducting Mister Neelix."

She looked to Neelix for support, or for forgiveness, or perhaps for just a glimmer of understanding, but he backed away from her, clearly stung by her betrayal. He melted back into the crowd, slipped through the checkpoint, and was gone. Kes looked back at Tuvok, her anger rising. "What did you do to me?"

He lowered his voice. "Let it suffice to say that before we helped you hone your powers, we took precautions to prevent them from being turned against us."

"Is it permanent?"

"That will depend on you." He helped her to her feet. "When you persuade me that you can be trusted to use your abilities wisely, we will discuss the deactivation of your neural damper." With his hand on her back, he gently nudged her into motion away from the checkpoint. "For now, however, we need to get you somewhere safe."

Apocalyptic thunderclaps split the air as the station rocked and shuddered, hurling Kes and Tuvok against a wall. Then the echoes of impact gave way to the angry bleat of alarms, followed by a voice declaring over the PA system, *"Red Alert! All hands to battle stations!"*

Kes glared at Tuvok. "You were saying?"

"The plan changes, but the goal remains the same." He reversed direction and pulled her back toward the checkpoint, quickening his pace from a trot to a run. "We must get off this station immediately, or else we are both going to die."

13

Alamo

No matter how many times Eddington and the other ship commanders had urged O'Brien to direct attacks from a safe remove, he had ignored them and ordered his crew to put the *Defiant* at the head of every formation. *You can't lead from the rear,* Sisko had always told him, and it was a lesson O'Brien had taken to heart.

Facing the collective might of the Cardassian military's Ninth Order, however, O'Brien wondered whether this might have been a good time for a change in tactics. Until that moment, the Terran Rebellion had limited itself to small-scale strikes, hit-and-run attacks, and guerrilla warfare. Now he and his people were about to try to hold the line against a full invasion force. Every shred of combat experience he possessed was telling him to retreat; the Alliance could mount dozens of efforts such as this, but the rebellion would likely survive only one. His conscience, however, knew that if he gave the order to retreat now, the people of Bajor would be the ones to pay for his cowardice.

I won't condemn billions to die just to save my own skin, he vowed. Leaning forward in his command chair, he put a confident edge in his voice and started snapping orders at his crew. "Bowers, take us in, full impulse, and meet the Cardassians' lead ship head-on. Ezri, target all weapons on that ship. Leeta, have *Kearsarge* and *Independence* guard our flanks." He thumbed open a channel to the engine room. "Muñiz! You're out of time! Do I have full power or not?"

"You've got it, sir. Just don't ask me how."

"Didn't plan to. Good work, Quiqué." He closed the channel.

Leeta looked up from the operations console. "Firing range in five seconds!" The buxom Bajoran first officer swiveled her chair to look across the cramped, dimly lit bridge at her wife, Ezri Tigan. "Lock torpedoes and phasers!"

The feisty young Trill was tensed for action. "Locked."

Bowers palmed a slick of perspiration from his smooth, dark-brown pate as he muttered grimly, "Here we go."

On the main viewer, the fleet of Cardassian ships became a wall of rust-orange hulls that blocked out the stars. Blinding lances of energy slashed and crisscrossed wildly between the fleets. Disruptor pulses flashed as they intersected with phaser beams and streams of charged plasma. Dense clusters of blazing torpedoes streaked past one another in both directions.

Defiant heaved and lurched as it was buffeted by Cardassian ordnance and friendly fire alike. All O'Brien could do was hang on and try not to get thrown from his seat as his crew, battle-hardened and lightning-quick from years of war, cheated death by infinitesimal degrees, over and over again.

In a matter of minutes, Bajor's orbit was littered with hundreds of shattered, burning starships. The wreckage of dozens of Cardassian battleships tumbled amid the broken husks of Talarian dreadnoughts and the glowing remnants of nearly half the rebels' hodgepodge armada.

As *Defiant* made a wide turn to prepare for its next attack run, O'Brien caught a glimpse of Bajor's surface. It had not yet been fired upon. Its surface-based artillery continued to hammer away at the Cardassian ships, with limited success, but so far the Cardassians had not yet retaliated.

O'Brien turned toward his first officer. "Leeta! Give me a big-picture look at the Cardies' deployment pattern!" As Leeta scrambled to compile the intel, O'Brien's eye was drawn back to the main screen by a blinding flash. He lifted a hand to shield his eyes for a moment until the screen compensated and filtered out the glare. "What the hell was that?"

Tigan looked up from her console. "The Talarians are making suicide runs!"

More explosions lit up the screen. O'Brien's heart sank. He'd hoped the prideful, stubborn Talarians wouldn't resort to such tactics, but the loss of their homeworld and territory had broken them as a people. Unwilling to live as refugees or nomads, they had chosen instead to die in battle, giving the last of themselves for the cause of vengeance. Though he had expected this outcome, he was disappointed to lose them as allies for the rebellion.

Can't cry about it now, he knew. *We've got bigger problems to deal with.*

"Captain," Leeta said, routing her strategic analysis to the display beside O'Brien's chair. "The Cardassians are focusing their attack on the station. Should we pull the fleet back to a defensive perimeter?"

O'Brien felt the blood drain from his face as he saw Leeta's report. As much as he wanted to protect the station—in other words, Keiko—he knew it would take away his forces' only advantages in this kind of battle, their superior speed and maneuverability at sublight. "No," he said, swallowing all his emotions. "Continue the attack. What's the next largest enemy ship?"

Tigan replied, "The *Ketaras,* bearing three-one mark five."

"Sam, intercept the *Ketaras.* Ezri, lock all weapons. Destroy that ship."

His crew snapped back into action, all eyes trained on the objective directly ahead of them . . . but all O'Brien could think of was the woman he had left behind.

The bridge of the *Geronimo* was ablaze. Smoke stung Neelix's eyes and flames licked at his arms as he barked, "Someone put that fire out!"

Seconds later the hiss of a fire extinguisher squelched the crackling inferno, and the haze hanging in the air went from smelling like burnt ODN cables to reeking of the chemical fumes left over from the flame retardant. "Thank you," Neelix said, then he turned his head to see Tuvok holding the extinguisher. "What are you doing on my ship?"

Before Tuvok could answer, a Tellarite at the helm cried out, "Incoming!"

"Evasive!" Neelix shouted. "Hard to starboard!" Detonations rocked the *Condor*-class raider, and burning phosphors rained from the overhead. A second barrage hammered the *Geronimo,* and a blast destroyed the helm console and sent its high-strung Tellarite pilot to the deck in a charred heap.

Tuvok leaped to an unmanned station and keyed in commands. "Rerouting helm control. Engaging evasive maneuvers."

There was no time to argue. Neelix looked over

his shoulder to his Cardassian-expatriate first officer. "Seska! Are the weapons back up yet?"

"Negative." She held a hand over her ear-mounted transceiver to block out noise while she listened to the damage reports from the aft sections. "Ziyal's still trying to seal the hull breach."

Neelix bit down on his rage. "Let me know as soon as we have weapons. We have to get back in the fight."

"Yes, sir." Seska turned away from him to focus on directing the ship's skeleton crew through the ever-growing list of emergency repairs.

"Mister Vulcan," Neelix said, "plot an evasive course that puts us outside the Cardassians' weapons range for the next few minutes."

"Plotted and laid in," Tuvok said.

"Engage." The raging battle on the main viewscreen spun and blurred as the *Geronimo* veered away at full impulse. As soon as Neelix was sure they were clear of the conflagrations that were rending both fleets, he sprang from his chair and loomed over the seated Vulcan. His voice was a strained, furious whisper. "Tell me what you're doing here, Tuvok."

Perhaps taking his cue from Neelix, Tuvok replied in a discreet hush. "Your ship was the only means of escape from the station when the attack began. Because I could not permit Kes to come to harm, I brought her aboard just before—"

He grabbed Tuvok's collar. "You brought her onto *my* ship?"

"It was the only logical solution to our dilemma, Mister Neelix."

"That's *Captain* Neelix, to you."

Tuvok made a humble nod. "My apologies, Captain."

"Where is she now?"

"Sedated, in the brig." He looked back at Neelix. "I regret what she did to you, sir, but at the moment we have more pressing concerns."

From the other side of the tiny command deck, Seska called to Neelix, "We have shields and weapons, Captain!"

Neelix let go of Tuvok, returned to his chair, and prepared himself to rejoin the fray. "Mister Vulcan, set a course back to the battle. Seska, find the biggest, baddest ship the Cardassians have left. I want it blasted to bits."

Keiko dodged between eruptions of fire and shrapnel as she crossed Ops, firing off orders each step of the way. "Maintain suppressing fire! Luther, transfer all power from the Habitat Ring to shields!"

Sloan grimaced as he jabbed at his console. "It's not enough! Shields buckling in all sections!"

A power relay in the ceiling high above them burst into flames and rained molten slag onto the central command table. Waving caustic smoke and noxious fumes from her eyes, Keiko called out, "Fire teams! Over here!" She climbed a few short steps to look over Sloan's shoulder in the engineering station. "Retract the shield perimeter to the core section and center decks."

"And sacrifice the pylons?"

She slapped his back as she moved away. "It'll buy us a few minutes. Best we can do." She passed two Terran men who carried small chemical fire extinguishers. With a great hiss, the portable devices filled the air with fog.

Bone-jarring impacts rocked the station, and the irregular percussion of detonations against Terok Nor's dwindling shields grew steadily louder. Keiko hunched over one of the few still-functional terminals at the command table. She tried to call up a tactical display and got nothing but hashed lines followed by a blizzard of gray static. "Someone get me an update on the fleet," she shouted to the room. "I need hard numbers, and I need them—"

There was no sound but the roaring blast, no sensation but the mad rush of free fall, nothing to see but the jerky tumbling of bodies caught in the strobed light of a sparking cable ripped from its junction. Keiko slammed against a wall and bounced away from it in a daze. Then pale yellow emergency lights snapped on, partial gravity returned, and Keiko plummeted to the deck. Echoes of the explosion lingered in the air and the deck, quaking in endless ripples through the skeleton of Terok Nor. As Keiko pulled herself to her feet, she saw that consoles all over Ops were flickering erratically. Only a few of her command personnel were still conscious. "Damage report! Anyone, talk to me. What hit us?"

At the science station, Lon Suder, a bug-eyed Betazoid man with a ragged mullet of gray hair, looked terrified. "The Cardassian frigate *Mostar*." He looked up at Keiko. "She rammed us. Went right through our shields."

From the tactical station, Sloan added, "We've lost the lower core. Main power and the central computer are gone. Shields and weapons offline, and we're venting atmosphere." He added with emphasis, "The Cardassians are coming around for another volley."

Keiko activated the emergency channel, which would broadcast to the station's PA system as well as to anyone within subspace radio range. "All hands, get to your ships or the lifeboats! Evacuate the station!" She switched off the channel and asked Sloan, "Transporters?"

"Offline," he said with a grim shake of his head.

He pointed toward the single lifeboat attached to Ops. "That's our only way out in time."

It was the worst news Keiko could have received. The Cardassian-made lifeboats had been designed for little more than a brief powered descent to a planet's surface. Unfortunately, during that descent, the lifeboats would be completely vulnerable, and if they failed to land or splash down on Bajor within twenty minutes of launch, they would become little more than orbital debris waiting to burn up on entry into Bajor's atmosphere. *At least the transporter would have put us on the surface before the Cardassians use us for target practice,* she lamented, but there was nothing to be done except the inevitable.

"All right," Keiko said, herding her people with broad gestures. "Time to go. Everybody in." She took one final look back and made sure no survivors had been left behind in Ops, then she stepped inside the lifeboat, shut the hatch, and gave Sloan the order: "Launch."

He pressed the button, and the lifeboat rocketed away from the station, into orbit above Bajor—and into the crossfire.

"Hit them again, Ezri," O'Brien said as he watched torpedoes from *Defiant* rend the hull of the Cardassian cruiser *Prisika*. "Leeta, get ready to change targets."

More crimson flashes raced away from *Defiant*'s bow and obliterated the crippled *Prisika*. As the rebel frigate punched through the firestorm of debris it had wrought, O'Brien heard Keiko's voice through the heavy chatter on the subspace comm: *"All hands, get to your ships or the lifeboats! Evacuate the station!"*

Terror froze him in place as the battle raged around him. All he could do was speculate about Keiko's fate.

Would she have beamed down to Bajor? He sprang from his chair and shouldered past Tigan to take control of the tactical console. He turned the *Defiant*'s sensors on what was left of Terok Nor. The station's lower core had been destroyed. Fires raged throughout the inner and outer rings, and the pylons were breaking apart. *No lower core—that'll mean no main computer,* he reasoned. *Which means no transporters.* He clamped a hand over his sweat-slicked forehead. *God, I hope she didn't use one of those shoddy Cardassian lifeboats. She'll be dead meat floating around in one of those things.*

Leeta grabbed O'Brien by the shoulder and pulled him up and around to face her. Towering over him, the redhead scowled and asked, "*Orders, sir?*" He knew that what she'd really meant was, *Get your head out of your ass, Captain.*

She was right—he wasn't doing anyone any good standing like a mute, least of all Keiko. He stepped in front of his chair and faced the main screen. "Leeta, tell the fleet to fall back and start rescuing survivors from the lifeboats. Work in threes, like we practiced—two cover while one transports."

Bowers looked back from the helm, dismayed. "What about the survivors still on the station?" No one on the bridge was cold-blooded enough to say what Bowers should have known: There were no survivors left on the station. All that remained now of Terok Nor was a smoldering husk on the verge of oblivion.

"Sam," Leeta said, "set a search-and-rescue pattern. Ezri, tell *Kearsarge* and *Independence* to stay close, this is gonna get ugly." The first officer looked up reflexively as she said, "Bridge to transporter bay! Get ready to beam in survivors, as many as you can find and we can fit!"

On the forward viewscreen, Terok Nor glowed like an ember in the night. Angry blazes of energy surrounded the disintegrating station with massive bouquets of fire, in a steady cycle of blooms and dissolutions. Pointing into the heart of the storm, O'Brien said with rock-solid calm, "Take us in, Sam." He turned to Tigan and Leeta. "Drop shields and begin transport."

Seconds felt like minutes and minutes like an eternity as enemy fire dealt the *Defiant* one thunderbolt after another. The tiny ship rocked wildly under a steady barrage of punishment that became only marginally less brutal when it raised its shields and served as a defender for one of its two wingmen. One by one the *Defiant*'s systems hiccupped and went dark. Bitter smoke choked the air, sections of the overhead fell in, and fried cables spilled from the bulkheads like viscera.

After each critical failure, Leeta asked, "Fall back?"

Each time O'Brien fixed his hard gaze on the fire. "Not yet."

For a moment, it seemed they might pluck a victory from the flames, as the few remaining Cardassian warships abruptly retreated.

Then a single, majestic blast whited out the viewscreen, and the shock wave sent the *Defiant* and dozens of other ships hurtling away on chaotic vectors. When the glare faded from the screen, there was nothing left of Terok Nor but a gray mist and a massive field of debris that would soon burn up as it plunged out of orbit.

Tigan laid a hand on O'Brien's shoulder. He looked back to see the young Trill regarding him with admiration and compassion. "We can't fit any more," she said, sliding her gaze aft. He followed her look and saw that the doors at the rear of *Defiant*'s bridge were open. Outside them, the narrow passageways were packed solid with standing refugees. Giving O'Brien's shoulder a gentle squeeze, Tigan added, "All ships report they're at maximum capacity. It's time."

He nodded, his mien solemn. "Sam, set a course for the Badlands. Leeta, order the fleet to regroup at Athos IV."

Leeta stepped close and spoke in a confidential whisper. "Sir, the fleet is heavily damaged. We'll be vulnerable all the way to Athos. Why not beam the rest of the lifeboat survivors to Bajor and then join them on the surface?"

"Because that'll give the Cardassians the excuse they need to lay waste to the planet. The only way Bajor avoids a major bloodbath is if we retreat."

Leaning closer, Leeta sharpened her tone. "And what about Keiko? What if she's still out there in one of those lifeboats?"

Her words twisted like a blade in O'Brien's heart, but he refused to permit himself the luxury of self-pity. "Give the order. Retreat and regroup." He dropped heavily back into his command chair. "This battle's over. We've lost."

"The order is confirmed," Seska said, wiping blood and black dust from her face as she swiveled her chair toward Neelix. "Retreat and regroup."

"I can't believe O'Brien would abandon all those people," Neelix said, unable to mask his anguish. "Once we leave, they'll be defenseless!"

Tuvok glanced cautiously back at *Geronimo*'s two senior officers and kept a civil tone. "With all respect, Captain, we have already taken aboard more people than we can support. Even if you wish to rescue more survivors, we have nowhere to put them. The logical course of action is to obey General O'Brien's order and withdraw." He entered coordinates into the helm. "Course plotted for Athos IV."

Neelix looked at the swarm of Cardassian-made lifeboats drifting away from the scorched flotsam of Terok Nor. He had no idea how many still harbored living people and how many had been turned into ovens by the station's explosion. Noting the small handful of Cardassian warships that had fallen back just beyond the range of Bajor's planetary artillery, he knew that O'Brien and Tuvok were correct: It was time to retreat, before enemy reinforcements arrived.

That didn't mean he had to accept it without a fight.

"Seska, scan the remaining lifeboats. If you find one with someone still alive inside, put a tractor beam on it." He nodded at Tuvok. "Mister Vulcan, engage."

Gul Domal stood on the command deck of the Cardassian patrol cruiser *Azanja*. Less than an hour earlier, Domal had been a single starship commander in a great fleet. Now, through the magic of attrition and good fortune, he was the senior surviving officer—and de facto commander—of Cardassia's Ninth Order.

Unfortunately, the Ninth Order now consisted of precisely four warships and a small handful of support vessels. Of those four ships of the line, none had a working warp drive, only two were fully maneuverable at impulse, and only the *Azanja* had escaped the fray without a major hull breach. Though an argument could be made that they had won the battle—after all, Terok Nor had been destroyed and the rebels were soundly routed—Domal knew that the pyrrhic quality of this victory would require him to be modest in his celebrations.

His third-in-command, Glinn Kirso, approached and handed Domal a data slate. "Damage reports, sir."

Domal accepted the slate and reviewed its slew of

jargon and numbers, the endless lists and conservatively inflated repair estimates. "How irritating," he said under his breath. His ship and its remaining battle group likely were strong enough to repel any counterattack the undermilitarized Bajorans might send against them, but without reinforcements, the *Azanja* would be unable to mount a successful invasion and occupation of the planet. He thrust the slate back at Kirso. "Dismissed."

As the junior officer hurried away, Domal joined his second-in-command, Glinn Teska, at the ship's tactical station. "Report."

"The rebels are in full retreat." He called up a star chart overlaid with course projections. "They're heading for the Badlands at maximum warp. Should we alert the patrol squadron at Koralis?"

"No. The rebels would either outrun them or outgun them. Alert the Central Command and let them formulate a response."

"Yes, sir." Teska switched the display to a magnification of the *Azanja*'s view of Bajor. "The rebels left behind several occupied lifeboats, as well as a large number of sublight spacecraft that are currently adrift in orbit of Bajor. Orders?"

Domal cracked a thin, malevolent smile. "Have the gunners use them for target practice." He shared a brief laugh with Teska, then stepped back. "If you need me, I'll be in my quarters, revising the invasion plans," he said. "As soon as the Seventh Order joins us, the conquest of Bajor will begin."

14

Shadows upon Shadows

Passions were high inside *Excalibur*'s nerve center. Faces were taut with fierce anticipation of the battle to come—none more so than that of its captain.

Mac slowly flexed his fist several times while watching the image of swirling multihued gases on the forward bulkhead's main screen. Somewhere beyond that opaque, lightning-slashed storm, an Alliance convoy was drawing near. Lying in ambush to greet it was every ship under Mac's command.

Soleta looked up from a sensor console. "Convoy is twenty minutes out." Mac glanced at her and responded with a barely perceptible nod.

Patience had not always been one of Mac's virtues, nor had it been prevalent among the Xenexian freedom fighters he'd recruited or the Romulan refugees to whom he'd given succor. He and they had always preferred action to words, deeds to ideas. In his youth, Mac had found his decisiveness to be an advantage. Whenever his enemies had made the mistake of wasting a moment to taunt him, he had used those precious slivers of time to seize the initiative.

Things change, he reminded himself. *Either we change with them, or we die.*

Leading an armada on a long-term military campaign

against overwhelming odds had taught him the difference between tactics and strategy. At the point and moment of engagement, the readiness to act was all. But in the grander scheme of a conflict, what mattered was knowing when *not* to act—when to bide one's time, wait for the enemy to make a mistake, maneuver for advantage, or avoid an unwinnable confrontation. Battles and wars, he was learning, often were won or lost before their first shots were fired. The key to survival was learning how to tell the difference between a lost cause and a call to glory before committing oneself to the fray.

"Nineteen minutes out," Soleta said.

The silence inside the nerve center was oppressive. Normally, Mac paid no attention to the low-frequency hum of the ship's ventilation system or the subtle feedback tones from the consoles. Without a steady, low buzz of comm chatter as white noise, however, he found himself tuning in to every tiny sound around him. The cadence of Jellico's breathing from the tactical station. The scuffling of someone's shoe on the deck as they shifted their weight. A distant, eerie howl of dense nebular currents buffeting his ship's hull.

Amid that stillness, the alert chirping on Selar's console was sharp in Mac's ears. The lithe Vulcan woman silenced the warning and began working at her station with unusual speed and intensity.

Mac turned his chair toward her. "Selar, what's going on?"

"I have detected several unusual readings inside the nebula."

Concerned looks passed among Jellico, Soleta, and Mac. It was the Terran who asked, "Can you be a bit more specific, please?"

"Numerous sudden changes in the expected fluid dynamics of the nebula's core currents," Selar said. "They appear to be displacements of sufficient mass and volume to affect the nebula's natural convection patterns."

Making an effort to remain calm, Mac said, "Sum up, please. Quickly."

"We are not alone inside this nebula."

Jellico frowned. "Of course not, our whole armada's out there."

"You misunderstand," Selar said. "I had accounted for our forces' effects on the nebula's currents. These are new disruptions." She pointedly looked away from Jellico to address Mac. "Captain, I think there is another fleet in the nebula."

He got up and stepped toward Selar. Soleta and Jellico joined him, and they surrounded the Vulcan woman's science console.

Discreetly, Mac asked, "How large a fleet?"

"At least equal in size to our own," Selar said.

Soleta's features hardened with cold fury. "A trap."

"That would be the logical assumption, yes."

Behind his mask of composure, Mac was furious. Keeping his voice down so as not to fuel rumors, he said, "If it's a trap, that implies the Alliance knew we were coming. That suggests they have a mole aboard this ship."

McHenry's telepathic voice answered inside his head with urgent sincerity. *Not possible, Mac. If anyone on this ship had treasonous thoughts, I would have heard them and warned you.*

Mac exchanged a knowing glance with Soleta, who he was certain had also heard McHenry's assurance. Soleta arched one eyebrow. "If McHenry is sure that our ship is secure from treachery, I believe him."

"So do I," Mac said. "But our fleet has a lot of ships."

I have monitored all comm traffic between, to, and from the vessels of our fleet, McHenry insisted. *Our transmissions have been secure and free of alien codes or embedded signals, and no one has let slip any details of our mission. There has been no betrayal, Mac.*

Soleta cocked her head to one side. "There is a simpler explanation." She waited for Mac to train his withering glare upon her. "Maybe the Alliance lured us into a trap, and we got careless and took the bait." Her proposition drew grudging nods of agreement from Jellico and Selar.

"*Grozit,*" Mac muttered. In retrospect, it seemed so obvious, but that didn't make it any less annoying. "Selar, patch into the tactical panel." He waited until she called up the display showing his fleet's position relative to the approaching Alliance vessels. "Now we've got a problem. If we show ourselves to take a shot at the convoy, their fleet inside the nebula will hit us from behind, and we'll end up caught between them and the convoy's defense squadron." He frowned and looked at Jellico. "That's a losing battle for us. We'd be out of position and outnumbered." With a few deft taps, he began reconfiguring the icons on the screen to illustrate his points as he made them. "As much as we were counting on the supplies from the convoy, we'll have to let them go if we want to leave here alive. But if we do nothing, we're just as screwed. Once the ambush fleet realizes why we haven't attacked the convoy, they'll recall the escort squadron and come after us from two directions. So we can't go forward, but we also can't stay here." He finished moving things around, then flashed a mischievous smile. "But that's no reason not to have some fun."

"I don't like it when you smile," Soleta said. "It's usually a bad sign."

"Not this time." He enlarged part of the schematic on Selar's screen. "We're going to use the nebula's natural convection patterns to our advantage. Ed, have all our ships release full torpedo salvos without propulsion into this thermal upswell. It'll carry the warheads right up into the center of the hidden Alliance fleet's formation. Soleta, after each ship has released its torpedoes, have them maneuver one at a time, on thrusters only, into this vortex. It'll push us toward the eye of the nebula, where we'll have more room to navigate."

Soleta caught on right away. "The torpedoes will be on delayed fuses."

"Precisely. It'll take us roughly an hour to deploy torpedoes and ride the vortex clear. Ed, have all ships set their launched ordnance for detonation at precisely 1744 hours fleet time."

His plan drew a sly, approving look from Soleta. "In the vacuum of space, such a near miss would rattle the Alliance ships but do little real damage. But inside the nebula—"

"The shock wave'll rip their unshielded hulls apart like tissue paper."

Jellico grinned. "That's diabolical."

Mac took a self-congratulatory half-bow. "Thank you."

Within minutes, the *Excalibur* had sent a dozen of its warheads into the upswell. An hour later, she lay at station inside the placid vacuum of the nebula's eye, surrounded by the rest of Mac's armada.

Standing at the core of the ship's nerve center, Mac listened with cold satisfaction to the reports of distant warhead detonations, and the subsequent aftershocks produced by Alliance starships as they imploded.

"I'm going to call that a good day's work," he declared.

Soleta grimaced. "We have a dissenting opinion on the comm."

"Let me guess. Hiren."

"Hiren."

A tired sigh. "Put him on-screen."

Flickers of static resolved into the image of Hiren. *"We should pursue the convoy,"* he said without salutation or preamble.

"An interesting notion. . . . No."

"We need those supplies, Captain!"

Mac shook his head. "No, we don't. They'd have been useful and would've made what lies ahead of us easier, but we'll survive without them. At any rate, we've clearly lost the element of surprise here. It's time to move on."

The former praetor of the Romulan Star Empire looked nearly apoplectic. *"We had a deal, Captain! You promised my people we'd plunder this convoy and deal the Alliance a shaming blow, not just a paltry black eye."*

"No, I let you *request* that, and I said I'd take it under advisement. But in case you haven't been paying attention, Hiren, we just left the Alliance with a lot more than a black eye. The fleet the Alliance sent after us got turned into scrap a few minutes ago. Judging from my crew's estimates of its size, I'd say the Alliance just lost most of its forces in the Acamar Sector." He stepped forward and stared down the fuming Romulan. "They won't have enough ships to patrol your former empire for at least a year. And in case you've forgotten, *that* is what I promised you I'd try to do. Now it's done—and so is this conversation. Stand by for new orders. *Excalibur* out." He turned his back on Hiren, and Soleta closed the channel before the irate ex-praetor could reply. Mac settled into his command chair. "Henna, set course for the B'hava'el system and relay coordinates to the fleet."

"Aye, sir," said the young Xenexian woman at the helm.

He looked over his shoulder toward the science station. "Selar." When the Vulcan looked up at him, he beckoned her. With dignified grace, she stood and crossed the bridge to stand beside his chair. He motioned for her to lean closer. "There's something I need you to do for me."

"If I am able, I will try."

"Without telling anyone else, I want you to send a message ahead of us to the Terran Rebellion. I've instructed McHenry to assist you as needed."

Selar asked in a whisper, "What message do you wish to send?"

"Tell whoever's in charge that I want to meet—and I want to join forces."

15

The Face of Anarchy

Corat Damar stands in the shadows, watching from a safe remove as his leader and best friend, Skrain Dukat, steps onto the balcony outside his office to make a rare public address to all of the Cardassian Union. It has always been this way between the two of them: Dukat has always been more at home in the spotlight, as the focus of attention, and Damar has been content to live as the éminence grise, the power behind the throne, acting as Dukat's right hand.

On the balcony, Dukat lifts his hands and basks in the roaring adulation of the crowd gathered in the plaza below. Applause crashes over him like a breaking wave. The people's worship of him is a tangible thing, a tactile commodity. Damar is certain that if only he had the nerve to step into the light, he could touch that glory with his fingertips and revel in its warmth.

"People of Cardassia," Dukat bellows, his voice soaring into the honeyed sky, his words resonating in the arid morning air. "Today we rejoice! A great thorn has been plucked from the side of the Alliance. The Terran Rebellion has been routed from the Bajor system, its stronghold destroyed, and its numbers slashed to a mere fraction of its former strength. Mark my words: The Terrans . . . are . . . FINISHED!" Throaty cheers answer him. Voices full of pride and fury echo off the dusky building façades facing the plaza. "Soon we shall avenge the traitorous secession of Bajor. For too long we have let that tiny world dictate our affairs. It's time the Alliance had a new master, one worthy of the role—and that master will be CARDASSIA!"

Hope and joy swell in Damar's heart. Dukat's call to arms inspires him. It is a vision of a future for which he has long devoutly wished. Unable to resist the summons to greatness, for the first time in his life Damar steps from the shadows, into the light, and onto the balcony.

He draws his sidearm and shoots Dukat in the back of the head.

The moment is one of horrified silence. Far below, the crowd is silent. They stand stunned, not knowing how to react. On the balcony, Damar is slackjawed. He watches Dukat's corpse sag to its knees and collapse at his feet. Though the hole in the back of Dukat's skull is modest, his entire face is gone, leaving only a charred and bloody cavity. Damar stares in horror at the gun in his hand.

Time slows. Nothing seems real. Damar feels like a spectator to his life, a puppet watching its own clumsy pantomime.

Angry cries rise from the plaza. A riot breaks out. Cardassian civilians turn against one another, and within moments the crowd, which had seemed so happy and united only moments earlier, descends into violent chaos.

Damar staggers back inside the Supreme Legate's office. He drops his weapon on the floor and struggles not to weep.

Standing in the middle of the room, holding a tray

with two beverages upon it, is one of Dukat's mousy Vulcan handmaidens. Her eyes are cold, passionless, and seem to Damar as if they are gazing straight through him to his essence.

He looks back at her, desperate in his grief. "What have I done?"

She answers without pity, "Only what was logical."

The rifle is warm in Legate Remok's hands, a reassuring totem of power, and its screeching as he holds down its trigger drowns out the screams and pathetic cries of his officers until he is the last one left alive on the command deck of the dreadnought *Ostrava*. They were traitors, he reminds himself, unworthy of mercy, undeserving of his remorse or remembrance.

He seals the hatches to the command deck and enters his command override codes into the ship's main computer. From every deck of his ship, reports flood in of officers turning against one another, enlisted men rising up against their officers, mutinies devolving into senseless mobs. The comm chatter among the other ships of the Seventh Order tells the same story, over and over again: a sudden descent into madness, a pandemic of irrational violence consuming each ship's crew.

There is only one solution, Remok decides. Only one way to defend Cardassia and the Alliance from whatever mindless fury has seized his men. Whether the madness lies in their blood or is being forced upon them by some malevolent force, he sees only one recourse.

The computer acknowledges his codes. "Override all command directives for the Seventh Order," he says, and the computer complies. "Initiate counterinsurgency protocol *Skurov* on all vessels."

"Protocol armed."

Remok takes no pleasure in what he has to do, but he permits himself a modicum of pride. This is his sworn duty, his solemn responsibility: to defend his people, even if only from themselves. "Arm all self-destruct packages. Command authorization Remok-three-*cheska.*"

"Confirmed. All packages armed. Set delay."

"Ten seconds, silent countdown. Execute."

"Confirmed. Ten seconds to self-destruct."

He drops his rifle to the deck, relieving himself of its burden. His task is complete, and what has been done cannot be undone. None of the starship commanders in the Seventh Order has the command authority to override Remok's directive—not that it matters, since none of them will know he has triggered it until after their ships have been reduced to fractured debris and free radicals.

Falling to his knees, Remok laughs and weeps all at once.

The mad compulsion fades, and in the final seconds of his life he is afflicted with a moment of terrible clarity: *Someone has done this to me.*

Everything he knows is transformed into white light—and then it's erased, lost in time's fathomless abyss, as if it had never existed at all.

Selona has devoted her entire adult life to science. Growing up in Lakarian City on Cardassia Prime, she consistently tested at the top of her class in mathematics, chemistry, physics, and biology. Despite her doting father's misguided emphasis on praising Selona for her beauty, she knew from a tender age that the real path to prominence in the Union and the Alliance was prowess—to be the best at something important, something valuable.

That understanding had propelled her into one of Cardassia's finest universities, where she'd excelled beyond all expectations, even her own. More than a year before receiving her doctorate in applied biochemistry, she had been deluged with job offers from corporations and the military—but she'd known the only position worthy of consideration was the one offered by the Obsidian Order.

Today, her work comes to fruition. Her lifetime of study and labor, and her years of isolation in a secret bioweapons lab, yield their bitter reward.

She disengages the lab's internal sensors and biocontainment systems. Using her supervisory code, she shuts down even its most fundamental safety systems. Then she dons a protective respiration mask and opens the valve on a large tank of cytozine gas. Odorless, colorless, and silent, it disperses swiftly through the laboratory and is pulled into the main ventilation system.

Within minutes, all her colleagues—people with whom she has worked, socialized, flirted, fornicated, and competed—fall dead en masse. Soon enough she is alone in the massive underground facility, carrying out an objective for which she has spent most of her life in preparation, though until this moment she had no idea that she was doing so.

Stored in the deepest recesses of the Obsidian Order's bioweapons lab, behind multiply redundant layers of interlocks, safeguards, and barriers, is a weapon unlike any ever used in all of known history: a metagenic pathogen. Unleashed into a planet's atmosphere, it will self-replicate and feed off every bit of DNA and organic matter it encounters, devouring all in its path. It is capable of destroying entire ecosystems and exterminating all organic life on an average inhabited planet within a matter of days.

Selona reprograms a phalanx of forty-eight missiles whose warheads are loaded with the metagenic pathogen. She sets their guidance matrices to target populated Cardassian planets purely at random once deployed. Then she launches them. As the sleek drones lift off and head for space, Selona draws a small disruptor from her pocket and destroys the missiles' control console.

One more task, says a voice in her head that she knows is not hers but that compels her obedience all the same.

She releases the last of the safeguards on the reserve stockpile of the metagenic pathogen and purges it into the atmosphere of Kora II. Based on today's weather reports, wind patterns will likely carry it first to the military academy, and afterward to the population centers along the seacoast.

It is finished, the voice says, and Selona breathes a sigh of relief. No more struggling, no more lying, no more playing the part of the puppet.

She strips the respirator mask from her face, breathes in, and sinks into a dreamless sleep without end.

Gil Penar has no idea what is happening. He is just a low-level officer, freshly minted by the military academy on Kora II, and he is all alone in a remote subspace comm relay station, in deep space between Orias and Sarpedion.

The comm network is going haywire.

Frantic reports fill him with terror: From every corner of the Alliance, he is receiving reports of Cardassian fleets being rent asunder by infighting. Senior officers are wiping out their crews, junior officers are betraying their commanders, soldiers of the Alliance are turning their weapons on one another.

Each passing minute brings more reports of greater madness from farther away. Insanity is spreading faster than the speed of light, devouring Cardassia's best and brightest. Lost in the cacophony are several planetary distress signals. Normally, Penar would relay those pleas for help, but as he watches his entire civilization descend into chaos, he realizes there is no one left to call.

T'Nara's face is wet with blood—not her own but that of her so-called mistress, Natima, the lady of the aristocratic Cardassian household into whose servitude T'Nara had been born decades earlier.

Decades have slipped past while T'Nara played her part as a meek and faithful servant, a pliant slave willing to submit to whatever depredations her host family chose to inflict upon her. For the patriarch, Damek, she has been a concubine; for Natima, a whipping girl; for their spoiled, vicious children she has been a cook, a maid, a nurse, a confidante, an alibi.

Tonight she is the dark whisper in Damek's ear, willing him to murder.

Planting the idea was a simple matter. Damek has always been a simple man, despite his prominence in Cardassia's government. So simple, in fact, that even now he thinks it was his idea to butcher his own family in their sleep, one by one. In all likelihood, he will continue to believe that pathetic untruth for the rest of his life, and it will cause him no end of misery and self-loathing.

T'Nara has no regrets. Too many times she has been forced to close her eyes and bury her rage while surrendering to Damek's ugly violations. His disgrace will send shock waves through the upper castes of Cardassian polite society, though it will be only one of countless such incidents that the people of the Cardassian Union will studiously avoid discussing ever again. Just as they do not suspect who drove them to this madness, they will probably come to believe that they gave this awful night its name, rather than admit it was given to them.

For centuries to come, T'Nara is certain, Cardassians everywhere will blanch when they dare to remember the atrocities of the Red Hour.

She opens the doors to a wide terrace off the townhouse's main room and steps outside into the night air, which is heavy with far-off cries of terror. Across the boulevard, on another terrace, stands another Vulcan, an older man. T'Nara has met him a few times. His name is Sanok. Like her, he is a portrait in spilled blood. It speckles his face and slicks his hands.

Though they are more than a dozen meters apart, Sanok and T'Nara are strong enough as telepaths that they can communicate in brief flashes. She shares a memory, only minutes old:

I crouch in the darkness beside Damek and Natima's bed. He kneels atop his wife and severs her carotid artery with a cooking knife. Blood sprays toward me, warm and wet, baptizing me.

Sanok nods, accepting T'Nara's memory for safekeeping. He entrusts her with one of his own:

I push my masters into a verbal confrontation like the hundreds they have had before, but this time I free them from all their inhibitions. I enable them to be what they truly are. Within minutes they race each other to pluck ancient, family heirloom weapons from their walls and cut each other down with wild abandon. The master of the house emerges victorious, only to be overcome with grief when he sees he has beheaded his wife. He begs me for death. I reverently place his wife's severed head into his lap and whisper, "No."

T'Nara accepts Sanok's memory and pledges to vouchsafe it as if it were her own. He bows his head in gratitude.

Around them, the night is rich with horrors. T'Nara is not blind or bereft of conscience. She knows that what is being done, and what must yet be done, is a cold and gruesome business—but her guilt is assuaged by the memories of the fall of Vulcan, of the Alliance's mechanical cruelty, its practiced barbarism.

Those memories, passed down telepathically from Vulcan parents to their offspring, will be preserved until the last of their kind passes from the universe. As slights go, it is a recent one, a new injury, a wound so fresh it has barely taken on the psychic equivalent of a scab, much less the venerable affect of scar tissue. But it is one that all living Vulcans have vowed to remember—and avenge at any cost.

Glinn Teska stands, paralyzed, as he watches the last four ships of the Ninth Order break formation and purposefully steer into one another.

He can't appeal to his superior, Gul Domal, because Domal has just inserted his blaster's muzzle into his own mouth and shot himself. Which is only appropriate, since the gul had just slaughtered all the other bridge officers, sparing Teska only because, Domal had said, "I want you to see what follows."

Teska activates the ship's secure internal comms. "Command to Glinn Kirso, Priority One. Kirso, respond." No answer comes. With no one to whom he can issue orders, Teska sprints to the flight controls and shoves aside the dead man slumped across the console. He tries to make his fingers enter the commands that will navigate the *Azanja* clear of the imminent four-way collision, but all the symbols on the panel seem to be written in gibberish. *Ignore them,* he tells himself. *You know the sequence by heart. Just do it—evasive to starboard.*

It's a rote pattern, one every officer learns during training. By now it is all but second nature to Teska. Nonetheless, his hands disobey him. He sees in his mind's eye the sequence he desires, but his hands refuse to execute his instruction.

The image inside the holographic frame is daunting. Very little space remains between the four warships; second by second they blot out the stars as they converge. Teska punches the console that he cannot adjust, certain that something is stopping him, thwarting his will, condemning him to die.

In the distance, Bajor is a flickering light, a taunting glimmer, a goal that Teska knows will remain forever beyond his grasp.

Azanja's engines fire one last time, imparting a final blast of thrust.

There is nothing for Teska to do but curse as the ship beneath his feet keeps its appointment with oblivion.

16

Blood for Blood

The Great Hall thundered with angry voices as the High Council of the Klingon Empire unanimously excoriated Regent Martok. In the flickering crimson light of braziers packed with coal and sulfur, the councillors' shadowy faces became fearsome masks, twisted and grotesque.

"You arrogant fool!" shouted Councillor Kopek, his voice rising above the din. "Nearly a hundred ships, more than sixty thousand warriors, blown to bits because of your stupidity!" He turned his back on Martok and faced the other council members. "It's a disgrace to the Empire!"

Martok sprang from his throne, his thick eyebrows knit with scorn, and threw Kopek violently backward to the floor. "How dare you insult the sacrifice of our warriors!" He stalked in a tight circle, cowing the councillors out of his path with his stare. "War is a fickle mistress—she bestows bounty with one hand, and with the other she tears it away."

Kopek regained his feet and confronted Martok. "The spoils of war weren't taken from your hand—you fumbled them!" Cheers of support roared from several of the councillors behind him. "You set a clumsy, obvious trap, and our soldiers were the ones who paid for it! Their blood is on your hands, Martok!"

Before the brash, loudmouthed politician knew what had hit him, Martok buried his *d'k tahg* deep inside Kopek's guts, gave the blade a savage twist, and bared his fangs. "Now I have *your* blood on my hands, Kopek." With a sharp tug he yanked his blade free, splattering the floor with Kopek's viscera. Wide-eyed and speechless, the councillor sagged at the knees and collapsed, dead, at Martok's feet. Prowling in another tight circle, Martok kept his bloody dagger at the ready, an open challenge to anyone with a mind to emulate his expired rival.

"Our honored dead will not go unavenged," Martok said, his voice as rough as a boot on gravel. "We're going to hunt down the rebel Calhoun and his Romulan *taHqeqpu'* no matter how far they run, no matter how long it takes."

From the back of the room, an unfamiliar voice asked, "What of Bajor?"

The circle of councillors cleaved itself in twain, and the two clusters stepped back into the shadows, leaving Martok alone in the harsh light that shone in the center of the chamber. Facing the regent from the hall's main entrance was a figure that Martok recognized even in silhouette: a one-armed warrior.

"General Klag," Martok growled. "You forget yourself. Only scions of the Great Houses are permitted to speak inside this hall."

Klag marched forward, his eyes gleaming in the darkness, matching Martok's stare with his own. "They and those they invite, Martok."

Martok chortled. "All right, then." He pivoted to one side and then the other, eyeing the councillors. "Which one of you invited this *yIntagh* into my hall?" His stare met nothing but averted eyes and downward glances.

The answer came from behind him. "I did."

Amusement turned to frigid hatred as Martok turned to see his chief of staff, General Goluk, looking back at him from his throne's dais. The grizzled old veteran stood proudly, chin lifted in defiance. Seething, Martok asked, "Why?"

"His request was honorable," Goluk said. "I granted him entrance out of respect for his standing as a fellow member of the Order of the *Bat'leth*."

Vile curses tumbled from Martok's lips. Any mention of that dusty, useless old brotherhood was enough to drive him to vulgarity. He despised its outdated devotion to a lesser incarnation of the Empire, and its members' snobbish secrecy. Disgusted, he spat upon the ground at Goluk's feet. "Had I known you belonged to that band of *toDSaHpu'*, I'd never have made you my chief of staff." Then he turned back to face Klag, who stopped just out of reach. Martok met him with a menacing grin. "Though it seems fitting that the Order of the *Bat'leth* would induct a member who can't even hold the weapon it's named for."

Klag drew a *mek'leth* from his belt and dropped it to the floor in front of Martok. The curvaceous short sword clanged brightly as it struck the stone tiles. Then the one-armed general drew another *mek'leth* from a scabbard on his back.

"Pick it up," Klag said, "if you dare."

That was all the invitation Martok needed. He maintained eye contact with Klag as he sheathed his *d'k tahg* and squatted slowly to retrieve the melee weapon. His hand closed on its hide-wrapped grip, and he straightened while waiting for Klag to strike. The weapon felt balanced and solid, and a quick test with his thumb verified that both its short and long blades were honed to razor-sharp perfection.

He beckoned Klag. "Lay on, One-Arm."

The two warriors circled each other, and the councillors surrounding them stepped back to stay clear of the fight. Klag tested Martok with a few quick feints. Impatient, the regent lunged, determined to draw first blood.

Klag ducked and whirled clear of Martok's blade, and the next thing the regent felt was a slash of heat across his back. Instinctual reflex led him to clutch at the wound, and his hand came away stained fuchsia with his blood. Recovering quickly, he lowered his center of gravity by crouching slightly as he pivoted to keep Klag in front of him.

The general looked pleased with himself. "Hurts, doesn't it?"

"Less than you think," Martok rasped. He struck at Klag's left side to draw his defense, then sidestepped and swung at the general's exposed right side. His blade rang as it was parried by Klag's *mek'leth*.

Of course he's learned to defend his open right side, Martok chided himself. *He wouldn't still be alive if he hadn't mastered that.* Feeling a slick sheen of blood coating his flank and leg, Martok knew he would need to regain the advantage soon if he was to win this duel. He mustered his strength, let out a battle cry, and charged at Klag, raining attacks down upon him with speed and ferocity. Mighty swings crisscrossed Klag's chest with bloody lacerations, and an aggressive lunge tore a chunk of meat from the ribs on his right side.

Time to end this, Martok decided. He brought his *mek'leth* down in a powerful stroke, and as he expected, Klag parried it and their blades locked together. With his free hand, Martok drew his *d'k tahg* and raised his arm to deliver the killing stroke. As his arm fell to land the fatal blow, Klag shifted his weight, forcing Martok off balance, and before the regent realized what was being done, his arms were tangled together, both his blades snared.

Klag snaked his leg behind Martok's knee and swept the regent's legs out from under him. As Martok fell, his *mek'leth* was torn from his hands. He saw a flash of metal and raised his *d'k tahg* in a desperate bid to block it.

The next thing he saw was his *d'k tahg* spinning through the air, followed closely by his severed hand and a gout of blood. He was screaming in rage as Klag's *mek'leth* plunged into his skull.

The rest was silence.

Klag left his blade where he'd put it: in the middle of Martok's head. Bits of the dead regent's brain and bone flecked Klag's arm and chest, and he stood surrounded by a swiftly spreading pool of blood.

If he had harbored the slightest regard for Martok—as a leader, a warrior, or even simply as a Klingon—he would have honored his demise with the *Hegh'ta*, prying open the eyelids of the vanquished and roaring as a warning to the legions of *Sto-Vo-Kor* that one of their own was coming to join their august company.

Instead, he planted his boot on Martok's chest. "Follow me now."

The councillors were silent. Some looked perplexed. Was he making a request? Extending an invitation? Giving them an order? He did not care how they interpreted his imperative, so long as none of them challenged him. If forced to fight them all, one by one, he would do so.

He did not fear them, nor did he fear death. Power or oblivion—either would be acceptable.

Goluk seemed unwilling to wait for the council to achieve consensus. He stepped down from the dais and handed the regent's scepter to Klag. His voice filled the Great Hall and shook dust from its rafters: "All hail, Regent Klag!" No one spoke in opposition, so Goluk repeated, "All hail, Regent Klag!"

A few voices answered the chant, followed by a few others. Within moments it was unanimous, and Klag climbed the dais steps and sat himself on the throne.

For the price of one monstrous life, the Empire was now his.

17

Gone to Ground

W hat a bloody mess." O'Brien shook his head. He and Eddington stood on either side of the situation table along the aft bulkhead of the *Defiant*'s bridge. Exhausted and aching, O'Brien was hunched, palms flat atop the reflective black interactive console. Eddington, as usual, maintained his perfect posture, but his eyes were bloodshot and his normally clean-shaven face was rough with stubble.

Rubbing his eyes, Eddington said, "I don't like the thought of leaving people behind any more than you do, Miles, but we lost too many ships back there. And without the station, we just can't support this many people at once."

O'Brien was too tired to be angry anymore. Enervated from days spent in disorganized retreat with ships packed from bow to stern with refugees, and tweaking every emission from the *Defiant*'s warp drive to avoid accidentally ionizing or igniting the gases in the Badlands, all he wanted to do was collapse into a bunk and sleep, preferably forever. He picked up his mug of cold black coffee and took a bitter sip. "So, we have no defensible base. No resources. And less than half the fleet we did a week ago. Am I missing anything?"

"Only the good news," Eddington said.

"There's good news?"

Eddington called up geological scans of Athos IV, above which the damaged remnants of their fleet lingered in orbit and to whose surface the majority of its refugees had been transported. "The abandoned mines are full of fistrium, which plays hell with long-range sensors."

"I know that," O'Brien groused.

"We can move our people underground to keep the Alliance from detecting them if they send a patrol this way."

Scratching an itch under his week-old beard, O'Brien sighed. "That's what passes for good news, now? We have a good chance of not dying if we crawl into a hole and keep our heads down? I'd hoped we'd have higher standards by now."

"We play the cards we're dealt," Eddington said. "The real question is: What are we going to do next? The other captains are getting restless, Miles."

"And I'm not?" He held up his hand, willing himself to stop before unleashing a harangue on Eddington, who he knew didn't deserve it. "Sorry. It's just so bloody vexing. I'm trying to keep their morale up so they can do the same for their crews, but really, what am I supposed to tell them?" He blanked the geological data from the situation table's display and looked at his haggard reflection in the black tabletop. "The station's gone, and we're back on the run."

"If the news out of Cardassia is true, they've got their own problems." Eddington leaned forward and lowered his voice. "This is the time to hit them, Miles. When they're distracted. When they think we're beaten."

"How do you know we're not?"

"Because you're still standing," Eddington said, and he sounded like he meant it. "If your enemy expects you to lie low and hide—"

"Attack," O'Brien said. He nodded, grasping the truth in it. The key to the rebellion's strategy had always been to embrace the unexpected and the utterly unconventional. To take the risks the enemy never would.

He called up a star map of Alliance territory. "If the Cardassians are having as much trouble as these recon reports say they are, the Klingons probably think we'll take advantage of that, and hit the Cardies where it hurts." He planted his index finger on the display. "That's why we'll hit the Klingons here, at Capella. If the Cardassians are already down on one knee, they aren't the ones for us to worry about. It's the Klingons we need to hurt."

"I agree," Eddington said. "But Capella's a hard nut to crack. It's a long way from here, and it's heavily defended. I don't want to sound defeatist, but I don't think we have the forces to go after a target like that—not yet."

Undaunted, O'Brien forced down another sip of coffee. "Let me worry about that. I'm not saying it'll be easy, but I'm willing to bet it can be done."

To his surprise, Keiko's voice answered from behind him, "That sounds like the Miles O'Brien I know."

O'Brien spun, face bright with hope, to see Keiko smiling at him. Throwing decorum to the wind, he grabbed her in a bear hug and spun her in a circle. "Keiko!" He peppered her beautiful face with grateful kisses. "Dear God, I thought I'd lost you back there." Leaning back, he felt an irrational surge of annoyance. "Where the hell'd you come from? Why wasn't your name on the manifests?"

"I was on the *Geronimo*," Keiko said. "Well, behind it, actually. Captain Neelix put a tractor beam on my lifeboat on his way out of the Bajor system."

The news brought a smile to O'Brien's careworn features. "Remind me to buy that man a drink. But that still doesn't—"

"The survivor lists are a mess, Miles," she cut in. "For every two people you have on your roster, there's probably a third unaccounted for down on the planet."

That was both bad news and good news to O'Brien. "I'll have L'Sen make a more complete census, starting tomorrow." He shrugged at Eddington. "At least we'll have crews standing by if we can ever get our hands on more ships."

"There is that," Eddington said, accentuating the positive. "Lord knows we could use more ships if we're going after Capella."

An Alliance news dispatch appeared on the edge of the situation table's display and caught O'Brien's eye. He opened it and was shocked. "Martok's dead. General Klag killed him in ritual combat. Klag's the damned regent now."

Keiko and Eddington looked as dumbstruck at the news as O'Brien felt. In the moment of pregnant silence, an idea took shape in O'Brien's imagination. He stepped back, kissed Keiko on the cheek, and said, "Stay here. I'll be back."

As O'Brien walked in a hurry, heading aft toward the transporter bay, Eddington asked, "Miles, where are you going?"

He paused in the open doorway, smiled, and said, "To see an old friend."

Cables twanged as the antiquated lift descended, shaking as if it suffered from palsy, its metal frame clattering, its every groaning protest echoing from the narrow rocky shaft that surrounded it. O'Brien stood in the center of the lift carriage and realized how much he took for granted the fully enclosed and nearly silent turbolifts that were de rigueur on most modern starships.

Above his head, the single fluorescent rod on the lift's ceiling flickered. When he'd beamed down from *Defiant* a short time earlier, he had found Athos IV's perpetually clouded atmosphere depressing. Bathed now in the lift's sickly chartreuse light, O'Brien felt a new appreciation for those dreary gray skies.

The descent was maddeningly slow, and O'Brien didn't relish having to make an equal or possibly longer return journey when his visit was over, but at least it afforded him some space, time, and privacy to think—a luxury he rarely enjoyed aboard the ship. He reflected on his conversation with Eddington, who had reminded him unnecessarily about the fistrium that made these abandoned mines impervious to sensors and transporters. It wasn't as if that was the sort of detail O'Brien would have forgotten—especially since it was why he had long ago chosen this place for a very special purpose.

A sharp bump and deafening boom marked the lift's arrival at the bottom of the shaft. O'Brien opened the safety gate, which folded aside like an accordion, torturing his ears with a piercing metallic screech that echoed in the tunnel ahead of him. He stepped out and walked at a quick step, grateful to be free of the steel cage. His footfalls were loud and crisp in the cool, dank air. The long, dark passageway was lit only at wide intervals by weakly burning orange bulbs along the ceiling. O'Brien passed from one pool of light to another and noted his shadow by turns stretching ahead of him or contracting to meet him.

It took him a few minutes to reach the end of the tunnel. Arriving at its terminus, he turned and faced the only cell in what he had named Badlands Prison. Seated inside the spacious accommodation, secure behind its duranium bars, was the rebellion's only prisoner of war. O'Brien nodded at him. "Hello, again."

Worf stood and regarded O'Brien with a glum frown. "O'Brien."

"I trust you've been treated well since my last visit."

The former regent of the Klingon Empire avoided O'Brien's gaze and folded his hands behind his back. He looked contemplative. "I have no complaints."

O'Brien nodded. "Glad to hear it."

Despite its name, Badlands Prison was a clean, comfortable, and relatively dignified facility, one that Eddington had insisted be made worthy of such a high-ranking prisoner. The furniture had been tailored to suit Worf's tastes, and great pains had been taken to secure a supply of traditional Klingon foods, to ensure the former regent received an adequately nutritious diet. Unlike the sickly lighting in the lift and corridor, the illumination in Worf's cell was warm and even, and as an added courtesy it had been placed under Worf's control, so that he could manage his own schedule. He had been allowed a traditional Klingon wardrobe, after the garments had been inspected by his captors to ensure they contained no hidden weapons. Reading materials had been made available to him, and his jailers had been handpicked by O'Brien for their calm dispositions and generally nonviolent natures. They had been trained to address Worf with respect, and to make every reasonable effort to accommodate him without compromising security.

To O'Brien's surprise, the relatively benign state of Worf's captivity seemed to have worn the Klingon down far more thoroughly than any torture ever could have. Standing before him, the ex-regent looked calm, even statesmanlike. He affected an air of boredom. "Why are you here?"

"I have news."

Worf smirked. "You wish to surrender? I accept."

"Not bloody likely. Martok's dead."

A disaffected grunt. "Good riddance." O'Brien let the silence hang between them while he waited for Worf to ask the obvious question. "Who killed him?"

"General Klag."

Eyes wide, brow furrowed, Worf bellowed, "KLAG?" He lunged toward the bars and gripped them white-knuckle tight. "That one-armed *taHqeq* is regent?"

O'Brien shrugged. "Sounds like he won fair and square."

Worf pushed himself back from the bars and paced the confines of his cell. "That *yIntagh* isn't fit to shine the boots of a regent, much less hold the throne for Him Who Shall Return!" His face went taut with rage. "How did it come to this? Klag is a coward and an opportunist. He has no business even standing in the Great Hall, much less sitting upon the throne of Kahless."

The tirade drew a chuckle from O'Brien. "And I thought you hated Martok."

"Compared to Klag, Martok was a giant among Klingons—and Martok was a *petaQ*." A deep growl of contempt rumbled in Worf's barrel chest. "Is this why you came, O'Brien? To punish me with this news?"

Crossing his arms, O'Brien said, "Partly."

The deposed regent shot a sidelong look at O'Brien, then turned and walked slowly toward the bars, studying his jailer with suspicion from beneath a ridged brow knit with concentration. "What is it you want from me?"

"I suspect that what I want and what you want are very similar right now."

A derisive snort. "I doubt that."

"I've heard you speak more than once about how much you despise Klag. Had he not been protected from on high, you'd have had him killed years ago."

"So?"

O'Brien saw through Worf's façade of disinterest. The mere suggestion of misfortune for Klag had put the fire back in Worf's eyes, kindled his spirit. "I think you *want* what I *need*—to make Klag look weak, stupid, and vulnerable."

Grasping the bars that separated them, Worf scowled down at O'Brien. "And how do you propose I help you do that?"

"Tell us how to attack Capella."

Worf gasped in disgust and walked away from O'Brien, shaking his head. "You will never learn. This is why your rebellion will fail."

O'Brien wanted to pursue Worf, grab him by the shoulders, and turn him around, but he knew well enough not to get within arm's reach of the regent's cell bars, much less make the fatal mistake of stepping inside with him. Toeing the line on the concrete floor one-point-seven meters from the bars, he called out to Worf. "What haven't I learned, Regent?"

His plaint turned Worf's head. "If you want to hurt Klag, you must deal him a defeat from which he can never recover."

Aghast at the implausibility of Worf's implication, O'Brien backed up half a step and stared at him, jaw agape. "You're not really suggesting what I *think* you're suggesting, are you?"

"You must blast the Great Hall out from under him."

Now it was O'Brien who had to shake his head in disbelief. "That's insane. I don't have anywhere near enough ships for a mission like that."

"Then get more ships."

He made it sound so simple, which was probably why O'Brien felt such a powerful urge to shoot him at that moment. "Let's say I get more ships. What then? What would we need to know if we wanted to glass the Great Hall?"

Worf considered the question, then he stepped away to the table where he ate his meals, picked up its lone metal chair, carried it to the bars, and set it down facing O'Brien. He sat down and crossed his arms.

O'Brien took Worf's meaning very clearly: This was going to take a while.

He stepped back from the line and pulled forward a chair that was usually occupied by one of Worf's around-the-clock guards, whom O'Brien had dismissed in the interests of privacy. He sat down and mimicked Worf's pose.

The Klingon smirked. "Let me tell you about Klag."

18

The Damnation of Memory

Neelix stood at the threshold of the *Geronimo*'s brig and watched Kes through the invisible force field. She looked troubled even in her sleep.

Once, I would've done anything to comfort her, he brooded. *Now all I can think about is wanting her off my ship.* He knew he was lying to himself. If he had really wanted to send her away, he could have beamed her and Tuvok down to Athos IV when the other rescued survivors of Terok Nor were dispatched to the surface. Instead, at Tuvok's request, he had agreed to let Kes remain aboard the *Geronimo* as his prisoner. It was a bitterly ironic state of affairs, in Neelix's opinion. When he had first met her she had been a prisoner of the Kazon-Ogla, and he had risked their wrath when he'd gone to Ocampa to set her free. Now he was her captor, the one from whom she hoped to escape.

Kes stirred and cracked open one eye. When she saw Neelix lurking just outside the cramped nook that served the tiny ship as its brig, she awakened instantly and sat up. "Neelix! How long have you been there?"

"A while." It had been more like an hour.

She stood and took a half step toward him, stopping well shy of the painful but unseen barrier between them. "Are you still angry at me?"

He sneered. "Can't you read my mind?"

"No, I can't. Tuvok and his people did something to me. A neural damper, he called it. It's blocking my abilities."

Neelix looked at his nervously shuffling feet. "Maybe that's for the best."

"For the best? Neelix, they put something in my brain! They violated me!"

"Like you violated me?" He shot an accusing stare that made her back away. "Kes, you made a slave out of me! You forced your way into my mind and took away my free will! Do you have any idea what that feels like? Do you?"

She blushed as she averted her eyes, clearly ashamed. "No."

"It was the worst thing ever done to me, Kes. And I've had a lot of bad things happen to me. But the worst part of it, what made it really hurt, is that it was *you* who did it to me." Tears welled in his eyes, and the bitter rage in his heart left him fighting for breath and control. "I loved you, Kes. I *trusted* you."

She looked up, her face contorted in anguish. "Neelix, I'm sorry. Please believe me. I never wanted to hurt you. I just wanted to save you, but you wouldn't leave with me, even though the rebellion's clearly doomed, and I—"

"We're not *doomed*," he snapped.

She blinked and recoiled in surprise. "Are you serious? From what I've heard, the rebellion just got slaughtered. You lost Terok Nor and half your fleet."

"Losing one battle doesn't mean we've lost the war," Neelix protested.

Kes folded her arms and struck a haughty pose.

"Some battles mean more than others, Neelix. This one was huge. Even you have to be able to see that."

"Even me? What is that supposed to mean? Are you implying I'm stupid?"

She rolled her eyes. "No, just deluded. You're a romantic. I could see it in your mind—you never know when to walk away. You've never been able to tell when you've already lost."

"Is that so?"

Holding up her hands in a pantomime of surrender, she closed her eyes and took a deep breath. When she put her hands down and continued, she struck a far more conciliatory note. "I apologize. I spoke rashly, and for that, I'm sorry. I don't want to fight, Neelix. I want to earn your forgiveness."

"So that I'll let you out of the brig?"

Her eyes became windows to sorrow. "So that we can be together."

"I don't know if I'm ready for that. Or if I ever will be."

She bowed her head. "I understand. I know that what I did was horrible. But all that I've done since I left Tuvok's people, I did so I could come home to you. That's all I ever wanted—to live far away from everyone else, away from all the wars and fighting and suffering and death, and spend my life with you."

Hearing her invoke the dream they had spoken of so many times made Neelix long for the past, for the days years earlier when he had believed such a fate might be possible, that he could leave behind his war-torn memories and begin again with Kes, just the two of them and a clean slate.

"I'm not sure what you expect me to do, Kes."

"You could talk to Tuvok for me," she said. "Convince him I don't need to be caged like an animal."

That sounded like a tall order to Neelix. When he recalled what it felt like to be manipulated like a puppet, he had to admit that he saw the logic in Tuvok's request that Kes remain not only in custody but under maximum control. Deflecting his concerns onto the Vulcan, he said, "I'm not sure Mister Tuvok places much stock in my opinion."

"Well, it's not as if you need his permission to let me out of the brig. After all, you *are* the captain of this ship. You can let me out anytime you want."

Neelix bristled at the transparency of her suggestion. "I see what you're doing! Playing to my ego, trying to make me assert myself by defying Tuvok's wishes. Maybe that kind of clumsy suggestion works when you have your fancy psycho-powers, but without them, it comes off as sad and obvious." He saw the anger and disappointment on her face, and it filled his heart with scorn. "You're just trying to use me again. I wonder if maybe that's the only thing you know how to do anymore. Tuvok's right—you belong in there."

He walked away, eager to put as much distance as he could between him and Kes. As he opened a safety hatch that led to the forward sections of the ship, Kes cried out, "Neelix! Come back! Please, I'm sorry! Don't go!"

A jab of his thumb against a control panel secured the hatch behind him.

I've heard enough lies for one day, he decided.

Keiko awoke when she heard the door of O'Brien's quarters hiss open. She sat up as O'Brien came in. He paused as he saw her squinting at him. "Sorry," he said. "Didn't know you were sleeping."

"It's all right." She knuckled the slumber from her eyes. "I wanted to be awake when you got back, but I drifted off."

He took off his jacket and dropped it on the deck. "I'm not surprised. It's been a hard couple of days." He sat down beside Keiko and stretched his arm across her shoulders. "I'm just glad you're all right. I don't know what I'd do without you." His scraggly whiskers tickled her as he kissed her neck.

She kissed his forehead and smiled. "That makes two of us." They sat together for a moment, and Keiko let herself enjoy the comfort of feeling her breathing rise and ebb in sync with O'Brien's. He was more than a lover to her, more than a wartime romance: He had become a part of her, one she couldn't imagine living without. They belonged to each other.

Succumbing to curiosity, she asked, "Was Worf helpful?"

O'Brien sighed. "Yes and no. He has no end of hatred for Klag, and he gave us some good intel that we can use to penetrate the Klingons' defense perimeter."

"So, if that's the good news . . ."

"The bad news is we don't have the strength to act on it, and I think Worf knows that. He's toying with me—giving me good advice he knows I can't use." O'Brien looked dejected and distracted, as if his thoughts were light-years away and dwelling on something disheartening. "I don't know if the rebellion's ever going to recover, Keiko. Not after a loss like this. The station, all those ships, all those people. It took us so much time to rebuild after Zek and Bashir's blunder at Empok Nor. Now it's all gone."

She pressed her palm softly to his cheek. "No, it's not. Not all of it. There are still plenty of people ready to follow you, Miles. People who believe in you." Leaning forward, she put her forehead against his. "I still believe in you."

"Belief's not going to win this war," he said, slipping from her grasp and standing up to pace inside the cramped quarters. "If we'd taken out Olmerak, we might've had a chance. But now . . . now, I just don't know."

There was so much Keiko wanted to tell him, but Saavik had forbidden her to reveal Memory Omega's existence to anyone. She knew it would raise his spirits if he knew that Memory Omega had plunged Cardassia into chaos, or that its agents were even then gearing up for a major coordinated action, but all of that was considered classified. There was, however, one bit of good news she could share with him. "Miles . . . what if I told you we didn't have to be alone in this fight?"

A wary glance from across the room. "What do you mean?"

"I still have access to confidential channels of information," she said, crafting her explanation with care. "From time to time, I get messages from old friends, former allies. One of them contacted me today—with a message for you."

"For me?" He looked alarmed. "What kind of message?"

Striving to sound upbeat yet diplomatic, Keiko said, "An invitation."

He ceased his back-and-forth ambulation. "To . . . ?"

"A meeting. To discuss the possibility of joining forces."

That didn't seem to sit well with him. "With whom?"

Keiko stood to meet him. "Someone who can help us."

He was becoming annoyed. "I need a name, Keiko."

"Calhoun."

Confusion creased O'Brien's brow. "The Xenexian? I thought he was just a folktale."

"No, Miles, he's very real. And he leads a huge rebel faction—practically an armada. You say we need ships? Well, he has them."

O'Brien dismissed the idea with a wave of his hands. "I don't think so. When something sounds too good to be true, that's because it usually is." Holding out one arm to stave off Keiko's reply, he added, "Even if this is for real, what if it turns into another Zek fiasco? If this Calhoun has as many ships as you say, then what does he need me for? What's to stop him from swooping in here and taking over, like Zek did?"

"I don't know," Keiko admitted. "Maybe nothing. But aren't you the one who said we can't let our egos get in the way of doing what's right? That the rebellion's never been about us, and can't be?"

She saw the muscles in his jaw tense as he bit down on whatever angry response had first occurred to him. Apparently stung by having his own words thrown back at him, he stewed for a moment before he replied. "I did say that."

"Then we should at least consider meeting with him."

O'Brien narrowed his eyes and frowned. "I still don't like it. The timing's too damn convenient. Just when we need reinforcements, he calls for a parley? What are the odds of that, Keiko? If you ask me, it sounds like a trap."

"I'm almost certain it isn't."

An accusatory glare. "*Almost?* So, you're not absolutely certain it's safe?"

Growing tired of his obstinate resistance, she dipped her chin and glowered at him. "There are no guarantees in life, Miles. Every decision carries a measure of risk. Some are worth it, some are not. I think this one is."

He half-turned away from her and thought it over for a few seconds. Then he cast a guarded look her way. "This old friend who contacted you. Who was it?"

"Her name is Selar. She's a Vulcan."

O'Brien nodded, his manner thoughtful. "Do you have a secure means of getting our answer to her?"

"Yes, I do. What should I tell her?"

He took a deep breath. "I'll meet with Calhoun, but I won't lead what's left of our fleet into a trap. The *Defiant* will go alone, and I'd appreciate it if he'd do the same—just one ship and whoever has the authority to speak. I'd rather not draw the Alliance's attention by putting everybody in one place at the same time."

"That makes sense," Keiko said.

He cracked a rueful smile. "Glad you think so. Let's just hope this meeting doesn't turn out to be the last, worst mistake of our lives."

19

Ambition's Debt

Behold, the future of the Empire!" Klag stood in the center of the High Council chamber, atop the trefoil emblem that adorned the black marble floor. Projected above his head was a three-dimensional holographic star map of explored space.

From the ring of councillors that surrounded him, a youthful voice said, "What are we supposed to be looking at?"

Klag sought out the speaker in the throng and recognized him at once. "Isn't it obvious, Hegron? What do you see when you look at this map?"

The black-haired councillor snarled and pointed at the hologram. "You call that a map? Where are the borders?"

"Precisely," Klag said, turning slowly to gauge the other councillors' reactions. "This is the future, my brothers. Local space without borders—because it will *all* belong to the Klingon Empire."

A few of the older councillors guffawed. A battle-scarred veteran named K'mpar raised his voice above the mocking laughter. "Not this old nonsense! What do you take us for, Klag—schoolchildren? Klingon hegemony is a fool's errand. A romantic fantasy at best, a dangerous delusion at worst."

"I am not saying it will be achieved in our lifetimes," Klag said. "But we will lay the foundation for this future with the actions we take here now." Making a slow circle of the room, he continued. "The tactical and political realities facing us are changing rapidly, more so than ever before. If we are to thrive as an empire, and survive as a people, we must expand. We must *conquer*."

Korvog, who hailed from one of the oldest of the Great Houses, looked down his long, narrow nose at Klag. His cultured accent dripped with disdain. "What an *original* concept, Regent. Who do you propose we conquer first?"

Using a small controller tucked inside his fist, Klag highlighted in bright red a portion of the holographic map. "Cardassia."

Murmurs of surprise and concern circuited the room. Klag savored the atmosphere of muted shock that followed, and he seized the moment to continue. "For too long, the Alliance has been a house divided against itself. We've clashed with the Cardassians, negotiated with them, bargained with them. By degrees they have eroded our authority, our autonomy, our *power*.

"Now their union is in chaos. Their ships fire upon one another. Their military scientists unleash atrocities on their own civilians. And that *petaQ* Damar, having publicly assassinated his leader in one of the boldest coups I've ever seen, cowers from the public, either unwilling or unable to wield the power he's stolen! The Cardassian Union is descending into anarchy.

"For the good of the Alliance, order *must* be restored. If the Cardassians themselves cannot or will not do so, we will."

K'mpar shouted back, "That's an expensive proposition, Klag."

"Perhaps. But it's nowhere near as costly as doing nothing. If we fail to fill the power vacuum in Cardassian space, the Taurus Pact powers will not hesitate to claim the Cardassians' possessions for their own." He highlighted two more sections of the hologram, in green and blue. "In case you've all forgotten basic astrocartography, the Breen Confederacy and the Tholian Assembly both share borders with the Cardassian Union's sovereign territory. They are better positioned to invade Cardassia than we are—which is why we can't risk hesitating."

Hegron looked half-awake. "So the Cardassians fall to them instead of us. What of it?"

To Klag's astonishment, Korvog spoke up to rebut Hegron. "If the Taurus Pact seizes Cardassia, it will have enough power to begin annexing what are presently shared possessions of the Alliance. Many of the planets we rely on for dilithium lie within the bounds of the former Terran Empire. I can think of at least six the Breen and Tholians would be poised to take from us if they had all of Cardassia's resources to feed their war machine."

"Well said, Councillor," Klag said. "We'll need Cardassia's strength if we're to stand alone against the Taurus Pact."

Another young councillor, Krozek, interjected, "What about Bajor?"

Klag met the impertinent question with a venomous stare. "What of it?"

"Its secession cannot be tolerated," Krozek insisted. "We must make an example of it, before other worlds follow its treacherous path."

"Bajor will pay for its insolence, I assure you," Klag said. "But for the moment, it's not a matter of concern. Governing is about priorities, Krozek, and Bajor isn't one. Stabilizing Cardassia is. And so is defeating the Taurus Pact."

K'mpar shot back, "What about the Terran Rebellion? Or the pirate Calhoun and his Romulan armada?"

"The Terrans are routed," Klag crowed. "They cower in the Badlands, licking their wounds. I expect them to disband any day now. As for Calhoun and his rabble—we'll hunt them down *after* we've dealt with the most serious threats to our security: the unrest in Cardassia, and aggression by the Taurus Pact."

His declaration provoked a tsunami of enraged protests. The wave of sound was so dense, so impenetrable, that he couldn't discern one criticism from another. He let the commotion go on for close to a minute, but then his patience waned. He pocketed the controller for the holographic projection and beckoned Goluk to bring him his ceremonial staff of office. It was an ancient thigh bone from some great beast of prey, its bottom tip jacketed in steel and its bulky length reinforced at regular intervals with bands of iron. Klag took it in hand and cracked its tip against the marble floor repeatedly, until the staff's sharp reports shocked the squabbling councillors into silence. "I will hear one of you, but not all of you." He pointed at Hegron. "Speak."

"We can't afford to wait before pursuing Calhoun," Hegron said. "He and his allies are a clear and present danger to the Empire, and they must be exterminated immediately and with prejudice."

Grumbled assents filtered down from all the other councillors, making it clear that Klag was outnumbered.

He could overrule the High Council and force his will into action, but the political cost of alienating every member of the council at once was too high for him to risk it.

"Support my campaign to secure Cardassia, and I vow we will destroy Calhoun and his fleet before we launch our conquest of the Taurus Pact."

His pledge sparked several sotto voce side discussions as the councillors debated whether these were terms they could accept personally as well as justify politically outside the Great Hall. Within moments, Klag had his answer.

Korvog stepped down from the circle to join Klag on the main floor. "We are at agreement, My Regent." He offered his left arm, and Klag took it in a clasp that bonded both men to their words. Unfortunately, Klag suspected that this compromise would ultimately prove to be a mistake.

Once again, these fools have made a decision based on passion rather than reason, he lamented. It was the same error that he believed had plagued the Empire for generations: The members of its elite leadership caste had a long history of leading with their hearts rather than their heads. *And now they shall drag me down with them. May Kahless forgive us all.*

20

The New Wind of Change

The transporter beam released its hold on Picard as he and Troi materialized inside the *Solomon*. Though it was a slightly smaller vessel than Picard's ship, its interior felt more spacious because its technology was so miniaturized and compact. The consoles were seamlessly wedded to the bulkheads, following their angles and curves, and rather than fixing certain functions to specific locations, all the interfaces were dynamic, reconfiguring on the fly as needed. In contrast to the many shades of gray that defined the *Calypso*'s compartments, the inside of the *Solomon* was a study in pristine black and white.

Standing beside a bulkhead-sized black panel were K'Ehleyr and Barclay. He was operating the controls projected on the panel while she greeted Picard and Troi. "Welcome aboard."

"A most impressive vessel," Picard said. "Her exterior is remarkable, but it doesn't prepare one for this. Are all of Memory Omega's ships like this?"

The question prompted a humble shrug from K'Ehleyr. "This is one of our older ships, actually. I'm told the newest ones are far more advanced." She looked at Barclay, who shook his head no. "We'll just be a moment," she added.

"I don't mean to be contrary," Troi said, "but couldn't you have just told us the coordinates and let us beam down from the *Calypso*?"

Barclay answered over his shoulder as he worked. "I'm afraid not, Miss Troi. We have strict orders not to release those coordinates to anyone. Ever."

"Basically," K'Ehleyr added with a humorous gleam, "we trust you, but not with the lives of everyone we know. To be honest, it's amazing we were allowed to bring you here at all."

Picard nodded. "I understand completely. We know the asteroid below is uninhabitable, and *Calypso*'s sensors detected no energy emissions, so the base must be deep underground. Something buried that deeply would be highly defensible as long as a foe doesn't know its precise position."

"Exactly," Barclay said. "Most starships don't carry enough firepower to blast open something this big. Even if an Alliance ship got this far, we'd either blow it to bits or be long gone before it ever got near us."

Troi had the wide-eyed expression of someone struggling to think of something nice—or at least not rude—to say. "That's quite something, Reg," was apparently the best she could come up with at that moment.

Outside the *Solomon*'s forward cockpit, Picard saw the *Calypso* hanging in orbit above the airless gray planetoid that dominated the view. He imagined what would happen if a random patrol noticed it floating derelict beside the *Solomon*.

"What will happen to my ship?"

K'Ehleyr took a reassuring tone. "Once we're inside the base, the control team will use a tractor beam to tow our ships inside a concealed landing bay on the surface. They'll be out of sight and hidden from sensors."

Barclay turned from the console. "All set."

"Here we go," K'Ehleyr said. "Huddle up."

The four of them moved together in the middle of the *Solomon*'s main compartment. A few seconds later, another transporter beam seized Picard and the others in its golden embrace, and a musical rush of white noise ushered him into a brilliant white haze . . .

. . . that faded to reveal a lush jungle oasis. He looked up and saw patches of bright blue sky through a shredded blanket of white fog. Shafts of intense golden light speared down through the low-lying cloud cover, dotting the rain forest canopy far below with shifting patterns of light and shadow. Picard realized he and the others were standing on a cliff beside a majestic waterfall's rushing plume. The fresh scent of green plants and clean water vapor filled his nose, and he breathed deeply and smiled. Beside him, Troi stared at the vista, amazed.

"It's incredible!" Troi exclaimed. "Where are we?"

"Inside the asteroid," K'Ehleyr said.

Troi gazed upward at the azure canopy of sky. "This is *inside*?"

She was answered by the voice of an older woman. "Yes, approximately two hundred kilometers underground." Everyone on the cliff turned to see the middle-aged Vulcan woman who walked out of a shadowy corridor cut into the rock wall behind the cliff. "Most of what you see is real—the rain forest, the waterfall, even the sunlight, such as it is. Our holographic engineers added the illusion of sky to stave off feelings of claustrophobia among some of our more neurotic residents."

"Remarkable," said Picard, who found it hard to

believe. He had seen holographic illusions before, but never anything so perfectly convincing.

K'Ehleyr stepped forward to make introductions. "Luc Picard, this is Saavik, the director of Memory Omega."

He bowed his head to the Vulcan. "Director."

She returned the gesture. "Welcome, Mister Picard."

Barclay joined the tight circle. "Director, this is Deanna Troi."

Troi shook Saavik's hand. "Director."

Saavik scrutinized Troi with an unnerving stare, as if she were peering straight through her, plumbing her depths. "Your empathic skills are even more finely honed than we were led to think," she said at last. "Most impressive for only a half-Betazoid." The two continued to clasp hands for several seconds while sustaining unblinking eye contact. Picard wondered what manner of confrontation he was witnessing. Finally, Saavik released her hold on Troi's hand and repeated, "Most impressive." Turning to Picard, she added, "Welcome to Memory Omega."

"Thank you," Picard said. "Now can you tell me why you asked me here?"

"In time." She stepped away toward a broad trail that led down the side of the cliff in a switchback pattern. "Walk with me." Picard followed her, with Troi close at his shoulder and K'Ehleyr and Barclay following at what seemed like a respectful remove. Saavik continued as Picard caught up with her and fell into step at her side. "How much have K'Ehleyr and Reginald shared with you about who we are and what our purpose is?"

"Only the broad strokes," Picard said, taking care to watch his step along the edge of the trail. His every step sent loose stones tumbling down the dusty path. "She told us Emperor Spock created your group to preserve the knowledge of the lost Terran Empire. She also said you have many bases and amazing technology."

Saavik steepled her fingers at her waist. "That is only part of why we exist."

Picard stifled a derisive chuckle. "Ah, yes. She also said you were trying to 'steer the galaxy toward a new age of freedom.'"

"Not *trying*, Mister Picard. It is happening as we speak."

"I'll believe it when I see it. What has any of this to do with me?"

They navigated the switchback turn with careful steps. A few more pebbles dislodged by Picard's feet tumbled over the edge and vanished into the mist.

"Memory Omega needs the Terran Rebellion," Saavik said. "Our strategy is predicated on their eventual victory over the Alliance."

This time Picard could not help himself. He let slip a short, mocking laugh. "Then your strategy is in serious jeopardy—because I doubt the rebellion will last more than a few months now that it's lost Terok Nor."

"True, they are in great peril. You can help change that."

He warded off her suggestion by briefly crossing his wrists into an X. "Not me. I left the rebellion years ago. Their misfortunes are not my concern."

"I see," Saavik said.

Over his shoulder, Picard caught a glimpse of Troi's disapproving frown. He averted his eyes and kept them on the trail ahead.

Saavik trained a sidelong stare upon him. "Do you

understand the real reason Memory Omega was created? Or why it wants to aid the rebellion?"

"I'm not sure I want to know," Picard said, fearing that he might once again be pulled into the service of something he would grow to hate.

The Vulcan woman's gaze was steady and profoundly unnerving to Picard. "You fear that we aspire to resurrect the Terran Empire," she said.

"I am concerned about that possibility," he admitted. "But as a scholar of history, I know that Spock himself abolished the empire and replaced it with a constitutionally ordered republic. It seems unlikely he would dismantle an empire with one hand while hoping to rebuild it with another."

"A most astute conclusion," Saavik said.

Unable to suppress his natural curiosity, Picard asked, "What is it, then? What is Memory Omega's goal? To rebuild Spock's lost republic?"

"Not at all." Saavik led him around the next switchback and started a descent into a thickening fog. "What is gone is gone. Spock charged us to remember the past, not repeat it. He directed us to lay the foundation not for a second republic but for something far better: for a future in which *all* sentient beings can live freely, not just some."

It was one of the most outlandish, absurdly idealistic fantasies Picard had ever heard. "I'm sure this utopia you've conceived looks lovely on the drawing board, but—"

"I assure you, Mister Picard, we are working to make it a reality."

"Is that so? Then what, pray tell, are you waiting for?"

Saavik shrugged. "The right time. It is not enough

to know merely *what* must be done; one needs also to understand *when* it must be done. Spock's plan was carefully timed to unfold over a span of more than a century. In the long term—"

"Long term?" Picard snapped. He stopped and turned to confront Saavik face-to-face. "Do you listen to yourself? You speak of long-term strategies and grand plans to change the galaxy, but you have no sense of the present! For all your talk of supporting the rebellion, you seem to have done precious little to help it. Those people are dying *now*. They need your help *now*. While you hide in this magnificent Shangri-La, real people are paying for their freedom with blood and tears. Don't tell me what you plan to do in the future—tell me what you're ready to do right now. Because *this* is your chance to act, and you're missing it! To hell with Spock and his century-old timetable! Now is the time for action, not words."

K'Ehleyr emerged from the mist behind Picard. "I thought you didn't care about the rebellion. Because it sure sounds like you do."

He looked back at her to find himself the object of three different stares. K'Ehleyr was amused; Barclay looked hopeful; Troi wore a mask of desperation. Picard looked back at Saavik. "I'll ask for the last time: Why am I here?"

Saavik was composed, calm, and dignified. She spoke without emotion or hauteur, but with simple, direct honesty. "We have watched you for a long time, Mister Picard. I believe that because of your history and your inherent good nature, you are the sort of person who can help us reach out to the Terran Rebellion, by carrying our offer of support and leadership to them. We need someone from outside our sheltered society, someone with a reputation beyond reproach who is known to the rebels, to act as our ambassador. I wish you to be that ambassador.

"And you are correct in your assertions about Spock's timetable. His projected timeline of events was off because he did not account for further interference in our affairs by persons from the alternate universe. Thanks to events that have transpired on and around Bajor, the future has taken shape far sooner than Spock expected. Consequently, we—and you—must act now, before this pivotal moment in history slips away from us."

Shocked and intrigued, Picard asked, "What pivotal moment?"

Saavik placed her hand upon Picard's shoulder.

"The one at which a rebellion becomes a revolution."

21

Under the Rose

The image on *Defiant*'s main viewer danced and crackled as sapphire lightning bolts ripped through the bruised-black tempests of the Arachnid Nebula.

O'Brien sat in the command chair, stroking his stubbled chin and upper lip while waiting for a call from the darkness. Eddington stood silently close by, leaning against the bulkhead on O'Brien's left, while Keiko lurked on his right, next to his chair. Like him, she stared anxiously at the screen.

She quipped sotto voce, "You always take me to the nicest places."

"You're the one who told me to take this bloody meeting," O'Brien said, teasing her with a gruff look before softening it with a half smile. "Let's just hope he actually shows up. Otherwise we spent a week coming out here for nothing."

The bridge was quieter than usual because the ship was "running silent," with most of its systems either offline or at minimum levels. Instead of the normal undercurrent of energy moving through the plasma relays and the light chirping of feedback tones, O'Brien heard the soft taps of fingers on muted consoles and the occasional shuffling of a boot on the carpeted deck. He had always thought of the *Defiant* as cramped, but this deathly quiet only made it more oppressive.

Leeta looked up from the sensor console. "Captain, I've detected a single tachyon ping from another ship inside the nebula." She checked her data. "Transmission time and frequency are correct."

O'Brien shot a nervous look at Eddington, who mirrored it with his own. The terms arranged by Keiko with her contact inside Calhoun's armada specified a precise time at which Calhoun's ship would generate a single tachyon pulse, as well as a frequency to indicate that all was well and another in case there was danger. Apparently, Calhoun's ship had sent the all-clear signal.

Now it was the *Defiant*'s turn.

"Leeta," O'Brien said, "transmit the response ping. Signal all-clear."

"Yes, sir." She entered the command into her console.

Tigan looked over from the tactical console. "Should I arm weapons?"

"No. This is supposed to be a friendly meeting." Old habits died hard for O'Brien, and a glance at Eddington's guarded expression convinced him that he was not alone in thinking caution might be warranted. He looked back at Tigan and added, "But keep your eyes open—just in case."

Leeta declared, "The other ship has entered sensor range."

"Give me a visual," O'Brien said. Moments later, the image on the main viewer magnified, and he saw a beautiful, streamlined vessel slice its way out of the murky violence of the nebula. It was a much bigger ship than the *Defiant*.

Bloody hell, he thought, *that's one serious piece of machinery.*

An alert chirped at the forward station. Bowers silenced it and swiveled his chair to face O'Brien. "Sir, they're hailing us."

O'Brien stood and stepped forward, flanked by Eddington and Keiko. He took a moment to straighten his shirt and jacket and palm the sweat from his forehead. "All right. On-screen."

The image switched to a crystal-clear transmission from the other ship. Looking back at O'Brien and his comrades was a man who looked human except for his vibrantly purple eyes. His dark hair was long, ragged, and worn loose. A fearsome scar marred the left side of his face, and his complexion was tan and storm-leathered. Deep lines creased his forehead. He looked to O'Brien as if he had been chiseled into existence by an angry god rather than born of a woman.

That has to be Calhoun, O'Brien surmised.

Flanking the black-clad living legend was an elderly Romulan man who O'Brien recognized from news vids as Hiren, the former praetor of the fallen Romulan Star Empire, and a strikingly beautiful and youthful Vulcan woman.

Calhoun spoke first. *"General O'Brien?"*

"That's right. You must be Captain Calhoun." He gestured to his left and right. "This is General Eddington and Colonel Ishikawa."

Calhoun nodded, then glanced at his people. *"I suspect you recognize Praetor Hiren of the Romulan Star Empire, and this is my second-in-command, Soleta."* Hiren and Soleta nodded their salutations.

"All right," O'Brien said. "You called this meeting. What do you want?"

"What do you think we want? We're here to combine our forces."

O'Brien's inner pessimist reminded him, *If it sounds too good to be true . . .* He made no effort to mask his suspicion. "For what purpose?"

Soleta and Calhoun traded perplexed looks, then Calhoun looked at O'Brien as if he were answering a trick question. *"To defeat the Alliance."*

Crossing his arms, O'Brien said, "I'm not sure that's possible—not even with the fleet I hear you've assembled."

"Maybe it is, maybe it's not," Calhoun said. *"If it is, we'd be fools not to try. And if it isn't, we'll just fight on the run till we go down in flames."*

O'Brien frowned. "I can do that now. At least on my own, I'm calling the shots. So why should I team up with you?"

Calhoun shrugged. *"So we can do more damage before we die?"*

Eddington cracked an embarrassed smile. He leaned over and confided to O'Brien, "I like the way he thinks."

Keiko tugged on O'Brien's sleeve and whispered with urgency behind her raised hand. "We should meet with him, Miles. Hear what he has to say."

It cut against O'Brien's instincts, but he felt the tide turn against him.

"All right," he said to Calhoun, "let's talk."

"We've prepared a banquet for you," Calhoun said. *"Let us know when you're ready to beam over. Excalibur out."* The transmission ended, leaving O'Brien with a view of Calhoun's monstrous ship nose to nose with *Defiant.*

Brow furrowed with contempt, O'Brien mumbled, "A *banquet*? What does he think this is? A cotillion?"

"Don't look a gift horse in the mouth, Miles," Keiko chided. "Even if we end up rejecting his proposal, at least we'll get a free lunch."

"Don't be fooled," O'Brien said. "There's no such thing."

Eddington spoke softly but with a steely resolve. "Whatever lunch ends up costing, Miles, think about paying it. Look at Calhoun's ship. Now remember that he has a whole fleet of Romulan military starships. You've been saying we need more strength to take back the momentum against the Alliance." He shot a wary glance at the *Excalibur*. "Well, there it is."

O'Brien knew better than to argue with Eddington after he'd made up his mind. There was no other course now but to go forward. "Fine. I'll meet you both at the transporter bay in ten minutes." He started aft.

Keiko asked, "Where are you going?"

"To change." He gestured at his clothes as he left. "You don't think I'm going to a fancy dinner dressed like this, do you?"

Keiko hurried from the turbolift into the port-side corridor on Deck 3 of the *Defiant,* keenly aware of each passing moment, knowing that if she was late meeting O'Brien and Eddington at the transporter bay on Deck 1, it would arouse suspicion and invite questions she would prefer to avoid. She also hoped no members of the crew crossed her path while she made this unscheduled detour.

The door to the starboard cargo bay was locked. She opened it with her access code and slipped inside, making sure to seal the portal behind her. The lights were dimmed inside the cargo bay, making the tight spaces between the stacked containers feel like a rat's labyrinth. Navigating it easily by memory, she found her way to a remote nook in the mountain of metal boxes.

Tuvok was there, waiting for her. "Thank you for coming."

"I don't have a lot of time," Keiko said. "What's this about?"

"There is a disturbingly powerful psionic presence aboard the *Excalibur*," Tuvok said. "I think it might be cause for concern."

His news sent Keiko's imagination spinning in wild directions. "What sort of presence? Are we talking about another Vulcan, or maybe a Betazoid?"

The brown-skinned Vulcan shook his head. "No. I have never before encountered anything like it. Not even Kes made such a profound impression."

Struggling to recall the details of years-old briefings from Memory Omega, she asked rhetorically, "Kes? The alien you liberated from Intendant B'Elanna on Stratos?" Tuvok nodded. "I thought she was the most powerful telepath known."

"Until now, she was." There was a dark note of warning in his voice. "Whatever it is that travels with Calhoun and his crew, I suspect its power far exceeds that of Kes—by at least an order of magnitude. Perhaps more."

Keiko pushed her fingers through her hair as she pondered the ramifications of what Tuvok was saying. "Aren't Vulcans usually touch telepaths?"

"Yes, though in some cases our gifts can be used at short range, and there have been documented instances in which—"

"Yes, yes," she said, cutting him off with a raised

palm. "So, if you're able to sense this entity from a distance, is it able to sense you?"

"Almost certainly," Tuvok said. "It is possible there are few, if any, thoughts among our crew that it is not privy to, if it wishes to be."

Panic clouded Keiko's judgment. "This is not good. Not good at all." She started to pace in the tight lane between container stacks. "So, not only is it possible that Calhoun already knows we have telepaths aboard, it's likely."

Tuvok nodded. "Correct. It would, therefore, be wise not to prevaricate on this matter. If questioned directly, we should not attempt to hide the truth. Doing so might be perceived by Captain Calhoun as a sign of bad faith on our part."

"Well, that's going to be a problem." She struggled to keep from shouting. "Miles and Michael don't know about the Vulcans' abilities. If anyone asks them about it, they'll probably deny it. And if Calhoun or his people ask me, I'd have to confirm it—and Miles will know I've been hiding things from him."

"Logically, it stands to reason that General O'Brien will learn of your lies of omission eventually." He paused as Keiko shot a scathing glare at him. He arched one eyebrow and soldiered on. "Regardless, it would be most awkward if the truth were exposed under these circumstances."

Keiko sighed and rolled her eyes. "*Awkward*. That's an understatement."

"Might I suggest we obviate the crisis by telling O'Brien and Eddington about Memory Omega, and our mission, before the meeting with Calhoun?"

A shake of her head. "We're under strict orders from

Saavik not to reveal anything to the rebellion until she says otherwise." She pressed her palm to her forehead; either her hand was cold or her forehead was hot. She chalked it up to a flush of frustration. "But I honestly don't think she or anybody else knew we might end up in a mess like this."

"If this meeting goes badly, it could doom the rebellion," Tuvok said. "The only hope either side has of long-term survival, let alone victory, is to unite with the other. But there is too much innate distrust in their natures, too long a history of betrayals and deceptions, for them to compromise easily."

"The bigger problem is that power-sharing doesn't work in a military hierarchy. Consensus is all well and good for a civil government, but it's a formula for disaster on a battlefield." She made herself stop. "But I'm getting ahead of myself. That's a longer-term issue. What we need to focus on right now is making sure this parley doesn't break down before it has a chance to get started." A thought occurred to her. "If I let you mind-meld with me, can you erect a short-term telepathic shield for my thoughts?"

Tuvok nodded. "I believe so."

"Good." She closed her eyes. "I have to be on Deck One in two minutes. Let's do this." Discipline alone enabled her not to flinch as Tuvok's warm fingertips pressed with gentle precision upon either side of her face.

"My mind to your mind," he intoned. "My thoughts to your thoughts. Our thoughts are merging. Our minds are becoming one. We . . . are one."

Keiko opened her thoughts to his—and hoped his telepathic gifts would be enough to hide her secrets from whatever entity he had sensed aboard the *Excalibur*. She felt like a spectator to her own psyche as Tuvok erected defenses from her childhood memories and coached her in how to create walls of psychic white noise. It seemed to take hours, but she knew that one's perception of time became malleable inside the mindscape of a Vulcan meld.

When he at last declared her ready and ended their telepathic union, she checked the chrono and saw that only one minute had elapsed. "Nicely done," she said. She reached into her pocket and took out her quantum transceiver, which was disguised as an ordinary utility tool. "Know what this is?"

"Of course."

"After I beam to the *Excalibur,* use this to contact Selar. She's our person inside Calhoun's group. You need to make her understand how important this meeting is—and then you need to get her to contact Saavik with you, so that the two of you can make a joint appeal for help."

He held up the tiny device in his hand and studied it with cold eyes. "What, precisely, do you wish me to ask of Director Saavik?"

"Whatever it's going to take for us to reveal ourselves to both sides of the rebellion and get them to work together. I've been through too much to watch all this go down in flames—and so have you, Tuvok."

"On that much, we agree." He pocketed the transceiver. "What if Saavik refuses to accede to our requests for intervention?"

Keiko sighed. "If it comes to that, we'd better hope Calhoun is a better diplomat than O'Brien."

O'Brien sat in the *Excalibur*'s sleek but austere conference room, flanked by Eddington and Keiko and facing Calhoun, Hiren, and Soleta. As best he could tell, the two groups of rebel leaders were separated by three feet of table, six untouched platters of food, and the unbridgeable gulf of Calhoun's ego.

"Of *course* it makes sense for me to take command of the united fleet," Calhoun said. "Most of it would be mine to begin with."

That got a chuckle from O'Brien. "Yeah? From what I hear, most of your fleet"—he gestured at Hiren—"is on loan from *him*."

"Then you heard wrong," Soleta said. "Hiren and his people are pledged to Captain Calhoun. No one *loaned* us anything." She lifted her goblet and drank deeply of her wine, but kept her baleful glare fixed on O'Brien as she did.

He pushed his plate away and leaned forward with his arms on the table. "Look, no offense to you, Captain, but I've been on the bleeding edge of the rebellion since the day it started. I fought with Ben Sisko until he died, and then I took over where he left off. That was seven years ago. So excuse me if I don't just step aside because some hotshot with a fancy ship tells me to."

"It's not as if we just joined the fight *yesterday*," Calhoun said. "We've been at this for five years. And I'm sorry if this sounds harsh, but I think we've gotten a hell of a lot more done in that time than you have."

Hardly able to believe his ears, O'Brien traded looks of shocked offense with Eddington and Keiko before returning his focus to Calhoun. "Oh, really? Just how do you figure that, then?"

The Xenexian shrugged. "I think our records speak

for themselves. Mine is a string of brilliant victories, yours a litany of heartbreaking defeats."

O'Brien was seething. "What a load of—"

"We've had our share of victories," Eddington cut in.

A gruff snort from Hiren. "Such as Bajor? You just lost your primary base."

Keiko shot back, "And *you* lost all of *Romulus*."

Calhoun kept his piercing purple stare fixed upon O'Brien, who refused to give him any satisfaction by looking away. "What *was* your last victory, O'Brien?"

"What was *yours*?"

"I destroyed ninety-five percent of the Klingon Empire's Fifth Fleet just over two weeks ago, in the Joch'chal Nebula." He smirked. "Your turn."

Suppressing the urge to answer with a string of curses, O'Brien said, "We blew up Vareth Dar, in the Cuellar system."

Soleta belted out a cruel laugh. "Two *years* ago!"

Calhoun added, "What have you done lately?"

Before O'Brien could unleash a tide of vulgar suggestions for Calhoun and his minions, Eddington answered, "Look, this isn't some kind of contest. It's supposed to be a parley. And in case you've forgotten, we're here at your request. *You* invited *us*. You asked to join *our* rebellion. If you want to be part of our war, you can do it on our terms."

The ultimatum left Calhoun brooding for a few seconds. Then he nodded. "Yes, I admit we contacted you. And we did present ourselves as wanting to become part of your rebellion. But I have to be perfectly honest with you, Mister Eddington: That was before we realized you were leading your people to their inevitable, certain doom."

"Go to hell," Keiko said, catching O'Brien off guard. "You have no idea what we've done, the risks we've taken, the sacrifices we've made. We've liberated millions of slaves throughout Alliance space."

"Yes," Soleta replied, "but you've recruited only the tiniest fraction of them into your movement. The rest have fled into deep space. That's not exactly a show of confidence in your rebellion, is it?"

"And even if they had stayed," Hiren added, "you don't have ships to put them on, or bases for them to defend. As a result, your numbers succumb steadily to attrition. In essence, you're bleeding to death, one soldier at a time."

Calhoun stood. "We believe in what you fight for," he said, circling the table, "but not in the way that you fight. Your tactics have been timid, your long-term strategies deficient and unambitious—and now those weaknesses have cost you." O'Brien stood as Calhoun neared him, prompting everyone else to stand as well. Towering over him, Calhoun added, "Face it, O'Brien: Without us, you and your people will be dead in a matter of months. Your rebellion is drowning, and we're trying to throw you a line. Do the smart thing for once."

Looking up at the Xenexian's leathery features and hard eyes, O'Brien knew without question that he was no match for Calhoun, but he wasn't going to let that stop him from speaking his mind. "You smug bastard," he said. "It's always easy to find fault from a distance, isn't it? You insult my tactics, my strategy—as if you'd have done any better in my place. I know your history. You started out in some backwater sector, out past the Romulan Empire. Captured this pretty little ship of yours. Recruited the entire population of Xenex into your service, even though you didn't have any ships to put them on.

"Me and my people? We've been caught between the Klingons and the Cardies from day one, taking fire from all sides with no safe place to go to ground. Nowhere to fall back, no idea where our next meal was coming from or when. We've had to risk capture and death to steal damn near every ship we have. But you? You inherited a Romulan war fleet. Not a bad reward for letting a whole world die. And then the rest of the Romulan Empire gave you safe ports, supplies, munitions, personnel. You've been blessed with a force ten times the size of mine, and what have you done with it? Nipped at the Klingons' heels.

"While you've been playing soldier, we've been waging a bloody two-front war with one hand tied behind our back. We've suffered seven years of living hell, Calhoun, so if you think I'm just going to step aside and let you take command of my people, you're out of your goddamned mind."

Calhoun snarled, "And if *you* think I'm going to take orders from someone whose entire career is a series of defeats, setbacks, and tragic errors, so are you."

Eddington stepped in and forced them apart. "This seems like a good time to take a break."

"Yes," Calhoun said, "sound the retreat, O'Brien. That's what you're best at, isn't it?"

O'Brien smiled. "Actually, Captain, my specialty is fixing things." Leading Keiko and Eddington out of the room, he lobbed a parting verbal grenade over his shoulder. "Call me if you want some help extracting your head from your ass."

22

The Name of Action

The situation is devolving rapidly," Tuvok said. "Yesterday's first meeting between O'Brien and Calhoun was contentious, to say the least. There is little reason to hope today's discussion will be any better."

"Unfortunately, I must agree," Selar said. The transceiver projected her holographic avatar life-size inside Tuvok's private stateroom on the *Defiant*. *"What is transpiring now aboard the* Excalibur *is not a meeting of minds but a clash of egos. I fear that before it ends, the two rebel factions might end up at war with each other rather than united against the Alliance."*

"This cannot be allowed to happen," Tuvok insisted. "Both these men and the forces they represent are essential to fulfilling Spock's plan for Memory Omega, but neither Calhoun nor O'Brien will yield his authority to the other."

"There is only one way to end their conflict. Memory Omega must intercede and present both sides with a leader they can accept."

"The time for influencing the rebellion from behind the scenes is past. If the rebellion is to have any chance of success, and if Spock's plan is to come to fruition, Memory Omega must take an active role in leading the rebellion."

Silence fell as Tuvok and Selar finished presenting

their case, and the holographic avatar of Saavik nodded as she weighed their arguments. *"You make a compelling case,"* the director said. *"I did not realize the two rebel factions were so bitterly at odds."*

"The factions themselves bear each other no ill will," Tuvok said. "Their leaders, however, seem to despise each other."

A thoughtful frown hardened Saavik's mien. *"Sadly, this outcome has long been expected. Ever since the interference from the alternate universe seven years ago, the tempo of events has accelerated, and we have not always kept pace."* She briefly touched her index finger to her lips. *"Though I am reluctant to use the same methods of manipulation on our allies as against our enemies, is there any way the two of you could get close enough to O'Brien and Calhoun to influence their thinking and resolve their dispute?"*

Tuvok tried to mask his chagrin but felt his brow knit, telegraphing his deep frustration with the situation. "Although General O'Brien treats me as a valued adviser, he has never seen fit to permit me, or any other Vulcan, into his inner circle. In many ways, he sees the rebellion as an inherently Terran undertaking."

"Interesting, since so many of his followers are non-Terrans," Saavik said. *"Selar? Can you reach Calhoun?"*

The younger Vulcan woman shook her head. *"Unlikely. He knows of my telepathic abilities, and he keeps me at a safe distance. Furthermore, he is protected by Soleta, whose gifts are substantial, though less honed than my own, and he maintains a telepathic connection with the entity known as McHenry. It has been difficult protecting my thoughts from McHenry, whose abilities steadily grow stronger and more nuanced. Any attempt to manipulate Calhoun psionically would be detected by McHenry, and I believe the consequences would be severe."*

"In any event, such a tactic misses the fundamental problem," Tuvok said. "In our estimation, neither man is actually fit to lead the united rebellion."

Concern lined Saavik's forehead with deep creases. *"Why not?"*

"Calhoun is a fine tactician and strategist," Selar said. *"However, he has on many occasions displayed a level of ruthlessness and brutality that is incompatible with our philosophy. While it is possible that he might, with our support, be able to lead a successful war effort and defeat the Alliance, I would fear for the regime he might raise in its stead."*

"At the other end of the spectrum is O'Brien. As much as I admire his idealism and compassion for those under his command, he has been less than effectual as a military commander. Despite his philosophical compatibility with Memory Omega's long-term goals, I fear he lacks the nerve to prosecute the war with sufficient zeal to secure victory." Tuvok and Selar traded reassuring glances, and then he added, "The only logical solution, Director, is for Memory Omega to anoint a leader that both rebel factions will follow."

Saavik nodded. *"We have been making an effort to recruit just such a person. Unfortunately, he does not seem to want the job."*

"One can hardly blame him."

"Indeed."

The mild cynicism did not appear to sit well with the director. *"Regardless, it represents a serious setback—one that could cost millions of lives unless we rectify it. I will continue in my efforts to persuade him. In the meantime, the two of you must do all that you can to keep O'Brien and Calhoun talking to one another."*

"Given their animosity, that might prove counterproductive."

"I assure you," Saavik said gravely, *"the alternative will be far worse."*

Picard stood in the sleek, antiseptic hangar where Memory Omega had berthed the *Calypso* and watched a pair of human workers guide antigrav lifters loaded with supplies and provisions into his ship. Troi stood beside him, paying no attention to their preparations for departure; her wistful gaze told Picard that her melancholy thoughts were light-years away.

"You should go say good-bye to him," he told her.

She pointedly avoided looking at him. "I already did."

It had been obvious to him that she had wanted to stay and throw in her lot with the Memory Omega people, but their proposition had failed to persuade him. It seemed to him like little more than a highly developed death wish. *The best thing I can do for Deanna right now is get her as far from here as possible.*

Troi muttered with naked bitterness, "Keep telling yourself that."

He cleared his conscious mind, hoping to avoid stirring up any further discord between himself and Troi before they were on their way.

Crisp footsteps echoed off the pristine metallic floors, walls, and ceiling. Picard turned to see Saavik and K'Ehleyr approaching him. He stepped away from his ship to meet them halfway. "Come to see us off?"

"No," Saavik said, "to make one last appeal."

He pursed his lips. "I'm sorry, but my mind is made up."

K'Ehleyr loomed over him, her arms crossed and her brow sardonically arched. "I'd hear her out, if I were you."

He lifted his hands to forestall counterargument.

"With all respect to you both, I've considered your offer most thoroughly. After weighing its risks against its rewards, I'm simply not convinced you can deliver what you promise, and I won't risk my life—or Deanna's—on your delusions of grandeur."

Saavik half-bowed her head and showed her open palms in a gesture of humility. "I understand your reservations, Mister Picard, but I implore you to grant us just one more hour of your time."

With a cryptic smile, K'Ehleyr added, "We have something to show you."

"You've already shown me a great deal, and I admit, it's breathtaking. I have no doubt that you possess marvels of science undreamed of by the Alliance. But that's a far cry from being prepared to wage a war against them."

"I quite agree," Saavik said. She gestured toward the nearest turbolift. "Just one more hour is all we ask. Not much longer than it will take us to finish preparing your vessel for departure."

Picard looked back toward Troi, hoping for some indication of what to do, but she still had her back to him and was bombarding him with waves of resentment. He sighed and looked back at the two women facing him. The half-Klingon beauty narrowed her eyes and beckoned him with a nod toward the lift. "Come on. Indulge us. I think you're gonna like this."

"Very well. One hour—no more."

"As you prefer," Saavik said. "Please follow us." She and K'Ehleyr led Picard across the hangar and inside the turbolift, which sped away with a pleasing drone of sound and a faintly perceptible vibration in his feet. In no mood for small talk, Picard savored the silence while it lasted.

The lift halted, its doors opened, and the two women led him out to a long corridor. At its end, a door sighed open at their approach, revealing a silolike chamber that stretched up, past the glow of lights on its ground level, into darkness. In the center of the vast space was a circular platform surrounded by a dozen glossy interactive control panels manned by white-coated personnel of various species—humans, Vulcans, a Tellarite, two Andorians, a Bolian, and a Denobulan. One of the Andorians, a very masculine young *thaan* with chiseled features and white hair, nodded at Saavik. "Welcome, Director."

"Good morning, Arrithar. Erebus Station, please."

"Yes, ma'am." Arrithar and the other scientists set to work, entering commands into their consoles as Saavik, K'Ehleyr, and Picard stepped onto the platform and moved to its center. Arrithar looked up to say, "Three seconds."

K'Ehleyr quipped to Picard, "Hope you skipped breakfast."

The annular confinement field of a transporter beam seized them, and it was more powerful than any Picard had ever experienced. It felt as if it were crushing him to death, and when the first surge of white light from the energizer coils enveloped him, he had only a split second to wonder if there had been some kind of malfunction. Before he could rage at the waste and stupidity of dying in a transporter accident, sensation was stripped from him for the merest flash, and then it flooded back in another blinding pulse of light from above.

He sucked in air as the confinement field released him. For a moment he was doubled over, inhaling greedily while waiting for the vertigo in his skull to abate. When he straightened and looked around, he could have sworn he was in the same room that he had been in moments earlier, except that all the stations were unmanned, and the only people present were himself, Saavik, and K'Ehleyr. The two women had left the platform and were waiting for him.

"Sorry," he said, composing himself and stiffly descending from the round dais. Looking around in confused wonder, he asked, "What is this place?"

"One of our dark sites," Saavik said. She led him and K'Ehleyr out into a corridor that was identical to the one they had traversed underground on the Zeta Serpentis asteroid. "This is where we conduct operations that would be too likely to draw notice if conducted within range of the Alliance—or any other civilization of similar or greater sophistication." She stopped at a door and entered a code on the keypad next to it. The portal slid open with a soft pneumatic gasp, and she stepped through it. K'Ehleyr stood aside and motioned for Picard to precede her.

He stepped inside to find a long observation lounge looking out on a vast shipyard. Legions of automated systems replicated parts, assembled them into spaceframes and hulls, and moved in and out of ships that looked ready for service in every way except that they were dark and apparently deserted. But as remarkable as the shipyard was, it was the view beyond it that left him speechless.

He pointed at it. "Is . . . is that . . . ?"

"Yes, Luc," K'Ehleyr said. "That's the Milky Way galaxy—as seen from a distance of approximately three hundred thousand light-years."

Picard spun to face Saavik. "What is this? One of your holographic illusions? Some kind of trick?"

"I assure you, Mister Picard, it's very real."

He clapped one hand atop his head. "How did we get here?"

"A subspace transporter," Saavik said. "We use them sparingly because they consume vast amounts of power and are highly unstable. However, I considered our present situation grave enough to merit its use."

Pondering the distance back to the tiny pocket of space he called home, his mind boggled at the calculation of travel times, even at insane multiples of the fastest warp speed he'd ever attained. "How do you propose to move this fleet hundreds of thousands of light-years in any reasonable period of time? Surely you don't expect me to believe you have a subspace transporter that can move ships."

"Of course not," K'Ehleyr said. "As for how we get from A to B, let's just say we haven't shown you all our best tricks yet."

It was overwhelming. Picard felt dizzy. "Why show me this at all?"

Saavik spoke more boldly than Picard would have expected of a Vulcan. "So you will understand that I am not exaggerating when I say we have the resources to challenge the Alliance—and most other powers in the galaxy. What we lack are the personnel to crew more than one of these vessels."

Craning his neck and pressing his face to the transparent steel window, he still was unable to see all of the automated shipyard. "How many are there?"

"Hundreds," K'Ehleyr said.

"*Mon Dieu.*" He shook his head in disbelief. "What do you wish me to do?"

"Captain one of our ships," Saavik said. "We'll provide

the crew. With their support, you'll carry our message to the rebels and rally them behind you."

"*Me?* Don't be absurd. I'm no leader of men."

K'Ehleyr flashed a knowing smile. "Don't underestimate yourself. I think that once you've had a taste of authority, you'll find it suits you."

"Quite the contrary." He nodded at K'Ehleyr. "You seem far better suited to this role than I. If you like, I'll join *your* crew, but—"

"I can't sit in the captain's chair, Picard! *Look* at me. I'm half *Klingon*. No matter what kind of ship I arrive in, I'll never be able to command the respect and loyalty of the *Terran* Rebellion."

Picard turned toward Saavik, hoping—perhaps foolishly—for some degree of support, but he found no comfort in her words. "Don't look to me for absolution," she said. "A Vulcan may have inaugurated this movement, but Spock knew that no Vulcan could finish it." She placed her hands reverently on either side of his head. "From the very beginning we have known that when the war finally came, this revolution would need a *human* face."

Mac was faced off once again with the two human men from the *Defiant,* in the *Excalibur's* officer's mess. He was starting to question why he had ever wanted to join the Terran Rebellion; in his opinion, people this stupid didn't deserve his help. "Why the *grozit* are you fighting me on this, O'Brien? Can't you see I'm trying to save your asses?"

"Nobody bloody asked you to save anything, you puffed-up sack of—"

"I think we're getting off topic here," Eddington interrupted, drawing angry stares from O'Brien and Mac. "Maybe there's some way we can work out a power-sharing agreement, or divide the responsibilities for—"

"Forget it," said Soleta. "What you're describing is a fine way to run a government, but a battle fleet is no place for a debate."

Hiren nodded. "She's right." He directed an imploring look at the humans. "Look at me. I used to be the praetor of an empire. But I lost my homeworld, and with it my right to assert power. It galled me to surrender my authority to Calhoun, but this is *his* milieu, and in it there can be only one leader. One commander. Any other path leads to chaos—and defeat."

"That's fine," O'Brien said. "When he's ready to follow, I'll lead."

Mac tossed up his hands, fed up with the humans' posturing. "This is insane. What's it going to take to make you see reason? You have barely enough ships to stage a hit-and-run raid on a soft target. You're on the verge of being exterminated. Is that what you want? To be erased from history?"

"It can't be much worse than being a footnote in a chapter written about you," O'Brien grumped. "And spare me your rant about how you can face the Alliance and we can't, because that's a pack of lies. You're not in the fringe territories anymore—these are the core systems. We can't just hit-and-run and skip back into friendly space, because *there is no friendly space*." He raised his hand as if to point at Mac, then thought better of it and made a fist, struggling visibly to keep his self-control. "Name three strategically significant targets in this quadrant aside from Cardassia."

"Qo'noS. The dilithium mine on Elas. The—"

"Wrong quadrant," O'Brien cut in. "Try again."

It took a few seconds for Mac to dredge up his memories of the Alliance's possessions in the Alpha Quadrant. This region of space was more than two hundred light-years from anything he had ever cared about, and until now he hadn't spent much time thinking about it. He decided to buy himself time by naming the most obvious target, which was the only one he had been able to think of so far. "Raknal Station, inside the Betreka Nebula."

"That's one," Eddington said. "There are plenty more to choose from."

McHenry's voice murmured in Mac's thoughts. *Excuse me, Mac, but—*

Not now, McHenry. I can do this on my own.

The *Excalibur*'s peculiar navigator was unusually persistent. *I'm certain you can, Mac. It's just that I—*

Please just let me think, McHenry! Mac hated himself for snapping at McHenry, who he knew meant well, but sometimes the telepath's intrusions into his thoughts were enough to turn a bad mood or a short temper into a burst of fury. He was excruciatingly close to extracting another bit of trivia from the dustiest nook in his brain when Eddington derailed his train of thought.

"Oh, come on. It can't be *that* hard, can it, Captain? The topaline mines on Capella? The zenite refinery on Ardana? The Cardassian shipyards at Olmerak?"

Soleta stepped to Mac's side and glared at Eddington. "Your point?"

"As fine a strategist and tactician as Captain Calhoun certainly is, he doesn't know where the enemy's vital targets are in this region of space."

Mac was not impressed by Eddington's ruse. "I can learn."

O'Brien replied in his gruff rasp of a voice, "Who's gonna teach you? Get this through your thick Xenexian skull: You may have all the muscle, but we have the brains. This war has to be fought and won here, which means *you* need to know what *we* know. Listen to your friend." He nodded at Hiren. "When you're forced to play on someone else's turf, you have to play by their rules. My turf—my rules."

Mac, this might not be a good time, but—

Not now! "Look, O'Brien. I know that in this fantasy life you've created, you're leading your people to freedom and glory, but from where I'm standing, you look like a kid playing soldier and doing a lousy job of it. Don't sit there and tell me that you alone possess the vital intel to win this war when it's obvious all that information hasn't done you or your people any damn good. What can you possibly tell me that I can't learn for myself?"

"How to penetrate the defense network that protects the core planets of the Klingon Empire—including their homeworld, Qo'noS."

Mac tried to hold a straight face, but a tiny snort of derision squeaked from one of his nostrils, and the edges of his mouth curved upward. "Really? And how, exactly, did you acquire that intel?"

"Worf, the former regent of the Klingon Empire, is our prisoner of war."

Not missing a beat, Mac asked Hiren, "What would your government have done had you ever been captured alive during your reign as praetor?"

"All my codes would have been nullified, my biometric access revoked, and all contingency plans to which I had been privy would be considered compromised.

Within hours, my successor would initiate new protocols to secure all military, political, economic, and communications assets of the Empire."

Sporting a taut smile of condescension, Mac looked back at O'Brien. "How long did you hold Worf before he coughed up this allegedly vital intel?"

Nervous, embarrassed looks passed between O'Brien and Eddington. Under his breath, O'Brien said, "Two years."

Hiren, Soleta, and Mac all laughed. It was impossible not to. The sheer stupidity of it, the cluelessness, the utter incompetence was so stunning that hilarity seemed the only rational response. The more they laughed, the angrier the two human men became—which served only to make Mac laugh even harder. He was almost to the point of pounding his fist on the table for cathartic release when McHenry put an end to the frivolity. *Mac, you have company.*

The door of the officer's mess opened, and two people walked in. One was O'Brien's comrade, Colonel Ishikawa. Behind her was Selar. Both of them looked deadly serious. "Enough of this," Keiko said. "A decision has to be made, and this is it. Neither of you is the right one to lead the rebellion."

Instantaneously, Mac and O'Brien redirected all their ire at Selar and Ishikawa. Mac also saved some small measure for McHenry. *Why didn't you warn me sooner?*

I am quite certain I tried.

Try harder next time. Imagining the worst, he added, *Within reason.*

O'Brien bellowed, "What the hell is *this,* Keiko?"

"Call it an intervention," she said.

Standing shoulder-to-shoulder with O'Brien, Mac

stared down his shipmate. "Selar, I trust you have a better explanation than that."

To his surprise, Selar looked at the human woman before she spoke. Only after receiving a nod from Ishikawa did Selar respond. "For two days, you have done nothing but argue among yourselves. We had hoped for an amicable fusion of your respective forces, but that now seems unlikely. Though both sides are needed for the war to come, they must be united beneath a single banner. Since neither of you can provide that, Memory Omega will."

The name meant absolutely nothing to Mac. With the deliberate pace of a glacier, he turned his head toward O'Brien—only to see the human man doing likewise, looking to him for some hint as to what the *grozit* was going on.

In a low voice, Mac asked him, "Would you like the honors?"

O'Brien's eyebrows climbed a millimeter higher on his forehead. "It's your ship, Captain. I think you should take it."

Despite being relatively certain he wouldn't like the answer, Mac asked the women in the mess doorway, "What's Memory Omega?"

Selar replied, "To use a human idiom, it is the cavalry riding to your rescue."

Ishikawa said, "Please join us in the nerve center. We have something to show you." They turned and walked away without a backward glance.

Reluctantly, Mac followed them. Soleta and Hiren followed him without needing to be prompted, as did O'Brien and Eddington. Moving at a quick step and in a tight cluster, they reached the ship's nerve center less than a minute later. Selar and Ishikawa stood at the forefront of the compartment, limned by the glow of the main viewscreen. After Mac and the others had gathered behind the duo, he said, "All right, we're here. What are we supposed to see?"

Ishikawa took a small, innocuous-looking cylinder from her jacket pocket, gently tapped commands into a miniature panel on its side, and spoke into it. "We're ready, Director." Then she put away the device and nodded at Selar. The two women stepped apart, ensuring that everyone else had an unobstructed view of the main screen, which for several seconds showed nothing but the churning violence of the Arachnid Nebula.

From the sensor console, Robin Lefler declared, "Gravitational anomaly, Captain—dead ahead, range fifty thousand kilometers."

"Source?"

Lefler shook her head, bewildered. "No idea."

Hiren moved to Lefler's side and peeked over her shoulder. "Maybe it's from the twin pulsars inside the nebula?"

"No," Lefler said, "I already checked that."

Then Soleta pointed at the main screen. "Look!"

Mac turned and saw the dark maelstrom spinning wildly into a vortex, transformed by some unseen force into a massive funnel of black emptiness, a yawning void spiraling wider by the second and threatening to swallow the *Excalibur* and the *Defiant* whole. "Shields up! Battle stations!"

Selar raised her voice over the chatter of people preparing the ship for combat. "That won't be necessary, Captain. Trust me."

Soleta scrambled to the science console and ran her

own scan of the terrifying phenomenon taking shape ahead of them. "It's a wormhole," she declared. "And it's abnormally stable, almost as if . . ."

"As if it were artificial," Mac said, with good reason.

Emerging from the center of nothingness inside the wormhole was a ship unlike anything he had ever seen. Its design was reminiscent of those favored more than a century earlier by the Terran Empire, but it was far sleeker. Its forward profile was sliver-thin, its lines graceful and fluid, its overall bearing one of speed and power. As it cleared the mouth of the wormhole, the phenomenon irised closed behind it, propagating shock waves into the nebula around them. The wave thundered as it passed over the *Excalibur,* and on the viewscreen Mac saw the *Defiant* bobble and yaw as it weathered the disturbance.

The new ship glided off its intercept course with *Excalibur* and *Defiant,* turning to show them its starboard side as it came to a halt nearby.

A signal warbled on Lefler's console. She silenced it, swallowed hard, and looked up. "Sir? They're hailing us."

Mac looked at O'Brien and with a sideways nod invited him forward. The two men stepped up and stood front and center, facing the main viewscreen. O'Brien nodded his readiness to Mac, who told Lefler, "Onscreen."

The main screen switched to an image of a starship bridge packed with sleek, high-tech consoles and crewed by personnel of many species. A Tellarite and an Andorian manned the forward stations. Bolians, Vulcans, Caitians, and Benzites worked at the aft consoles, and a woman of partial Klingon ancestry stood at a panel not far from the center chair. But it was the middle-aged human man in that center chair who commanded Mac's full attention.

Lean and bald, he had a weathered, worldly look that his black-and-gray uniform couldn't hide. His face was etched with the lines of a lifetime of sorrow, but in his dark brown eyes burned the light of a powerful intellect. He stood and with a small tug smoothed the front of his uniform jacket before stepping forward. Everything about him—his stride, his carriage, his expression—conveyed an unmistakable air of dignity and gravitas.

He introduced himself in a rich baritone, with words that Mac would remember for the rest of his life:

"Greetings. This is Captain Jean-Luc Picard, commanding the free starship Enterprise.*"*

PART II

Deballare Superbos

2378

23

Crowns of Blood and Fire

Rise for Him Who Holds the Throne for Him Who Shall Return!"

The announcement reverberated in the cathedral-like space of the Klingon High Command's strategic command center, where hundreds of the Empire's most skilled war planners and tacticians directed the movements and activities of its armed forces. Few things could compel these professional warriors to set aside their duties, but a rare visit by the Regent of the Empire was one such occasion.

Klag strode onto the main floor flanked by his retinue of advisers and selected members of the High Council. The one-armed head of state gave only a cursory upward glance to the tiers of officers who had risen to honor his arrival. "Resume your duties," he said, enabling the busy staff to go back to work, their obligations to protocol fulfilled. The regent and his entourage joined Goluk at the center of the situation floor, which was a transparent steel surface above a deep pit inside which was projected a holographic map of local space. Klag stood beside Goluk and eyed the map. "What news of the Terran rebels, General?"

"Still no sign of them, My Lord." Goluk used a data tablet to manipulate the projection beneath their feet, magnifying different areas as he continued. "The Sixth Fleet converged upon Athos IV as you ordered, but found the rebels' camps deserted and all their ships long since departed."

"Departed? For where?"

Dreading the regent's inevitable harangue, Goluk said, "Unknown. None of our listening stations or patrols have detected any large-scale fleet movements in or out of the Badlands in months."

Klag squinted at the star map. "Could the rebels have evaded our sensors if they'd left a few ships at a time, on different vectors?"

Goluk considered that scenario. "In theory, yes. Assuming they had foreknowledge of our surveillance patterns, they might have done so."

Pointing at the projection, Klag said, "If they regroup, it will most likely be inside the Rolor Nebula or the Argolis Cluster."

"That was our conclusion as well, My Lord. General K'mdar and his battle group are positioned inside the nebula, and the cluster is being patrolled by the Third Fleet under General Torgoth. However, neither has reported any activity in the past six weeks."

That news put a broad grin on the regent's face. He turned to his crowd of sycophants and cronies. "You see! Just as I predicted—the Terran Rebellion has scattered, gone to ground like frightened voles! O'Brien and his malcontents are finished." Looking back at Goluk, he asked, "And what of Calhoun's armada?"

"We've been unable to locate them, My Lord."

Klag's grin became a scowl. "What? A fleet that size? Are you telling me that many ships escaped the Joch'chal Nebula without being detected?"

It was hard for Goluk to preserve his air of detachment with Klag shouting in his face, but he did so because, as a professional soldier, he had too much respect for the chain of command and the demands of decorum to break them for the fleeting satisfaction of upbraiding a Regent of the Empire. To Goluk, the High Command was a place for cold facts and hard numbers, not politics. Not so long ago, Klag had shown this place the same respect, but he had since exchanged a life of war for one of words, and the traditions of honor for the trappings of power.

"It is unlikely that Calhoun's fleet could have left the nebula without registering on our sensors," Goluk said. "We've spent the past several months bombarding the nebula in random patterns to flush them out. However, we've not yet seen any evidence of a direct hit." He added in a low deadpan, "Perhaps you could declare victory over Calhoun's forces as well, My Lord."

The regent shot a hateful, narrow-eyed stare at Goluk. "Perhaps I will." He banished his anger with a low growl, then turned his attention back to the map. "If the rebels have removed themselves from our equation, all the better. We have a more important threat on our doorstep." He held out his hand, and Goluk handed him the control pad for the star map. Klag centered it on the Empire's border with the Gorn Hegemony. "The Taurus Pact grows bolder with each passing day. Taking advantage of the unrest inside the Cardassian Union, the Tholians have seized control over no fewer than ten star systems between Rudellia and Vanden, and the Breen have planted their flag on Lazon II, claiming its mineral rights for themselves. Now they're threatening to move on Arawath.

"Ten hours ago, Gorn troops landed on Ogat. This error in judgment will be their undoing." He thrust the control pad back at Goluk. "Tell me how you plan to respond to this brazen assault on our empire."

Goluk magnified the sector surrounding Ogat. "The Second Fleet is en route, My Lord. The Gorn sent only a small expeditionary force, most likely to gauge our response. I doubt they expect to be able to hold Ogat once we counterattack."

"So, they're testing us, is that it?" Noting Goluk's nod of confirmation, Klag's eyes widened and his brow arched with malice. "Then let us show them more than they expect. While the Second Fleet forces them from Ogat, we'll retask the Fourth and Eighth fleets for a full-scale invasion of the Gorn Hegemony."

The regent's entourage received his insane order with a chorus of approval, which only made Goluk's role as the voice of dissent that much more difficult. "My Lord, redeploying the Fourth and Eighth fleets will leave our border with the Romulans undefended."

Klag swatted away Goluk's opinion as if it were a bothersome insect. "Irrelevant. Romulan space is under our control, and whatever military it once had has vanished along with that miscreant Calhoun."

"With all respect, sir, Romulan space will remain under our control only so long as we patrol it. Shifting our forces to the far side of the Empire to invade the Gorn will leave the Romulans' territories open to annexation by the Kinshaya, the Thallonians, the Grigari—"

"I wasn't soliciting opinions, General." Klag let his rebuke settle in for a moment, and Goluk was keenly aware that the political tide had shifted against him with alarming haste. Klag continued in a more confidential manner. "I set the policy, and your duty is to carry it out. Is that clear?"

Goluk's grim visage was as steady as if it had been hewn from bedrock. "Absolutely, My Lord."

Ostensibly satisfied, Klag turned his attention back to the map. "The Breen and Tholians are too remote for us to deal with right now. If Damar can rein in the madness that grips his people, we'll let them defend their own borders. For now, our primary goal is to make an example of the Gorn. We need to make them pay in blood for this trespass. Failure to retaliate will only invite further aggression."

Moving the pieces in his imagination, Goluk envisioned the logistical challenges the regent's new agenda presented. "Our forces can be deployed under cloak to attack positions within five weeks."

Klag nodded and looked pleased. "Excellent."

"But you should know, My Lord, that what you propose will be costly, and it will involve a high degree of risk." He illuminated sections of the map with various icons and symbols as he laid out his case. "If the Tholians come to the Gorn's aid, we could find ourselves on the receiving end of a pincer assault."

"If you think the Tholians are getting involved, pull the Ninth Fleet back from Talar and open up a new front on the enemy's rear flank."

"Very well. But there is another concern." He scrolled the massive display in a swift blur to the far side of the Empire. "If the rebels should reappear in or near Romulan space, many of our most important systems in that sector will be defenseless. Narendra, Khitomer, Mempa—"

Leaning almost close enough to touch his nose to Goluk's, Klag said in a whisper laced with menace, "I've already told you: The rebels are *finished*. They're *gone*, Goluk. Forget about them, and don't make me repeat myself."

Steady as a man of stone, Goluk said, "Yes, My Lord."

Lifting his voice to address the room, Klag declared, "With Cardassia foundering, the future is ours to take— so let us take it!"

Klag's megalomania was rewarded with the blood-thirsty roars of great warriors. Goluk hoped that Klag proved luckier as regent than Martok had been—or else those roars would soon be calling for Klag's head on the end of a *bat'leth*.

The mental image made Goluk smile. *We should be so lucky.*

Supreme Legate Corat Damar stood at the three oval windows behind his desk and watched a hazy dusk paint Cardassia City in shades of crimson.

For the first time in months, the metropolis was quiet. All of Cardassia Prime was at peace. The capital of the Union was once again a place of unity and calm. One world, one people. On every planet under Cardassian rule, order had been restored—and all it had cost Damar was his soul.

Night's purple cloak stretched languidly across the heavens, making its way by slow degrees toward the far horizon, while Damar stood motionless and stared into the distance, searching for himself in the deepening shadows.

He had suspected from the beginning that the plague of madness and violence that had ravaged the Cardassian

Union had been inflicted upon his people by an external enemy. At first, he had sought to fix the blame upon the Alliance's new political and military rival, the Taurus Pact, but the available intelligence about the powers involved had made that seem unlikely. Then, while reading reports of recent riots, Damar had noted an interesting fact: None of the incidents ever involved direct harm to the alien servants of the wealthy and powerful who had suddenly run amok, or to the alien assistants of the Union's preeminent scientists, or to the aliens who served as slaves for elite members of the military.

Then he had remembered Dukat's Vulcan hand-maiden at his back on the day he had inexplicably assassinated his best friend in full view of the public.

He had made his decision then without hesitation, despite knowing it would haunt him for the rest of his life, whether it proved to be correct or a grievous error. Issuing his first executive decree as Supreme Legate of the Cardassian Union, he had ordered every non-Cardassian servant and every alien slave summarily executed, without trial or delay, on every world, colony, and ship of the Union.

Within a matter of days, millions of slaves, most of them members of species that had been part of Spock's fallen empire, had been slain. By the end of the first week following Damar's order, the number of the slaughtered exceeded fifteen million. For nearly three weeks "the Purge" had continued. Allegedly, the Union's last alien slave had been exterminated just that day. The final body count, according to the military, was just over thirty-one million, most of them Vulcans. Damar was surprised the streets weren't awash in blood. He knew that in his nightmares, they would be.

That evening's news feeds had been devoid of ill tidings. It was a day on which the billions of surviving Cardassians across the Union had breathed a collective sigh of relief—and it filled Damar with a toxic brew of shame and guilt. He was no stranger to war or violence; he had willingly employed both for the good of the state on more than one occasion and had suffered no remorse.

But this felt different to him. The Purge had been a slaughter unlike any in his lifetime, a premeditated mass murder on a grand scale. It offended him as a soldier and as a man of conscience and principle. He had served as Dukat's right-hand man all those years in the hope of mitigating his late friend's more brutal tendencies. The irony cut him to the quick.

I finally attain high office, and my first executive action is one of genocide.

Tired of waiting for night to finish its descent, he plodded to the liquor cabinet in the corner and filled a low glass with a generous pour of the most potent *kanar* he could dredge up. He emptied the glass in one toss down his throat, and then he refilled it. Another mindless guzzling, another refill, and a third mouthful for good measure. He felt the alcohol suffuse his bloodstream, softening the edges of his perception, bleeding the colors and muffling the sounds. For just a few minutes, he savored the ability not to care so much, but his pleasure was dulled by the knowledge that it was all temporary, and that no amount of *kanar* would ever be enough to let him forget what he had done. It didn't cure shame.

Darkness fell at last. Damar donned a robe and pulled its hood low over his face as he slipped out of his office, got out of the lift a few floors above ground level, and left the Detapa Council headquarters through its kitchen service entrance. Stepping outside into the stifling night, he was careful to check over his shoulder and make certain no one was following him.

The streets of the Tarlak Sector were sparsely trafficked. Not many civil servants worked this late at night, and there were few other attractions in that part of the capital—certainly none that would be worth the risk of violating curfew. Though he knew it would have been faster to take the main thoroughfares to his destination, discretion was Damar's chief concern that evening, so he restricted his movements to side streets, service alleys, and little-known shortcuts.

Despite his detours and circuitous route, he reached the Munda'ar Sector in less than half an hour. Much like the Tarlak Sector, which was dominated by government offices, the Munda'ar Sector was dedicated almost exclusively to one function: industrial storage. At night its clusters of warehouses made Damar think of great leviathans huddling in the desert for warmth. He knew from experience, however, that one needed to tread carefully in that part of the city, because the Obsidian Order frequently used some of the warehouses as black sites, for brutal interrogations and assassinations. Crossing the path of the wrong person at the wrong time in the Munda'ar Sector could be a fatal mistake.

Fortunately, he had been there many times, and he knew by heart which streets to avoid. As he neared his destination, he followed a route that was devoid of surveillance systems, and arrived at an unmarked door.

A soft knock and a moment's patience.

At eye level, a small metal bar slid open, revealing nervous eyes. "Yes?"

"I've lost the way," Damar said.

The eyes narrowed. "Did you ever know the way?"

"Yes," Damar said, careful to keep his face hidden inside the hood. "I heard it once, in the song of the morning."

He heard the soft, deep clack of heavy metal bolts retracting. The door was pulled open, swinging inward in a way that concealed the person behind it and left only one direction for Damar to go: to his left and down a steep flight of stairs into darkness. He hurried inside and down the steps, and heard the door close behind him. At the bottom of the stairs was an antechamber with two doors. One was an exit that let out on a street far from the entrance, in a concealed back alley not monitored by cameras or sensors; the other led to the Tabernacle.

Beside the second door was a long table stacked with generic masks. Damar picked up a mask and secured it over his face, then pulled back his hood and stepped through the door to join a few dozen of the anonymous faithful.

On a raised dais at the front of the room, a man and a woman, each wearing an ornamental recitation mask, stood facing the congregation. Behind them on the dais was a table, directly below a wall-mounted sculpture of the winged goddess Oralius. Two plain masks lay on the table. The speakers were in the latter half of the opening ritual, as the man finished his recitation from the Hebitian Records:

"That can destroy his body with my hand,
Reduce his spirit with my hate,
Separate his presence from my home:

To live without Oralius,
   Lighting our way to the source,
   Connecting us to the mystery,
Is to live without the tendrils of love."

Having completed the salutation, the man and woman faced each other in silence for a moment, and then they turned their backs to the congregation as they removed their recitation masks and replaced them with the plain masks that had been on the table. Once again anonymized, they sat down several seats apart from each other in the front row. Blessed, perfect silence filled the room.

In a few moments, Damar knew, someone would begin to hum, and that resonant sound would be answered by a contrapuntal harmony, and then others, until the music washed away every thought in Damar's mind for a few exquisite minutes. But until then, alone with his thoughts in that brief moment of stillness, he prayed to Oralius and begged her to cleanse his heart of murder's black stain.

24

Agents of a New Dawn

All eyes were on Picard as he stepped onto the dais inside the *Enterprise*'s main cargo bay, which had been cleared for his en masse briefing of all the rebel commanders and their senior personnel. He felt the pressure of their expectations and their hunger for inspiration. Against his advice, Memory Omega had set him up as the leader of this untamed rabble, and now it was incumbent upon him to live up to the role in which he had let himself be cast.

Heaven help us all.

"Thank you all for coming," he said, his voice sounding deeper than he'd imagined as it boomed from the overhead speakers and echoed inside the vast compartment. The crowd before him settled into expectant silence. "We have arrived at a threshold moment. Until now, you all have been limited to waging defensive battles or small-scale guerrilla attacks. Large-scale offensive operations have been beyond your purview. No more." He pointed over their heads, through the enormous open doorway and its invisible force field, at the fleet of ships gathered outside, around Erebus Station. "Training simulations have been completed for the crews you've provided, for the ships that Memory Omega built. We now possess sufficient numbers, in both ships and personnel, to engage the Alliance from a position of strength. Approximately one day from now, that is exactly what we are going to do."

He stepped aside to the edge of the dais and nodded at K'Ehleyr, who activated the interactive hologram she had prepared. The first images to take shape depicted a heavily fortified and well-patrolled star system. "This data is based on reconnaissance scans of the SoHcha system, deep inside the Klingon Empire," Picard said. "It is the site of their largest, most advanced, and best defended shipyard. This is where the Klingons have been reverse-engineering the Romulan-made cloaking device that they captured from the *Capital Gain,* after the battle of Empok Nor." He smiled at O'Brien. "And you, General O'Brien, are going to lead the attack to destroy it, denying the Klingons a major advance in stealth technology and crippling their military infrastructure for most of the next decade."

O'Brien cast a dubious look at the hologram. "Am I, now?"

"Yes, you are. And the *Enterprise* will be there with you, as will several of her sister ships." Picard updated the hologram with a complex overlay of tactical diagrams. "Taking full advantage of our wormhole-based propulsion methods, our attack force will emerge inside the Klingons' defensive perimeter. Based on our analysis of the Klingons' response times and tactical protocols, we believe this will enable us to destroy the shipyard while minimizing our losses."

Calhoun, who stood beside O'Brien at the front of the crowd, sounded concerned. "What kind of losses do you think we'll suffer?"

Picard's mask of optimism faltered. "Memory Omega

estimates our losses at ten to fifteen percent of all ships committed, and casualties of thirty percent among all crews that survive." Looks of dismay spread like a virus through the rebel leaders. "This will not be an easy victory, but I believe it will be worth the price we pay for it. Without the SoHcha shipyard, the Klingons will be hard-pressed to replenish their fleet—and that will be the advantage we need going forward. Unless we accomplish this objective first, all others will remain out of reach."

The Xenexian captain studied the plans with a sharp eye. "I'd like to have a bit more time to study these before I commit the *Excalibur* to the attack."

"We welcome your tactical advice, Captain," Picard said, "but you and your crew will not be part of the SoHcha mission." He glanced at K'Ehleyr, who switched the projection to the next part of his briefing. "The *Excalibur* will be leading a second, simultaneous attack. Your mission is to liberate Earth."

Looking as if Picard had just slapped him, Calhoun said, "What?"

"While the *Defiant* leads the strike against SoHcha, the *Excalibur* will crush the Alliance garrison on Earth and declare that world's independence."

Nervous murmurs burbled up from the throng. Calhoun waved for quiet, and the crowd hushed. "Why Earth? It has no strategic value. As a matter of fact, it's completely surrounded by the Alliance. Why plant our flag there?"

"Because we can," O'Brien quipped in his raspy Irish accent.

Picard nodded. "Exactly. It's true: Earth presently has no strategic value—at least, none recognized by the Alliance. But it has great *symbolic* value, Captain Calhoun. First, by liberating the former homeworld of the Terrans, we give them cause to celebrate. Reason for hope. It might seem frivolous to you, but don't underestimate its importance to a people enslaved. Second, by launching coordinated attacks on targets hundreds of light-years apart, we will be demonstrating to the Alliance—and all other powers in local space—that we possess the means and the will to project military force on a galactic scale."

Anger gave Calhoun a fearsome aspect. "But at what cost? How many lives are we sacrificing by splitting our forces for two attacks? I think we should hit SoHcha with everything we've got, with overwhelming force."

It was an argument for which K'Ehleyr had prepared Picard. "Tactics that seem obvious are sometimes wrong, Captain. We've conducted countless battle simulations in preparation for the attack on the shipyard. The fleet being deployed with General O'Brien is, we believe, of optimal size. A larger force will impede its own ability to maneuver at close range against the station. The result would be a sharp increase in friendly fire damage and casualties, and easier targeting for the Klingons." He added with an ironic smile, "Bigger is not always better."

Calhoun opened his mouth to respond, but his executive officer, Soleta, cut him off by muttering, "Don't even say it."

Picard lifted his eyes to take in the sea of faces, committing them to memory. "Not all of us will survive what comes tomorrow. But know this: If you should be among those who fall in the war to come, your names and your deeds will not be forgotten. This is no longer a humble resistance, no mere insurgency. For far too long, we have all lived in the darkness, alone in the night. But that time is coming to an end. We who have gathered here, hundreds of thousands of light-years from the nearest star, will be the agents of a new dawn."

O'Brien turned and offered Calhoun his hand. "Good luck, Captain."

Calhoun shook O'Brien's hand and smiled. "Good hunting, General."

In his best voice of authority, Picard said, "Man your ships!" The commanders dispersed, heading for the exits, and Picard watched them depart, wondering in pained silence how many of them he had just sent to their deaths.

Miles O'Brien returned to his stateroom aboard the *Defiant* in a contemplative mood, his thoughts burdened with grim anticipation of the mission upon which he and his crew were about to embark. As the door of his spartan quarters opened, he halted at the sight of Keiko. She had been pacing, but stopped and turned to face him as he stood in the doorway, regarding her as if she were a stranger.

She wrung her hands into a knot. "Hello, Miles."

He was momentarily lost for words. "Keiko."

"I apologize for dropping in unannounced."

He couldn't bear to look her in the eye. "What do you want?"

Her voice was tight with remorse. "I just wanted to see you. Before . . ." She gestured vaguely away, toward the unwritten future. "Just . . . before."

"Well, you've seen me." He stepped back and aside, then beckoned her out of his cabin. She looked shocked, hurt, and angry all at once.

"You won't even talk to me?"

O'Brien stood with his jaw clenched shut, fighting the urge to let loose a torrent of rage that would do no one any good. He pulled one hand down over his rough-whiskered mouth and chin, buying time in which to master his fury before he spoke. "What for, Keiko?"

"It's been weeks since we've seen each other."

Noting some crewmen rounding the corner at the far end of the corridor, O'Brien stepped inside his quarters and let the door close behind him to keep his conversation with Keiko private. "Not bloody long enough, in my opinion."

"How many times can I say I'm sorry?"

He crossed his arms. "I'm not sure it matters."

Stubborn as ever, she sat down on his bunk, uninvited. "Why not?"

A low growl rolled in his throat, a sound of pure vexation. This was not a conversation he wanted to have, and he resented that it was being forced upon him. "What can you possibly say to make me forget that you've been lying to me for two years? How can I forget all the lives that might've been saved if you'd told me the truth?"

Exasperated, she shot back, "You *know* why I couldn't do that."

"What? Because you were under *orders*? Is that supposed to excuse all the people you let die? All the people the other Ghemor murdered when she fragged Ashalla? All the folks who died when the Cardies took down Terok Nor?" He shook his head and looked away, fed up with her. "Makes me sick."

Grief had a stranglehold on Keiko's voice. "It makes *me* sick, too, Miles. Don't you think I *wanted* to save all those people? You have no idea how many times I begged Memory Omega to speed up its timetable, to step in and help."

"Fat lotta good it did."

"Damn you." She got up and faced off against him. "I made myself feel every one of those deaths, just like you did. I owned them, took responsibility for them. I won't let you act like I'm some heartless bitch and you're the patron saint of foot soldiers. I lost the same friends and cried at the same funerals you did, so don't you dare lecture me about the lives I might've saved—*because I know every one of them by name.*"

O'Brien still couldn't meet Keiko's gaze, but now it was because he felt ashamed. He recalled those nights that the two of them had lain awake, sharing memories of friends and acquaintances lost in action, or vowing to erect memorials to the fallen someday when the war was over and they had made a life someplace safe. Those were sad but cherished memories, but they felt tainted now by Keiko's deception, and as much as O'Brien wanted to ignore what he knew and live in the time that had been, he knew he was cursed like everyone else to live in the present.

"I don't doubt that you mourn those people now every bit as much as you did then," he said. "And I even believe you when you say you begged for Memory Omega to do something to help us. But that doesn't change the fact that you didn't tell us"—he corrected himself—"that you didn't tell *me*."

Keiko walked toward the door, and for a moment O'Brien thought she had surrendered her moral high ground. Then, as the door opened ahead of her, she stopped and looked back. "You know what it means to belong to something bigger than yourself. To fight for a cause that matters more than you do, and more than the people you love. Well, so do I, Miles. I was born into Memory Omega. I grew up in one of its secret bases. I was trained to be a field operative, to observe and report and not get involved. When I was sent to Terok Nor, I was just supposed to watch and listen. But after I met you, I couldn't sit by and do nothing. Helping you, fighting at your side, risking my life with you—*that* was my choice, Miles. Even when Memory Omega told me not to, even when they told me to walk away, I didn't, because I'd made my choice. *You* were my choice. You still are." She wiped a single tear from her cheek. "And you always will be."

He turned away, shamed by his own misting eyes. He brusquely sleeved the tears from his cheeks, then looked back at her. "You know I still love you."

"And I love you." A sad smile made her all the more beautiful. "The question is, can you forgive me?"

"If we survive the attack on the shipyard . . . ask me again tomorrow."

25

Nor Shall My Sword Sleep in My Hand

Despite the importance of the SoHcha Fleet Yards to the Empire's war machine, they afforded no prestige to the officers and enlisted personnel who served there, much to the chagrin of their commandant, General Roka. Klingon culture glorified combat experience above all else, and it had little regard for the behind-the-lines technical expertise it took to make the Empire's victories possible. Some days, Roka cursed whatever genetic quirk had gifted him with an aptitude for engineering rather than a talent for wielding a *bat'leth* or a knack for tactical planning, but his resentment was assuaged by the fact that he had been promoted into the only position in all of the Empire that permitted an engineer to attain the rank of general.

And with rank came privileges—not the least of which was the right to abuse one's subordinates with absolute impunity.

"How did you get this posting, J'mek? Did you blackmail someone?" Roka flung a data slate at the lieutenant, who was so young he could barely sport a full beard on his trembling chin. "I asked for results, not excuses!"

J'mek fumbled the data slate, dropped it, then scrambled to pick it up and resume his at-attention stance in front of Roka's desk. "Yes, General."

"Yes, what? *Fek'lhr*'s beard, boy—say something useful!"

The flustered lieutenant stammered, "The, um, tests of the cloaking device are, um, scheduled to resume to-morrow after the power fluctuations are fixed."

"Very well." He shooed the junior officer away. "Out."

Looking relieved, J'mek made a hasty retreat from Roka's office. As the door slid closed, the general stood and turned to look out the wide viewport that dominated the bulkhead behind his desk. The block of transparent aluminum had a microscopic layer on its interior surface that acted as a polarizing filter, to cut the harsh glare reflecting off the facility's numerous construction frames and the hulls of the starships being built around them. Though it would have been a necessary feature at nearly any orbital facility, it was especially critical at the SoHcha Fleet Yards, which had been constructed in relatively close orbit of its name-sake star in order to draw upon its nigh-endless re-serves of raw solar energy.

Just two more years and then I can retire, he reminded himself. The Klingon ideal of dying heroically in battle had never held any appeal for Roka, since the warriors had never seemed to have much regard for him. Freed of the illusion that he was destined for a place in *Sto-Vo-Kor*, he had dared to plan a very different kind of future. Though the Empire had little use for privatized industry, the Cardassians respected an individual's right to profit from dealing with the military. For the better part of the last decade, Roka had been planning a post-military career as a defense contractor inside the Cardassian Union. Though the recent troubles inside the Union had given him a moment of concern, Damar seemed to have restored order in a relatively expeditious manner, reviving Roka's confidence that he could enjoy a stable and reasonably affluent life on a Cardassian world.

He considered it a shame that he couldn't take the cloaking research with him when he left. The capture of the Romulan device, which had been far more advanced than anything the Klingons had possessed up to that point, had launched a flurry of analysis, reverse-engineering, and new developments. Design plans for entire fleets had been scrapped so that their spaceframes and warp geometries could be optimized to work with the new cloaking systems. And to ensure that the Romulans didn't make another quantum leap in the science of stealth before the Klingon Empire deployed its adaptation of their stolen cloak, an elite force had unleashed a thalaron weapon on Romulus, incinerating the homeworld and capital and transforming the few Romulans who survived the calamity into nomads.

Somewhere in the dark corners of Roka's imagination, he concocted the beginning of a plan to smuggle a copy of the cloak's schematics with him to Cardassia—and then a proximity alarm jolted him back into the moment. He spun and hurried out of his office into the command center just outside. Harsh white lights had snapped on, which meant the facility was at full alert. Moving into the center of the room, Roka barked, "Lankar! Report!"

His executive officer was hunched over the tactical display, apparently having shouldered aside the junior officer who normally manned the post. "Severe gravimetric disturbance, General!"

"Charge perimeter defenses," Roka ordered. "Arm all weapons and stand by to relay target coordinates to our patrol fleet!" He moved closer to Lankar. "What's causing that disturbance, Commander?"

"Unknown," Lankar said, his attention fixed on his console. "Distortion increasing, bearing five-eight mark nine. Range eighteen-point-four *qelIqams*!"

From a nearby weapons station, J'mek exclaimed, "That's *inside* the defense grid!"

"On-screen," Roka snapped, turning toward the main viewer. As the image switched to a view of the shipyard, the general's jaw slowly went slack. A wormhole spiraled open like a fiery blue flower unfurling in the night, and a fleet of ships raced from its mouth, weapons blazing. The command center quaked as one blast after another hammered its shields. Roka recognized a handful of the ships' designs, but several that led the attack were of a type he had never seen before. Reasoning he would identify them after they were dead, he shouted, "Return fire! Tell our fleet to engage and destroy!"

Disruptor blasts and torpedoes, fired from weapons platforms spread across the shipyard, converged on the enemy ships. Several were vaporized instantly, and others peeled off, burning and crippled. The ones that Roka didn't recognize, however, weathered the tempest of fire with ease. One barrage after another flared against those vessels' shields but did nothing to slow their advance.

An explosion ripped through the command center, peppering Roka, J'mek, and Lankar with shrapnel. The general collapsed to the deck with a white-hot chunk of twisted duranium protruding from his gut. He clutched impotently at the wound, unable to touch the burning-hot metal even as it seared his organs and cooked the skin of his abdomen black.

J'mek lay just out of arm's reach from Roka. The

lieutenant pressed his hands to his ravaged, bloody face. Roka feared that the wet, gurgling noise coming from the young engineer's throat was a scream with no larynx to give it voice.

Lankar clawed his way to his knees and clung with fierce pride to his failing console. "Critical hits, sir," he said. "Shields gone. Targeting sensors offline."

"Order gunners to use manual targeting," Roka said, choking out the words between agonized grunts. "Send all logs to the High Command, now."

"Transmitting," Lankar said, hanging on to his station with one hand and entering commands with the other. "The enemy is blocking our comms." Another thunderous concussion rocked the command center, knocking out the white action lights. Emergency lights activated, suffusing the center with the sickly green glow of chemical illumination. "Main power hub destroyed," Lankar said.

Roka watched the main viewscreen, horrified, as the shipyard's primary power-collection facility plunged toward the star that had fueled it. He knew that when it reached the corona, it would trigger a gargantuan stellar-mass ejection. For a moment he hoped he might at least have the satisfaction of knowing his killers would perish with him. Then he saw a new wormhole open, and the surviving enemy vessels vanished into it, abandoning the SoHcha facility to its fate. Roka wanted nothing more than to curse them as they fled, but his mouth was filling with blood welling up from his esophagus.

As the wormhole twisted shut and vanished, a blinding flash on the surface of the star served as the portent of Roka's imminent demise. He spat the blood from his mouth and laughed. "A warrior's death, after all," he spluttered. He grinned at Lankar. "I'll see you in *Sto-Vo-Kor*."

A moment later his world turned white, and his prediction came true.

It had been nearly a decade since Worf, the former regent, had exiled Miral to Earth for rejecting his crude advances. He had disguised Miral's banishment as a promotion by appointing her Intendant of Earth, a title of honor on most worlds in the Alliance. Earth, however, was a useless rock, a low-value Klingon possession long since stripped of precious elements. Its chief export now was cheap human slaves, culled from the few native survivors of the Alliance's conquest of their homeworld decades earlier.

Miral, however, had been shrewd enough not to let on that she viewed her so called punishment as a gift. The reason Worf had sent her to Earth, of all places, was because he had mistakenly believed he could embarrass her by calling attention to her sexual fetish for human men. From her point of view, he had simply granted her the one thing she desired more than anything: an endless supply of male human slaves to feed her insatiable appetite.

Stretched out on the massage table in her solarium, she had everything she had ever wanted. Two buff, young human men—one golden brown with raven hair, the other pale and blond, both shirtless—to massage her, one on each side. Another beautiful young man, barely old enough to no longer be a boy, his skin dark like *raktajino* and his head shaved smooth as glass, fetched Miral's drinks and served her meals. At night, she enjoyed her most exotic specimens of human manhood: One was as tall, broad, and muscled as a Klingon, with hair the color of fire and a ruddy complexion; the other was effeminate and slender, his body nearly hairless even though he had flowing brown tresses to rival Miral's own. When Miral wanted a challenge, a bit of exercise, she used the ginger male; the *be'HomloD* she reserved for nights when she wanted to be pampered and adored.

Exiled in paradise, Miral reflected, luxuriating under the touch of her magnificent masseurs. *How lucky I am that Worf was a fool.* Outside her sunroom, wavetops tore themselves to pieces across a seabreak of jagged rocks, and the hissing of sea foam whispered the secrets of the deep into Miral's waking dreams.

Then the squawk of an alarm shattered her bliss to pieces.

Cursing, she pushed herself up and off the massage table. Her slaves backed away, well practiced at avoiding Miral's wrath when she was in a hurry. The dark brown man-boy hurried forward from wherever it was he stood awaiting her summonses, and he held open her bathrobe. She slipped into the loose-fitting garment of brushed Bolian linen and let the slave dress its line across her shoulders, then she tied it shut and stepped into her sandals. "This had better not be a false alarm," she muttered, stepping briskly toward her private transport pad.

In a cascade of golden light accompanied by a mellisonant hum, Miral went from her beach house in the Maldives to her office at the Klingon Consulate in Okinawa. Erected atop the ruins of Spock's former palace, the Empire's patch of sovereign soil on the homeworld of its former rival was little more than a bunker, but it was as secure a headquarters as Miral had ever seen.

She stepped out of her office and started shouting questions and orders. "What the hell is going on? Somebody activate the planetary defense screens, and power up the nadion-pulse cannons." Spotting her chief of staff lurking on the far side of the situation room and trying not to be noticed, she directed her ire at him. "Szopa, you Cardassian bug, get over here!"

The long-limbed, gawky Cardassian man rushed to heed Miral's call, but she found his gait so awkward and ungainly that she could hardly bear to watch him. He arrived at the steps leading to her office and looked up at her. "Yes, Intendant?"

"You're out of breath," she said with disgust. "Do you need a medic?"

"No, Intendant." Composing himself, he added, "We're under attack."

"You don't say." She descended the stairs in quick strides and shouldered Szopa out of her path. "By whom?"

He followed her to the central command table. "The lead ship matches the description of the rebel dreadnought *Excalibur*."

She spun around to glare at him. "Calhoun's ship?" As soon as Szopa gave her the first hint of a nod of confirmation, she cried out, "Destroy that ship the moment it's in range!"

"That's what I'm trying to tell you, Intendant: It's already—"

A deafening boom, like the strike of an angry god's hammer, drowned out every other sound inside the command center. Screens and consoles went dark, and the ground beneath Miral's feet continued to shake for several seconds.

Miral pounded the side of her fist on the nearest console until it stuttered back to full function. Then she looked down and saw Szopa cowering on the floor. "Stand up or I will kill you like the vermin you are."

Szopa got to his feet with terrible reluctance. "As I

was saying, Intendant—the attack fleet appeared out of nowhere, from a wormhole in orbit above us."

More blasts rocked the consulate, and dust rained down from the fractured ceiling, coating all the consoles in fine gray powder. Furious, Miral grabbed Szopa by his armored breastplate and pulled him down so his nose was against hers. "Our orbital platforms should be *shredding* that fleet! Why aren't they firing?"

"They're trying," he said. "We all are, but there's an error in the system. We can't get any of our weapons to fire."

She threw him against the console. "Tell the gun crews to fire manually!"

"They can't!" He was hyperactive from panic. "They all keep saying they can't make their hands work the controls! They try to obey, but they can't!" He pointed at the flood of emergency bulletins flooding into the comm stations. "There are slave uprisings all over the planet! What are we going to do?"

It was impossible, but it was happening. Every incoming signal brought news of a new revolt, another mass murder of the planet's Klingon masters by their slaves, another gun battery or military installation blasted into slag by Calhoun's ship and its attack fleet. In less time than it would have taken for Miral to order dinner from her kitchen, her private paradise had been laid waste.

She stepped back from the console and pushed Szopa forward to take her place. "Organize a counterattack. I'll contact Qo'noS for reinforcements."

Before he could protest or ask questions, Miral was moving up the stairs, back into her office. There was no time to waste. She activated her personal transporter and set it to send her back to her beach house. The flurry of light and sound enveloped her, and then she savored the fragrance of warm air off the sea. She sprinted across her poolside terrace toward the landing pad on the west side of the compound, where she kept an unmarked personal shuttle for just such a crisis as the one that was engulfing her. *No time to pack,* she told herself, burying the pangs of regret she felt at abandoning her wardrobe, as well as several mementos whose value was purely sentimental but whose loss stung keenly all the same.

As she rounded the corner of her villa, she saw her coterie of beautiful men gathered at the entrance of her shuttle, waiting for her. *How adorable,* she thought as she ran to them. *As loyal as gelded* targs.

Half a breath before she could tell her ginger man to open the shuttle's hatch, the *be'HomloD* drew a disruptor from his loosely drooping sleeve and aimed it at her. Miral had just enough time to wonder what the pretty man was doing but not enough time to ask before he pulled the trigger and shot her in the chest.

The blast brought her to a halt. A moment later her legs started to feel like weak rubber, and she dropped to her knees. Her bevy of male slaves prowled toward her, all of them except the *be'HomloD* drawing knives from under their tunics. Their eyes were hard and cold, just as vengeance demanded.

Miral did not beg for mercy. It would not have become her as a Klingon.

Her slaves set upon her with the savagery of wild animals, their blades ice-cold as they plunged into Miral's body again and again, an orgy of violence many years in the making. As she vanished beneath their flurry of betrayal, her final thought was of her missing and disgraced half-human daughter, B'Elanna.

I should have slain her in the womb.

26

A Price Paid in Blood

O'Brien was roused by the distant comfort of human voices. Pinned beneath half a ton of warped metal and sparking cables, he could barely breathe, let alone move. Except for intermittent flashes from a severed plasma line or an occasional fall of sparks from somewhere overhead, all he saw was darkness. He wasn't certain how long he'd been unconscious after the overhead of the *Defiant*'s bridge had caved in, but he had awoken to the falling hum of the ship dropping out of warp and maneuvering on impulse. Several long, agony-filled minutes later he had heard the buzzing and clanging of rescue teams beginning work somewhere above him.

They'll get to you, he told himself, willing his spirits not to flag. *Just hang on.* He took comfort in the familiar racket of groaning metal and crackling hisses, which he knew from experience meant that someone with a plasma torch was cutting their way down through the wreckage to him. He sucked air through dry teeth and realized that his mouth was parched and he was thirsty as hell. That wasn't a good sign, he knew. It probably meant he had suffered an internal injury. For a moment he hoped that some impatient soul would simply lock a transporter onto his life sign and beam him out from under that heap of duranium. Then he remembered that beaming someone out of a mess like this—without knowing whether their body is depending on a penetrating piece of debris to prevent them from bleeding to death in the span of a breath—could be disastrous.

He tried to dredge up his last memory from before everything had come tumbling down, but his mind felt foggy, scattered. Conjuring images of ships dodging artillery fire while maneuvering at breakneck speeds through tight spaces in a shipyard felt right, but he couldn't be certain he hadn't imagined it.

White light bent its way through gaps in the junk pile atop O'Brien's chest, as if the beam itself were searching for him. More pulses of bright light made him wince and left him seeing purple-black afterimages. He kept his eyes closed as two more cutting tools tore through metal with small, fiery jets of energy. The voices that had roused him back to consciousness drew closer and became clearer. Someone shouted, "Lift!" Grunts and groans of painful exertion accompanied a sudden decrease in the pressure on O'Brien's sternum. He sucked in a full breath like a drowning man breaking through the surface of a black sea, and he savored the sensation of profound relief.

Ponderous slabs of the ship's inner hull were dropped to the deck with resonant clangs, or dragged aside with a hellish screech of metal on metal. Several beams of blinding light converged upon O'Brien's face as someone asked, "General O'Brien? Are you all right, sir?"

All he could say was, "Get me out of here."

Silhouetted figures worked in a frenzy, and within minutes they exhumed O'Brien from what he had feared might become his tomb. A male Tellarite kneeled beside him and scanned him with a medical device. "You have internal injuries," said the porcine-faced physician.

"I figured as much. Can I get some water?"

The doctor waved over a human woman. She crouched beside O'Brien and lifted a small canteen to his lips. "Drink slowly," she said. "Small sips."

It took all his willpower not to wrest the canteen from her hand and guzzle it empty in one swallow. He restrained himself to half a mouthful at a time. After his second swig, his eyes had partially adjusted to the light. Squinting at his caregivers, he noticed they both were wearing the black and gray uniforms of Memory Omega personnel. "What ship are you from?"

"*Enterprise,*" the Tellarite said. "I'm Doctor Mov, and this is Nurse Milioti."

Looking around, O'Brien saw that not much of the *Defiant*'s bridge was intact. Bulkheads had buckled inward, deck plates had heaved and bent, and most of the overhead had crashed down. A thick haze of dust lingered in the air, and the air was sharp with the acrid tang of burnt circuitry and overheated metal. "How did we get here?"

"Through a wormhole generated by the *Enterprise,*" Mov said.

"No. I mean, how did *Defiant* survive the battle?"

"Your chief engineer, Muñiz. He and his team transferred helm and weapons control to engineering and navigated clear of the crossfire. They saved your ship."

O'Brien nodded. He was proud of Quiqué, but his face felt slack, and he couldn't muster any praise more effusive than, "Good man."

Milioti said, "You're in shock, General. Stay still until we can transport you to the *Enterprise* for surgery."

Two men, a Vulcan and a Bolian, carried another

survivor out of the wreckage and laid him with tender care beside O'Brien. As the rescuers stepped away, he saw that the man at his side was Samaritan Bowers. Through years of war, O'Brien had learned to recognize the fading light in a dying man's eyes, and he saw it now in Bowers, who asked in a weak, rasping shade of his rich voice, "Did . . . did we make it?"

Mustering all his strength, O'Brien lifted one hand and rested it on Bowers's shoulder. "Yes, Sam. We made it. Well done." The news seemed to give Bowers a measure of peace as his life slipped away from him.

A cry of rage and sorrow filled the bridge. Fearing what he'd see but knowing he had to look, O'Brien turned his head toward the bitter, funereal keening and saw Ezri draped over the scorched and twisted body of her wife, Leeta. As Ezri's wails shrank to small, desperate sobs, listening to the young Trill weep beside her beloved became more than O'Brien could bear. His stoic mask cracked and then crumbled, and heavy sobs shook his chest. Tears rolled from his eyes and cut warm trails across his grime-covered cheeks. These people were his family, and they lay strewn around him, shattered and bleeding, and there was nothing he could do to help them, no words of comfort he could offer. Worst of all, there was no solace he could grant himself, because he had led them there.

Bereaved and broken, all he could think about was Keiko.

Doctor Mov stepped between O'Brien and Ezri as he said, "One for transport directly to sickbay. Energize."

O'Brien had just enough time to palm the tears from his face before the transporter beam snared him and whisked him in a wash of light and sound from the bridge of the *Defiant* to the sickbay of the *Enterprise*. He materialized on a state-of-the-art biobed, a few meters away from a team of surgeons in smocks and masks who were getting ready to perform the latest in that day's string of medical miracles. He turned his head as he heard Picard's voice.

"I'm glad you're still with us, General." Picard stood at O'Brien's bedside, his uniform pristine and untouched by the battle. "We've scored a great victory."

Sick with grief and seething with anger, O'Brien lay down and rolled onto his side, away from Picard. "Not from where I was standing, we didn't."

Barely able to see where he was going, Tuvok navigated by memory as he carried Seska toward sickbay. The corridors inside the *Geronimo* were pitch dark and curtained with smoke, and the turbolifts had stopped working after the ship lost all power to primary and secondary systems, forcing him to carry the wounded over his shoulder while he climbed steep emergency access ladders one-handed.

He stepped over the body of a person who had died mere paces from the ship's tiny medical bay. From what he had seen while searching for survivors, the dead outnumbered the living aboard the small attack ship, and judging from the blood-soaked spectacle that greeted him in sickbay, he suspected many of those currently counted among the wounded soon would join the ranks of the fallen.

The ship's Denobulan medic, Tropp, noted Tuvok's arrival—and the unconscious Cardassian woman in his arms—with a tired glower. "Put her over there," he said, gesturing toward an empty spot on the deck by the aft bulkhead.

Tuvok eased Seska to the deck and then joined Tropp, who was performing a crude job of abdominal surgery on one of the ship's mechanics. "Is there anything I can do to assist?"

"Stop bringing me wounded," Tropp grumbled. "I can't help most of 'em, anyway. Might as well save time and space 'em now."

Looking around, Tuvok had his doubts regarding the accuracy of Tropp's diagnostic skills. "Perhaps I could perform basic triage and prioritize the—"

"The ones who really need my help are as good as dead. We're out of most drugs, half my surgical tools don't work, and we have no blood for transfusions. Tell me who has superficial wounds, and I'll do what I can for them."

Hiding his contempt for Tropp's fatalism, Tuvok surveyed the room full of injured people. "Seska has serious burns, but a dermal regenerator should suffice to repair most of—"

"Fine, she's next. Who else?"

"That man's leg is broken. If we fix it, he—"

"Osteofuser's busted. Best I can give him is a splint."

Tuvok eyed the scarce supplies that were at hand. He reached into a nearby cabinet and took out a medkit. "May I borrow this?"

Tropp replied with defensive suspicion, "For what?"

"I intend to see if anyone on the bridge requires medical attention."

The medic harrumphed and returned to botching his surgical procedure. "Fine. While you're up there, see if you can get us moved up in the queue for help from those *freknarka* at Memory Omega."

"I will see what I can do." Medkit in hand, Tuvok

abandoned Tropp to his impromptu abattoir and made his way forward.

In the passageway that led to the bridge, Tuvok was halted by the echoes of desperate sobbing followed by bitter, muffled screams. The hatch was ajar, and he edged toward it, his steps light and all but silent. Sidling up to the doorway, he peeked through it.

Neelix was slumped limply in the center chair, his head tilted sideways at an unnatural angle. Kes kneeled in front of him, with her arms wrapped around his torso and her face against his chest as she wept. The rest of the bridge crew lay on the deck at her feet, their bodies torn and blackened, their eyes open but unseeing.

At a loss for words, Tuvok lurked outside the doorway, reluctant to intrude upon Kes's grief. He chastised himself for his absent-mindedness; overwhelmed by the relentless clamor and confusion of the battle, and then by the severity of the damage to the ship and the sheer number of casualties, it had never occurred to him that the loss of main power would lower the force field on Kes's jury-rigged cell, or that she might be loose and wandering the ship. *It is of no consequence,* he decided. *The issue of her confinement can be revisited later, at a more appropriate time.* He backpedaled slowly from the hatchway, intending to leave Kes in peace.

Her voice was low and raw and laced with bilious fury.

"I know you're there, Tuvok. I can hear you."

The challenge in her words was implicit. Tuvok stepped forward and slipped sideways past the half-open door. He met her stare of cold hatred with humbly downcast eyes. "I am sorry for your loss."

"No you're not." She stood and stalked toward him.

"You're a Vulcan. You don't *let* yourself have feelings. Not for him, not for me, not for anyone." Though she was many centimeters shorter than Tuvok, she was fearless as she invaded his personal space to confront him. "You have no idea how much he meant to me, how deeply I loved him. I would have gone anywhere to find him, given anything to be with him. And now he's gone forever, because of you. He's *dead* because of you!"

"You are mistaken. I did not kill Captain Neelix."

"Oh, *yes, you did*." Kes stabbed at Tuvok's chest with her index finger. "*You* flipped the switch on whatever this thing is that your friends put in my head. *You* took away all my power. If it hadn't been for you, I could have *saved* him, Tuvok!" She pointed at the bodies surrounding them. "I could've saved them all! And everyone else in our fleet who died today! But you didn't let me—so now their blood's on your hands. And I will *never* forgive you for that."

"Your accusation would be far more damning if I believed for a moment that you would actually have used your abilities to aid the rebellion, and not just to flee from known space with Neelix as your telepathically enslaved love object."

She spat in his face. "You disgust me!" As Tuvok wiped the spittle from his cheek, Kes stormed past him and darted through the half-obstructed doorway.

He listened to her receding footsteps. Hoping her sensitive Ocampa ears could still hear him, he replied, "I assure you, the feeling is mutual."

27

The Wine of Desolation

Though Klag had entertained his share of foul moods over the years, few equaled the one that animated him as he stormed through the doors of the High Command's strategic command center. The cause and object of his wrath, General Goluk, stood waiting for him in the center of the situation floor.

A guard noted Klag's unheralded entrance and snapped to attention as he shouted, "All hail Him Who Holds—"

Klag snapped, "Shut up, you *petaQ*!" He fixed his rage-knit brow on Goluk. "When I'm roused in the middle of the night, I expect to hear a reason why, General." A glance at the holographic map of the Empire beneath his feet revealed several active areas of interest. "What in the name of Kahless is going on?"

"A great deal, My Lord," Goluk said. "Excellent news from the Gorn border. We've crushed their forces on Ogat with ease, as I predicted. Meanwhile, the Fourth and Eighth fleets have begun their invasion of the Hegemony. Several planets have already fallen, including Seudath, Karazek, and Ozannot. If we push on, we can expect to land forces on the Gorn homeworld in six weeks."

"What do you mean *if* we push on?"

Goluk gestured into the heart of the Empire's territory. In a sepulchral voice, he said, "There have also been less fortuitous developments in the past few hours. The rebels are back—and they've destroyed our primary fleet yards at SoHcha."

Certain he must have misheard the general, Klag said, "They did what?"

"It's confirmed, My Lord."

"How extensive is the damage?"

The question seemed to pain Goluk. "The facility isn't *damaged*. It's been completely destroyed, along with every starship it was building."

It was simply unbelievable to Klag. "How? It's located in the center of the Empire. It's surrounded by the First Fleet and four tachyon pulse networks that can detect cloaked ships. How did they get anywhere near it?"

"Our intel is incomplete at the moment, but some survivors report seeing the rebel fleet arrive and withdraw through an artificial wormhole."

The more Klag learned, the more he wished he'd ignored Goluk's summons and stayed in bed. "Where in *Fek'lhr*'s name did Calhoun get his hands on that kind of technology?"

"That's the next fact of interest," Goluk said. "This attack was led by the *Defiant*—and supported by ships of a kind none of our people have seen before. The same kind of ships that participated in the *Excalibur*'s attack on Earth."

"There was an attack on Earth?"

"Yes, My Lord. At the exact same moment as the attack on the shipyard."

Dread churned sour bile from Klag's gut up his

throat into his mouth. "Let me guess. They, too, appeared without warning from a wormhole."

Goluk nodded. "Correct. The fact that both forces are using the same previously unknown technology suggests that one of our worst-case scenarios has come to pass: The two rebel factions have joined forces and become exponentially stronger as a result." He tapped commands into a data slate and shifted the display beneath them to a long-range scan of the Terran system. "Earth's orbital defenses have been wiped out, and its surface artillery has been captured. We've also received reports that Intendant Miral deserted her post during the battle."

"Have her executed immediately."

"She's already been murdered by her slaves."

Klag frowned at the missed opportunity. "Pity." Seeing several other star systems ringed in flashing white symbols of distress, he asked, "I presume you're far from done giving me bad news."

"Unfortunately correct, My Lord. In addition to losing the fleet yards, we've also lost the prototype for the recently captured Romulan cloaking device, as well as all its specifications."

"What about the backup copies? The ones in the lab on Ty'Gokor."

The general's face darkened with shame. "Erased— by accident, or so the research team claims."

That news stank of a betrayal. "Have them executed immediately."

"Yes, My Lord." He switched the hologram to the Tiburon system.

Dreading the answer, Klag asked, "What's happening there?"

"Slave uprising. The first of many, on several worlds across the Empire." Widening the scope of the star map, he added, "There have been revolts and riots on Ajilon, Korinar, Krios, and Cambra."

If there was a connection, Klag didn't see it. "Those worlds are all dozens of light-years apart. How can they all suddenly become madhouses at once?"

"We don't know," Goluk confessed.

"Never mind the cause, then. Focus on the solution. How long until we bring those worlds back under control?"

Embarrassed, Goluk averted his eyes as he answered, "We're unable to say at this time, Regent. Infighting has slowed our military response to the crisis."

The scenario unfolding before Klag started to sound ominously familiar. "What sort of *infighting* are you referring to?"

"Irrational violence," Goluk said. "Regiments plunging into battle frenzies for no reason and going on blood-drunk rampages, slaughtering civilians and one another. Starship crews opening fire on one another. Utter madness."

Klag nodded. "Yes, General. I think that's exactly the right word: *madness*." The grand-scale picture of what was transpiring became clear to him, and it troubled him greatly. There seemed to be no unifying element to all the reports of chaos engulfing the Empire, but there was no mistaking its pedigree. The Cardassians had figured it out, Klag realized, but only after it was too late.

It was all about the slaves.

He wasn't sure how the slaves were involved, whether they were the cause or merely the impetus for an external political actor's intervention, but he no longer cared about that distinction. If the slaves were the problem, he knew the solution, and it was one he was more than happy to implement. Klag had never liked the Empire's institutions of domestic slavery—not because he thought it immoral but because he believed it made strong warriors soft. Slaves made life too easy, too comfortable, and those were the kinds of sins that Kahless had long ago warned would dull any warrior's fighting edge. Having spent his life as a soldier, Klag had never been able to afford a personal slave until he became a general, and by then he'd had no wish for one. Sadly, the same could not be said for many of his peers; he had known far too many members of the Klingon elite who had succumbed to the temptation of enhancing their social standing by adorning their household with a Vulcan slave or a Terran eunuch.

Now fate had given Klag a chance to purge the Empire of that abominable vice, and he resolved not to waste the opportunity. He filled the massive chamber with his voice. "This is how the troubles began inside the Cardassian Union. It cost them entire worlds, whole fleets. I won't see us suffer the same fate."

Goluk and several other officers inside the command center exchanged worried glances. The general asked warily, "What do you propose, My Lord?"

"We'll solve this problem the same way the Cardassians did." He flashed a malevolent smile. "We just won't wait so long to do it."

Damar politely acknowledged the Cardassian handmaiden who removed his empty dinner plate and then moved on to clear the setting to Damar's left. Though he had always loathed the picayune details of decorum that governed formal dinners with the senior members of the Detapa Council, his inherited role as its Supreme Legate made his attendance at the state function a necessity rather than a formality.

He sat with his back to the window and feigned an air of polite regard for his three dining companions. To his left was Councillor Rajak, a blunt-faced man of middling years whose girth was exceeded only by his bluster. Opposite Damar sat Gulal, who at the age of thirty-nine was the youngest of the three senior members and was also the only woman currently serving on the council. Seated on Damar's right was Councillor Menaar, the tall and gaunt elder statesman of the group. As was customary, they waited for the servants to leave before resuming any talk of sensitive matters of state. When the last server had exited, Rajak was the first to pick up the conversational baton and run with it. "Quelling the slave revolts was only the first step to security," he said. "You've seen the latest briefings, yes?"

"Of course," Damar said.

Gulal leaned forward, her mien conspiratorial. "Then you must see what's happening. Prominent council members disappearing. Captains of industry and major executives being assassinated by unknown professionals." She cast knowing glances at Menaar and Rajak. "It's the Obsidian Order."

"We don't know that," Menaar cautioned.

Indignation animated Rajak's fleshy face. "Of course we know that, you old fool! Who else would it be? Who *could* it be?" He looked at Damar, as if expecting support or at least affirmation. "It's a coup in the making! You see that, yes?"

"I see unsolved crimes that are still under investigation." Damar picked up his glass of *kanar* and affected an air of nonchalance. "I think it would be imprudent to leap to conclusions in the absence of evidence."

Menaar raised his own glass in salute to Damar. "Wise counsel."

Gulal seemed poised to make a counterargument when two servants returned from the kitchen carrying the evening's desserts. Conversation halted while the young female server set plates of *huseka,* a traditional and decadent dessert, before the four politicians, and her male colleague refilled everyone's glasses with *kanar*. Afforded a moment to collect his thoughts, Damar reminded himself to err on the side of caution and discretion in conversations such as this. One never knew when or where the Obsidian Order might be listening, or who might be acting as their agent. For all he knew, Gulal might be spouting her conspiracy theories as a lure, seeking to entrap Damar into uttering a seditious remark. Of course, what troubled him most about her line of inquiry was that he feared she might be right—that the Obsidian Order was moving in the shadows to assert control over the Union during its moment of weakness and confusion. All the same, no good would come of talking about it.

As the servants returned to the kitchen, Damar decided another change of subject was in order. "I think we can all agree that recent events present us with more pressing challenges. After months of eluding us, the rebels have struck two decisive blows at once. I can't recall them ever being so bold before."

"The bad news," Menaar said, "is that the two rebel factions have united into one, and wield new technologies of unknown origin. The good news is that both attacks hurt the Klingons far more than they hurt us." He shoveled a heaping spoonful of *huseka* into his mouth.

Gulal looked offended by the elder politician's remark. "You speak as if the Klingons were our enemies instead of our allies."

Rajak looked askance at her. "Look at the latest intelligence from the border. The Klingons are gearing up to invade our space and turn us into a protectorate. If it weren't for the new insurgency by the Talarians, we'd already be at war." He pushed away his untouched dessert. "The Klingons think we're weak and ripe for conquest."

Menaar cast a hard look across the table at Rajak. "We *are* weak."

Sensing an opportunity, Damar said, "Which is exactly why we should be consolidating our strength. It's time to regroup and choose our battles with greater care. I agree with both of you—the Klingons know they have us at a disadvantage, and they hope to reinforce their own weakened position by destabilizing ours."

"Let's say you're correct," Rajak said. "What do you propose we do?"

All eyes fell upon Damar, who set down his spoon and folded his hands on his lap as he leaned back, attempting to appear relaxed and thoughtful. "Clearly, the rebels have made significant advances in their technology and numbers, and the new political axis of the Taurus Pact has left us on the defensive. If we had the support of the Klingons, these threats might be surmountable. But if our allies betray us, we can't prevail against such odds. One of these conflicts needs to be resolved—or at least postponed—by political means rather than military force."

"Half the legates in the Central Command want to

make a preemptive assault on the Taurus Pact," Menaar said. "The other half want to launch a sneak attack against the Klingons. Which would you choose, Damar? If you had to."

Damar hadn't expected to be put on the spot so blatantly, but the deed was done. He sipped his *kanar* as a stalling tactic while he considered his answer. "The Klingons," he said, setting down his glass. "Facing them will entail fighting on a single front. Engaging the Taurus Pact would mean establishing three fronts nearly a hundred light-years from one another."

Gulal shook her head. "You're forgetting something, Legate. The people overwhelmingly favor the invasion and conquest of Bajor. They see its secession and the defeat of the Ninth Order as a slap in the face of all Cardassians."

"That's because they've been brainwashed by Obsidian Order propaganda," Damar said. "The Order wants us to overextend ourselves and be humiliated on Bajor so that they'll have an excuse to seize power." Reining in his contempt for the easily manipulated masses, he continued in a calmer vein. "I won't rule out a future retribution against Bajor, but this is not the time. Our first priority has to be preparing for war with the Klingons. To that end, we need to broker a truce with the Taurus Pact."

Rajak asked, "Why them? Why not with the rebels?"

"That's a terrible idea," scolded Menaar. "We can't afford to legitimize the rebels as political actors. Besides, even if we wanted to do something so ridiculous, we don't have any trusted diplomatic channels to the rebellion."

Gulal pressed her palms on the tabletop and leaned

forward to harangue Menaar. "As if your way is any less insane? Negotiating our own peace with the Taurus Pact would abrogate our treaty with the Klingons. The Alliance would be dissolved, and the Klingons could rightly lay the blame at our feet. Then their attack would be seen as reactive rather than preemptive."

Damar was baffled by her reasoning. "So what? To whom would such a distinction make the least bit of difference? The point in all of this, Gulal, is that our fight with the Klingons is inevitable. If we're to survive it, much less emerge triumphant, we need to avoid splitting our focus. We must fight one war at a time."

Her frown was unyielding. "The conquest of Bajor can't be sidelined so casually, Supreme Legate. The people want revenge—and if they don't get it, incumbents such as ourselves will face serious consequences in the next election."

"If we lose our war with the Klingons, there won't *be* a next election."

Gulal broke eye contact and poked distractedly at her dessert. "I hope you can be so cavalier when the people go to the polls to vote us out."

"Relax, Gulal. The Obsidian Order rigs the results, anyway." Damar looked at Rajak. "Contact your friends in the foreign service and have a covert diplomatic mission sent to the Taurus Pact. I want a cease-fire in place before the Klingons cross the border." He turned toward Menaar. "Talk to Legate Temar at Central Command. Tell him I want to see new invasion plans for Bajor immediately, and make sure that request gets leaked to the press. That should keep the people *and* the Obsidian Order placated while we negotiate with the Taurus Pact."

Menaar downed the last of his *kanar* and swallowed with a gratified exhalation. "And if the Central Command should play its part too well and actually launch an invasion of Bajor? What then?"

Lifting his own glass to take a desperately needed drink, Damar said, "Hope the Terrans choose that moment to hit the Klingons again."

Regent Klag had entered the shadowy swelter of the High Council's chamber inside the Great Hall expecting to be assailed by a storm of self-righteous outrage, and the councillors did not disappoint him. They surrounded his throne in a dense knot, so that no matter what way he turned he was met by a wall of angry faces.

Declarations of "You had no right!" overlapped with cries of "How dare you make such a decision without the council!" Klag let the waves of fury wash over him, paying them no heed. He had done what he'd known was right, and he had no regrets. He could have endured the council's rebuke for hours—until K'mpar, the young hothead, made the mistake of grabbing Klag's ceremonial stole.

"Who are you to order the executions of millions?"

Klag seized K'mpar's hand, twisted it till the wrist snapped, and stood from his throne, forcing the young councillor to the floor. "Who am I? I am the Regent of the Klingon Empire! I am He Who Holds the Throne for Him Who Shall Return! I am the agent of Kahless in this world!" He let go of the younger man's wrist and kicked him in the face. Teeth and fuchsia spittle flecked the robes of the councillors nearest K'mpar, who crumpled in a stunned heap. Meeting the stares of the council with his own unwavering gaze, Klag addressed them in a voice of pride and power. "I had the Empire's slaves put to death as a matter of imperial security. I had reason to suspect they were acting as a fifth column inside our civilization, providing aid and comfort to our enemies, and fomenting chaos and violence among our people. For the good of all Klingons, I had these disruptive elements neutralized."

"You mean you had all our slaves executed," Hegron raged. "Tens of millions of them, all over the Empire, cut down in the streets!"

"Better them than us," Klag said.

Korvog shouldered his way forward and pointed a finger at Klag. "And are you prepared to pay for all those slaves, Klag? Do you have that kind of fortune?" He turned and played to the room. "With one word, he erased billions in profits from our Empire!" Looking back at Klag, he added, "How *generous* you are, Regent, when you're spending everyone else's wealth!"

"Never mind the economic losses," added Councillor Qolka, a crooked-nosed, blister-faced horror of a man whose face made even hardened warriors flinch. "What about the blow to our prestige? Suddenly, we're not strong enough to keep our slaves in check? We're so afraid of our servants that our only recourse is to put them down like rabid *targs*? Damn you, Klag, you've made us the laughingstocks of the galaxy!"

One councillor after another piled on, reading lists of factories and agricultural colonies that would be unable to meet their quotas without their armies of slaves. Shortages of everything from fuel and food to raw materials and weapons were prophesied with absolute certainty. Klag listened to them drone on, maligning him as if he had just written the Empire's epitaph rather than delivered it from an enemy that had been hiding in plain sight, killing it from within.

Finally, his patience expired. He stood and slammed the end of his ceremonial staff three times on the dais. The ear-splitting cracks silenced the councillors and gave Klag the floor. "Stop whining," he said, his voice rough with contempt. "A true Klingon doesn't care about money, or what the *novpu'* think of us. What matters is that an enemy has been slain, and the Empire is secure."

Korvog shot back, "*Secure?* The rebels destroyed our main fleet yard! They've liberated Earth! We're under siege by the Taurus Pact, and our allies are powerless to help us. Each day our foes grow stronger, and we lose ground. You call this security?"

"He's right," Hegron said. "Not since the loss of Praxis have we been this compromised." He pointed at Klag. "And it happened on *your* watch, one-arm."

Qolka added, "The loss of Earth and the fleet yard has our rivals talking. If we can't defend a world in the heart of our own territory, they say, which of our other possessions are ripe for the taking? Where else have we overextended our reach? Already, the Kinshaya are moving fleets toward the former Romulan Star Empire. And thanks to your blunders, Klag, there's nothing we can do to stop them."

"That's not the least of his failures," said Hegron. "The rebels' victory at Earth has given them credibility. Several of the neutral powers in local space are beginning to talk of supporting the rebellion if it can carve a new nation out of ours. All the rebels would need is a few more systems under their control, and powers such as the Taurus Pact might start treating them like equals."

Klag felt a dangerous shift in the room's mood. It was tipping over the edge that separated simple anger from all-out revolt, mere dissension from violence. Unless he turned its tide away from himself and against an external enemy, it soon would swallow him whole, and he would find himself without allies while facing one challenger after another for the throne. *And even if I defeat those willing to face me in open combat,* he knew, *the others will resort to assassination.*

He needed to assert his dominance and demonstrate his leadership of the council and the Empire, and he needed to do so quickly. "The rebellion will not have a chance to gain that foothold," he said. "Their strikes on Earth and SoHcha were bold, but make no mistake about this—they suffered heavy losses for their victories. They didn't escape those battles unbloodied." He waved his staff in an arc that forced the councillors to step back from his dais. "They don't have the numbers or the *yoHjaq* to do anything more than hit and run. They're nothing but brigands. Pirates. Well-armed harriers."

"Harriers that have left us without our primary shipyard," Qolka said.

"For now," Klag said. "And I hear the same rumors you do—of our galactic neighbors whispering behind our back in support of the gnat that buzzes our ears. But that will all come to an end soon enough, I assure you. I've set a plan in motion. One that will guarantee no other power in local space will dare to offer the rebels their support ever again. And when the rebels see what we're capable of, and what we're prepared to do, that knowledge will bring them to their knees."

28

Love in Wartime

Three weeks had been more than enough time for Memory Omega's automated repair bots at Erebus Station to rebuild the *Defiant* inside and out, but it had felt like nowhere near enough time for O'Brien to rebuild his crew's confidence—or his own. No matter how many times Picard and those backing him insisted that the rebellion had stunned the Alliance, all that O'Brien could think of were the people he had lost, the lives that had been sacrificed to score tactical victories of dubious merit. The dead weren't statistics to him; they had been his friends, the only ones he had ever really known. To him, they were his only kin.

Reliving days and moments long past, he walked the corridors of the station's residential quarters, following the signs to a meeting he had avoided for as long as possible but that could no longer be postponed. He arrived at his destination and hesitated. For a moment he considered turning away, going back the way he'd come, and trying to make do with what crew he had left. *Don't be stupid,* he castigated himself. *This is no time to break in a novice*. He pressed the door signal and waited. Several seconds passed with no response from within. Thinking he'd misread the chrono, he checked it again. He was on time.

I've come this far. Might as well give it one more try.

He pressed the door signal again. Moments later, he heard Tigan's faint voice from behind the door. "Come in."

The door unlocked and slid open with a soft hiss. O'Brien stepped inside Tigan's quarters, which were as generic as everyone else's. All the lights were off except one in the corner, behind a chair. As he moved farther inside and heard the door close behind him, he squinted into the heavy shadows until he found Tigan sitting at a small square table on the far side of the room from the light. He took a few steps toward her, then stopped. "Okay if I sit down?"

Her entire affect was deadpan, as if she were numb. "Sure."

O'Brien eased himself into a chair diagonally across from her. He looked at her for several seconds, but she made no effort to acknowledge his presence. She just stared straight ahead, her expression slack, her eyes fixed upon something unseen in the darkness. He folded his hands atop the table. "How've you been?"

"How do you think?"

He hadn't expected her to make this easy, but he'd hoped for a bit more engagement than this. "I don't know. That's why I'm asking." His gentle coaxing seemed to have no effect. She just went on staring at the wall. "What I do know is that I'm worried about you. A lot of us are."

"Why?"

"Are you really gonna make me say it?" He leaned forward and cocked his head, trying in vain to attract her gaze. "I'm sorry for your loss, Ezri. We all are." He had no idea what else to say. "You know I cared about her, too."

"Not like I did." Anger revived Tigan's face as she shot a hard look at O'Brien. "Don't you dare compare your loss to mine."

Leaning back and lifting his palms, he said, "I wasn't. But it's not a contest, Ezri. Just because I miss her, too, doesn't mean you miss her any less." He relaxed a bit as he added, "I just wanted you to know you're not alone."

Tears welled in her eyes. "But I am alone, Miles." She buried her face in her hands, and grief strangled her voice. "Leeta was all I had left. My mother and my brother Janel are dead, my younger brother Norvo's an Alliance stooge . . ." She began to cry. "I've lost everyone I've ever cared about. They're all gone." Eyes and jaw clenched shut, she struggled not to break down completely.

Unsure how she would react, but desperate to offer some consolation, O'Brien stood and reached toward Tigan's shoulder. He figured that if he didn't invade her space too abruptly, she might accept that small gesture of comfort.

At the first touch of his hand, she got out of her chair and embraced him, nestling her face between his neck and shoulder. Reacting to an instinct he hadn't known he possessed until that moment, he hugged her and gently stroked her greasy, unwashed hair with one callused hand while she cried.

Several minutes slipped away while he let her express her grief without question or interruption. All she seemed to want was someone to care, to accept her grief in its pure form. That was something he knew how to do.

When her outpouring of emotion at last tapered off, he asked in a husky whisper, "You all right?"

She leaned back and sleeved the tears from her cheeks, then looked up at him with puffy, reddened eyes and nodded. "I think so. For now."

He wrung his hands, dreading her reaction as he said, "I'm sorry that I have to ask you to do this, but I need you back on the *Defiant*."

"No." She shook her head furiously, reacting violently at the idea. "No, absolutely not. I never want to see that ship again." There was desperation in her eyes. "I can't go back aboard that ship, Miles. I'll see her everywhere."

"We all will," O'Brien said. "But we don't have a choice."

"Yes, we do. Let someone else command *Defiant*. Pick another flagship."

O'Brien shook his head in gentle refusal. "All the other ships have captains. *Defiant*'s our boat, Ezri. It's our duty to take her back into service."

She got up and retreated from him. "That's a load of crap, and you know it. You're one of the leaders of all this. If you told one of the captains to switch commands with you, they'd do it."

"Maybe. But the other crews have all earned their ships, just like we earned ours. I've never asked any captain who joined us to give up their ship, for me or anyone else. I don't plan to start now." He followed her around the room as she backed away from him, but he was careful to keep his distance. "This war's a long way from over, Ezri—but now there really is an end in sight. And everyone else is counting on us to help them get there." She backed herself into a corner, so he stopped and raised his hands, palms out, doing all he could to allay her fears. "Picard and the Memory Omega folks have a plan for the next phase of the war, and they need *Defiant* to be part of it."

Tigan shrugged. "So? Go. Nothing's stopping you."

"I need a good first officer, Ezri, one I can rely on." He cracked a lopsided smile. "I need you."

As he'd feared, the suggestion that Tigan take the position that had belonged to her late wife brought her back to the edge of tears. What he hadn't expected was that she would also be smiling. "Me? Your XO?"

"That's what I said, isn't it?"

She covered her mouth with her fingers. Miraculously, that tiny gesture seemed enough to dam up the flood of her emotions. "I'm not sure I'm ready."

He stepped forward and gently took her by the shoulders. "I am. Big things are coming down the pike, kid. I can't do it alone. Come with me."

All at once, the young Trill woman looked humbled but proud, terrified but relieved, torn apart by grief but buoyed by courage. Mustering a faltering and crooked smile, she nodded, then lifted her chin. "I won't let you down, General."

Overcome by his own turbulent blend of anxiety, pride, and affection, he gathered her up in a fatherly embrace. "I know you won't."

Keiko stood in the observation lounge and felt dwarfed by its ten-meter-tall transparent steel wall that looked out on the starship construction yard. From her vantage point she had an unparalleled view of nearly half the ships docked at Erebus Station, and, beyond them, the majestic spiral of the Milky Way and the intimidating gulf of the intergalactic void.

Several meters behind her, people passed by on the

level's main concourse. Some of them were O'Brien's people from the Terran Rebellion, and others were from Calhoun's armada. Only once in a great while did she catch a dim reflection of a fellow Memory Omega member, most of whom had sequestered themselves out of habit. Amid the great commotion of moving bodies, Keiko remained still. She had hoped that arresting her body in space might bring her tranquility of spirit. So far, it did not appear to be working.

She inhaled and made herself savor the sweetness of unpolluted air. *I'd forgotten the small pleasures of living in a civilized place. After so many years on Terok Nor, I guess I just became accustomed to foul odors and tepid showers.*

There had been no end to her litany of criticisms of Terok Nor, but now that it was gone she regarded its memory with a peculiar fondness. She found herself thinking of the nights she'd celebrated with the rebels after hard-won battles, or the moments of tenderness she'd shared with Miles, and suddenly all of the old station's shortcomings fell away, forgotten.

Letting go of her reverie, she felt a change in the air, a subtle presence. She couldn't describe the sensation. She wasn't psionically talented; she didn't pick up surface thoughts or read emotional auras. Most of the time, anyone with a light step could creep up on her with little difficulty. But there was one person who made the world feel different simply by virtue of being nearby.

She caught her own reflection on the transparent wall and forced herself to suppress her hopeful reaction before she turned around. Then she pivoted and looked over her shoulder.

Miles O'Brien stood alone, an island among men, and looked at her. His lifetime of hurts was etched into every line of his face, and the horrible burdens of wartime leadership showed in the deep worry lines that creased his forehead.

The two of them regarded each other for several seconds, neither speaking nor moving. Keiko understood the moment perfectly, despite the silence. A profound loneliness yawned between them, an aching emptiness. She had heard about the casualties his crew on the *Defiant* had suffered during the attack on the Klingon fleet yards, and the toll his grief had taken on him was plain to see.

Knowing he would not take the first step, she did.

She moved with caution, as if fearful of scaring him off. He held his ground and let her come to him. Traversing the last few inches between them with trepidation, Keiko stopped a hair's breadth shy of touching her forehead to his, and she looked up into his eyes. "I'm sorry," she said, "for every—"

"No." He looked at his feet for a moment. "You don't have to be sorry. You did what had to be done. You don't owe me anything."

She felt ashamed. "I just wanted to explain why—"

"It doesn't matter." He reached over and took her hand. "No more apologies, no more explanations. I'm done with them. We don't have time for grudges."

Keiko nodded. "No more *woulda-coulda-shoulda*."

"Exactly." His shoulders slumped as he sighed. "To hell with pride, too. I'm miserable without you. I had forgotten how lonely I used to be before I met you. Then I pushed you away, and I had to learn it all over again." He looked over her shoulder, out at the ships, the distant galaxy, the endless cosmos. "None of this is worth a damn without you."

She squeezed his hands tightly. "I feel the same way. Without you, all I do is go through the motions." She reached up one hand and stroked his stubbled cheek. It rasped like fine sandpaper beneath her touch. "Missed you."

"Missed you, too. Can you forgive me for being an ass?"

Favoring him with a smile, she said, "No more apologies, remember?"

He chuckled nervously, then asked in a small voice, "Can we start again?"

She kissed him. "We never stopped."

He kissed her, and this time it lasted long enough for him to gather her up in his arms, a homecoming in the form of a bear hug. When they came up for air, he leaned back just far enough to look her in the eye. "Any more secrets to tell?"

"None," she said. "We're on the same page, now."

Her answer put a pensive look on his face. "I guess this means we're in this together, now. For the duration, I mean."

She kissed him again and held him close. "All the way to the end."

Two Months Later

29

The Last Argument of Kings

Ensconced in the center seat of the *Enterprise*'s bridge, Jean-Luc Picard hoped no one ever caught on to what an impostor he was.

The ship rumbled and pitched as it blasted its way through the debris field of ruined spacecraft that littered Andoria's equatorial orbit. On the main viewer, torpedoes hammered the defending Alliance warships as phaser beams flensed sections of hull from their exteriors. All but defenseless before the superior firepower of the *Enterprise* and her sister ships, *Intrepid* and *Courageous,* dozens of Klingon and Cardassian battleships had been reduced to fiery scrap and now plunged, broken and ablaze, into Andoria's vast La'Vor Sea.

And all Picard had done to make it happen was utter a single word: "Fire."

Behind his left shoulder, K'Ehleyr was the true tactical mastermind behind the rebellion's latest victory—and those that had preceded it. She and the other Memory Omega–trained personnel were the architects of these strategies, yet everyone else treated Picard as if he were the champion of the rebellion, a savior who had come to lead them to some long-imagined promised land.

He hated living a lie, but revealing the truth would do more harm than good. The rebellion needed a hero, now more than ever, perhaps just as much as it needed Memory Omega. Without a symbol for its aspirations, a face and a name in which to invest its hope, the fragile insurgency would splinter and collapse. It didn't matter that Picard wasn't the military genius they'd been led to think he was; what mattered was that they believed they could change the galaxy by putting aside their fears and selfish desires long enough to follow him to victory.

They wanted to be deceived, Picard realized, *and so they were.*

Cognizant that lives depended upon him playing his part, Picard kept his back straight, his chin up, and his eyes trained on the battle. He shot a look at K'Ehleyr, as if to imply that he was involved in what she was doing.

She noted his stare and played along. "Yes, sir. I see it." Moments later she unleashed a barrage on the last enemy ship holding the line above Andoria, and reduced it to ionized gas and free radicals. "Target destroyed, sir."

"Well done, Commander," Picard said. "Secure from Red Alert."

Picard occupied himself watching the main viewer until K'Ehleyr relayed to the screen beside his chair the damage and casualty reports from their ship and throughout the fleet. The damage to the *Enterprise* had been moderate, mostly to its shields. Several rebellion ships had suffered far worse, unfortunately. While he read the summary of the battle, she stepped forward to stand beside his chair. "We're receiving subspace comms on multiple channels," she said.

He looked up, unsure if he should feel alarmed or curious. "From who?"

"Groups of escaped slaves in stolen ships, looking to join the rebellion." K'Ehleyr nodded at the damage reports on Picard's screen. "And just in time. We could use some reinforcements."

"I doubt any of the ships they've procured will be able to take the place of the warbirds we've lost," Picard said. "But we're in no position to turn them away. Where are they assembling?"

"Earth." She smiled. "It's become the new rallying point for the rebellion."

Picard found K'Ehleyr's good mood infectious. "Remarkable. I'd thought Saavik mad when she said that liberating worlds such as Earth and Tellar and Andoria would galvanize support for the rebellion—but there it is."

"Never underestimate the value of a symbolic victory." She handed him a data padd. "There's something else. It's important."

Intrigued, he took the padd and read the message she had called up on its screen. When he finished reading it, he blinked and then read it again. Then he looked up at her, his eyes wide with disbelief. "Can this be true?"

"We just verified it with three sources. It went out on a general frequency."

He marveled at the good news. The Ferengi Alliance had just declared its support for the Terran Rebellion, recognizing the worlds it had liberated as its new sovereign possessions—in other words, it considered the Terrans a new nation. With that recognition came an offer of alliance—funding, safe passage, and trade agreements. "Could this be the turning point?" He looked up at K'Ehleyr. "Might this be the moment when the rebellion's hopes are, at last, vindicated?"

"Maybe," K'Ehleyr said. "Maybe not. But at the very least it's an opportunity, and one we need to start using as soon as possible."

"Agreed." Picard swiveled his chair and looked back at the aft duty stations. "Lieutenant Troi, send out a message on all frequencies. Declare Andoria's new status as a free world—and then acknowledge the support of the Ferengi Alliance."

Troi, whom Picard had appointed as the *Enterprise*'s chief of security, looked up from her console with a polite nod. "Aye, sir."

Picard turned forward and looked up at K'Ehleyr, who remained at attention. "Order the fleet to regroup and prepare for return to Erebus Station. As soon as all ships report in, have *Intrepid* open a wormhole and make the jaunt."

"Yes, sir. Will we be joining them?"

"No. Our orders are to remain here and assist in the repatriation of free Andorians to their homeworld." Picard looked at the blue-gray, Class M moon orbiting the massive gas giant Andor and realized he had just helped write a new chapter in its history. Its conquest by the Alliance decades earlier had led to the genocide of nearly the entire Andorian species. He had no idea whether enough survivors of that endangered race remained to repopulate their world, but he felt a sudden swell of pride in knowing that he had given it back to them, regardless. *We all deserve a second chance in life. Let us hope this can be theirs.*

He watched the main viewscreen, which showed the rebellion fleet gathering into the optimal formation for group passage through the artificial wormhole the *Intrepid* was about to generate. *A year ago, who would have believed such unity was possible among such a diverse and motley collection of people?* It amazed him to think that he had played any part in it, however manufactured his role might be, and he felt the faint stirrings of a feeling he'd never thought to find again.

It was hope.

Captain Krona slouched in the command chair of the *Vor'cha*-class battle cruiser *I.K.S. Ya'Vang*. He saw no reason to expend effort on posture, reasoning that he'd sit up or get up if and when the situation called for it. Until then, he considered it one of the perks of command that he could enjoy the musky atmosphere and low buzz of activity on his bridge in comfort. "Helm," he said, "time to target."

Ronak, the flight controller, answered, "Two minutes."

A grunt of acknowledgment from Krona was enough to make Ronak turn away and resume his duties. This was the way Krona thought a ship should be run: loose, simple, and quiet. The *Ya'Vang*'s previous captain had been Kurn, who had followed Intendant Kira of Bajor to the *I.K.S. Negh'Var*—a move that had seemed advantageous at the time but later proved to be Kurn's undoing. His death had come as no surprise to Krona, however. He'd always suspected Kira was trouble.

Krona watched his first officer, Commander Garvig, lurk from one console to the next, checking each crewman's work and collecting information. Unlike the *Ya'Vang*'s lean and sinewy commanding officer, Garvig was a hulking brute, even by Klingon standards. His biceps and thighs were too massive to fit in most standard-issue garments, so rather than have him tatter and stretch a new pair of breeches into rags every day, he had been granted dispensation to dress in an ancient style of battle tunic. The one-piece crimson garment reached to his knees and was cinched at the waist by a leather belt. His unusual attire, coupled with his peculiar reddish mane and beard, had once prompted a Terran to compare Garvig to something called a *vyqIng*. Despite having no idea what a *vyqIng* was, Krona had interpreted it as a compliment.

Garvig spent a few moments questioning the ship's comely young communications officer, Beqar, before parting from her company with a leer and smile. He approached the dais of Krona's chair and leaned on its lower tier. "No change in comm traffic, Captain. No sign they've detected us."

"Good. Stand by to drop the cloak on my order."

The first officer nodded and stepped away to man the cloaking controls himself. Krona respected that kind of hands-on leadership. He distrusted officers who were too quick to delegate rather than do important work themselves.

Ronak said over his shoulder, "One minute to target, Captain."

Krona turned toward the tactical officer. "Qeyhnor, arm the warhead."

"Arming sequence engaged," Qeyhnor said. Garvig and the other officers often mocked Qeyhnor for being "too handsome to be a warrior," but despite all their jests, the man had proved himself repeatedly as an exemplary soldier and a shrewd battle planner. "Beginning trajectory computations."

"Beqar," Krona said, "tell Hervog to stand ready. As soon as we fire, we'll need the warp drive back online." He watched the target grow larger on the main viewscreen while Beqar passed his orders down to the chief engineer.

"Thirty seconds," Ronak announced.

So close now. Krona straightened his back and centered himself in the seat, tensing for the culmination of months of secret planning and preparations. The *Ya'Vang* was the only ship in the fleet currently equipped with these special new munitions, and only a handful of his crew had been briefed on the true nature of their mission. Regent Klag had made it expressly clear that every facet of this operation was to be considered top secret, and its details shared only on a need-to-know basis. Even here, on the bridge, the only officers who fully understood what was about to happen were Krona, Garvig, and Qeyhnor. Ronak knew only a set of coordinates to which he'd been ordered to guide the ship. Outside of the *Ya'Vang*'s crew, only the regent and a handful of the most senior generals at the High Command knew the horror they were about to unleash.

For his part, Krona was eager to see how this scenario would play out. He had long advocated for this sort of weaponry and these kinds of ruthless tactics, but until now no one on Qo'noS had seemed inclined to support them. *Amazing how much faster things get done when you put a general on the throne,* he mused.

"We've reached optimal firing position," Ronak said.

"All stop," Krona ordered. He got up and leaped down from his dais, eager to be in the heart of the action when the decisive moment arrived. "All hands, stand by for battle stations. On my mark, drop the cloak, fire the missile, and set a reverse course away from here, at maximum warp." He watched Garvig make a final circuit of the bridge, confirming that everyone was ready to act. Then the first officer took his post at the cloaking station and nodded at Krona. The captain bared his teeth and declared, "Mark!"

In a rush of action, the bridge lights snapped from red to blinding white, and Krona heard the primary systems hum back to full power as the cloak disengaged. Barked orders and confirmations overlapped, fast and sharp, between Garvig and the other officers. Then, over the din, Qeyhnor announced, "Missile's away!"

Krona slapped Ronak's shoulder. "Helm! Get us out of here!" Ronak pivoted the ship hard about and jumped it from a dead stop to maximum warp in a matter of seconds. Knowing they might not outrun the subspace shock wave, Krona snapped at Qeyhnor, "Raise shields, all power aft!"

Garvig commanded, "Aft viewer!" The main screen switched from streaking stars to the fiery trail of their trilithium warhead–equipped missile arcing into the orange dwarf star known to the Alliance as Ventarus Idrilon, and to the residents of its fourth planet as Ferengal.

Moments later the star dimmed and went dark, collapsing into a dark pinpoint. Then it detonated in a brilliant flash that washed out the main screen for half a second. Krona watched with morbid fascination as a faster-than-light subspace shock wave erupted from the slain star, expanding outward in a deadly sphere that turned the system's four rocky inner planets to dust in a matter of seconds and sent its three outer gas giants spinning off into interstellar space, orphaned rogue planets condemned forever to roam the darkness.

In a word, it was *glorious*.

One minute later, Ronak reported, "We're clear of the shock wave."

"Secure from battle stations," Krona said. "Reengage the cloak and set course for home, warp seven. Beqar, send the following message to General Goluk at the High Command: 'Mission accomplished. Ferenginar has been destroyed.'"

30

Blood on the Scales

The fierce, scarred visage of Regent Klag glowered from the main viewscreen on the *Enterprise*'s bridge. *"By now your long-range sensors can confirm what I'm about to tell you: The Ferengal star system, and with it Ferenginar, the capital of the Ferengi Alliance, has been destroyed—wiped entirely off the star charts."*

Picard listened, mute with horror, to the message Klag was broadcasting throughout the Alliance and to all of local space. *"We, the Klingon Empire, have done this to warn all who would dare to support the criminal slave uprising known as the Terran Rebellion: Do so at your own peril. Any world that knowingly harbors ships or members of the rebellion will share Ferenginar's fate. There will be no hearing, no trial, no chance to beg for clemency. From this moment on, you are either with the Alliance or against it.*

"To the rebellion, I issue this further ultimatum: Any world or star system that you claim as your own will be destroyed as Ferenginar was. And unless all your forces surrender to us immediately and unconditionally, and hand over the secrets of your wormhole propulsion technology, we will unleash our new trilithium warheads upon every populated star system in the former Romulan Star Empire. We will destroy one system after another until you comply with our demands. You have three days. After that, Fek'lhr take you."

The transmission ended, and the screen went dark for a moment. Then Troi patched in four other signals, side by side. On the far left was O'Brien, transmitting from the *Defiant,* which was deployed to Tellar. To his right was Eddington, commanding the jaunt ship *Liberty,* which had just ousted Alliance forces from Vulcan. Next was Saavik, who was secure on Erebus Station and communicating via a relayed quantum signal. On the right was Captain Calhoun, who was in orbit of Earth aboard the *Excalibur,* organizing new recruits into the rebellion.

Most of the rebellion's leaders shared a grave mood, Picard observed with a scholar's dispassionate perspective. Saavik, as usual, was alone in betraying no emotional reaction to Klag's screed. Eddington appeared thoughtful, as if he were parsing the Klingon's diatribe for hidden nuances. Calhoun, on the other hand, looked ready to explode at the slightest provocation. O'Brien was pale and visibly shaken; he was the only one of the commanders who chose to sit down.

Saavik spoke first. *"We have confirmed that Ferenginar was destroyed by the detonation of trilithium munitions inside its star. Given that the Klingons have already deployed this weapon once, it seems very likely that they will do so again. The only question now is, where do they plan to strike?"*

The enraged Calhoun replied, *"That's the only question?"* He pointed forward. *"Here's a better one: What planet of the Klingon Empire do we frag first? And which three do we blow up after that?"*

"That is not a productive line of inquiry," Saavik said, her affect cold and businesslike. *"Though we are more than capable of engaging the Alliance in a war of attrition on this scale, doing so is antithetical to our long-term objectives."*

Calhoun snarled like a wild animal reacting to captivity. *"Long-term objectives? Are you serious? Unless we give the Klingons a reason to stop, this'll never end. They'll lay waste every world a Terran's ever set foot on."* He pointed his finger aggressively. *"Listen to me, Director. I've fought the Klingons for a long time. I know how they think. If you want them to back down, you need to show them we can burn worlds, too."*

O'Brien mumbled something, but no one seemed able to make it out, because his mouth was covered by his hand. Confused looks passed among the rebel leaders. Finally, Picard asked, "What did you say, General O'Brien?"

The stout, haggard man lowered his hand. He looked stricken. *"I said, 'It's Ashalla all over again.'"*

Eddington winced at the mention of the vaporized former capital of Bajor. Calhoun scowled in frustration. Picard emulated Saavik and held his poker face.

The Xenexian replied, *"This won't be a repeat of Ashalla for one very simple reason: We're not going to surrender this time."*

"That's not fair," Eddington said. *"You weren't there. You didn't have to choose between losing the station and sacrificing billions of innocent lives."*

"Correct me if I'm misremembering this," Calhoun shot back, *"but weren't you the ones who were supposed to be holding Bajor hostage? Wasn't it you who spent years threatening to glass its surface if the Alliance moved against you? So how did you go from that to total surrender when the Alliance shot at Bajor first?"*

Eddington grappled a moment with his temper. *"It was complicated."*

"This isn't."

"The hell it's not," O'Brien said. *"Millions died in Ashalla when our bluff got called. Billions just died on Ferenginar be-*

cause they dared to support us. We didn't pull the trigger on those
people, but that doesn't mean we just get to wash their blood off
our hands. And it damned sure doesn't mean the answer is to
slaughter billions more."

Disgust twisted Calhoun's features. *"What's your solu-*
tion, little man? Lay down our weapons, give the Klingons our
wormhole tech, and let them win?"

Picard was done listening to them argue. "That's
enough." Calhoun opened his mouth to retort, but
Picard silenced him with a stern glare and prevailed in
the test of wills. "I understand why each of you feels as
you do. But to be perfectly blunt, you're both wrong.
This is a time for neither surrender nor vengeance. Captain Calhoun is correct: We cannot allow the Alliance to
possess wormhole technology. And frankly, given their
history, I see no reason to believe they would keep their
word even if we capitulated to their every demand.

"On the other hand, I'm sympathetic to General
O'Brien's point of view. We must not allow our desire
for victory to blind us to the suffering of the innocent.
This is not some parlor game, not some abstract exercise
in theory. This is war, and real people are at stake. We
owe it to those who have put their trust in us not to be
cavalier with their lives." He moved forward, cognizant
that he had become the focus of attention, both for the
others on the channel and on his own bridge. "Surrender is not an option, but neither is genocide. We need to
target this new capability of the enemy and neutralize it,
while minimizing collateral damage."

Eddington betrayed a shadow of doubt in his worry-
creased brow. *"That'll be difficult now that the Vulcan agents*
inside the Empire have been executed."

"There are other ways of gathering intelligence,"

Picard said. "We need to start using them. Captain Calhoun, prep your crew for a quick raid into Klingon space. We need to capture one of their communication relays. O'Brien: If I get you aboard a Klingon relay station, could you hack its encryptions and access their network?"

O'Brien shrugged. *"Probably."*

"That's a start. My crew will pick the target. Be ready to strike within twenty-four hours. I'll expect updates hourly until we deploy. That is all."

Calhoun, O'Brien, and Eddington acknowledged Picard's orders and signed off in quick succession. None of them looked happy with Picard's middle path forward, but they seemed resigned to it, and that would have to suffice, he decided.

The last person left on the channel was Saavik. She gave Picard a sly look. *"Well done, Captain."* Before he could reply, she ended her transmission.

Settling back into his command chair, Picard realized he had not been briefed or coached in advance of this impromptu conference; there had been no prior discussion of addressing the lingering tensions between Calhoun and O'Brien. The situation had arisen, and Picard had, by instinct alone, dealt with it. *I've played the part of a leader for so long that I'm starting to become one,* he realized with amusement. Despite himself, he smiled. *It's about time.*

Klag did not receive the welcome he expected upon his return to the Great Hall. Where he had anticipated songs and fanfares worthy of a hero of old, he found only manic shouts of denunciation.

Hegron spit at Klag's feet. "Where is the honor in detonating a star?"

"You've launched an arms race without precedent," added K'mpar. "Our predecessors signed treaties to *prevent* this kind of madness."

Klag growled at his detractors. "K'mpec was a fool to trade away our power. I've taken it back, for all of us!"

"No," Hegron bellowed, "you've doomed us, you stupid *taHqeq*!"

Other councillors followed Hegron and K'mpar's lead, and their voices bled together into a wall of noise. Klag rapped the steel-jacketed end of his staff on his dais so many times that he lost count, and he kept on pounding it until they shut up. "Don't cry to me about honor! This is war! All that matters is victory. This has always been our way, and so it will remain."

"For how long?" asked Korvog. "It's only a matter of time until the Taurus Pact develops its own anti-stellar munitions."

Councillor Qolka added, "If they don't, the Kinshaya will."

"All the more reason to act now, while we hold the advantage," Klag said. "With trilithium warheads in our arsenal, we can bring all those second-rate powers to their knees and wield supreme authority over all of known space!"

K'mpar recoiled in contempt. "Have you forgotten about the rebels, Klag? They control *wormholes*. That kind of technology doesn't happen in a vacuum. If they can fold space, what else can they do?"

"If they had some mighty superweapon, they'd have used it by now!" He spread his arms in a gesture of invitation. "Let them come! I'll break their bones and drink their blood! I long for the day when at last I face Calhoun in battle."

"Face *me* first."

Klag knew that voice rumbling from the shadows, at the far end of the room beyond the cluster of councillors surrounding him. It was familiar, one he had met before but that his memory now struggled to connect with a face or a name. "Who dares challenge me in my own hall?"

Heavy footsteps drew near. The knot of councillors unraveled, and the approaching figure stepped into the light. It was a warrior in the prime of his life, wearing a general's insignia and carrying a *bat'leth* in each hand. He tossed one of the large, curving swords to the floor, and it clanged to a stop at the regent's feet. Only as its echoes died in the smoky haze that wreathed the ceiling did Klag realize who was calling him out for a duel.

"Duras, you filthy *petaQ*! You have no standing here!"

The general raised his blade and took a ready stance. "That's for the council to say. But whatever they decide to do with me, I am going to kill you for leading this empire into disgrace." He nodded at the *bat'leth* on the floor. "Pick it up."

Klag set aside his staff, stepped off the dais, and crouched to grasp the sword's hide-wrapped center bar. Then he stood and struck a defensive pose, his blood racing with the call to battle. "Lay on," he said.

The general let out a battle roar and charged.

The regent blocked Duras's first crushing downstroke, but the impact drove Klag to his knees. He intended to roll right and then feint to open up Duras's defenses, but he never got the chance. The general's second blow was a brutal swing that all but knocked Klag's weapon from his hand.

Before Klag could regain his feet he found himself skewered on the tip of Duras's *bat'leth*.

Staring wide-eyed at the blade in his chest, he struggled to draw breath for a final curse at Duras, but failed. Robbed of honor and title, Klag sank into darkness clinging to his hatred—only to despair as death stole that from him, as well.

Hegron was the first to declare, "All hail, Regent Duras!" The other councillors roared in approval. Rather than bask in the moment, Duras despised it.

He tore his blade free of Klag's chest. "Enough of this madness," he said, ascending the dais and seating himself upon the throne as if it were a matter of no great consequence. "We never should have let this power-mad fool lead us down a path to destruction. It's time to chart a course back to sanity."

The councillors gathered around the dais. Korvog asked, "How?"

"By setting rational priorities," Duras said. "Cardassia gears for war. So does the Taurus Pact. And Klag's idiotic violation of the Raknal Accords might have just sparked an arms race for trilithium weapons. These are real threats—but the Terran Rebellion isn't. It's our least important foe, but it has become powerful enough to make a nuisance of itself. Satisfying as it might be to swat at it, we can't afford to be distracted from our real enemies, not with so much at stake."

K'mpar asked warily, "How do you propose we deal with the rebels?"

"A cease-fire," Duras said. "I'll rescind Klag's foolish ultimatum, and mollify the rebels by granting them the systems they've already captured."

Qolka was outraged. "Give up worlds of the Empire? To that scum?"

Duras quelled the protest with a raised hand. "Only temporarily. We also need to broker a truce with the Taurus Pact so that we can focus on bringing Cardassia to heel." He leaned back and relaxed onto the throne. "These are all wars we can win, my friends. Just not all at the same time." He sighed. "Someone prep a subspace broadcast on all frequencies: I have a message to deliver."

O'Brien sat in his command chair and felt his blood pressure rise as the bridge crew of the *Defiant* pressed forward toward the main viewscreen, all eager to view the message being transmitted from the Klingon Empire's newest ruler, Regent Duras. Unable to see or hear clearly through the wall of bodies, O'Brien cleared his throat with as much volume and menace as he could muster. Abashed, the bridge crew retreated to their assigned stations as the transmission began.

The face of Duras appeared on the screen. He sat upon his throne inside the shadowy chamber of the High Council. Behind him, a Klingon banner adorned the wall, flanked by free-standing braziers crowned with golden flames. *"Fighters of the Terran Rebellion, hear my words: The Klingon Empire offers you a cease-fire. My predecessor, Klag, betrayed our code of honor with his cowardly crime against Ferenginar. You have my word that we will commit no further such atrocities—on the condition that your rebellion also pledges to honor this cease-fire. If you accept our terms, keep the worlds already under your flag and rule them as you see fit; if you reject our offer . . . then may you die well.*

"You have two days to respond."

The signal ended, and the screen switched back to a

view of warp-bent stars. Standing at the port-side sensor console, Tigan scrunched her face with contempt. "*Pfft.* Does he think we're that stupid?"

Swiveling around from the helm and operations console, the *Defiant*'s new flight controller, Prynn Tenmei, also sounded a doubtful note. "Why would the Klingons let us keep captured star systems?"

"The bigger question," added weapons officer Kirsten Perez, a lean and muscular human with blond hair who looked younger than her forty years, "is, will the Cardassians honor promises made by the Klingons? I can't imagine they'd just let them give away entire star systems—especially to us."

"Those are all good questions," O'Brien said, pondering what he'd heard. "My guess is that it's a trap. Duras wants us to settle on a few planets and let our guard down so he can box us in and kill us all in one massive assault."

Keiko, who had been listening from the aft situation table, stepped forward to stand next to O'Brien's chair. "You're all wrong," she said. She waited until everyone looked at her, then she continued. "The cease-fire he offered is genuine. And if he's looking to trick anyone, it's the High Council and the Cardassians."

O'Brien wondered whether his beloved was pranking him and his crew. "Oh, really?" he said. "What makes you so sure?"

A devilish smile brightened her face. "Because Duras is one of us."

31

Aggressive Expansion

Their cease-fire with the rebels is clearly a prelude to an invasion of our space!" Councillor Menaar punctuated his thought by pounding his fist on Damar's desk. As soon as he'd done it, he sheepishly backed away, obviously aware of his faux pas. "Forgive my exuberance, Legate."

Damar let the older man squirm a moment before he let him off the hook. "Think nothing of it, Councillor. Passions are bound to run high at times such as these." He measured the reactions of the others gathered before him: Councillors Gulal and Rajak, and Legates Temar and Parn. They each were careful to avoid eye contact with Damar, lest they find themselves embroiled in Menaar's error. Satisfied that he had them at a momentary disadvantage, Damar capitalized upon it. "It is not the Klingon Empire's sudden change of leadership or even Duras's offer of a cease-fire to the rebels that concerns me. What troubles my sleep is knowing that they've dispatched an ambassador to broker their own truce with the Taurus Pact. I, for one, find it highly unlikely that the Gorn, the Tholians, and the Breen will negotiate in good faith with both the Klingons and us. Even if both treaties are signed, history suggests only one will be honored."

"Very true," said Legate Temar, a tall, broad-shouldered, square-jawed man whose profile looked as if it had been hewn off some celebrated monument in the heart of the Tarlak Sector. "The Taurus Pact will honor its truce with the power they believe poses the greatest threat to them. If we wish to claim that honor, we need to crush the Klingon Empire, take its brawn for ourselves, and leave enough of its ragged carcass for our foes to scavenge that they don't set their sights on us."

Around the room, everyone nodded. "Unfortunately," Damar said, "the Klingons are doing everything in their power politically to make certain we remain engaged on as many fronts as possible. By offering the Terrans a cease-fire, they make us the rebels' sole remaining target, and they've sent a negotiator to the Taurus Pact, undermining our own efforts at diplomacy and increasing the risk that our borders will remain under siege by the Breen and the Tholians. It's the Klingons' way of making sure we're too dispersed and off balance to defend ourselves when they launch their own attack."

Legate Parn, a man whose bulging physique tested the limits of his uniform, interjected, "Any significant incursion of Klingon forces into our sovereign space would be a disaster for us."

"I am well aware of that." Damar shot a glare at Parn's superior, and Temar passed the silent reproach along to Parn, who wisely stifled himself.

Councillor Gulal stepped in to fill the conversational gap. "The military implications of a Klingon invasion would be nothing compared to the political ramifications, Legate. Popular support for this regime is deeply fragile at the moment, and the loss of confidence such an invasion would bring would almost certainly make our continued governance untenable."

Her verbosity made Damar smile. "You mean the people will throw us out if we let the Klingons in. Thank you, Councillor, for that remedial lesson in politics." He picked up a glass from his desk and sipped *kanar* that was almost as sweet as the look on Gulal's face was sour. Setting down the glass, he asked Temar, "How does Central Command recommend we stop the Klingons?"

"By taking Raknal Station," Temar said. He lifted a portable data tablet and pointed at the interactive display surface that covered one wall of Damar's office. "With your permission, sir?" Damar nodded his assent, and Temar uploaded his strategic briefing to the wall screen with a tap of his finger. As he continued, he illustrated his points with broad sweeping gestures. "Raknal Station is the single most important strategic asset in this quadrant. Its central position, fortification, and concealment within the Betreka Nebula all make it a prime location from which to command and control interstellar traffic from the Terran system to Cardassia Prime to Qo'noS. At the moment, the garrisons stationed there are split evenly between our people and the Klingons' personnel. If we move now and make a decisive first strike, I believe we can capture the station."

Damar eyed the battle plan and interior schematics of the station with a dubious eye. "Perhaps. But doing so is certain to provoke a Klingon retaliation. Are we prepared to repel such an assault?"

"Not at the moment," Temar said. "Our proposal calls for the redeployment of all available forces to reinforce Raknal Station pending the Klingon retaliation."

The three councillors appeared troubled by Temar's

suggestion. Rajak was the first to respond. "Legate, what if you've misjudged the Klingons' response? What if instead of trying to retake the station, they attack Cardassia Prime?"

"Or any of a number of strategically valuable worlds," Menaar added, "such as Chin'toka or Setlik III?"

Temar nodded at Parn, who replied, "From our vantage point on Raknal Station, we would be able to see any incoming attack before it reached our core systems. Any deployment out of Klingon space will register on the station's long-range sensors. The Klingons won't be able to move against us without being intercepted en route."

"What if they're cloaked?" asked Gulal.

With a sideways glance, Parn deflected the question to Temar. The senior legate answered, "Raknal's sensors were built by the Klingons, Councillor. With its resources at our disposal, the Klingons' cloaking devices would be rendered useless. The advantage would be ours."

"Be that as it may," Rajak said, "what you're proposing is a commitment of nearly all our remaining military forces. Even if we prevail, we might be crippled."

The legate shook his head. "I doubt that, Councillor. Assuming we take Raknal from within and then turn its defensive systems against the Klingons, the brunt of the battle will fall upon the station. Our forces will simply be there to prevent their escape and mop up the stragglers."

"I certainly can't fault you for a shortage of optimism," Damar said. "What kind of losses do you project in a full engagement?"

"No more than thirty percent, sir." He raised his

hands to forestall a tempest of protests. "I know those numbers aren't inconsequential, but after we emerge victorious, we'll still have enough strength to set the political agenda in all of known space—starting with the eradication of the rebellion."

Damar reclined his chair and weighed the risks of Temar's plan against its potential rewards. Menaar interrupted his deliberations with a desperate plea. "Please don't tell me you're actually considering this insanity?"

"It seems reasonable and proportionate to the challenge facing us."

Waving his arms at the wall display, the older man verged on hysteria. "It's a recipe for disaster, Damar! Sending all our forces to Raknal on a gamble? Have you considered the price we—and the people—will pay if Legate Temar is wrong? I beg you not to approve this plan."

Training a suspicious stare on Temar, Damar asked, "How do you respond, Legate? What if we lose our stand against the Klingons, and they retake Raknal?"

Temar was relaxed and smug. "That won't happen, sir. The Obsidian Order has obtained intelligence from a reliable source that will guarantee our triumph at Raknal Station. As a great philosopher once said, 'The secret to victory in war is to win the battle before it is fought.' And I assure you all"—he smiled not just at Damar but at the three councillors, as well—"this battle is won."

"For all our sakes, and that of Cardassia, I hope you're right," Damar said, steeling his resolve. "Seize Raknal Station and prepare for war with the Klingons."

Picard checked the status report from the *Enterprise*'s engineering department for the tenth time that hour.

It remained unchanged from his previous nine reviews. He knew that refreshing the computer screen on the desk inside his ready room would do nothing to accelerate the process, but anxiety lately had been driving him into strange patterns of behavior.

His ready room had been his refuge since his first day aboard the massive, intimidating starship. Before taking command of the *Enterprise,* the only ships on which he had spent any significant time had been the *Stargazer* and the *Calypso,* a small runabout and an outrider, respectively—starships made for crews whose members could be counted on one hand. Inside the multilevel labyrinth of a ship such as the *Enterprise,* Picard felt lost and disoriented. He was unaccustomed to having so much interior space in which to roam. Consequently, when he wasn't expressly needed on the bridge, he passed his hours sequestered in his quarters or cloistered in the privacy of his office.

Dissatisfied with the dearth of new information on his computer, he got up and strolled to the window behind his desk. Looking out at the once-thriving moon of Andoria, whose curve dominated his view but was itself dwarfed by the mass of its gas giant parent, Andor, Picard watched as crews in small spacecraft worked as quickly as possible to construct orbital defense platforms. Though he could not see the planet's cloud-blanketed surface from orbit, he knew that other crews down there were laboring just as diligently to install dozens of artillery batteries on every major landmass. It was all part of a long-term defensive strategy prepared by Memory Omega during the decades it had spent in hiding. *Tragic that it comes far too late for the vast majority of people who once called this home,* he lamented, recalling the historical accounts of the Cardassians' slaughter of the Andorian people. Despite the cease-fire with the Klingons, it was the lingering threat of renewed hostilities with the Cardassians that gave urgency to the rebellion's efforts to erect formidable defenses for its new possessions.

He suppressed a twinge of melancholy and turned away from the window. For a moment, he thought about using the ship's replicator to procure a cup of hot tea, then his door's visitor signal warbled. He moved back to his desk, sat down, and picked up a data slate that he pretended to read. "Come."

K'Ehleyr entered with a bold stride. "Captain? You called?"

Feigning distraction, as if he were reading something important, he took his time looking up at his first officer. "What's the latest estimate for the completion of Andoria's defenses?"

"The same as the last estimate." She looked suspiciously amused. "Something bothering you, Captain? Or do you always try to read a data slate while it's turned off?"

He frowned and dropped the slate on his desk. Then he exhaled angrily, stood, and smoothed the front of his jacket. "I don't know what to call it," he said. "Wanderlust, perhaps."

"That's your old self talking." She sat on the edge of his desk. "You spent a lot of years on your own, as a roamer. Old habits are the hardest to break."

Picard turned toward the window and stepped away from K'Ehleyr, and he wondered if it was because there was truth in what she said. "I keep thinking we've spent too much time here. We should move on."

"Not yet. There's still a lot to do. It takes time to build a nation."

Hearing her put the thought into words crystallized it for Picard, and he turned to face her. "Yes, that's it, isn't it? That's what we're doing now. Not just fighting a war, not just struggling to get out from under a government—but working to erect a new one." The scope of it all compelled a smile from him. "All the years that I fantasized what it would be like to see the Alliance overthrown, I never once stopped to imagine what would come after it." Conducting a stark and honest inventory of his feelings, he confessed, "Probably because I never believed a rebellion would ever get this far."

"Well," K'Ehleyr said, picking up the data slate from his desk, "then you're going to love this." She activated the device, accessed a screen of data, and handed it to Picard. "The latest tactical report from Memory Omega."

He skimmed the classified briefing, eyes wide with shock. It said that Cardassian forces aboard Raknal Station had betrayed their Klingon counterparts and seized control of the base. Lowering the pad, he asked her, "Can this be right?"

"Confirmed on long-range sensors. Both sides are deploying everything they've got for a battle royal inside the Betreka Nebula. Looks like the Alliance is officially history, and the Cardassians and Klingons are going to war."

Picard was stunned. "What do we do now?"

K'Ehleyr laughed. "Get out of their way."

32

Keen and Bloody Swords

If there was one truism that had served General Kaybok well throughout his decades of service in the Klingon Defense Force, it was that paranoia always paid the best dividends. One could never count upon the support of anyone else in times of trouble. Allegiances shifted, loyalties could be bought or sabotaged, and some people were simply no damned good to begin with. The idea found its truest expression, however, when dealing with non-Klingons—particularly those who deigned to call themselves the Empire's allies. It had long ago been distilled into a saying that every Klingon learned in childhood: *You can trust an enemy to act against you—but only a friend can betray you*. Taking that lesson to heart had saved Kaybok's life many times over.

The bridge crew of Kaybok's flagship, the *I.K.S. bortaS,* worked with the quiet, lethal focus of deep-forest hunters. The *Vor'cha*-class battle cruiser was under cloak, moving at one-tenth impulse inside the eye of the Betreka Nebula, just beyond the natural concealment of its turbulent, iridescent gases. Several million *qelIqam*s away, but looming large on the *bortaS*'s main viewer, was Kaybok's designated target, Raknal Station.

The facility had all the classic hallmarks of Cardassian design. Its disc-shaped central hull was surrounded by curving pylons, giving it an arachnoid silhouette as it orbited the daylight side of Raknal V, the planet for which it had been named years before Kaybok had been born. It was seven kilometers in diameter and possessed more firepower than an entire fleet of warships.

Nonetheless, Kaybok was resolved to see it captured or destroyed.

"Gunner," he said, his voice like a rumble of falling rocks. "Report."

Tevog, a young soldier whose face was still devoid of whiskers or scars, looked up from his console. "As you predicted, General. The Cardassians are still scanning for our old cloaking wavelengths."

That was welcome news to Kaybok. "Finally, it seems those *petaQpu'* in the Great Hall did something right for a change." It had been more than five decades since the Empire and the Cardassian Union had united to construct and jointly operate Raknal Station. Each side had claimed that it was installing its best and most advanced armaments and defenses on the station. Fortunately for Kaybok's battle group, the Klingon Empire's leaders had lied about that. It was in anticipation of a scenario exactly such as this that the Empire had for decades made certain that Raknal's information about Klingon cloaking technology was at least one generation out of date— and also why the Defense Force conducted regular war games to practice attacking and boarding the station.

"Commander Logar," he said, beckoning his executive officer, "order *Razheel* Squadron to set their cloaks to the old wavelengths," Kaybok said. "Then have them maneuver to attack Raknal head-on, along its orbital plane."

Logar snapped his head in a curt nod. "Yes, General."

Kaybok trusted the commander of *Razheel* Squadron

to obey his orders in spite of the fact that they would prove fatal for him and his men. The general did not regret sending them to their deaths. They all would perish in glorious battle, braving the enemy's most fierce assault, while ensuring the Empire's eventual victory. No Klingon could ask for a more noble demise.

Only seconds after the order was given, Logar returned to Kaybok's side. "*Razheel* Squadron is in position, General."

"Good." He jabbed commands into the touch screen interface beside his elevated command chair. "As soon as the Cardassian fleet engages *Razheel* Squadron, initiate alternating wave attacks from their flanks, and from above and below them on the z-axis." Keying in his final directives—a prioritized list of targets on Raknal Station itself—he said to Logar, "Commence attack."

The lights flared bright white as the *bortaS* went to battle stations, and all around Kaybok the battle unfolded with swift precision. He watched without emotion as *Razheel* Squadron uncloaked and made a daring frontal assault on Raknal Station. As he'd hoped and expected, the Cardassian fleet defending the base converged like insects on a dropped morsel, all of them so eager to share a taste of what seemed like an easy victory that they broke formation and left their aft quarters vulnerable. Caught in the crossfire, the ships of *Razheel* Squadron vanished in a storm of fire. Kaybok smiled. *It is a good day to die.*

He nodded at Logar, and the second phase of the assault began.

The *bortaS* led the attack, swooping in under cloak, uncloaking, firing disruptors and torpedoes, then cloaking and veering off on seemingly random trajectories, in a practiced pattern that quickly reduced the Cardassian fleet to utter chaos. Over and over, Klingon warships appeared like spectres, dealt punishing blows, and then vanished.

Several times each minute, a lucky salvo from the Cardassian fleet or from the station tore through a cloaked Klingon ship, reducing it to flames and debris, and a few glancing shots rocked the *bortaS* and even breached the hull in its engineering section. It amused Kaybok that Raknal's formidable defenses actually worked against its own defending fleet, many of whose vessels blundered into its terrifying barrages. Despite starting the battle with superior numbers, in minutes the Cardassian fleet found itself whittled down to a handful of badly damaged stragglers huddled within the defensive radius of the station.

The station, Kaybok brooded. *Now we separate the fortunate from the dead.* There would be no easy or painless way to overcome the station's defenses. The mere act of closing to within firing range would put the *bortaS* and every ship in its fleet squarely within the station's impressively thorough firing solution. Being cloaked would confer no advantage at that range. Any ship close enough to attack the station would have to endure a firestorm unlike any other in the galaxy. Taking down this base would be nothing less than a suicide mission.

"Logar," Kaybok rasped, his voice harsh and loud in the muted environment of the *bortaS*'s bridge, "order the fleet to remain cloaked until after we drop Raknal's shields. When I give the order, all ships are to fire torpedoes only, from outside the station's disruptor range."

"Yes, General." Logar relayed the order to the communications officer, who informed the fleet. This had been the plan since the mission was launched: Eliminate the defending fleet, then withdraw to a range of ten lightseconds, outside disruptor range, and hammer Raknal

Station with a nonstop barrage of torpedoes. The one piece of the puzzle that was not general knowledge within the fleet was the special weapon the *bortaS* was about to deploy, one whose development Kaybok's patrons in the House of J'Gol had personally financed and shepherded into service. "Gunner, arm a full salvo of phase torpedoes, and target the station's defense screen generators."

Tevog initialized the experimental weapons, then looked back at Kaybok. "Torpedoes armed and locked, General."

"Fire."

The *bortaS* dropped its cloak just long enough to unleash a dozen prototype munitions, which followed drunken, corkscrewing paths toward Raknal Station—and then promptly blinked out of phase. Kaybok wondered what the Cardassians aboard the station had made of that unprecedented sensor data: twelve torpedoes simply vanishing. Next would come the proof of concept, and if his gamble proved to be a losing wager, this assault would be all but over.

Massive detonations lit up the base, one after another, obliterating its shield generators. Just as Kaybok had hoped and his engineers had intended, the torpedoes had shifted seven *terzIqar*s out of phase within seconds of being launched from the *bortaS,* took advantage of their phase-shifted status to penetrate the base's shields, and returned to normal phase a fraction of a second before making impact—with spectacular results.

The executive officer declared, "The station's shields are down."

"All ships, begin torpedo barrage."

Kaybok smirked. The station's size and weaponry no longer mattered. At this range, its disruptors were ineffectual. It could fill Raknal V's orbit with torpedoes, but none of the Klingon ships uncloaked long enough for the torpedoes to lock on and connect. And with its shields down, the massive base, which was tethered by gravity into a geosynchronous orbit, was the galaxy's biggest target.

Exactly as my war game scenario predicted, Kaybok gloated. *We'll knock out its weapons platforms and then begin boarding operations.*

It all was going perfectly—and then it all went to *Gre'thor.*

Without warning, torpedoes fired from Raknal Station began finding cloaked targets with unerring accuracy. One after another, Klingon warships were revealed in the moments of their destruction. Kaybok bolted from his chair and seized Logar by his lapel. "They have our new cloak wavelength! All ships, withdraw and regroup!" Moving on to the gunner, he added, "Ready another salvo of phase torpedoes." He was about to go back to his chair when the communications officer beckoned him. Marching toward the man, he snapped, "What is it, Miklor?"

"Intercepted signals, sir," the frazzled, middle-aged Klingon replied. Nodding at his screen, he added, "From the *Ya'Vang* to Raknal Station!"

"On speakers!"

"It's just noise, sir," Miklor protested. "Raw data."

Hunching menacingly over the slightly built man, Kaybok demanded, "What *kind* of data?"

Miklor worked in frantic motions, applying filters and translators to parse the signal he'd snared. Then the gibberish on his screen resolved into clear code, and he replied, "Our new cloaking wavelength, General."

For a moment, the news seemed unthinkable. Then Kaybok remembered the bitter lessons of youth: *Only a friend can betray you.* "Who sent that signal?"

"Captain Krona," Miklor said.

Kaybok ascended the steps and reclaimed his command chair. "All ships! Locate and destroy the *Ya'Vang*! She and her crew are traitors to the Empire!"

Tevog the gunner pounded the side of his fist on his console. "The *Ya'Vang* has broken formation, sir! She's on the other side of the station and accelerating away. I can't get a lock on her."

"Note her heading and send a burst transmission of all logs to the High Command on Qo'noS," Kaybok said.

After sending the signal as ordered, Logar approached the general's dais. "Withdraw and regroup, sir?"

"Too late for that," Kaybok said. "We can't go to warp inside the nebula, and at impulse, their torpedoes can rip us to shreds. We can't fight, and we can't retreat." He entered coordinates into the terminal beside his chair and relayed them to the helm of the *bortaS*—and to those of every other ship in the fleet. "Those coordinates at maximum warp, on my mark." The flagship's bridge went silent. Kaybok's intention was clear to all. He held up his head with pride, resolved to enter *Sto-Vo-Kor* with a warrior's bearing. "*Qapla'*, sons of Qo'noS! *Mark!*"

The helm officer engaged the warp drive. Kaybok's last hope was that some great poet would one day pen a glorious song to tell the future how he and his men rammed Raknal Station at three thousand times the speed of light, destroying it and Raknal V for the everlasting glory of the Empire.

Captain Krona saw the flash on the *Ya'Vang*'s viewscreen, and he knew that both Raknal Station and the majority of two nation's fleets had just been annihilated. *Good riddance,* he decided. The aid of the Cardassians had been more a matter of tactics and convenience than one of fealty. They had been a means to an end, nothing more.

Arrowing through the prismatic fury of the nebula, the *Ya'Vang* was on its own, a ship without a country for as long as it took to restore sanity to the regency. Krona had known the risk he and his crew would face by following a renegade path, but once it had become clear that the new regent lacked Klag's clarity of vision and indomitable resolve, he had been unable to see any other way forward.

"Helm," he said, "time to target."

Ronak replied without looking at his console. "Six hours, eleven minutes."

"Qeyhnor, is the next trilithium warhead ready?"

The weapons officer replied, "It will be armed before we arrive, sir."

Krona was pleased. He swiveled around toward the communications officer. "Beqar, send the following message back to Qo'noS." He thought a moment. "Belay that. Send this directly to Regent Duras: 'Because you lack the will to do what must be done to defend the Empire, my crew and I shall do it for you. Today, we strike a blow for pride, for strength and honor, for the Klingon way. On the blood of my father, I swear that I will make Bajor pay for its treason—and give the galaxy reason to tremble before us once more.'"

Duras stood half-awake in his bedchamber and stared aghast at the vid screen on the wall. "What in the name of *Fek'lhr* is that *yIntagh* doing?"

General Goluk answered over the comm from the Great Hall. *"He seems to think he is defending the honor of the Empire, My Lord Regent."*

As he entered his second minute of consciousness since being roused from a sound sleep, his memory came back in fits. "The *Ya'Vang* is the ship with those damn trilithium warheads, isn't it?"

"Yes, My Lord." New information appeared on Duras's screen as Goluk continued. *"New intel indicates dozens of ships whose commanders are loyal to Krona are en route to rendezvous with him just outside the Bajor system."*

The new regent's face burned with rage. "Who do we have left that can intercept them?"

"No one. We lost most of our combat-ready forces in this quadrant in the attack on Raknal Station, as did the Cardassians—not that they've shown any desire to stop Krona, even if they were able to do so."

A male Klingon servant opened Duras's bedchamber door and entered with a fresh set of robes. Behind him, a female Klingon entered carrying a tray on which sat a pot of *raktajino* and a plate of raw *targ* meat, sliced paper thin and salted.

Brusquely waving away the servants, Duras said to Goluk, "We need to issue some kind of warning to Bajor."

"Why?"

"Because Krona is acting in open defiance of my public pledge. If we don't disavow his actions and those of his accomplices, we'll appear to be sanctioning their crime. At which point, my word as regent will become worthless."

"I see." Goluk sounded as if he was trying to persuade himself of Duras's argument. *"It's not the result of Krona's mission we need to deal with, but its political blowback. Most wise, Lord Regent. I'll issue the warning immediately. After all, it's not as if it will affect the outcome."*

His adviser's nonchalant tone gave Duras new cause for alarm. "Why not?"

"Because the I.K.S. vaQ'taj *is holding station four hundred million* qelIqam*s from Bajor and blocking all subspace signals in or out of the B'hava'el system."*

Now Duras understood Goluk's rationale. He thought that Duras wanted to issue a warning solely for the purpose of banking political capital. Realizing it would not be wise to press this matter further with his chief of staff, he feigned agreement. "Very good, General. See to it the message is sent immediately."

"Yes, Lord Regent."

"And do not bother me again before morning unless Qo'noS itself comes under attack. Understood?"

Goluk sounded duly rebuked. *"Yes, My Lord."*

As soon as the channel clicked off, Duras deactivated the comm system completely, and then he barred the door to his bedchamber. As soon as he was certain he was alone, he retrieved his quantum transceiver from its hiding place inside the grip of his *bat'leth*. The precious Memory Omega communications device had been given to him only weeks earlier, by a middle-aged Vulcan woman who had declined to share her name with him, in preparation for his bid to replace the megalomaniacal Klag as regent. Using the device as she had taught him, he first scanned his room for surveillance devices and was unsurprised to detect five of them. Next, he disabled the bugs and established a field of white noise as a defense against eavesdroppers at his door. Then he opened a channel to Memory Omega and hoped that his warning would reach them in time to prevent Bajor and its people from sharing Ferenginar's tragic fate.

33

The Hour of Fire

Mac strode into *Excalibur*'s nerve center at a quick step, followed moments later by Soleta. The pair of them were still coitally rumpled, having been roused from their bed by McHenry's urgent telepathic summons. "Report," Mac snapped as he moved toward his chair.

Jellico studied Soleta and Mac through narrowed eyes, and Lefler seemed unable to conceal the ghost of a smile as she looked their way. Selar arched one eyebrow into a curve of elegant jest. "Forgive us, Captain," the Vulcan woman said. "We did not realize the two of you were—"

"Resting," Soleta cut in. "We were *resting*."

"The urgent message, Robin," Mac said. "On-screen. Now."

Lefler worked her console. "*Courageous* is relaying a signal from Erebus Station." She looked up with anticipation at the main screen. "Here it comes."

Saavik's face replaced the image of Earth's northern hemisphere on the *Excalibur*'s forward screen. "*Thank you for joining us, Captain Calhoun. General O'Brien and Captain Picard are also on this transmission.*" The screen divided into three equal, vertical panels. O'Brien and Picard bookended Saavik. "*Minutes ago, we received a priority alert from Regent Duras. He informs us that a rogue battle group of Klingon warships led by the Ya'Vang is preparing to destroy the*

*star B'hava'el just as it annihilated Ferengal—which means
every living soul on Bajor is minutes away from extermination."*

It was easy for Mac to recognize the anguish in
O'Brien's eyes as he heard the news. The human's horrified stare was the same one Mac had seen in the eyes
of every survivor of the Klingon-triggered holocaust on
Romulus. Glancing to his right, he caught Soleta's fleeting wince of remembrance, as well. *I've seen the Alliance
burn too many worlds,* Mac decided. *No more.*

Picard said, *"Enterprise is starting calculations for a jaunt
to Bajor. We can have our fleet there in two minutes.* Courageous *and* Ardent *have begun their own calculations."* He
looked away for a moment, then asked, *"What do we
know about these trilithium weapons the Klingons are using?
How do we stop them?"*

*"Once they strike their target, the chain reaction is irrevers-
ible,"* Saavik said. *"Our only hope of preventing a catastrophe is
to either destroy the Ya'Vang before it fires a trilithium weapon,
or intercept the torpedo in flight to its target."*

That suggestion left O'Brien aghast. *"Shoot down a
warp-capable torpedo in flight? That's practically impossible!"*

*"Then I suggest you concentrate on identifying and destroying
the* Ya'Vang *as quickly as possible,"* Saavik said. *"We are sending you the last recorded energy signature for the* Ya'Vang, *but it
might no longer be accurate."*

Mac nodded. "Understood. Captain Picard? General O'Brien? I think our best bet is to deploy our fleet
in a dispersed blockade along the Klingons' most likely
vectors to the star. If we emerge from our wormholes
within fifty million kilometers of B'hava'el, we should
be able to get ahead of the attack."

*"Generating a wormhole that close to a star can be highly dan-
gerous,"* Picard said. *"However, it seems we have no other choice."*

O'Brien was openly skeptical. *"Defending Bajor would be hard enough—its star is a million times bigger. How are we supposed to guard every possible attack vector the Klingons might use?"*

"We don't," Mac said. "Most of our fleet will have to engage the *Ya'Vang*'s escorts. The *Excalibur* will stop the *Ya'Vang,* one way or another."

Soleta discreetly clutched Mac's arm and whispered, "Mac, what are—"

"Trust me," he whispered back. *McHenry, I'll need you at your best.*

You'll have it, Mac.

"Time's wasting," Mac said. "Let's get moving. *Excalibur* out." The screen switched to a view of the free starship *Courageous* spinning up a new artificial wormhole, and Mac returned to his seat. "Soleta, sound general quarters, all hands to battle stations. We're going hunting."

Defiant emerged from the wormhole generated by the *Ardent,* which by necessity would be the last vessel in O'Brien's battle group to make the jaunt to the Bajor system. As soon as *Defiant* cleared the wormhole's event horizon, O'Brien began checking the updates on the command screen beside his chair.

So far, so good, he assured himself. All the active ships under his command had completed the jaunt while remaining in formation, and the *Ardent* was following close behind them, pulling shut the wormhole behind it.

"Perez," he said, snagging his weapons officer's attention. "Are Picard and Calhoun here yet?"

"Yes, sir." She routed data from her screens to his. "Bearing two-three-two mark four, range nine hundred thirty-six thousand kilometers." She added over her shoulder, "Their fleets are moving into battle formations."

O'Brien frowned as he examined the deployment pattern. It was far too widely spaced and riddled with gaps for his comfort, but it couldn't be helped. Recapturing the former core worlds of the Terran Republic had taken a heavier toll on the rebellion than it had let on. Memory Omega's amazing wormhole-driven ships were fast and powerful but far from invincible. Several had been lost in the battles for Vulcan and Tellar, along with dozens of vessels from Calhoun's and O'Brien's fleets. Most of the rebel starships that had survived those battles now were docked at Erebus Station, undergoing extensive repairs and refits.

This is the worst possible time for us to be forced into a major battle, he thought with grim anticipation. *If it was any world other than Bajor . . .* He caught himself. *You'd be doing the same damned thing, and you know it.* "Ezri, signal our fleet to cover sector grids twenty-five through fifty," he said. Poking at his command screen, he wondered if it was malfunctioning, or if he was simply reading it incorrectly. "Perez, where's the *Excalibur*?"

"No idea, sir," said Perez. "We had her on sensors for a few seconds when we first arrived, then she went dark."

"Must be in stealth mode," Tigan said. "What's Calhoun doing?"

O'Brien smiled. "Lying in ambush for the *Ya'Vang*."

Tenmei turned from the helm. "Won't *Ya'Vang* be leading the attack?"

"Of course not," O'Brien said. "She's the one carrying the trilithium warheads. She won't show herself until she's ready to fire." New orders from Picard arrived on O'Brien's command screen. "In the meantime, here comes her battle group to punch a hole in our blockade. Shields to maximum, set attack pattern

Oscar-Delta. And Perez, remember: zoned firing solutions. Don't try to target the Klingons as they uncloak, you won't have time. Just use the phasers to make a no-fly zone between us and the *Takagi*."

Perez nodded. "Got it."

Seconds passed with excruciating languor as O'Brien watched the main viewscreen for any sign of activity. The sensor readings said the Klingon fleet was out there and coming in fast, but all he saw were stars.

Then came a blur of gray-green metal and a crimson flash of disruptor energy. *Defiant* pitched and echoed from a thundering impact against its shields.

And away we go. "Fire at will!"

Pulses of phaser energy tore away into the endless night, in what seemed like a futile display. Tenmei pivoted and yawed the *Defiant* while Perez laid down a wide arc of suppressive fire. Then flashes of contact brought Klingon cruisers and birds-of-prey stuttering briefly out of their cloaks and into view for a few seconds before they veered off, away from *Defiant*'s free-fire zone.

The hits rapidly became less frequent, then stopped. O'Brien couldn't see the Klingon fleet, but he could feel its commanders adjusting their tactics to undermine the zone defense. "Attack pattern Whiskey-Alpha!" he called out, sensing disaster at hand. "Come about bearing two-seven-one—"

Defiant pitched violently as a thunderstorm of impacts rocked its hull. Fighting to maintain her balance, Tigan staggered to the engineering console. "Heavy damage to the ventral shields," she reported. "Main power dropping!"

"Helm, dip the nose ninety degrees! Perez, return fire!"

More blasts shook the *Defiant,* and the lights on the

bridge flickered and dimmed. O'Brien caught the sharp bite of smoke in the air. "Damage report!"

"Power overloads," Tigan said. "Bridge to engineering! Quiqué, we're losing power to the phasers!"

"Nothing I can do, bridge," Muñiz shouted back over the clamor of panicked voices and wailing alarms. *"The plasma relays are slagged!"*

Another brutal hit overloaded the ship's inertial dampers and all but launched O'Brien from his chair. He scuttled across the deck and pulled himself up with both hands on his command screen. Glancing at the display, he caught short blips of Klingon ships uncloaking during their fly-by assaults, each of which dealt the *Defiant* another pummeling blow. "Dammit, get me defensive fire!"

"Phasers are at half power and falling," Perez snapped. "The Klingons are too fast for me to lock torpedoes!"

Tigan lunged across the bridge to loom over Perez's shoulder. "Look at their attack pattern!" She pointed at two points on the targeting display. "With those speeds and headings, they'd need to regroup somewhere between there and there. Give me a full launch of torpedoes right there, spread pattern Victor."

Perez locked in the target and fired. "Torpedoes away!"

The projectiles streaked away, twisting and spiraling as if at ghosts—then they all detonated at once, and half a dozen Klingon ships were knocked out of cloak and left shattered and smoldering, adrift in space. Tigan patted Perez on the back. "Target those ships and fire at will."

As Perez blasted the hobbled Klingon ships to bits, Tigan returned to O'Brien's side. "That'll buy us fifteen seconds while they regroup."

"We need to close ranks or we'll get killed," O'Brien decided. "Prynn, move us closer to the *Enterprise*. She's got damage on her port side, and we've got a breach to starboard. Let's see if we can give each other some cover."

Tigan hurried to the comm station. "I'll alert Picard."

Tenmei acknowledged from the helm, "Coming up alongside *Enterprise*."

A massive explosion behind the *Enterprise* silhouetted the majestic vessel. Seconds later, maydays from three different vessels overlapped on the rebellion's encrypted subspace channel. "What happened?" O'Brien demanded.

"*Courageous* is gone," Perez said. "*Ardent* just lost her shields, and the *Uzaveh* is losing antimatter containment." Checking her readings, she added, "Five Klingon ships just uncloaked and are starting an attack run on *Enterprise*."

"Helm, hard about," O'Brien said. "Weapons, target the lead Klingon ship."

"I can't," Perez said. "*Ardent*'s in the way." She shot a horrified look at O'Brien. "They're on a suicide run!"

"Helm, put us between *Ardent* and the *Enterprise,* and roll on the z-axis to show them our topside. Ezri, match *Enterprise*'s shield frequency! We have to take the hit or else it'll rip that breach in their hull wide open."

No one protested or questioned O'Brien's orders, and for that he was proud.

Tigan sounded the collision alarm. "Brace for impact!"

On the main viewer, the *Ardent* rammed the attacking squadron of Klingon cruisers head-on. The sleek Memory Omega starship exploded and consumed three of the Klingon ships entirely while leaving the other two tumbling away erratically into the void. Moments later, huge chunks of twisted, blackened starship debris slammed against the *Defiant,* which shuddered and pealed like a church bell as each slab of duranium made impact, one after another.

"Damage report," called O'Brien. "Talk to me, people."

Tenmei slammed her palms in frustration on the helm. "Warp drive's gone, helm's not responding!"

O'Brien glared at Tigan and tilted his head toward Tenmei. The first officer took the cue and scrambled forward to help the novice pilot patch in the auxiliary helm controls. *That'll get us back in motion,* he knew, *but it won't fix the warp drive.* He opened a channel to engineering. "Quiqué! How long for warp?"

An unfamiliar male voice answered. *"Chief Muñiz is dead."*

"Who's this?"

The engineer answered in a halting voice, *"DeCurtis, sir."*

"Well, listen up, DeCurtis. We need weapons and warp speed on the double, or we're all dead. We're counting on you now, so find a way, and get it done."

"Yes, sir."

"Bridge out." O'Brien closed the channel with a jab of his thumb. *That was the worst pep talk in history. We're all gonna die.* "Tactical, report."

Perez fought to coax useful intel from her console. "We're dead in space, the phasers are offline, and if we fire torpedoes, we'll have to target manually." Something began flashing rapidly on the long-range sensors. "Trilithium warhead signature! Range, ninety-three-point-five million kilometers." Her face was bright with terror as she faced O'Brien. "It's the *Ya'Vang*! They've targeted B'hava'el!"

"Bloody hell," O'Brien muttered, slumping in his

chair. *I hope to hell Calhoun knows what he's doing,* he fumed. *Because without warp drive, we'll be as good as dead if the Klingons set off one of those warheads.*

One Minute Earlier . . .

Patience had never been Mac's forte. Lurking millions of kilometers from the battle for B'hava'el and keeping the *Excalibur* in its minimum-power stealth mode was excruciating for him. As he watched his allies make one valiant sacrifice after another in their stand against the Klingons, bloodlust thundered in his temples; his fists curled white-knuckle tight and his brow knit with fury. He wanted to be in the thick of the fight, unleashing the full might of the *Excalibur* against its enemies.

His command team mirrored his pent-up desire to wade into the fray. Soleta stood close at Mac's shoulder, her fingers steepled and her unblinking stare fixed on the distant carnage pictured on the viewscreen. Jellico was hunched over his console, his thin lips all but vanished into a taut frown. Lefler was anxious and distraught, and even the normally unflappable Selar was perched on the edge of her seat, her countenance focused into a portrait of fierce intensity.

A comm signal on Lefler's console distracted her from the mayhem on the screen. "*Ardent*'s gone and the *Enterprise* has been hit," she said, her voice a fearful vibrato. "*Defiant*'s in trouble, too." She shut her eyes, unwilling or perhaps unable to take any more bad news from the battle.

The rest of the crew looked expectantly at Mac, as if he might suddenly reverse his decision and plunge into the crossfire. "Be patient," he said, projecting a calmness he didn't feel. "The *Ya'Vang* waits for her moment. We wait for ours."

No one looked placated by his words, and he didn't blame them.

An alert buzzed from Jellico's console. He reacted immediately and began punching in commands. "New energy signature! Trilithium warhead being armed! Bearing eight-five mark twelve, range one hundred sixteen point one thousand kilometers." He checked his data again. "Ship uncloaking—it's the *Ya'Vang,* sir!"

Mac cracked a gloating smile. *Right where I knew she'd be.* He sprang from his chair and stalked forward, feeling the thrill of the chase. "Full power, shields up! Lock all weapons and fire!"

The crew turned Mac's words into actions with speed and efficiency. The ship surged to life, emerging from stealth mode with a vengeance, and less than a second later the crew hammered the *Ya'Vang* with every ounce of *Excalibur*'s fearsome arsenal. Selar relayed new data to Jellico as the Klingon cruiser veered off into an evasive maneuver, and McHenry anticipated the *Ya'Vang*'s every turn and yaw, enabling Jellico to deliver one devastating shot after another. A barrage of return fire strafed the *Excalibur*'s shields, shaking the sleek warship but dealing it no serious damage.

"Her shields are down," Selar announced.

Soleta pointed at the underside of the ship's aft quarter. "Hit her main reactor, then her targeting array."

"On it," Jellico said, launching a storm of torpedoes.

Half a second later, the *Excalibur*'s crew cheered as multiple explosions tore through the *Ya'Vang,* breached her hull at multiple points, sheared away one of her warp nacelles, and set her adrift in an uncontrolled tumbling roll.

That's more like it, Mac rejoiced. He returned to his chair, lifted his chin, and put on his mask of stern command. "Lefler, send to *Ya'Vang* on all frequencies: 'Attention, commander and crew of the *Ya'Vang*. This is Captain Mac Calhoun of the free starship *Excalibur*. Surrender and prepare to be boarded.'"

"Sending," Lefler said. A moment later, her eyes opened wide, and she looked back at Mac. "Captain Krona's responding, sir."

"Put him on-screen."

The main viewer changed to a static-hashed image of the smoky, wrecked bridge of the *Ya'Vang*. Flames crackled in the background, framing the scorched visage of Captain Krona. He bared his teeth in a bloody, predatory grin. *"You think you've won, Calhoun? You think I didn't plan for this? Then you're a fool."* A blast of static crackled over the speaker as the transmission broke up and ended. The viewscreen reverted to the image of the burning husk of the *Ya'Vang*.

Before Mac could wonder aloud what Krona had been implying, McHenry's telepathic voice drowned out his thoughts with a frantic interruption. *Mac! The* Ya'Vang *is a decoy! I saw it in Krona's thoughts!*

Soleta spun and faced Mac—she, too, had heard McHenry's warning. Focusing his thoughts, Mac asked, *A decoy for what?*

He put some of his trilithium warheads on a bird-of-prey that took a wide course around the blockade. I'm sending its coordinates to Soleta's panel.

She turned and activated her console as Mac rushed to her side. One look at the data was enough to wipe all jubilation from her face. "I've got the bird-of-prey on sensors. It's less than two million kilometers from the star"—she frowned and looked at Mac—"and it just armed a trilithium warhead."

Jellico was crestfallen. "It's beyond disruptor range, and even if I fire a torpedo now, it won't reach them till after the warhead's away."

Tears shone in Lefler's eyes. "Then that's it. Game over, Klingons win."

"Not yet," Mac said. "We have one thing faster than a torpedo: us."

Soleta grabbed Mac's arm and hissed, "What're you doing?"

"What needs to be done." Though he normally communicated telepathically with McHenry, he decided the crew needed to hear his next order. "McHenry? I know you can push this ship to speeds we can't imagine. You can reach them before they fire."

McHenry responded aloud over the ship's PA system, much to the crew's surprise. "Mac, they're about to launch. You won't be able to fire before they do."

Calhoun nodded with grim, quiet resolve. "That's why I want you to ram them, at maximum warp. We need to destroy that warhead."

"Are you sure about this, Mac?"

"I am."

McHenry asked in a plaintive voice, "Soleta?"

She looked into Mac's eyes, and for perhaps the first time since he had known her, she looked at him with something greater than lust or affection or even mere respect. He knew that she had, at that very moment, come to love him.

"Yes, Mark," she said. "Do it. Before it's too late."

"As you command. Prepare for maximum warp."

Soleta took Mac's hand. Then she said, "To hell with decorum," and pulled him into a passionate kiss, right in front of everyone.

Locked in her embrace, savoring their emotional farewell to the flesh, Mac realized that his life's first truly selfless act was also about to be its last. *That's all right,* he concluded. *Always best to end on a high note.*

The *Excalibur* leaped into warp, on a collision course with fate.

One Minute Earlier . . .

"Get me more power!" Picard shouted toward the overhead speaker. He had taken over at the helm after the pilot, a Tellarite named Pog, had been struck unconscious by a falling hunk of the bridge's overhead. "I need full impulse, Mister Barclay!"

The harried chief engineer hollered back, *"Well, if you know some secret to unmelting a drive coil, now would be the time to share it, Captain!"*

"Dammit, Reg," K'Ehleyr chimed in from the tactical console, "we can't do combat maneuvers on thrusters alone! If the impulse drive is gone, say it now—because if you can't fix it, we need to abandon ship!"

Unintelligible cries of distress and a muffled explosion drowned out Barclay's first attempt at a reply. As the commotion receded, he said again, *"We can do it. Give us twenty minutes."*

"You've got five!" Picard snapped, wiping blood from a small shrapnel wound in the middle of his left eyebrow. "Bridge out!"

An explosion rocked the ship, and Picard clutched the sides of the helm panel to avoid being thrown from his chair. Aftershocks rumbled through the *Enterprise* as he looked back at K'Ehleyr. "What hit us?"

"The *Ardent,* sir. She's gone—and the only reason we didn't go with her is that *Defiant* turned itself into our shield." She switched the angle on the main viewscreen to show the *Defiant* holding station off the *Enterprise*'s port side, its own hull dented, scorched, and perforated.

Picard waved a drift of noxious gray smoke out of his eyes. "Remarkable," he said under his breath, impressed by such a display of valor from a people he himself had been all too willing to dismiss months earlier as a lost cause.

The forward turbolift doors opened, and a quartet of radiation-suited damage-control personnel rushed out. They split up and made quick work of extinguishing the small plasma fires inside several of the aft bulkheads. Moments later, a medical team emerged from a different turbolift and rushed to the aid of the fallen bridge personnel, who lay strewn about Picard and K'Ehleyr.

An alert shrilled at K'Ehleyr's station. "Trilithium warhead signature," she said. "It's the *Ya'Vang,* bearing—hold on, *Excalibur*'s emerging from stealth mode and moving to intercept! She's firing!" Half a second later, the half-Klingon woman pumped her fist. "Yes! They got her! *Ya'Vang* is down!"

"Excellent," Picard said, breathing a sigh of relief. "Tell Captain Calhoun I said, 'Well done.' Now let's see if we can finish off the rest of these—" He paused as he watched K'Ehleyr's good mood turn to horror. "What's happened?"

"A second trilithium signature," she said. "Bird-of-prey at point-blank range to the star. They must've known we'd go after the *Ya'Vang*."

He stood up. "Who's close enough to stop the bird-of-prey?"

K'Ehleyr shook her head. "No one. They're powering up their forward launcher. We have less than twenty seconds to get out of here."

"Alert the fleet. Order all ships that have warp speed to retreat."

She started to open the channel, then stopped and reacted to a new alert. "Massive energy reading from the *Excalibur*! She's going to warp! She's on a collision—" A blazing flash of light near the southern pole of B'hava'el washed out the *Enterprise*'s main viewer for several seconds. As it faded, K'Ehleyr finished her thought. "She was on a collision course with the bird-of-prey."

The news hit Picard like a fist. "Is . . . is the *Excalibur* . . . ?"

K'Ehleyr was somber. "Both ships are gone, sir. Completely destroyed." Reacting to more incoming signals, she added, "The *Ya'Vang* just exploded."

Picard didn't know what to say. Celebration felt grossly inappropriate, but his heart swelled with admiration for Calhoun and his crew. Never before had Picard witnessed an act of such amazing personal sacrifice. It left him speechless.

His moment of reverent, bereaved silence was broken by the chirp that preceded the opening of an internal comm channel. From an overhead speaker he heard Troi's voice. *"Captain, the crew of the* Excalibur *is in Hangar Bay One."*

Stunned and baffled, he looked at K'Ehleyr for an explanation, but all she had to offer was a confused shrug. Realizing that Troi was his only source of information at the moment, he asked, "How many of their crew made it aboard?"

It was Calhoun who replied sadly, *"All of us. . . . Except one."*

"Remain where you are, Captain," Picard said. "We'll send a medical team to assist you as soon as possible. Bridge out." He threw a hopeful look at K'Ehleyr. "Inform Mister Barclay I want impulse power in five minutes. It's time to finish this battle while we have the upper hand."

As if he had spoken a curse or invoked a jinx, an unwelcome sight rippled into view on the forward screen: Several dozen *Keldon*-class Cardassian warships uncloaked within visual range of the war-torn rebel fleet and cruised toward it at full impulse, grouped in a standard battle formation.

K'Ehleyr magnified the image and stared in confusion at the Cardassian ships. "I don't recognize those markings. What fleet are they from?"

Picard knew the ships' markings all too well, from his years of discreet service to Gul Madred. "Those ships don't belong to the regular Cardassian military," he said, his voice low with dread. "They're from the Obsidian Order."

"So much for having the upper hand," K'Ehleyr said.

Walking back to the helm, Picard said, "Tell Mister Barclay he now has one minute." He sat down. "Because I don't plan to die while standing still."

Alone in the brig of the *Geronimo,* Kes had only her imagination to tell her what was happening as concussions pounded the ship and the lights stuttered and failed. Alert klaxons wailed, and from the corridors outside her cell she heard shouts followed by explosions and the moans of the wounded and dying. The din of combat continued for several minutes, and each hit the tiny frigate suffered thundered more loudly than the last.

Then came the bone-jarring thunderstroke that plunged the ship's interior spaces into darkness. The force field on her cell went out, but the magnetic restraints binding her to the bulkhead remained stubbornly locked. Smoke billowed in from outside, and she dropped to the deck to avoid it and find breathable air.

Tuvok's voice echoed down the passageways as he shouted to the surviving crew members, "Abandon ship! Get to the escape pods!" Moments later, she heard his running steps and saw him stumble into her cell. "Kes! Are you all right!"

"I'm—" She choked on a mouthful of smoke and coughed. "I'm here!"

He crouched at her side, unlocked her restraints, and pulled her to her feet. "Stay with me! We need to abandon ship!" Using his tremendous Vulcan strength, he dragged her like a rag toy out of the brig and toward an outer corridor, where the escape pods were located.

"Tuvok, stop! What's happening?"

He answered without slowing or missing a step. "Our ship is dead in space, *Enterprise* and *Defiant* are surrounded by Cardassian warships, and most of the fleet is gone, including the *Excalibur*." They rounded a corner so quickly that Kes rebounded off the far wall as she struggled to keep up with her captor.

A booming impact rocked the *Geronimo* and momentarily pinned Kes and Tuvok against a bulkhead. The ship continued to tremble, and Kes could tell that the next serious hit the *Geronimo* suffered would be its last. As Tuvok pulled her back into motion, she pleaded, "Stop, please! I can save us!"

"It's too late," he said, opening the hatch on the

corridor's only remaining escape pod. "This battle is lost. I need to get you to safety."

Marshaling her strength, she pulled free of his grasp. "Why save me at all?"

"I swore to defend you," he said.

"What about the rebellion? Isn't it more important than me?" She could see from the doubt in his eyes that she was getting through to him. "If Calhoun's gone, the rebellion can't afford to lose Picard and O'Brien, too!" She grabbed his shirt with both hands. "Losing *all* its leaders in *one* fight? Tuvok, they'll never recover from that! *Never,* no matter how many super toys Memory Omega has. If you don't let me save them, the rebellion dies, here and now."

He took his hand off the escape pod controls. "Your point is logical."

"Tuvok, I'm *begging* you. Turn off the chip in my head. Let me help."

"As the only alternative is to accept the failure of everything for which I and millions of others have fought and sacrificed . . ." He let that thought trail off as he took the psi-damper control device from his pocket. And pressed its master switch. "Our fate is now in your hands, Kes."

Her power returned in a dizzying rush, as if a titanic dam that had been holding back an ocean was shattered all at once. Overcome with vertigo, she staggered backward and slumped against a bulkhead for balance. As she recovered her composure, the flat barren universe in which she'd been held prisoner vanished and gave way to one that was luminous with psionic energies and invisible forces. Thousands of minds, gravitational waves, cosmic strings, and extradimensional pockets of dark energy all were hers to wield.

She flashed a diabolical smirk at Tuvok—then bent the cosmos to her will.

During his long career in the Obsidian Order, including more than two decades as the intelligence agency's director, Enabran Tain had rendered many acts of patriotic service to the Cardassian Union and the Alliance, none of which would ever be publicly known. It did not trouble the obese, thick-jowled old Cardassian spymaster that he would never receive honors or accolades for any of those many accomplishments—because he was about to guarantee his place in history as the one who crushed the Terran Rebellion in one fell swoop.

"All ships, target the *Enterprise* and the *Defiant*," Tain said. "Keep the other ships at bay, but focus on destroying the two lead vessels." His subordinates nodded, then parroted his orders down the chain of command.

Watching the pair of hobbled rebellion ships loom large on the main screen inside the combat information center of the *C.D.S. Koranak,* Tain felt vindicated. He had broken half a dozen laws by authorizing the Obsidian Order to build its secret fleet of warships, but now that the majority of the Cardassian military had been left in ruins by the incompetent leadership of Supreme Legate Damar and his stooges on the Detapa Council, only Tain's forces stood between the Union and its enemies. And, as he was about to demonstrate, the Obsidian Order was better equipped to defend Cardassia's interests than the Central Command had ever been.

Pythas Lok, a slender and youthful-looking senior operative who served as Tain's second-in-command, approached the director and confided, "All ships report weapons lock—but Gul Drocan asks whether you wish to offer the Terrans terms of surrender."

"Why? So they can stall for time and find a way to escape?" Tain growled in frustration. "No terms will be offered. Order all ships to open fire, and when this battle's over, have Drocan eliminated."

Lok dipped his chin and backed away. "Yes, sir."

Tain turned toward the main screen, eager to see the rebellion end in fire. Its agents had slain his illegitimate son, Elim Garak, years earlier. Though Tain had never been able to risk acknowledging Garak as his scion, not even to Garak himself, he hated the rebels for denying him the chance to ever set things right.

Now you die, he raged behind a malevolent glare.

The *Koranak* flew apart, and the air was ripped from Tain's lungs as he was hurled without warning into zero-g vacuum. He was surrounded by a silent storm of twisted metal and flailing bodies cast into space, all scattering like flakes of ash on a volcanic gale. Feeling his blood boil as his vision purpled, Tain saw the rest of his magnificent fleet suffer the *Koranak*'s fate—dozens of state-of-the-art warships ripped to shreds as if by the invisible hands of the gods. Moments later, the same merciless power crushed the remaining Klingon ships into flotsam.

Surrendering to the cold grip of space, Tain spent his last ounce of strength composing curses he could never utter.

O'Brien pulled himself off the deck and massaged the wound on the back of his head. His hand came away sticky with half-dried blood, and he wiped it clean across the front of his shirt. Looking around the *Defiant*'s smoky bridge, he saw Tenmei at the helm, pressing a hand over the bloodied left side of her face. Tigan and Perez were at the weapons console, conferring in excited whispers. He stepped over a chunk of wreckage and staggered toward them. "What's going on?"

The two women looked up, their faces bright with hope and disbelief. "It's over," Tigan said. "Something tore the enemy ships to pieces."

"Care to be a bit more specific?" He hunched over Perez's left shoulder while Tigan leaned over the right.

Perez shook her head. "I wish we could, but we have no idea what happened. One minute the Cardassians had us dead to rights, and the next—we're floating in the middle of an Alliance starship graveyard."

The news drew an amused grunt from O'Brien. "Every time I think Memory Omega's run out of tricks . . ." He shook his head and patted Perez's shoulder. "Hail the *Enterprise* and put it on-screen." He stepped away and situated himself in the center of the bridge, facing the main viewscreen. As the image switched from the *Enterprise*'s battle-torn hull to its half-demolished bridge, O'Brien marveled that any of its crew were still alive. "Captain Picard? Are you there?"

Picard stepped into view. His face was smudged with soot, and a nasty laceration had bifurcated his left eyebrow. *"Yes, General. Are you all right?"*

"Thanks to you, we are. I don't know what you did to that fleet, but I wish you'd done it a hell of a lot sooner."

His praise seemed to befuddle Picard. *"General, we had nothing to do with stopping the Cardassian fleet."* He traded a worried glance with K'Ehleyr. *"In fact, we were just about to ask* you *what happened."*

Confusion turned to alarm in O'Brien's imagination. "But if it wasn't us . . ."

The comm signal wavered and broke up. Behind O'Brien, Perez protested, "Something's jamming all frequencies. I can't—wait, I have an incoming signal." She turned toward O'Brien and added, "It's on all channels."

He turned back toward the viewscreen as the garbled mess of fluctuating colors and scratching noise resolved into the crystal-clear, rock-steady image of an attractive young blond girl with curiously shaped ears. Her face had an innocent beauty, but the sinister gleam in her eyes belied that sweetness. O'Brien had never seen her or her species before, but he could tell in a glance that the girl was trouble.

"Who the hell are you?"

She answered with a haughty arrogance that gave O'Brien chills. *"My name is Kes, and I'm the one who just saved your lives—and your rebellion."*

O'Brien felt as if the girl were staring through him and directly into his soul. He tried to swallow his fear, only to find his throat as dry as the Martian desert. "I guess we ought to say 'thank you,' then."

The girl sneered, her contempt as cold as space. *"I don't want your thanks. I demand your obedience. As of this moment, you all exist to serve me."* Her smile made O'Brien shiver with terror. *"I'm your new empress."*

34

Fury's Reign

Crushing pressure enveloped Tuvok's skull. He'd collapsed facedown on the deck of the *Geronimo*'s bridge after staggering there in pursuit of Kes, who had stunned him with her first psionic jab. This time she hadn't even deigned to look in his direction before smashing through his telepathic barriers with humbling ease. He clutched the sides of his head and writhed in agony, the pain so great that his vision blurred and nausea twisted his stomach and churned sour bile up his esophagus.

"Kes," he gasped. "Please stop."

The lithe Ocampa crouched over him. "Not much fun to be the one without control, is it?" He dug his hand inside his pocket, but found it empty. She held up the control device for the psi-damper chip inside her skull. "Looking for this?" Before he could beg her to stop, she puffed a breath across the small metallic cylinder, which turned brittle and disintegrated into powder that dusted Tuvok's face. She clapped her hands clean. "Too bad."

"You . . ." His eyes felt as if they might burst. "You don't have to do this."

Raising herself up to her full height—which wasn't much, but from Tuvok's vantage point lying on the floor was more than tall enough to be intimidating—she adopted an imperial countenance. "I don't *have* to do anything, Tuvok. I'm doing this because I *want* to. That's all the reason I need."

He struggled to keep his voice steady and his thoughts calm. "Power like yours can show mercy."

His attempt at calming discourse sparked an eruption of temper from the young woman. "Like the mercy you showed me when you kept me from Neelix? Or when your people cut me open and used me like a lab specimen? Or the kind of mercy that left me trapped in the brig while Neelix died?"

Another lightning bolt of fiery torture blazed through Tuvok's conscious mind. When his vision refocused, he blinked and realized Kes was kneeling over him and holding him by the collar of his jacket. Her face was deformed by rage into a sick parody of itself, and her voice broke as she screamed, "You took me from him! You made me give up the only thing I ever loved! You lied to me!"

"I did what was necessary for the greater good."

She slapped him hard enough to gouge his cheek with her fingernails. "You and this whole sick corner of the galaxy deserve to pay, and I'm going to make sure every last one of you suffers like I have, only a thousand times worse. I'll bring you all pain and sorrow and death, and you'll worship me for it, because the ones who appease me best will get to die *first*."

He stole a glance at the chrono on the front of the helm console, then met Kes's hateful glare with his dispassionate gaze and said simply, "Forgive me."

"I already told—" She caught herself, realizing perhaps that something in his tone had changed, that his words had been pregnant with a terrible implication. She locked one hand around his throat. "What are you hiding from me, Vulcan?" Tuvok felt Kes's telepathic intrusions stabbing at his psychic barriers, and he summoned every psionic defense he knew to mask his thoughts.

The harder he fought for his privacy, the angrier she became. "You told me once that I couldn't kill you. You said every member of Memory Omega was trained to block the psionic wavelengths I use to kill." She exploited a weakness in his defense and sent a jolt of white agony down his spinal column. "That was a *lie,* Tuvok. You thought if I believed it was futile, I'd stop trying. That I wouldn't find out how powerful I really am." With a few synaptic tweaks she fooled his body into believing it was on fire. His screams were hideous and involuntary. No matter how he tried to block the pain as a mere illusion, Kes forced the signal through. "Tell me what you're hiding, Tuvok, or I'll make sure your death is a slow one."

Overcome by his mind's betrayals, Tuvok lost control of his defenses and felt Kes invade his deepest thoughts. As he'd feared, it had never been a real contest. His lifetime of skill was no match for the unstoppable force of her mind.

Like a mental spectator, he stood on the black shore of his psyche and watched as Kes dredged the truth from the dark, still waters of his suppressed memories. It glittered like a jewel in her hand as she unraveled its secrets.

"The psi-damper chip," she whispered in the physical world, her breath warm on his face. "It had a failsafe . . ."

"With a three-minute countdown," Tuvok muttered as she exhumed the details from his brain, "to an explosive charge . . ."

She let go of him and pushed herself away, scrambling about on all fours in a desperate search for the control device, which she now knew was the only way to stop the chip from completing its lethal final function.

Pawing at the silvery dust on the deck, she whimpered, "The controller . . . Tuvok, help me!"

Tuvok watched impassively as Kes struggled in vain to reassemble the powder into the device it once had been. Unfortunately for Kes, even Tuvok had not known its secrets, or in what part of her brain the chip had been implanted—only that her conditioning during her convalescence at the base inside Regula had rendered her permanently blind to that part of her own mind. Her eyes were bright with tears and terror as she looked at him. "Tuvok?"

"There is nothing I can do to help you now."

She shut her eyes, balled her fists, and mustered a scream of furious denial—which caught in her throat as a tiny explosion inside her head was betrayed by a muffled *pop* and a tiny wisp of gray smoke from her left ear.

Her eyes were still open as she slumped onto her right side, lifeless and limp. As Tuvok freed himself and crawled out from beneath her, he saw a thin trickle of blood escape from Kes's right nostril. The banality of the moment struck him as both ironic and unjust: The greatest psionic power in the galaxy had just been murdered by an induced aneurysm. Her death, despite being necessary and at least partially self-inflicted, filled him with regret—not for his actions or omissions, but for the simple, grotesque wastefulness of it all.

I must accept what I cannot change, Tuvok reminded himself. He reached over, gingerly nudged Kes's eyelids closed, and stood to leave, knowing that in his own estimation, he had failed her in every way possible—and that her death would be his shame to bear for as long as he lived.

"Good-bye, Kes."

35

Blood and Bones

Delivered from the coruscating embrace of the transporter beam, Picard was awed by the natural beauty of the Elemspur Monastery and its surrounding wilderness preserve. Located in Hedrikspool Province in Bajor's southern hemisphere, the millennia-old religious retreat was considered by many scholars to be one of the most significant archeological sites in the quadrant. Despite his long service to Gul Madred, Picard had never been able to obtain permission to set foot on Bajor, never mind the monastery's grounds, while in the Cardassians' employ.

Now he stood on its ramparts as an invited guest. He drew a deep breath of the muggy air and reveled in the lush bouquet of the Bajoran rain forest. Peaty, earthy qualities blended with floral fragrances. Then he turned and admired the monastery's ornate stonework, lofty towers, and graceful arches. Bathed in the amber light of dawn, it was one of the most magnificent places he had ever seen.

He heard the footsteps of people climbing the stairs to his left. With a quick tug he smoothed the front of his uniform jacket and then turned to greet Captain Calhoun and General O'Brien, who strode toward him side by side. "Gentlemen," Picard said, shaking

O'Brien's hand first, then Calhoun's. "I trust you're well."

"I've been better," Calhoun said.

O'Brien shrugged. "Can't complain."

Picard eyed Calhoun. "I've been meaning to ask you, Captain: How *did* you and your crew survive when your ship rammed that bird-of-prey?"

"I wish I knew," Calhoun said. "I suspect the credit belongs to my navigator, but since he's the only one who didn't make it out alive . . ." He shook his head.

The general glanced skyward and asked Picard, "How's it going up there?"

"Every ship that's still intact has been towed into orbit," Picard said. "Most of the survivors have been beamed down to sanctuaries here on the surface. We've left skeleton crews aboard a few ships to work on repairs."

Calhoun nodded. "What about reinforcements?"

"I spoke with Saavik," Picard said. "She'll be able to send replacement crews on a ship with a working jaunt drive in about thirty-one hours. Once they arrive, they'll open a wormhole and escort us back to Erebus Station for repairs and refits." Noting the pained look on Calhoun's face, he added, "And in your case, Captain, reassignment—if you're willing to helm a new ship."

The Xenexian captain let slip a rare hint of a laugh. Exorcising all trace of a good mood from his face—except for a mischievous gleam in his purple eyes—he replied, "Yes, I think I could be talked into that."

"Saavik thought you might."

Tilting his head toward the stairs to the monastery's courtyard, O'Brien said, "We're supposed to bring you down to the temple hall. Kai Opaka and her friends are waiting for you."

"Lead on, then."

Picard followed O'Brien and Calhoun down the weathered, rough-hewn stone staircase to a grass-covered, rectangular courtyard surrounded by a cobblestone walkway. Taking care to stay on the stone path, O'Brien noted, "Don't walk on the grass. The locals seem to take that kind of personally."

"Noted," Picard said. They passed through an open archway into a long covered promenade, which led to a pair of tall, dark wooden doors with brass fittings. O'Brien pushed open the doors, which protested with high-pitched shrieks. Then he stood aside and let Picard lead the way inside the temple.

The main hall of the Elemspur Monastery had a high, domed ceiling adorned by antique murals and mosaics. Sturdy metal stands held tall white tapers whose flames danced madly as the three men disturbed the air with their entrance. Curved benches were arrayed in a 240-degree arc facing an elevated dais, upon which stood a short altar of rough granite, two marble tables topped with small items of religious paraphernalia, and a lectern of cold-wrought iron. The entire room was suffused with a pleasing, honeyed light, and reverberated with the distant mellisonance of deep voices chanting in forgotten tongues.

Standing before a row of candles to Picard's right was Kai Opaka. The stout woman busied herself reigniting wicks snuffed by the breeze that had followed the rebel commanders into the sanctum. It was to her credit, Picard thought, that she appeared perfectly serene in the performance of her task. Trailing her by a few steps was

Vedek Winn, and seated on a bench at the back of the room, observing from a distance, was Iliana Ghemor, the Cardassian woman who, to Picard's surprise, had been accepted by the Bajoran people as their prophesied messiah, the long-awaited Emissary of the Prophets.

Opaka used a lit candle to relight an extinguished one, then set the first back into its place. She nodded at Winn, who stepped forward and continued the task as Opaka walked over to greet the visitors. "General, Captains," she said with a broad and genuine smile. "We're so glad you're all still with us."

"So are we," O'Brien said.

The kai let the quip pass without comment. "We've quartered your personnel as best we can, given the continuing ecological damage inflicted by the destruction of Ashalla, but I assure you they'll all be well fed and comfortably sheltered—as will you and your senior personnel."

"As long as the Cardassians don't take another shot at us," Calhoun said.

Opaka shook her head. "Not likely. Between this battle and the one at Raknal Station, they've suffered great losses in a short time. I suspect it will be months before they have enough ships in this sector to mount a new offensive."

Winn added, "And even if they did, our surface-based artillery would make them think twice about closing to weapons range." She folded her hands in a beatific pose that was at odds with her bellicose rhetoric. "You're safe here."

"And for that we are tremendously grateful," Picard said. "We promise not to overstay our welcome. If all goes as planned, we'll be gone by tomorrow."

Taking hold of Picard's arm with a feather touch, Opaka asked, "So soon?"

"I'm afraid so. We've suffered significant losses and need to regroup."

The news provoked a look of concern from Winn, who asked the three men, "How badly were your forces hit?"

O'Brien answered, "Very. We lost a lot of ships and a lot of good people."

Opaka turned her soulful gaze toward Calhoun. "I'm told you sacrificed your ship to save our world." She reached slowly toward his left ear, and when he reflexively pulled away, she asked with a smile, "May I? Please?" He nodded his assent, and Opaka gently cupped his ear in her hand, closed her eyes, and squeezed the lobe. She winced, then opened her eyes and stared with reverence at Calhoun. "You and your crew did not expect to survive. You thought you were sacrificing yourselves—not just your ship."

Her proclamation made O'Brien and Picard face Calhoun and regard him with new respect. Calhoun, for his part, seemed uncomfortable with the attention. He gently removed Opaka's hand from his ear. "We did what we had to do."

Winn looked as if she was on the verge of tears. "You risked your ships, your lives, and the fate of your rebellion—all to save us? Why would you risk everything for which you've fought and sacrificed, for just one world?"

Picard, O'Brien, and Calhoun exchanged hopeful looks, and in that moment Picard was certain that they all had arrived at the same answer. As Calhoun spoke and O'Brien nodded, his belief was proved correct.

"We did it," Calhoun said, "because it was the right thing to do."

The air in the temple was charged with equal parts excitement and anxiety, but O'Brien felt only the latter. He and the vast majority of the remaining commanders of the Terran Rebellion had gathered in the sacred hall of the Elemspur Monastery at the behest of Director Saavik, whom he had been told would be making a personal visit to address them. The news hadn't seemed especially noteworthy to O'Brien until Keiko had explained that no director of Memory Omega had ever done anything remotely like this in its century-long history.

Sensing the enormity of the moment, O'Brien had shaved and made an extra effort to find a clean shirt to wear to the meeting.

Milling about the domed hall were people he'd known for years, and some he knew only on sight but not by name. Picard and Calhoun stood off to one side, conducting a discussion in whispers. Keiko stood with a circle of Memory Omega operatives that included Selar, Tuvok, and L'Sen. Eddington held court for a few of the rebellion's senior commanders, including Ezri Tigan and Alan Kistler. O'Brien spotted Picard's first officer, K'Ehleyr, and her shipmates, Troi and Barclay, lurking along the room's periphery. Near the back of the room, Calhoun's first officer, Soleta, was engaged in a muted but intense conversation with former Praetor Hiren and four of his Romulan commanders. Dozens of others packed the rows of seats, filling the room with a hushed undercurrent of worried voices.

The euphonious hum of a transporter beam halted

the overlapping dialogues and drew everyone's attention to the front of the room, where a prismatic swirl of particles coalesced into the white-garbed and eminently dignified shape of Saavik. She wasted no time on a preamble. "The *Valiant* has arrived in orbit and begun preparations to shift your vessels back to Erebus Station. Replacement crews are being beamed aboard your ships to assist in repairs."

Calhoun interrupted, "You didn't come all the way here just to tell us *that*. What's the real news?"

The Vulcan woman lifted one brow a quarter of a centimeter, and O'Brien read the subtle shift in her expression as one of annoyance—and then decided he probably was just projecting his own feelings onto her. Raising her chin, Saavik directed her reply to the room at large, not just to Calhoun. "The captain is correct. You have been gathered together so that we can plan the final stage of this revolution. The good news is that our cease-fire with the Klingon Empire seems likely to hold, and might soon develop into a formal truce. The bad news is that peace with the Cardassian Union seems all but impossible. Recent intelligence suggests that Damar personally would prefer to end this conflict, but he is under extreme pressure from his people, their civilian government, and the Cardassian military to press on, despite their recent losses."

It definitely was not the news O'Brien wanted to hear. "So, what now?"

"As noble—and fortunate—as your defense of Bajor was, it will leave the Cardassians' appetite for revenge unsatisfied. Regrettably, this war will not end until Cardassia's collective will to wage it has been broken."

Picard stepped forward to stand at O'Brien's side as

he asked Saavik, "What, precisely, are you suggesting that will entail?"

"We must lay waste every major military and political target in the Cardassian Union—starting with their homeworld, Cardassia Prime."

Fatigue robbed O'Brien of his strength, and he rubbed his eyes as he exclaimed, "No." He repeated that single word so many times in rapid succession that he lost count of how many times he'd said it. "That's not the answer. It can't be." The war-weary general shook his head. "I've seen too much killing, too many worlds left in flames. It has to end. Someone needs to be the first to take the high road. I can't believe the only path to victory is paved with blood and bones."

"It has ever been thus," Saavik said, "and so it shall remain."

Moving forward to join the debate, Calhoun raised his voice for the benefit of the crowd. "She's right. This is no time to shy away from hard choices."

"No one's *shying away*," O'Brien said. "If anything, choosing peace is the hard way. We've all lost people we care about, we all want our pound of flesh, an eye for an eye. But some lines, once they've been crossed, can't be uncrossed."

Standing between O'Brien and Saavik, Picard looked torn. "Miles, I share your revulsion at the notion of genocide, but I spent a good portion of my life living among the Cardassians. I know their temperament well, from first-hand experience. They're a ruthless, almost amoral people. Saavik may be right—the only way to slake their thirst for war might be to drown them in it."

The crowd pressed inward, and heated voices started shouting at one another from all directions. Some people argued for hope, others for cynicism; for each person who counseled diplomacy, another cried out for blood. Voices were raised, fingers were pointed, and epithets shot back and forth like flights of poison arrows, wounding egos as they tainted the discourse.

Pushed to his limit, O'Brien took to the dais, placed himself before the altar, and faced the raging throng with his arms upraised. "Enough!" he shouted, his roar cutting through the noise like a surgeon's blade. "Listen to me!" A hush descended upon the crowd, and everyone gave their attention to O'Brien. "What have we been fighting for all these years? I said it before, on Terok Nor, and I'll say it again here. This rebellion hasn't just been about slavery or freedom. It hasn't been about revenge. We fight for a belief. For the idea that we can all live together as equals under the law, no matter who we are or where we came from. Our goal hasn't been to bring back the Terran Empire, or even the Terran Republic, but to build something new, something *better*. It's been about making *ourselves* better, so that we can deserve to live in this new world we're fighting to create.

"What's been suggested here tonight—wiping out most of Cardassia to make a point and break their will—is the sort of thing our ancestors would've done. It's what the Terran Empire would've done. And that's exactly why we shouldn't do it. Embracing this kind of merciless, scorched-earth warfare would be a major step backward. And progress is about moving *forward*.

"Before we decide how to end this war, we need to know what kind of civilization we want to build when we're done—because the choice we make now will define that decision for us. You can't build a noble society, a just society, on a foundation of genocide. That's not a legacy I want to be known for. But if we do what Saavik is suggesting, anything born of this revolution will forever be tainted by that crime. History will never forget it." He frowned and heaved a sigh. "That's all I have to say. You tell me what kind of people we are."

His speech was met with a long, shamed silence.

Then a woman called out from the back of the crowd, "You're right." The members of the crowd turned as one to see Iliana Ghemor, the Emissary, standing in the open doorway of the main temple hall. She strode toward the front of the room as she continued, and the rebellion's rank and file parted before her. "With all respect, Captain Picard, the Cardassians aren't ruthless because of their biology—they learned that trait from their culture. If you really want to put an end to this war, mass murder isn't the solution." She reached the front of the room, looked O'Brien in the eye, and favored him with a subtle, hopeful smile. "If you'll let me, I can help you find a better way."

It was midnight in Cardassia City, which sprawled beyond the oval windows of Supreme Legate Damar's office. He stood alone with the lights off and gazed at the dim outlines of the capital as he downed a glass of his best *kanar*. *Might as well finish it off while I still can,* he reasoned, stepping to the liquor cabinet in the corner for a refill. *Tomorrow this could all be gone.*

Pouring a triple measure of the syrupy liquor into his glass, he wondered how many more it would take to submerge his melancholy in an alcoholic slumber. The *kanar* had become his only refuge in a world gone to pieces. Central Command and the Obsidian Order were both in utter disarray, each blaming the other for its latest high-visibility defeat. All but a few standing units of the Twelfth Order had been obliterated at the battle for Raknal Station, leaving the Central Command barely able to patrol the Union's outermost borders. Meanwhile, the Obsidian Order—which Damar had been livid to discover was operating a secret fleet of military starships—had squandered its hidden arsenal in a failed bid to wipe out the Terran Rebellion at Bajor.

With both arms of the Union's security apparatus broken, the people were in an uproar. The financial markets were crashing, interstellar commerce had been halted because the trade routes were no longer safe to traverse without armed escorts, and the media had slipped its government leash and was excoriating the Detapa Council in general and Damar in particular as "incompetents" who were steering the ship of state aground. Predictably, instead of uniting to weather the storm of public opinion, the incumbent members of Cardassia's political class had begun pushing one another overboard. It was easy to see why: Metaphorically speaking, there was blood in the water, and everyone assumed the citizenry would be happy to feed on whomever it got hold of first. What Damar suspected but hadn't said was that he feared the mob wouldn't be appeased by a few token sacrifices, not this time. *They won't stop until they devour us all,* he brooded.

He turned away from the dark metropolis and sank into his chair, glass in hand. Lifting it to down another mouthful in the hope of dulling one more iota of his bitter mood, he saw someone move in the shadows between him and the door. To his own surprise, he did not panic or cry out. Instead, he sipped his drink and set it down, then smiled at the unannounced visitor. "Are you an assassin?"

"No," she said. "A messenger."

Her voice was familiar, but he couldn't place it. He leaned forward and eased the lights up to one-quarter brightness, revealing her face. "Iliana Ghemor." His smile broadened into a grin. "Are you sure you're not here to kill me?"

She stopped in front of his desk and stood before him, empty-handed. "I'm just here to talk. There's been far too much bloodshed already."

"Strange words from a member of the Obsidian Order."

"That's not who I am anymore."

He sipped his drink. "Oh, yes. I forgot. You're a Bajoran demigod now."

The lithe, attractive woman circled around his desk. "I am to them what I am to you: a messenger. That's what it means to be an *emissary*."

He chortled; the implications of her statement were preposterous to him. "What are you saying? That the Bajorans' magical 'prophets' sent you to me?"

"In part, yes." He saw in her eyes that she was quite serious. She continued. "I'm here to help you do the right thing as a member of the Oralian Way."

Panic clouded his thoughts and made his heart race, but he froze his expression in a mask of vapid amusement. "I think you've mistaken me for—"

"There's no mistake, Damar. I know you're a true believer in Oralius, that you were secretly raised in the faith by your mother. Even your father never knew that you were brought up with the song of the morning."

How can she know this? A terrible possibility occurred

to him. *She was in the Obsidian Order. They must have vetted me when I came up through the ranks. But that would mean they know everything!*

Ghemor rested a hand on the back of Damar's chair as she leaned over him. "I can see that you're scared, Damar. Don't be. No one knows this but me . . . yet."

"But how did you . . . ?"

"The Prophets reveal many things to those who know how to listen." She beckoned Damar to his feet, and he stood. With a gentle hand on his shoulder, she turned him to stand beside her and face out his windows. "I know that the Oralian Way is alive and growing as an underground movement throughout the Cardassian Union. It's the philosophy our people used to live by, before the time of the Change. And it's what we need to return to, if we're to survive as a species and as a culture."

He backed away from her. "You must be out of your mind! After all these centuries? There's no going back now."

"Then why put your faith in it? Why worship Oralius if she has nothing to offer?" She seized Damar's forearms and pulled him back to the window. "Don't run from this, Damar! This is your chance to do what Dukat never would have done, and what no one else in your place could do: You can bring the Oralian Way out of the shadows. You can usher in a Second Hebitian Age."

"No!" He struggled to pull away from her, but her grip was ferocious. In his futile effort to break free, he dropped his glass, which shattered and drenched their feet in *kanar*. "The people aren't ready! If the disciples of the Way reveal themselves now, they'll be slaughtered in the streets! And me with them!"

"You're wrong, Damar, and I'm going to tell you why. Our people respect one thing above all else: strength. We value family, but we love power."

She was a madwoman, he was certain of it. "So? The Oralian Way's not about power. It's about peace and compassion for others."

"So is the Bajoran religion, which now has a link to its divine source—and I'm that link, Damar. Want to know what else I've learned from the Prophets?"

As desperately as he wanted to escape her clutches, he was deeply curious to hear what she had to say next. "What?"

"The Bajoran faith and the Oralian Way share a common heritage. They're both linked to the ancient Hebitians, and to the Prophets. I'm not just Bajor's emissary—I can also be Cardassia's." She let go of him, but he no longer felt the urge to flee. She pressed her palms to his face. "I can shed new light on your faith, on our true history, and even our future. That's the kind of power I can give you—the kind no one else on Cardassia has: the truth."

The burden of his doubt was oppressive. "I'm not sure that will be enough to spark the kind of change you're hoping for."

"I am," Ghemor said. "The Prophets have seen it. It's coming."

He wanted to trust her; he was desperate to believe her words. "Asking the people to accept a change of this magnitude after everything that's happened in the last year could be the tipping point. It might cause our society to implode."

"If so, that will be your chance to rebuild."

Staring out the windows across the Tarlak Sector, he

envisioned a thousand ways this risk could end in catastrophe. "If I were to attempt something so rash and ill-advised . . . where would I begin?"

"First, you need to end the war with the Terran Rebellion."

"And how am I supposed to persuade the council to do that?"

Ghemor's countenance turned grim. "Tell them the truth. Your military's been gutted, and the rebellion is still heavily armed. Unless you sue for peace in the next three days, the rebels will destroy every planet in the Union—starting with Cardassia Prime." She cracked a sardonic smile. "After they swallow that little nugget, legalizing the Oralian Way will probably seem like no big deal."

Damar shook his head and collapsed into his chair. "This is ridiculous. You ask the impossible, Ghemor. You want me to transform our entire society all but overnight, and almost entirely by myself. One man can't change the world."

"Wrong. It takes only one man with a vision to summon the future. You can *be* that man, Damar. More important, Cardassia *needs* you to be that man." She offered him her hand. "And if you let me . . . I will help you."

Mac and Soleta followed Saavik down a broad, two-kilometer-long corridor that was lined on both sides with spacious observation lounges. Next to each lounge was a hatch to a gangway that led to a docked starship. Some of them were new wormhole jaunt ships constructed by Memory Omega, and others were vessels from the rebellion armada that had been brought back to Erebus Station for repairs—or, in the most extreme cases, total rebuilds, from the spaceframes out.

"It's not much farther," Saavik said.

Soleta replied, "You might consider putting in moving walkways."

"We did. We decided that promoting exercise was more beneficial." The Vulcan woman continued a few paces ahead of Soleta and Mac, and didn't see the dismissive glances that passed between them. After a few more minutes of walking, she detoured toward an observation lounge on their right, stopped at the towering transparent wall, and turned back to face the duo. "Here it is."

Stepping up to the window-wall, Mac looked out at one of the sleek jaunt ships that Memory Omega had built. This one was white and pristine, and he suspected that even if he were to inspect every inch of its hull with a magnifying glass, he wouldn't find so much as a scratch on her. "She's a beauty," he said.

"Very impressive," Soleta added.

A friend's voice echoed in Mac's thoughts: *Over here. Behind you.*

In unison, he and Soleta turned, alerting him that she had heard the same telepathic summons. Without explaining themselves to Saavik, they walked away from her and crossed the corridor to the observation window on the other side. After a moment of confused hesitation, Saavik followed them.

They arrived at the other transparent wall and gazed together at a Romulan starship docked at the end of the gangway. It was a *Mogai*-class warbird, one of the Romulan military's newer designs, but this ship clearly had been through hell. The distinctive feathering pattern of its green hull was scorched and pitted, and large sections had been replaced with unsightly gray patches. A team of robots were hard at work replacing its charred warp nacelles.

Without prompting, Saavik volunteered, "This is the *Valdore,* one of the ships salvaged from the Battle of Bajor."

Staring at the sleek raptor of a vessel, Mac focused his thoughts. *McHenry, is that you? Are you on the* Valdore?

Yes, Mac. It's me. Hello, Soleta.

Mac glanced to his right and saw Soleta smile. *McHenry, what happened at Bajor? How did we end up on the* Enterprise? *How'd you get here?*

The navigator sounded abashed and distracted. *It's a long story, Mac. I saved you by creating overlapping folded pockets of space-time and shifting our temporal constant. Do you really want me to go into detail?*

Trading an exasperated look with Soleta, Mac projected back, *No.*

As for myself, I waited until the nanosecond before the Excalibur *struck the bird-of-prey, then severed my consciousness from my physical form. Fortunately, these new Romulan ships are using bioneural computer cores, so when I found that the* Valdore's *crew was gone, I took over its main computer. And here we are.*

Ever the practical sort, Mac asked, *Does the cloak work?*

Of course, McHenry responded.

Soleta smiled, and Mac knew what to do.

He turned to Saavik. "We'll take this one."

The director arched an eyebrow. "Are you quite certain? We can restore this ship's systems, but one of our jaunt ships would be far more powerful—and better suited to a figure of your stature within the rebellion."

"We're sure," Mac said, "on one condition." Despite himself, he smiled. "I'm renaming it *Excalibur.*"

Miles O'Brien walked alone through the empty corridors of the *Defiant*. The ship had been docked at Erebus Station for nearly three weeks, and its latest round of repairs and refits was nearly complete. Its ablative armor had been improved, and its new transphasic munitions were expected to deliver nearly six times as much firepower as the quantum warheads they were replacing.

Not that any of that mattered anymore.

Wandering the deserted corridors on the starship's lower decks, O'Brien felt dazed and insubstantial. The rhythm of his own breathing filled his ears, and his footsteps seemed to land without sensation, making him feel as if he were afloat. He still couldn't make sense of the news that had just been relayed to the fleet by the Memory Omega crew that manned the station. Though he'd watched it three times over, and had heard every word with perfect clarity, it still seemed surreal.

Supreme Legate Damar had decreed on an open subspace channel the acceptance of a cease-fire with the Terran Rebellion and an uneasy truce with the Klingon Empire—both of which had been confirmed immediately by Regent Duras. Though the Alliance remained dissolved, both powers had signed nonaggression treaties with the Taurus Pact, which in turn had surprised O'Brien by recognizing the Terran Protectorate as a nascent state.

It had been less than three hours since ambassadors from the Klingon Empire and Cardassian Union had met in secret on the neutral Orion homeworld with a representative of the Terran Rebellion to sign the Tripartite Armistice. In a surprising gesture of good faith, Ambassador M'Rod of Qo'noS had been the first to sign the document. Next, Ambassador Broca of Cardassia had affixed his seal on behalf of the Union, after which Representative Eddington had completed the ceremony by signing on behalf of the rebellion.

In addition to ending hostilities among the three powers, the armistice had formally ceded more than two dozen worlds in a twenty-light-year radius around the Sol system to the rebellion's autonomous control and established a ten-light-year-wide Neutral Zone around the new independent territory. Despite the fervent objections of the Klingon ambassador, the armistice also restored the sovereignty of the Romulan Star Empire and compelled the Klingons to withdraw their forces from Romulan space without delay. Then, while the ink was still wet on the armistice, the rebellion had signed a treaty of alliance and mutual defense with the Romulan Star Empire, which was represented by Hiren, its once and future praetor.

After seven interminable, blood-soaked, and sometimes ostensibly hopeless years . . . the war was over. The rebellion had won.

Roaming the empty spaces of his battle-torn ship, O'Brien was overcome with melancholy. Everywhere he looked he saw reminders of the past, and he began to count the dead. His heart grew heavy as he remembered Leeta and Sam, and Muñiz and Luther Sloan. He mourned Sisko, who had started him down this long and bloody path, and Neelix and Seska, and Cal Hudson, and Kasidy Yates, and thousands of other patriots who had given everything for people they would never know. He even let himself grieve for men like Zek and Bashir, who had acted more like his rivals than his allies but who had died for the cause.

They, and tens of thousands of others he couldn't even name, had made this day possible. It pained O'Brien to think that none of them would see the new world that had been paid for with their lives.

We owe it to them to make sure it's a good one, he decided as he neared the door to his quarters. For all the times he had professed to hate the Klingons, or the Cardassians, or the Alliance, or even the war itself, he knew that none of those were the real object of his scorn. What he hated most was what he had become because of them. He vowed to himself that he would honor the sacrifices of the fallen by laying down his arms and never killing again.

He arrived at his quarters, and the door sighed open. As he stepped over the threshold, Keiko rushed forward and wrapped him in her loving embrace. There were tears of joy in her eyes as she kissed him.

"We made it," she said. "All the way to the end."

He kissed her, then smiled. "No, this is just the beginning. . . . Marry me."

PART III

Post Tenebras Lux

January 2379

36

Pax Omega

TRANSCRIPT START
OBSIDIAN ORDER SIGNAL INTERCEPT
   4891–19-*Orutal*
SUBSPACE FREQUENCY: 3.247 KT
SOURCE: UNKNOWN

WOMAN'S VOICE (VOICEPRINT PROFILE 561-
   Nexot-979183)
Attention, all worlds within range of this signal. The
   following is a warning from Memory Omega.
   We serve as the advisers and defenders of the
   new independent state formed by the Terran
   Rebellion. For nearly a century we have labored
   in secret, developing new technologies, and we
   shall continue to do so. However, our new goal is
   to guide this burgeoning civilization in a peaceful
   and logically sustainable direction.

We assure you all that the new political entity we have
   nurtured into being will not behave aggressively
   toward you or the worlds over which you reign. It
   will, however, welcome into its ranks any planets
   or species that wish to defect from yours—and
   you are going to permit this. You also will suffer

this new government's need to explore in peace beyond its borders and expand its territory to include new worlds and new civilizations.

Many of your nations have signed treaties with this new government. It is our hope that these pacts will be honored in good faith. Unfortunately, history is our guide, and it teaches us that it can be difficult for nation-states to resist the temptation to act treacherously when doing so is to their advantage. We have found that the only effective means of discouraging such opportunistic behavior by large-scale political actors is to make sure that the cost of such action outweighs any potential benefits.

To that end, we have prepared a demonstration. Your long-range sensor stations will be able to confirm what we are about to show you.

[VID SIGNAL ACTIVATED ON SAME FRE-QUENCY: *Image from high orbit of a Type Nine planet.*]

This is the planet Rhenvara V, a Class G world in an unpopulated star system that lies just beyond the Terran Neutral Zone, inside sovereign Terran space. It has no natural resources worth exploiting, and its lack of indigenous life-forms is well documented.

[*A bright object streaks toward the planet.*]

This is the Genesis Device, a technology we mastered nearly a century ago.

[*The object makes impact and detonates. A fiery shock wave expands from the blast point, spreads at hypersonic velocity, and engulfs the entire surface of the planet. The planet's equatorial region becomes a verdant rain forest.*]

Genesis is capable of transforming lifeless worlds like Rhenvara V into lush, Class M worlds capable of supporting humanoid life—not over the course of years or even months, but in a matter of hours. Check your sensor readings of Rhenvara V, and you will discover that what we have told you is true.

Know this: If a Genesis Device is deployed on a world where life-forms already exist, it will destroy such life in favor of its new matrix. And remember that our mastery of wormhole propulsion means we can deploy these devices at any time against any world in the galaxy.

The rest of this galaxy is yours to explore in peace— but do not interfere with the worlds under our protection. This will be your only warning. We strongly recommend you do not test our resolve.

TRANSMISSION TERMINATED
TRANSCRIPT END

ADDENDUM
LONG-RANGE SENSOR REPORT: RHENVARA V
OBSIDIAN ORDER OBSERVATION STATION
KELGOT
GUL LEOBEN, COMMANDING OFFICER

As requested on 23 *Hamarak* 4891, this station conducted a thorough examination of the planet Rhenvara V, located at coordinates 15.02.076.12. Consistent with the data provided by the Signals Intelligence Unit (SIU), the planet, which had been documented as a Type Nine world with no atmosphere or indigenous life-forms, now registers as a Type Five habitable planet with an oxygen-nitrogen atmosphere. With permission from Gul Trokal, we requested that *O.S. Osskol* conduct an independent survey of the planet. *O.S. Osskol* has confirmed our readings.

37

Severed Bonds

Just as O'Brien had expected, Worf was on his feet and facing him as he arrived outside the former regent's cell. Thanks to the mine's natural deposits of fistrium and some active sensor camouflage installed by the rebellion, the Alliance had not found the underground prison during their scouring of the Badlands for O'Brien and his people after the destruction of Terok Nor. And so Worf had languished here, beneath a filled-in mine shaft, with only a small detachment of guards and a larder full of stolen Alliance military rations to sustain him.

The Klingon folded his hands behind his back. "O'Brien."

"Worf." O'Brien took a control device from his jacket pocket, and with the press of a button, unlocked and opened the gate of Worf's cell.

All at once, Worf tensed, and his thick brows knit together. He let his arms fall loosely at his sides, and he stared at O'Brien with a murderous glare tempered by the obvious suspicion that he was being goaded into a trap. "What is this?"

"The war's over," O'Brien said.

Apparently still leery of a ruse, Worf remained still. "I do not believe you. Klag would never surrender. He is too stubborn."

"Klag's dead. Duras is the new regent."

Worf bellowed, "Duras? That *petaQ*?"

O'Brien nodded once. "Afraid so. He and Damar signed a treaty with the rebellion, giving us control of everything within twenty light-years of Earth."

Heaving a deep sigh, Worf closed his eyes and bowed his head. Several seconds passed while he let O'Brien's news sink in. Then he looked up, his expression grave. "What is to be done with me?"

O'Brien reached under his jacket and pulled out Worf's long-confiscated *d'k tahg*. He offered the dagger hilt-first to Worf. "You're free to go."

Worf reluctantly took the blade and stared at it. He turned it over as he studied it, seized its grip with both hands, and plunged it into his own chest. A thick gurgling rattled deep inside him as he collapsed to his knees, his massive hands suddenly coated in his own fuchsia blood. The light was fading from his eyes as he looked up at O'Brien and weakly rasped, "Thank you."

"Least I could do," O'Brien said. He stayed and watched over Worf until the man stopped breathing, and then he walked away. With his final obligations to both the rebellion and the Klingon's tarnished honor satisfied, he turned his thoughts, at long last, toward the world he had finally earned the right to call home.

Ezri Tigan debarked from the *Defiant* and crossed the gangway to Erebus Station. This was her first visit to the station since the ship's last refit, months earlier, and the vast facility's quiet passageways seemed even emptier than before. That came as no surprise to her; every place had seemed desolate to her since Leeta's death, and the *Defiant* had become even more so following O'Brien's resignation, which had resulted in her being promoted to captain at the tender age of twenty-four.

Who in their right mind could possibly think this was a good idea? she wondered. The daily rigors of starship command, especially in the uncertain postwar era, when no one had any idea what they were supposed to be doing or to whom they were supposed to answer, was taking a terrible toll on the young Trill. Most nights she barely slept. Just that morning, after she'd showered and dressed, she had looked at her reflection in the mirror and been astonished to count her first few gray hairs, just above her left ear.

She stepped off the gangway to find Director Saavik waiting for her, just as the invitation had specified. The Vulcan woman held up her hand, fingers spread in the V-shaped Vulcan salute. "Welcome, Captain. I trust your rendezvous with the *Odyssey* was free of incident."

"Yes," Ezri said. "Your jaunt ship was right on time, as always."

"Good." She beckoned Ezri with a subtle nod as she started walking. They strolled for nearly a minute down the massive passageway before Saavik asked, "How are you adapting to your new role as *Defiant*'s commanding officer?"

Ezri hadn't been prepared to face such a direct inquiry, and she suddenly became paranoid that members of her crew might have gone over her head. Masking her anxiety with a smile, she said, "I'm doing fine, thank you."

"Welcome news." Saavik glanced Ezri's way. "O'Brien was right about you. He assured me that you were a dynamic individual of great potential."

Feeling unworthy of the praise, Ezri avoided looking

Saavik in the eye. "I do the best I can, Director." She
buried the truth as deeply as she could. Her days were
filled with loneliness. Losing her wife had been a shattering blow, but then to also bid farewell to O'Brien,
who had been more like a father to her than anyone else
she'd ever known, had left her feeling directionless . . .
lost.

Saavik led her through a tall set of doors, which slid
apart as they drew near. On the other side was a cavern-
ous, silolike space filled with glossy consoles that ringed
a large elevated platform. White-jacketed technicians of
several species manned the various consoles, and one
of them, a dignified-looking graybeard of a Tellarite,
smiled when he saw Saavik. "Good evening, Director."

"Good evening, Doctor Treg." Saavik stepped onto
the platform and moved to stand near its center. "Omega
Prime, please."

"Right away, Ma'am."

Ezri hesitated at the circular dais's edge. "What is
this?"

"A subspace transporter. It will send us to Memory
Omega's headquarters."

Taking half a step back, Ezri said, "I thought *this* was
your headquarters."

"This is merely a staging ground," Saavik said.
"Come."

Uncertainty quickened Ezri's pulse, and a rush of
adrenaline made her shake like a leaf on the verge of
quitting its branch as she stepped onto the dais.

The director nodded at the technicians. "Energize."
To Ezri she added softly, "Brace yourself. Subspace
transport can be jarring."

Ezri had just enough time to draw a deep breath

before the confinement beam crushed it out of her. A hideous flash of white light erased her very essence from existence for a fraction of a moment, then she returned from oblivion into an excruciating spasm as the viselike grip of the transporter beam abated. Free to move, she dropped to one knee and gasped for air. Once she'd regained her bearings, she looked up to find herself in a room identical to the one she'd left. All that seemed to have changed was the technicians manning the consoles.

An Andorian *thaan* nodded at Saavik. "Welcome back, Director."

"Thank you, Arrithar," Saavik said, leaving the platform. She gestured for Ezri to follow her. "Quickly, please. There isn't much time."

Spurred by the sudden urgency in Saavik's tone, Ezri composed herself and hurried off the dais. Saavik led her out of the transporter chamber and down a long passageway that closely resembled the ones on Erebus Station. Then they turned a corner and stepped out into something completely different.

It was a tropical paradise inside a cave. Ezri and Saavik stood on a cliff high above a basin valley packed with a lush rain forest. Beside them, a plume of white water fell hundreds of meters and vanished in a great cloud of mist. Overhead, a golden sun burned at the apex of a cloudless blue sky. Humid air teased Ezri's nose with floral scents and the rich fragrance of untamed wildlife.

Mastering her surprise, she asked, "Where are we?"

"Inside a large asteroid in the Zeta Serpentis system."

It took Ezri several seconds to process the implications of Saavik's answer. "All of this is artificial?"

"Yes. It was created with a more primitive version of the Genesis technology we demonstrated last month for the benefit of our galactic neighbors." She stepped aboard a parked hovercraft and motioned for Ezri to join her. "Please, Captain."

Ezri did as Saavik bade her, and she continued to marvel at the self-contained ecosystem during the brief ride from the cliff to a cluster of buildings hidden deep beneath the rain forest's canopy. As soon as the hovercraft touched down, Saavik led her away from it and inside a building whose cool, antiseptic-smelling interior immediately identified it as an infirmary.

The windows all were shaded, and the beds in the main ward were empty. Though she and Saavik were alone, something about the setting made Ezri whisper as she inquired, "Why did you bring me here?"

"You will see in a moment."

The two women passed through a pair of doors and a sterilizing field before entering the operating room. A team of blue-smocked medical personnel stood gathered around one table, on which a patient lay covered by a teal blanket. Another bed lay empty beside them.

Saavik announced to the medical team, "She is here."

The team pivoted to face Ezri and Saavik. As they turned and stepped slightly apart, Ezri saw the face of the man lying on the operating table. He was an elderly Trill, his eyes milky with age, his skin so mottled and brown that she couldn't tell where his spots ended and his melanomas began. His breath came in labored wheezes, and when he lifted one wrinkled hand, it trembled.

Ezri turned her back on him and grabbed Saavik's sleeve. "I don't understand."

"His name is Curzon," Saavik said. "For more than a century, he has lived among us as both a prisoner and a living embodiment of history. He also bears within him the last member of a species that once lived in harmony with yours—a symbiont." Lowering her voice, she added, "He's dying, Ezri."

"That's not my problem."

"No, it's not. It's your chance to become something greater than yourself." Saavik looked at the old man. "It's also my way of making amends for my crime against your people." Ezri caught a flicker of sadness in the Vulcan's eyes as she continued. "Ninety years ago, in the waning days of the Terran Empire, I was the captain of the *Enterprise*. Emperor Spock sent me to your homeworld to gather intelligence about the symbionts. When I discovered that they had been infested by a hostile alien parasite, I ordered their extermination for the safety of not just the Empire but the entire galaxy. Emperor Spock carried the measure a step further: He ordered the genocide of every Trill symbiont. All save one." She gently guided Ezri through a slow turn to face Curzon. "He was an ambassador, one of the Empire's senior diplomats. Spock spared him by imperial decree, and he has resided since then in Memory Omega's custody as a living memory of the truth, a fair witness to history. We have extended his life far beyond its likely natural end, but it is time for us to let him go. When that happens, his symbiont will need a new host—and I think it should be you, Ezri."

The suggestion filled Ezri with horror and revulsion. "Me? Are you crazy? I don't want that . . . that . . . *worm* inside me, using me like a puppet!"

From his deathbed, Curzon gasped, "It's not like that." His feeble, whispered interjection captured Ezri's attention. He beckoned her, and she felt compelled to answer his summons. She drifted to his bedside and leaned down to listen to him. "It's a union. A . . . partnership. You . . . will still be you. But you'll be . . . *more*." His sightless eyes stared past her as he flailed weakly for her hand. She clasped his bony fingers to spare him the indignity of pawing at empty air. At her touch, he smiled. "Lifetimes . . . become yours. Centuries of knowledge." Mustering what felt to Ezri as if it must be the last of his strength, Curzon squeezed her hand. His palm felt brittle and desiccated, like onion skin. "Some part of me will live on . . . in the symbiont. Bond with it . . . and part of you can live on . . . after you leave this world."

His hand went slack, and his head rolled away from her as he lost consciousness. The medics swooped in, chattering their jargon and wielding their subtle instruments, and shouldered Ezri out of their way. She backed away from the table, uncertain what to do. She'd grown up hearing horror stories about the evil parasites, but she'd also heard of benignly "joined" Trill in the alternate universe. *That's a whole different universe,* she reminded herself. Curzon had seemed lucid enough—but what if he had been lying? Wasn't that exactly what a parasite would say if it wanted to possess a new host?

Saavik stopped Ezri's retreat with a gentle hand against her back. "It's time. They need to remove the symbiont from Curzon now, and they have only a short time in which to join it to a new host. You need to decide."

Aware of precious seconds bleeding away as the surgeons cut open Curzon's abdomen, Ezri asked Saavik, "If I join with it, can I change my mind later?"

"No. Once the bond is made, it cannot be prematurely terminated without killing the host." One of the surgeons turned and shot a questioning look at Saavik, who gestured for the doctor to be patient. Then she said to Ezri, "Choose."

"I'll be someone different after it's done . . . won't I?"

"Yes," Saavik said. "But you will also never be alone again."

Those words struck a chord in Ezri's grieving soul, and she purged herself of fear. "All right. I'm ready." She walked to the second table and climbed atop it. One of the surgical assistants lifted Ezri's shirt to expose her belly and applied a quick wipe of antiseptic mixed with a local anesthetic. As her abdomen went numb, she asked, "Aren't you going to put me under?"

"No," said the technician. "General anesthesia interferes with the neural bonding process. You need to be conscious when the link is formed."

New waves of fear rolled through Ezri's thoughts, but she refused to let them control her. She pursed her lips and nodded to show she understood.

Moments later, the team of medics surrounded her table. While the nurses and technicians monitored her vital signs, one of the surgeons began making an ultra-fine incision just below her solar plexus. Ezri's eyes were locked on the ruby-red beam that was slicing her open until the second surgeon stepped into the circle, holding the viscera-slicked vermiform symbiont in his hands. Despite the mask over his mouth and nose, she could tell that he was smiling.

"Ezri," he said, "meet Dax."

July 2379

38

An Epitaph to War

Captain Picard stepped out of his ready room and let the hum and chatter of orderly activity on the *Enterprise*'s bridge wash over him. Over the past several months of peacetime service, he had learned to enjoy the patterns and rhythms of daily life on a crowded starship. It had been a difficult adjustment for him at first, after a lifetime spent traveling and living in solitude, but the experience had begun to grow on him once the additional stresses of life during wartime had been removed from the equation.

As he moved toward his chair, Troi stepped away from the forward operations console to walk beside him. Her black-and-gray uniform flattered her. "We just got news from Deneva," she said. "Our government finally has a name."

He settled into his chair, cocked his left eyebrow, and teased her with a smile. "And . . . ? Don't keep me in suspense, Deanna."

"The Galactic Commonwealth. It passed by a majority vote this morning."

Picard repeated the name under his breath, then approved it with a half nod. "I like it. Describing itself as *galactic* might seem a bit self-aggrandizing, but one has to respect the ambition in it."

Troi folded her arms and struck a haughty pose. "I just

like that they omitted the word *Terran* from the name."

"Well, that seems only fair, wouldn't you agree? After all, it wasn't just Terrans who fought to make this new order. It belongs to all of us—and the whole idea is to share it with anyone who wants to join."

The half-Betazoid woman stifled a chuckle. "If you say so. I think it's more important that they chose to start from scratch. A clean slate never hurts."

"Very true," Picard said. "In fact . . ." He was about to underscore the point by regaling Deanna with one of his examples from ancient Iconian lore when the turbolift door swished open, and Reg Barclay stepped out.

Barclay swiveled his head like a predator on the open plain, froze when he spotted Troi, and smiled. The pair hurried to greet each other with a quick kiss that Picard imagined they thought was discreet but which had been noted with varying degrees of disquietude and amusement by the rest of the bridge crew.

Taking Troi's hand, Barclay asked, "Busy?"

"No more than usual. Why?" Troi suddenly beamed with delight, apparently having read good news from her paramour's surface thoughts. "You finished it?"

"Just this morning," Barclay said. "Cargo Bay Six is fully converted."

"So now it's a . . ." She came up short of a word. "What did you call it?"

"A holodeck. Just like we had in the Genesis Cave, but a lot smaller."

Troi seemed positively giddy at the news. Struggling to put on a professional demeanor, she looked over her shoulder at Picard. "Excuse me, Captain? Would it be all right if I finished my shift a few minutes early today?"

"Go," Picard said, eager to have the fawning couple

off his bridge. "Please. Lieutenant ch'Sallas, take over at Commander Troi's station." As the Andorian junior officer stepped in to relieve Troi, she and Barclay headed for the turbolift.

Picard picked up a data slate and pretended to ignore the departing couple while he reviewed the *Enterprise*'s latest orders from its new civilian government: a six-week patrol of the Neutral Zone, followed by an autonomous, one-year exploration mission that he could hardly wait to begin.

Once the lift doors closed, K'Ehleyr sidled up to Picard's chair. "Are you sure it's a good idea to let the chief engineer date the chief of security?"

"I don't care whether it is or not. I'm just pleased to see Deanna so happy."

K'Ehleyr sat down in her own chair, leaned toward Picard, and cracked a sardonic smile. "I'm kidding. Frankly, I'm relieved he finally found someone to moon over besides me. I was getting tired of having a pet."

"We all have our crosses to bear, Number One."

The half-Klingon first officer scrunched her face in disapproval. "I'm sorry—what did you call me?"

Picard set down the data slate and responded with a jovial, sidelong glance. "I called you 'Number One.' It's a term from ancient Terran naval practice. It was used by captains as a nickname for trusted first officers."

She cocked an eyebrow at Picard's slyly implied compliment, then played it off as if it were no big deal, in case any of the bridge crew was eavesdropping, which they all very likely were. "If it makes you happy," she said with a coy smile.

He took a moment to appreciate the turn his life had taken, and couldn't help but smile back. "Yes," he said, "I think it does."

January 2380

39

People of Hope

Sevok was only a child when the Cardassians invaded Vulcan, took him from his family, and made him a slave. Today he is a man of middle years standing on the surface of a world he has not seen in over eight decades.

The wind is rich with the clean scent of the deep desert as it moans and shaves the crests off sand dunes, along the outskirts of a heap of rubble once called ShiKahr. On either side of Sevok, lines of repatriated Vulcans stand mute, holding a silent vigil in remembrance of their ancestors who died here to protect the promise carried off-world by Spock's army of sleepers.

Though it is not the Vulcan way to indulge in emotion, they have become a people of hope. Other liberated species of the Commonwealth have pledged to help the Vulcans rebuild their world. Even the Terrans and the Andorians, who both lost so much more, have sworn oaths to see the world of Surak restored.

It will be a long time, Sevok knows, before those oaths can be called fulfilled. He expects that it will not be accomplished in his lifetime, but he has reason to think this generation's heirs will see it achieved. That thought gives him pause, during which he collects himself to prevent an unseemly show of grief. He has come home, but his mate and children have not. They were caught up in the Cardassians' great Purge, rounded up and put to death before Sevok could ferry them off Chin'toka II to safety. When the time comes, he will see their names inscribed on memory stones in his city's main square—along with tens of millions of other sons and daughters of Vulcan who perished in the Alliance's holocaust.

He finds no solace in knowing he is not alone in his grief. If anything, it leaves him with no one from whom to seek condolence. On a world where all are in mourning, no one remains to give comfort.

Eager to put his sorrows behind him, he steps out of line and begins the trek toward the fallen city of his forefathers. There is work to be done.

L'Tal is only a child, just shy of turning seven, but she is old enough to sense that she is in the middle of something important. The sun is setting, and the red sky has become a dark shade of purple. Her mother, Sakara, holds her hand and leads her through a city she says is called Vulcana Regar.

Most of what L'Tal can see of the city has been half-buried by the desert's creeping sands. Wild animals roam freely through narrow vales that Sakara insists were streets. A fierce, growling roar echoes from somewhere close by, and L'Tal can see that it makes all the adults around her nervous. "That was the cry of a *le-matya*," her mother says. "It is a very dangerous creature."

Sakara leads L'Tal inside a low building, and the other dozen or so members of their group follow them inside. A pair of men and two adolescent boys begin gathering stones and other heavy objects to barricade the entrance. Sakara and three other women retrieve food and water from their backpacks.

"It is time to rest," Sakara tells L'Tal.

After dark, the air grows cold, and howling winds hurl sand through cracks in the walls and gaps in the makeshift barrier. Soon the refugees and all they own are coated in dust the color of curry. Outside, the night is alive with animal cries that will haunt L'Tal's dreams.

Dawn comes all too soon, and L'Tal is bleary-eyed as the men dismantle the barricade and lead the group back out into the sun-bleached ruins of Vulcana Regar. L'Tal sees other groups of Vulcans emerge from other buildings in the distance. Confused, she looks up at her mother. "Where do we go now?"

"Nowhere," Sakara says. "Now we rebuild." She reaches out and gently strokes L'Tal's straight black hair. "This is our home, now."

Vulcan's Forge at midday is an anvil of fire, and the blazing orb of Nevasa is the hammer, striking down the weak and ill-prepared who dare to pit themselves against the Forge's power. Robed-and-hooded Vulcans trudge slowly through a desert canyon, following their leader, Sarok. Even by Vulcan standards the heat of the Forge is extreme, but Sarok masters his discomfort, for he knows it is only an illusion of the mind. That is a core teaching of Surak, whose aeons-old wisdom is preserved inside the minds and memories of Sarok and his fellow disciples of the Seleyan Order.

As they follow a hand-drawn map to their destination, Sarok silently laments the loss of the Temple at Mount Seleya. As significant as the site is, it will not be possible to rebuild there. The Alliance was quite thorough in its devastation. Nearly a century after their barbaric ravaging, the planet lies in ruins. Its cities are broken into rubble, its most revered monuments and landmarks have been vaporized or defiled, and many of its greatest natural wonders have been blasted sterile. It will take several generations to rebuild.

The scope of the challenge does not daunt the Vulcans. They are a patient people. And so the work to reclaim their planet begins.

Sarok and his fellow disciples have made the arduous journey into the Forge to do their part for Vulcan's future. In this nightmarish place, where constant geomagnetic distortions and electrically charged sandstorms wreak havoc with sensors and navigational devices of all kinds, the safest method of travel is on foot—with *safe* being a relative term. No one comes here without a compelling reason. Many people Sarok knows will not make this journey for any purpose. For Sarok and the others, this trek is a long-overdue *kahs-wan*—a coming-of-age ceremony, a threshold moment in their passage to adulthood and independence.

A swift and terrible darkness blots out the horizon ahead. Lightning flashes, green and angry, inside the fast-moving sandstorm. Sarok knows they must hurry and reach their destination before the storm hits. Pain is an illusion, but the damage inflicted by Vulcan sandstorms is not. Without wasting precious breath on spoken orders, he starts running, sprinting over the rocky ground, trusting his native Vulcan stamina and years spent as a manual laborer in a Klingon-run dilithium mine to carry him through the deadly swelter to safety.

The canyon echoes with the rapid patter of running feet, assuring him that his fellow disciples are keeping pace with him. Overhead, the radiant, cinnamon-hued sky dims as the sandstorm begins to engulf them. Forks of viridescent electricity light up the soot-black clouds of volcanic ash, and a thunderstroke splits the air and rains a flurry of loose rocks down upon them from the cliffs above.

Rounding a bend in the canyon, they see their safe haven a short distance ahead, an ancient temple hewn from the rock: the T'Karath Sanctuary. Sarok reaches it first and beckons the others to hurry as the storm scours them. He counts the number of people who pass by him, and when he is sure that all are inside, he calls out over the wind noise to two of the adepts, "Tovar! Kaleris! Seal the entry!"

The young Vulcans hurry back to Sarok with portable force field generators, and they set them to create overlapping fields that will shield the interior of the sanctuary from the storm. Satisfied that they are secure, Sarok pulls back his hood, and the others in his entourage do the same.

Compared to the Seleyan leaders of ages past, they are all too young. Some, such as T'Eama and Kalok, would once have been barely old enough to qualify as adepts. Tovar and Kaleris are only novices, but so few initiates had survived the Exile that they all are needed now to lay the foundation for a new beginning. Of those gathered there with Sarok, his only peers in age and experience are Sturek and T'Ren. He motions for them to accompany him to the lower sanctum.

As they descend the carved-stone stairs into hand-cut tunnels beneath the sanctuary, no one speaks. They know why they have come.

In the deepest recesses of the sanctuary, they find the sepulcher wall. It is intact and untouched, exactly as their predecessors had hoped.

Contrary to the annals of history, the elders of Mount Seleya did not perish in fire with their secrets. All but a small handful had long since vanished into other identities by the time the Alliance came. In their place, they had left behind willing impostors, pawns to be sacrificed in Emperor Spock's epic game of galactic chess. Memory Omega preserved written copies of the ancient texts, and even a few of the original documents. The old knowledge perseveres and has been brought home to Vulcan to guide the reconstruction of the people's cultural identity. Safe in the minds of Seleya's few remaining acolytes are the arcane mysteries of *fal-tor-pan* and the *Kolinahr*.

Now all that remains is for Sarok and his peers to ensure that Vulcan's greatest treasure has survived its long abandonment in the desert. With care, he and T'Ren and Sturek press the symbols in a sequence only they know, thereby retracting the massive, internal dead bolts that hold the sepulcher wall in place. The final bolt withdraws with a heavy scrape.

The trio step back as the wall sinks into the floor, revealing a secret for which tens of thousands of Vulcans have laid down their lives since it was smuggled, piece by piece, from the Halls of Ancient Thought at Mount Seleya: the vast trove of *katric* arks, representing millennia of preserved Vulcan memories and personal essences, the single most sacred charge of the Seleyan Order.

Sarok dares to let his fingertip brush one ark, and it glows with ancient power. "The wisdom of Surak taught us to create these arks," he says, his voice resonating deeply off the dusty stone walls, floor, and ceiling. "The wisdom of Spock enabled us to save them. Hallowed be Spock's name."

T'Ren and Sturek reply in unison.

"Hallowed be Spock's name."

2381

40

Peaceable Kingdom

*H*istory must never glorify me,* said the enormous holographic projection of Spock's careworn face, which hovered like an angry god above the members of the Commonwealth Assembly. *"Do not applaud me because I claimed to have noble motives. Do not venerate me if one day my plan should come to fruition. Instead, remember me for who and what I really am: a villain."*

The recorded message ended, and the ghostly visage of Spock vanished, leaving behind an uneasy silence in the amphitheater-style meeting chamber.

And then Bera chim Gleer, the Tellarite delegate, ruined it, in Michael Eddington's opinion, by standing up and speaking as if he knew what the hell he was talking about. "While I don't deny that was a very *moving* speech, I think we should keep in mind the *context* in which it—"

On the main dais, Eddington stood and banged his gavel, halting Gleer's tirade before it could pick up steam. "Point of order, Delegate Gleer. Parliamentary procedure requires you to receive the recognition of the Chair before speaking."

"May I be so recognized, Mister Chairman?"

"No. Sit down." Eddington's rebuke provoked gales of laughter throughout the assembly, and he rapped his gavel once more to quash the frivolity. "That's enough.

This message from the late Emperor Spock was not presented today by coincidence. It was shown here on this, the second anniversary of the ratification of the Tripartite Armistice, at the request of our benefactors, Memory Omega. It's important that we remember how far we've come—and that we work together to make certain we never repeat the mistakes of the past.

"Spock's warning to us is clear. We have to be vigilant against those who would seek to divide us, to turn us against one another. Even more important, we can't let one person seize all the power. Our government— our civilization—belongs to all of us. It needs to serve all of us, not just our strongest or most privileged. All our people, every last individual, have a right to equal treatment under the law. And we must never forget that as the elected agents of our people, we are here to serve them—not the other way around."

As Eddington permitted himself the briefest pause to draw a breath, the Andorian delegate stood. Realizing he could not stall discussion forever, he set down his gavel. "Delegate zh'Faila of Andoria is recognized for five minutes."

"Thank you, Mister Chairman," said the regally dignified Andorian *zhen*. "If I might be so bold as to presume to distill your message to its essence?" She looked at Eddington, who nodded his assent. "I believe that what Spock and you wish us to understand is that evil is a choice. Our ancestors embraced evil because it was the easier path—but in the end it led them to destruction. Rejecting evil is the far more difficult road to follow, but it is the one we must choose together." She favored him with an almost imperceptible nod. "I yield."

Eddington stood and reclaimed his place at the lectern. "The delegate yields the balance of her time." Min Zife stood, and Eddington nodded to the softly spoken, bald, blue gentleman. "Delegate Zife of Bolarus is recognized for five minutes."

"If it please the Assembly, I would like to open a discussion regarding Resolution Four-Nineteen, which deals with the allocation of terraforming resources among the worlds of the Commonwealth. While the people of Bolarus recognize that worlds such as Vulcan and Earth have more urgent need of these technologies than do Bolarus or other member planets, we feel that the apportionment of atmosphere-processing hardware has been disproportionately weighted to those two planets, to the detriment of their Commonwealth partners. If you'll all please refer to the presentation I've uploaded to the comnet . . ."

A collective groan filled the hall, and Eddington knew that this day—despite starting off with a powerful and historic message from the past—was about to devolve into a long, loud, obnoxious, messy, and utterly wonderful exercise in representative democracy. The thought of it made him smile—then he reminded himself to take every moment of this government seriously, because if history was any guide, it would last only as long as he and people like him could defend it from those who would do anything to subvert it, corrupt it, and tear it down.

Let them come, he decided, reclining as he listened to Zife drone on about optimal allocation strategies for civil engineering personnel and resources. *I'll be here for the long haul.*

In seven years of war, the Alliance had never once brought O'Brien to his knees. Now a small patch of hardscrabble ground humbled him like a penitent fifty times a day. Genuflecting on his rock-infested soil, he dug with rough hands through the cold earth and ferreted out large stones that were obstructing his effort to plant a row of potatoes. He cursed under his breath as he cast each one into a wicker basket that he dragged behind him while he worked, but in his heart he found the process deeply satisfying.

Standing straight, he clapped the dust from his hands and looked up at a sky masked by clouds like white marble. It was late spring by his reckoning, but the weather remained stubbornly cold and overcast, with the occasional random drizzle to keep everything damp and dreary.

It's my own fault, he scolded himself. *I could have put my farm anywhere, but I chose here.* Grimacing good-naturedly at his bleak surroundings, he considered his decision a triumph of nostalgia over common sense. He and Keiko had built a house on Inis Mór, a small isle off the western coast of a Terran island nation once called Ireland. The isle was hard country, in the finest Irish tradition. Its rocky soil was overgrown with brush and weeds that were hardy from surviving long, harsh winters at high latitude, and the countryside was a patchwork quilt of centuries-old stone walls, most of them crumbling and carpeted in moss.

Several ancient stone forts, the handiwork of a people known as the Celts, still served as the tiny isle's key landmarks. O'Brien had situated his home and farm on the site of a deserted village known as Cill Mhuirbhigh, at the bottom of a path that led up a hillside to Dún Aonghasa, "the Big Fort." His nearest neighbors were more than six kilometers away, in Cill Rónáin, near Dún

Dúchathair, "the Black Fort," and that was just the way O'Brien liked it. He had come to Inis Mór for the solitude and, most of all, the quiet.

In the mornings, lying in his bed, he could hear the sound of his border collie trotting up the gravel road from Cill Rónáin from half a kilometer away. Some evenings, after dinner, he walked the trail up to Dún Aonghasa and laid himself down on the grassy field inside its walls. The fort was walled on only three sides, with its western face open above a dizzyingly tall cliff whose base was pounded day and night by the relentless sea. Lying in the grass, O'Brien had finally been able to hear himself breathe, and for the first time in his life he'd known peace. In a way no other place had ever been, Inis Mór was his home.

O'Brien looked back on the progress he'd made preparing this plot of soil for planting. As best he could tell, he had cleared only two of the eight rows he intended to plant in that afternoon. *Time to get back to it, then.* He lifted his garden hoe and resumed his steady chopping at the hard, cold ground. Just as the hoe's blade struck another rock with a grating scrape, he heard the back door of his house open. He turned and saw Keiko standing in the open doorway, balancing their infant daughter, Molly, on her hip.

"Someone's coming up the road," Keiko called out. "On foot."

He sleeved the sweat from his brow. "Did you see who it is?"

She shook her head. "No, but it doesn't look like Maggie or Aidan."

In addition to being Miles and Keiko's closest friends on the island, Maggie and Aidan McTeague were also the ones who brought them fresh supplies from the cargo shuttles that visited Cill Rónáin on the first Monday of each month. None of the island's other residents had visited the O'Briens since they built their home in Cill Mhuirbhigh, so an unexpected caller at the front gate was cause for curiosity. O'Brien set down his hoe and made his way out of the fields, then followed the path that circled his house until he reached the front gate.

He arrived in time to see the visitor, a lone figure in an off-white hooded robe, rounding the curve on the steep incline that led up to his house. Observing the traveler with a trained eye, O'Brien concluded that it was a woman, and that she likely wasn't armed. He waved to her. "Hello, there. Can I help you?"

She pulled back her hood. It was Saavik. "Greetings, General."

"Don't call me that," he said, waving away the honorific as if it were a bad odor. "I'm just Miles now. Or Smiley, to people who 'knew me when.'"

Saavik nodded. "As you prefer, Miles." She continued walking toward him, and he ducked through the planks of his fence to step out and greet her. They met in a light but friendly embrace. "Are you and Keiko well?"

"Very," he said.

"And your child?"

"Molly's great. A bit colicky some nights, but nothing we can't handle." The wind picked up, and he tucked his hands into his pockets to keep them warm. "What're you doing here? Is something wrong?"

Folding her hands together in a way that made the drooped sleeves of her robe overlap to block the wind, Saavik arched one brow. "I had meant to ask you the same thing. I was surprised to find you here rather than at the Assembly on Deneva. I'd expected you to join Mister Eddington in the new government."

O'Brien shrugged. "Earth only needs one delegate, and I figured Michael was the better man for the job."

She cocked her head, ostensibly confused by his reply. "There are other positions in which you could serve besides delegate. You were a leader, Miles. People looked up to you. They respected you and followed you. Why walk away now, after all you did to bring this new order into being?"

Overhead, the cloud cover broke just enough to let some sunlight dapple the countryside. Squinting up at the golden beams and a patch of blue heaven, O'Brien squinted. "Honestly? I feel like I've done enough leading." Out of the corner of his eye, he saw Keiko and Molly watching him through one of the bedroom windows. He smiled at them, then looked back at Saavik. "Now I just want to *live*."

"I understand," Saavik said. She lifted her hand in the V-shaped Vulcan salute. "Live long and prosper, Miles Edward O'Brien."

He tried to emulate the gesture, but his fingers refused to obey. Saavik, however, didn't seem to mind. "May the road rise to meet you, Saavik, and may the wind be ever at your back."

For a moment, he thought he saw the ghost of a smile on her face. Then she nodded at him, lifted her hood, and walked back the way she had come, her steps crunching on the gravel as the wind whispered its valedictions between them.

EPILOGUE

The Far Side of Night

The Honored Elder crossed the bridge and snapped to attention at Eris's side. "We have reached the co-ordinates."

The slender, violet-eyed female Vorta turned toward him and lowered the holographic eyepiece of her command headset. "Well done, First." She quickly accessed the Dominion battle cruiser's sensor logs and super-imposed the trajectory of its long-range sensor probe over the latest readings gathered by her crew. "Have your men found any evidence of the high-energy phenomenon the probe detected?"

"None."

Eris was not ready to abandon the investigation. "Check for gravitational anomalies within ten light-minutes." A nod from the First to his Second initiated the new sensor sweep.

Perhaps the anomaly has vanished or moved, she speculated. *It would be a shame if we missed such a rare event.* Years had passed since the deep-space probe had recorded the massive subspace fluctuation less than five light-years from the Idran system. Because of the event's great distance from Dominion space, its verification and analysis had not been considered a priority.

The First conferred in a low voice with the Second,

then he returned to face Eris. "No gravitational anomalies detected." He waited a moment, apparently to see if Eris had further orders. "May I make a recommendation?"

"By all means, First."

He lowered the eyepiece of his own headset and used it to relay data in real time to Eris's display. "Navigator Rogan'agar reported disruptions to our subspace field as we dropped from warp to impulse. I suggest we check for deformations in the local fabric of subspace."

Eris graced the First with a fleeting smile of approval. "An excellent idea, First. See it done." With a glance he delegated the task to his Second. Eris knew it was no mere accident of fortune that the First had become an Honored Elder among his kind. He was a gifted thinker condemned to live among the cannon fodder. She also admired his unshakable loyalty to the Founders; though he had been born without the normal Jem'Hadar dependency on ketracel white, he took it with thanks each day. He considered it part of his duty as First to accept the gift of the Founders with gratitude, as an example to his men.

He returned to her, looking pleased. "We have found something."

"Route it to my display, please." She waited as the sensor data appeared, complete with annotations, in her holographic matrix. A storm of neutrinos silhouetted a funnel-shaped gravity well. "Is it stable?"

"Preliminary readings are inconclusive. May I recommend we launch a new probe to gather detailed telemetry from the anomaly's interior?"

Flush with excitement, Eris nodded. "At once, First." More quick looks were translated into efficient action. Seconds later, a flash in Eris's display signaled the launch of the probe. She watched with rapt attention as it arced into seemingly empty space. Then a cerulean bloom spiraled open to swallow it whole, like a leviathan devouring an amoeba. The wormhole was a majestic vortex of matter and energy, hypnotic in its invitation. It took all of Eris's willpower to resist ordering the First to plunge their vessel in after the probe.

"Readings are steady," the First said. "The wormhole appears stable. Verteron nodes inside it may be a navigational hazard. Shielding on our warp core might be required for safe passage." The wormhole irised shut and vanished from sight, leaving only stars and darkness. The First confirmed his findings with the Second, then he turned back toward Eris. "We have lost contact with the probe."

She lifted her eyepiece back to its standby position. "Ready a secure channel. I need to report this discovery at once." The First nodded. Eris stepped away, intending to make her report from the privacy of her quarters. She paused in the open doorway, looked back, and smiled at the First. "You've done well, Taran'atar. I'll be sure to mention you by name when I speak with the Founders."

Consummatum est

Acknowledgments

It has been my practice since my first direct-to-paperback novel to thank my wonderful wife, Kara, for her support during the writing of this book, and it remains as right and proper on this, my twentieth book, as it did on my first.

I also wish to extend my thanks to the editors who helped bring this project to life. Margaret Clark first commissioned this novel from me; Jaime Costas shepherded the book through the approvals process; Marco Palmieri offered me sage advice on the outline and helped me smooth some of the tale's rougher edges; and Ed Schlesinger guided the finished manuscript through editing and revisions to help it become the tome you now hold.

My agent, Lucienne Diver, also deserves her measure of my gratitude for keeping up with the business side of my endeavors and making sure all my paperwork is dotted and crossed to perfection in triplicate.

In keeping with the collaborative nature of a shared universe, I am indebted to two authors who assisted me before, during, and after the writing of this manuscript. The first is Peter David, who graciously agreed to vet the chapters in which I used characters he created for his *Star Trek: New Frontier* series. The second is Keith R.A. DeCandido, who gave me ideas and let me bounce some of my crazier notions off him. I also tip my hat to the very long list of authors who contributed tales to the *Star Trek Mirror Universe: Shards and Shadows* anthology that built upon and expanded the mythology and backstory of the secret cabal known as Memory Omega.

Also, I'd be remiss if I did not acknowledge the inspiration of Jerome Bixby, writer of the *Star Trek* episode "Mirror, Mirror," which spawned this whole concept, and Michael Piller and Peter Allan Fields, whose *Star Trek: Deep Space Nine* episode "Crossover" dragged the alternate universe kicking and screaming into the twenty-fourth century—and my imagination along with it.

Along the way, I relied on many fine reference works to help me keep my facts straight. Topping the list are *The Star Trek Encyclopedia* and *The Star Trek Chronology,* both by Michael Okuda and Denise Okuda; *The Star Trek: Deep Space Nine Technical Manual* by Herman Zimmerman, Rick Sternbach, and Doug Drexler; *Star Trek: Star Charts* by Geoffrey Mandel; and the wiki-reference websites Memory Alpha, for canonical *Star Trek* information, and Memory Beta, for information from the world of official licensed *Star Trek* literature and more.

Lastly, I continue to be thankful for you, the readers and fans who keep the dream of Gene Roddenberry alive. May you all live long and prosper.

About the Author

David Mack is the national bestselling author of more than twenty novels and novellas, including *Wildfire, Harbinger, Reap the Whirlwind, Precipice, Road of Bones, Promises Broken,* and the *Star Trek Destiny* trilogy: *Gods of Night, Mere Mortals,* and *Lost Souls.* He developed the *Star Trek Vanguard* series concept with editor Marco Palmieri. His first work of original fiction is the critically acclaimed supernatural thriller *The Calling.*

In addition to novels, Mack's writing credits span several media, including television (for episodes of *Star Trek: Deep Space Nine*), film, short fiction, magazines, newspapers, comic books, computer games, radio, and the Internet.

His upcoming works include the new *Vanguard* novel *Storming Heaven,* and a *Star Trek* trilogy scheduled for late 2012. He resides in New York City with his wife, Kara.

Visit his website, www.davidmack.pro/, and follow him on Twitter @DavidAlanMack and on Facebook at www.facebook.com/david.alan.mack.